Deception

A Derrick King Novel: Book 7

By Daniel L. Copeland

Deception
A Derrick King Novel, Book 7
Published October 21, 2023
First Edition

ISBN: 9781970773071
Ingram Spark Edition
Published by Chipping Away Publishing

Dedication
To all those doing their best to improve their community and the world.

Acknowledgements:
It is difficult to adequately express my gratitude to everyone who has helped me with the Derrick King series. I could not have completed the books without the assistance of several people who read, edit, and comment on my work. Special thanks to those who have provided feedback and guidance: Rod Leonard, Kristy Steen, and Elizabeth Barbee.

Part One

1

Friday, April 9, 6:01 p.m.

SHERIFF COLLINS, DONNA, AND JASON listened to Patel's one-sided conversation. They waited for him to finish his call, speculated who he was talking to, and wondered if they'd find out before the missile hit. Allen sighed and studied his computer screen, seemingly oblivious to the intensifying anxiety in the room.

Not that Allen wasn't relieved. He was thankful beyond words. Miriam, Rebekah, Anna, and Derrick were alive, the missiles were headed out to sea, and his upload was complete. Yet the feeling of dread persisted. He wasn't sure why. Perhaps the adrenaline rush that fueled his fight-and-flight reaction had not yet subsided. Maybe because he knew safety was a temporary condition.

Or his dismay might have been because of the expression on Jason Maxton's face.

The danger wasn't over. It was just beginning.

"Allen, are you going to tell us what just happened?" Collins asked.

Allen nodded but said nothing. Instead, he typed. After a few moments, he closed his laptop. "Sorry, I had to send an e-mail to my colleague, letting him know the upload was complete. I was talking to Miriam. They are alive, and they diverted the missile. Potterville is safe, for now."

"You don't look as happy about that as one might expect. Is there something else?"

"Is it L. Linda?" Jason asked.

"Nothing about L. Linda. Miriam asked if we had seen her. I'm sorry, Jason."

Donna said, "I hope she's okay."

Jason said, "She can take care of herself."

Collins said, "Jason, it's okay to be worried about her."

"I know that, but you don't understand."

Donna said, "I'm still confused about why we are not celebrating."

Allen said, "I don't understand it myself. You probably gathered that there's a problem. However, the kids are okay, and we are okay. My emotions are run amuck because I have not recovered from the adrenaline."

Donna said, "I can relate to that."

"Why was the military here?" Collins asked.

Jason said, "Painting the town."

"Huh?" Collins and Browning asked simultaneously.

"Locking coordinates to ensure the most efficient location for the missiles to strike."

Allen said, "Missile. There was only one missile intended for Potterville."

Jason shook his head. "City killer."

Collins said, "They'll soon know the missile didn't hit us, which means they'll be back. I think it's time to evacuate the town."

Jason said, "I don't think the military will be back."

Collins said, "Okay." Stretching out the word. "You don't appear to be any more at ease than Allen. What am I missing?"

"Assassins. You have forgotten about assassins."

2

Friday, April 9, 6:15 p.m.

IN AN OLD CAFÉ IN A SMALL BORDER TOWN, Derrick downed his second glass of ice water and poured a third. Rebekah took the empty pitcher to the counter to ask for a refill. Rebekah vaguely understood someone would be around because she had witnessed how it worked a few times since she and Miriam escaped from Pacific Edge. However, she was too parched to be patient. The waitress returned from the kitchen and handed her two full pitchers but said nothing, as if thirsty people here weren't unusual. Rebekah understood because a thermometer near the front door read 101, and it was after six o'clock.

A bell over the door rang, and Derrick jumped to his feet, spinning to face the sound.

Rebekah said, "Relax. It's just Miriam."

Rebekah set one pitcher in front of Derrick and then refilled Anna's glass and then handed the pitcher to the soldier. "What's your last name, Kevin?"

Derrick still found it hard to believe a soldier from the missile unit in Mexico was with them. He wasn't sure it was a good idea. However, he was sure killing the kid would have been a bad thing.

Kevin took a long drink and then said, "Schell."

Miriam returned from the ATM and sat next to Derrick.

"Did you get it?" Derrick asked.

"Yes. Did you think I would forget how?"

Derrick said, "No. I worried they'd figure it out and took their money back."

"Who'd figure it out?" Miriam asked.

Derrick said, "I don't know. Whoever you took the money from."

"Least of our worries. Do we order at the counter?" Miriam stared at three young girls and a man wearing a dirty white apron who were huddled listening to a radio.

Rebekah said, "A girl brought us water, but we told her we were waiting for another person. I had to go back for more water. She's kind of ignoring us."

Miriam said, "You should have ordered. We need to keep moving."

Derrick said, "We couldn't order. We have no money."

Miriam said, "I told you I'd get money. Don't you trust me?"

Derrick glanced around. "Lower your voice. Of course, I trust you, but I don't trust them. As I said, I was afraid they might have figured it out and had taken their money back." He paused. "Whose money is it, anyway?"

Just then, a girl, younger than they were, arrived. "Sorry, I didn't notice your friend came in." She paused, fighting back tears. "It's just with all that's happened. It's awful, isn't it?"

"What happened?" Derrick asked.

"How could you not know? It's on all the channels."

The girl's name tag read: Alice. "Alice, we're trying to get home, and our truck has no radio." Derrick motioned toward the street.

Alice turned. "Dean, turn on the TV."

A giant monitor mounted on the wall behind the bar flickered to life. The sound was too low to hear, but hearing was unnecessary. The news lady was crying as she spoke. On the Breaking News banner running across the bottom of the screen, it read, "The President and Vice President have been assassinated. Prime has taken control of the country and declared martial law. Prime vows revenge on those responsible. Preliminary evidence points to Mexico."

"Plan B?" Miriam asked.

Derrick said, "Looks like it."

"What are you talking about?" Alice asked.

Miriam started to say something, but Kevin interrupted her. "Just an inside joke. We are not big fans of the current administration." He paused. "Any administration."

Alice gave him a weak smile and then pretended to close a zipper on her mouth. "Your secret is safe with me."

Kevin said, "Can we get food? I know you're upset, but we have a long drive ahead. We'll make it simple, just burgers and fries." He looked at the others, hoping he had not done something wrong.

Alice studied Kevin for a minute. "Double-cheese burgers for the boys and regular burgers for the girls? Large fry for each of you? And what to drink? Soda or milkshake?"

"Can you bring each of us a chocolate milkshake now and then large sodas when our food is ready?" Kevin asked.

"Do you want the food to go?" Alice asked.

Kevin looked at Miriam.

Miriam said, "We'll eat here."

Alice went behind the counter and speared their order on a spindle above the kitchen counter. Then she started making milkshakes.

Miriam said, "Why did you do that, Kevin?"

Kevin was now wearing a white t-shirt, having donated his army shirt to a desert tortoise crossing the road just north of the border. "I'm sorry. I panicked. I was afraid you might say something that would make them suspicious. I'm AWOL."

"AWOL?" Derrick asked.

"Absent without leave. That's a court-martial offense, and they are not taking it lightly, I've been told," Kevin said.

Miriam said, "Thanks, Kevin. We don't know how people talk out here. You may have saved us some trouble."

Kevin said, "I hope what I ordered was okay. I have money and can help pay."

"It was perfect," Miriam said. "How much money do you have?"

"Fifty bucks."

"Bucks?" Derrick asked.

"I think that means dollars," Miriam said.

Kevin said, "You're the ones, aren't you?"

Miriam looked puzzled for a moment. "What ones?"

"The ones who escaped from Pacific Edge."

Kevin looked at Derrick. "You're Derrick King."

3

Friday, April 9, 6:25 p.m.

COLLINS TOLD DONNA TO CLOSE EARLY. Donna insisted on taking soup, sandwiches, and pastries for everyone at Jack's shop. While she worked in the kitchen, Jason went to get Jack from the watchtower. Patel studied something on his laptop.

Jack walked through the door. Lori Martinez followed, then Browning, and finally Jason.

Jack said, "Smells like Donna's baking. Sign says closed."

Collins said, "Jack, have you ever tried to talk Donna out of doing something?"

Jack poured himself a coffee. "Can't say that I have."

Collins said, "Don't bother trying. She's made a pile of sandwiches. It was a slow day, so there's plenty of soup too."

Jack said, "Still don't explain why she's baking when she should be closed."

Collins said, "Jason wants us to return to your shop. Donna intends to feed everyone, and she didn't think she had enough pastries, and she believes a good pastry will cure just about anything."

"She can't keep doing this. No business all day, then feeding all of us." Jack pulled his wallet out. "I don't have much cash." He pulled out two tens. "I got more stashed at the shop."

Collins threw a twenty alongside Jack's two bills. "I'll go to the bank tomorrow."

Martinez said, "I'll do the same. I only have a five on me."

Jason said, "Donna will appreciate the gesture, but it's not important right now. No one is making a trip to the bank."

Collins said, "Look, Jason, I appreciate you wanting to help, but you're not in charge. People are free to do what they want to do."

Jason stared out a slit in the blinds. "We'll talk about it at Jack's."

Donna backed through the saloon doors, carrying a tray laden with freshly baked cinnamon rolls. "I'll let these cool just a little before icing them, and then we can head to Jack's. I hope I have enough food." She looked at the small pile of bills on the counter. "What's this?"

Browning said, "We're pitching in to pay you. We'll get more when we can go to the bank tomorrow."

Donna said, "Keep your money. I'm doing this because I want to. I can't help like you all, so this is my part. Don't take it from me."

"Nobody's trying to take anything from you, Donna," Browning said, "but you can't afford to do this."

"You let me worry about that," Donna said.

Allen said, "Donna, what you've done for us is wonderful. I think perhaps we forget how hard this is on our families. It was kind of Jack to let us stay in his shop, but it's not like home. Add the fear that we might not have a future." He paused. "I'm struggling to get my head around it."

Collins sat across the table from Allen. "Speaking of getting your head around something, I'm confused about this VPD thing."

"VPN."

"Right. That. You said the Resistance used it for years," Collins said.

"That is correct."

"Then why do you need Derrick and Miriam's father or keeper, whatever he is? Why does he need half of the code?" Collins asked.

Patel nodded. "Very observant. Lawrence King got scared when they exiled Derrick. It was all coming apart. He kept the program going by convincing the Tribunal to send Derrick here as a continuation of the test, I suppose. Lawrence hoped to control Derrick using the 1984 chip but was concerned that it wouldn't work."

"Because it failed before? Like when Derrick hit that Carver kid?" Browning asked, scooting his chair closer to Allen's table.

"Exactly. When Miriam escaped, Lawrence did too. He took the VPN as insurance. Leverage to use in the future."

A knock sounded at the door. Collins pulled his gun. "Now what? Everyone to the kitchen."

Browning said, "I'm staying."

"Not the time for an argument," Collins said, motioning them toward the kitchen as he eased toward the door. When everyone except Jason Maxton had cleared the room, Collins opened a slit in the blind. "For hell's sake. It's okay. You can come out." Collins unlocked the door, swinging it open just enough for Mark Grealy to slide in sideways.

"I figured I might find you here," Grealy said.

"Not a good time, Mark," Collins said. Donna closed early. If you're looking for Derrick for a guitar lesson, he's not around.

Grealy ignored him, walking toward Patel and pulling a cell phone from his pocket. "You've got a call coming soon." Then glancing at Collins, Grealy said, "I know more than you might think."

Patel took the phone, turning it over. "Burner phone? I thought you went to Los Angeles."

"That I did. Lots of shit going down." Grealy surveyed the room. "I guess you all know that."

"Call from who?" Patel asked.

Grealy motioned. "Up north. Having trouble with Lawrence. John wants you to talk with him."

"I doubt that will help. Lawrence won't trust anyone, not even me. I can't blame him," Patel said.

Grealy said, "You need to convince him. It won't sit well with John if he doesn't cooperate."

"You think John will turn him in?"

"No. John isn't like that. John is more of a tie Lawrence to a boxcar wheel and toss him into the river sort of guy."

4

Friday, April 9, 6:40 p.m.

OUTSIDE THE LIGHT WANED AND THE western sky glowed orange and red. The waitress brought food on a large platter balanced on one hand. She placed a basket containing a hamburger and mountain of french fries in front of each of them, and said, "I'll get your drinks."

Kevin said, "Thanks, Alice."

"You're welcome."

Derrick said, "I was thinking. If Prime controls New America Media, why are they talking about the president and vice president being assassinated? That seems more honest than I anticipated."

"Fair question," Miriam said. "First, I would say we don't know exactly what controlling the media looks like. Does that mean one Prime site does that? Like it is that location's job? Or is it more of a directive? Do this and don't do that. If they stray off course, Prime nudges them back on track. But in this case, Prime wants everyone to know. Prime is in charge, and those who might have stood in his way are dead."

Derrick said, "That makes sense. So, if we destroy the Prime that controls the media, more accurate reporting might occur."

"When, not if, brother. And maybe, but doubtful," Miriam said.

Rebekah said, "It's so much to take in. I'm not sure I can comprehend it all. I just want to play soccer."

While Alice filled drinks at the counter, Miriam whispered, "Eat. We need to get out of here. Do you think we can trust her?" She nodded toward Alice.

Derrick said, "I don't know, but what choice do we have? It's not like we can kill them."

Miriam said nothing.

"Well, it's not," Derrick said.

"We may have to do many things we don't want," Miriam said.

Rebekah said, "You can't be serious."

Anna said, "She's serious, and she has a point. I'll do it. Soon as we finish eating."

Kevin said, "She's joking. Right?"

Derrick nodded toward Anna. "That one doesn't joke much. We aren't killing anyone. Relax."

Anna fired back. "Who made you the boss?"

Miriam said, "That might be my fault. Someone has to lead, and I think it's Derrick."

Anna said, "How did that become your decision to make? Shouldn't we at least vote on it?"

Miriam glared at Anna. "It's not a democracy. If I remember correctly, you joined us recently. After someone came to save you. Besides, it would be a tie. You and Rebekah vote for you. Derrick and I vote for Derrick. Tie. Then what? We fight to the death?"

Rebekah said, "I would vote for Derrick."

Anna stared at her. "Why?"

"Because he hit Marcus Carver. He wasn't supposed to do that. He went against whatever controls they had over him." Rebekah looked at Derrick. "I trust him."

Anna stood. "And what? You don't trust me?"

Derrick said, "Sit down, Anna. I don't want to be the boss or leader, whatever you call it, but Miriam is right. Someone has to."

Anna plopped into her seat, arms folded.

Derrick said, "There may come a time when you must follow my orders without hesitation."

"What do you mean?" Rebekah asked.

"There may come a time when the risk is too great. I won't let any of you go further. I'll do it myself."

Miriam said, "Don't be dramatic."

Derrick said, "As if I know what that means."

"It doesn't matter. We are in this together. I'm not letting you go it alone," Miriam said.

"I wasn't asking permission."

"Could you guys stop bickering?" Rebekah asked. "I don't see how it helps. Let's eat and get out of here. Sitting still makes me nervous."

"Me too," Kevin said.

Everyone stared at him.

"What? I can't be nervous? Or I'm too stupid to understand what's happening?"

"No one said that," Derrick said.

"How long will it take us to get to where we are going?" Kevin asked.

Derrick said, "I don't know."

Miriam said, "About eight hours."

Derrick looked at her. "How do you know that?"

"I looked at a map of California."

"When?" Derrick asked.

"When I was in Technical Services."

"When was that?" Kevin asked.

"March 15th."

"That's like three weeks ago. You're joking. Right?"

"I am not."

Kevin said, "That's not possible."

Rebekah said, "It's possible. I'll bet she's within 15 minutes."

"Eight hours to where you are dropping us off. It will take you longer to get to where you are going. You can stop and get some rest. No big rush for you to get to Potterville. It's better if you don't roll into town in the middle of the night," Miriam said, pulling her burner phone out and turning it over in her hand.

"What are you thinking?" Derrick asked.

"Thinking about turning this on. I wonder if someone has a charger. Almost dead," Miriam said.

Derrick said, "I thought you only called Allen at six."

"Correct." Miriam walked over and said something to Alice. Alice ducked behind the counter, coming up with a charger, which Miriam plugged into an outlet under the table at their booth, and then she powered it on.

"I thought it was dangerous to leave them on," Rebekah said.

"It is," Miriam responded.

"Then why did you turn it on?" Rebekah asked.

"A feeling."

"A feeling? I thought you operated using logic," Rebekah said.

"That's what I prefer. Following a feeling sucks."

"Who are you going to call?" Derrick asked.

"I'm not calling anyone. Someone is calling me, I think."

"Who?" Derrick asked.

"Allen, I suppose."

Derrick shook his head. "You're doing this because of a feeling?"

"I know. It sucks."

5

Friday, April 9, 6:45 p.m.

SCOTT KEY, AKA, LAWRENCE KING, SAT in front of a rundown hotel on an old plastic chair he assumed was once white in a previous life. The air smelled of pine and was fresh in a way he'd only experienced during his trek here on the Pacific Coast Trail.

Scott had resigned himself to the 8:30 appointment with John, the beer maker. John's man, Bob, the guy who drove Scott to the haircut lady, sat 20 yards distant, watching him. Running wasn't an option, and when he thought running, he meant escaping. Scott waved to Bob. Bob motioned toward the brewery. Apparently, when John said 8:30, he wasn't firm on the time. Scott didn't know John's last name. He didn't even know if his name was John.

Scott assumed Bob would drive him to the brewery, but perhaps not. Deciding to take control of what little he still could, Scott stood and started walking. Bob followed, keeping a constant 20-yard separation. Scott didn't know if that was good or bad, but he felt certain he would soon learn just how dire his situation was. John-the-Brewer had never swayed in his conviction that Scott was Lawrence King. Scott had accepted that John would not be swayed. What John was capable of was the question.

It was dark. Sparsely placed streetlamps dimly lit the streets. Fog drifted on the light breeze, creating an eerie scene. Nothing about the situation raised Scott's hopes. This was probably the end. He should have been honest with John. Too late now. Scott doubted a change of attitude would alter what was coming.

In that, he was not wrong.

6

ALLEN PATEL STARED AT THE PHONE. Mark Grealy had disappeared into the kitchen without explaining why Patel was left holding a phone, other than saying someone would call and a lot of shit was going down. The only information was that someone was calling him rather than him calling somebody. He had already heard from Miriam at their designated time. Grealy said John wanted to talk, but it didn't sound like the call was coming from John.

A few minutes later, Grealy dashed out of the kitchen with a sandwich stuffed in his mouth, and lettuce and mayonnaise dropping to the floor in his wake. He mumbled, "Why ain't you got it turned on? I told you someone was going to call."

Allen remained calm. "Who is calling?"

"Turn on the phone and find out."

Allen picked up the phone, frowned, and pushed the start button. The phone signaled a familiar chime. The phone had just finished booting when it rang. "Hello?"

"Yes, this is Allen Patel. To whom am I speaking? —

"I see. I do not know anyone by that name. —

"We have never met. —

"Oh. I see. Yes. I have heard of the Wizard. —

"Okay. Just Wizard. What can I do for you, Mr. Nist? This is a dangerous time, and I don't feel comfortable speaking on the phone with someone I don't know." Allen listened, nodding his head from time to time. After a moment, he held his hand over the phone and mouthed, "It's Wizard."

Collins said, "What's he talking about?"

"Hell, if I know," Browning said.

Grealy held up one hand, chewing savagely. Swallowing, he said, "Lloyd Nist, they call him Wizard. He's a genius and way up the chain in the Resistance."

Allen said, "I see. —

"Yes. —

"I do. —

"But she won't answer. We have already talked at our designated time. Her phone will be turned off until 6 p.m. tomorrow. —

"I understand that would be too late, but I can't make her turn her phone on. I don't even know where she is. —

"Sure. I'll try. Yes, every 30 minutes, but I don't see how that will help. —

"Then we may well be doomed. —

Everyone stared at Patel. He lowered the phone. "He wants me to call Miriam."

"Then what are you waiting for?" Grealy asked, making a hurry-up motion.

"She only turns her phone on once a day to contact me at our designated time. She won't turn on until tomorrow evening."

"What did Wizard say to that?" Grealy asked.

"He wants me to try anyway and keep trying every 30 minutes."

Grealy waved his hand again. "Do it then!"

Patel punched the number into the phone. His eyes widened. "Miriam?"

7

MIRIAM HAD JUST TURNED ON HER CELLPHONE a few moments before it rang. The conversation was brief, and for everyone at the table, it was one-sided. Miriam didn't look happy. She set the phone on the table but did not turn it off. Then she took a bite of her hamburger.

"Well?" Derrick asked.

Miriam held one finger up and chewed. Finally, she said, "I hate it when that happens."

"When what happens?" Derrick asked.

"When I do something based on nothing more than a feeling, little more than a whim, yet it works out. That was Allen."

"And?"

"And he told me to leave the phone on."

"Damn it, Miriam. Do you always have to make things difficult?" Rebekah asked.

"Not always."

"Are you going to tell us what this is about, or should we guess?" Anna asked.

"You'd never guess correctly."

Derrick sighed. "Then tell us already. Why is the phone on? Isn't that dangerous?"

"It is on because I'm expecting a call, and yes, it's not a good idea."

"Who?" Rebeka asked.

"Sorry. I don't mean to be difficult, but I'm a bit discombobulated."

"Discombobulated?" Derrick puzzled.

Miriam said, "Confused, upset, anxious. You need to expand your vocabulary, brother."

"I'll get right on it if the world doesn't end."

"Stop already," Anna said. "Who is calling?"

Miriam looked at Kevin and then at Derrick. "Lloyd Nist called Allen and relayed a message." She paused. "Father is calling me."

8

Friday, April 9, 6:55 p.m.

SCOTT CONTEMPLATED MAKING A RUN for the bridge, but that would only result in exhaustion and cost him any chance of enjoying a cold beer and juicy hamburger before John-the-Brewer, chopped him into fish food and tossed him in the Columbia River. Although it had always been a long shot, Scott had hoped to survive. He liked to think he was smart enough to escape, but he wasn't as smart as a legion of Resistance fighters or an army of Prime's security forces. So, Scott braced against the chill of the fog and conceded his escape attempt was over. He could only hope that John would inflict a quick death and not turn him over to Prime, because that monster would show no mercy.

Not for Lawrence King.

The fog thickened quicker than any Scott ever witnessed in Pacific Edge. When the brewery finally came into view, he knew something wasn't right. There were no cars in the lot or on the street. It wasn't closing time yet. It was only a few minutes past seven, and the brewery should be open till nine and perhaps later on Fridays.

The front door opened.

John waved him inside. "Quickly, man, before someone sees we are here."

A closed sign hung on the door read: Closed. Sorry, Short Staffed. Once inside, the scent of grain, hops, and a potato baking filled the air. "Smells wonderful," Scott said.

"I hope you're hungry. I decided a good steak and a baked spud were better than a hamburger on such an occasion. This is an important moment. Don't you agree? Like a crossroads. Anyway, it's somewhat difficult cooking in the dim lighting, but Henry's a topnotch chef. Most cooks would be pissed if asked to cook under such conditions. But Henry understands what's happening. I trust all my employees. That's important. Right? Trust. Don't worry though, Henry hasn't started the steak. Don't want to overcook them." John turned on a flashlight, shielding it and letting a little light leak through his fingers. "We'll go down to the basement."

John walked toward a doorway Scott had not previously noticed.

With his back turned, John said, "First, we have business to take care of."

Scott didn't ask what business that might be. He didn't want to know the answer because he could not imagine any scenario where the answer was good, not for Lawrence King. His time was ending. Very soon.

At the bottom of the stairs, John led Scott down a dark hallway, stopping at a door where he inserted a key into a lock and punched a code into another device. "This room is secure. Only one other person has the key and code, and that person is 500 miles from here."

The room was dark except for dozens of blinking red and green lights. John didn't reach for a light switch, but the lights flickered to life as he stepped into the room. Scott hesitated at the door. The smell of electronics filled his nostrils. Banks of computers lined one wall. A workstation with three monitors, one chair, and one keyboard sat next to the computer modules.

John walked to a desk at the far end of the room. He moved behind the desk and sat. "Sit down."

Scott sat. "I didn't expect this," he said, looking around the room. Although this room was astonishing, it cemented that Scott's time on earth was limited. John would not let him live after seeing this, whatever it was, and since Scott didn't believe in the golden city in the sky promised for the chosen and a few special commoners, he knew when the end came, he would no longer exist. With nothing to lose, Scott asked, "What is this place?"

John glared at him. "First things first."

"Okaaaay. What's first?" Scott asked.

"We are waiting for a call. Then you'll make a call. After which, I'll decide whether you'll learn anything about this place."

"A phone call? Is that safe?"

"It is here. Safe as it gets, which isn't a guarantee, so we try to avoid them, but these are desperate times. Wouldn't you agree?"

Scott nodded. He was desperate. That much was true. "Who's calling?" He had decided to drop the, *you have the wrong guy routine.*

The phone rang. John pushed a button. "You're on speaker. Your guy is sitting here."

Allen Patel said, "Hello, Lawrence?"

Scott said, "AJ?"

"Yes. I go by Allen away from Pacific Edge. That's my first name."

Scott said, "I'm going by Scott."

Allen said, "Good choice. It suits you."

"What's this about?"

"The VPN—we need it back. Why did you take it?" Allen asked.

"I didn't take it. You still have it. I thought you would realize that by now. I only password-protected it." Scott took a breath. "Sorry, I needed some insurance. You know, if I made it to Canada. Some leverage to get in. I hoped that might help."

The line was silent for a moment. "What do you mean, I have it?"

"I slipped a hard drive into your briefcase."
Silence.
Leaning forward, Scott asked, "You found it, right?"
Allen whispered. "I don't have my briefcase."
"Where is it?" Scott asked.
"In my office." Allen paused. "In Pacific Edge."

9

ALLEN PATEL SAT SLACK-JAWED AND PALE, holding a phone halfway between his ear and the table. Over the phone's tiny speaker, a man's voice, thin and as if transmitted from a distant galaxy, said, "Allen? Are you still there? Allen? AJ? Can you hear me?"

After a few moments, Allen raised the phone to his ear. "I'm here. I thought you took it. Things went south. I left in haste and didn't return to the tech building."

Scott said, "I guess you'll have to do without it."

Allen said, "I can do without it, but it's vital for the Resistance. Especially now."

Scott said, "I understand how important it was for the Resistance. I planned to give you the code when I got to Canada, if they were to let me in. If they didn't, I hoped it would provide enough leverage to change their minds." Scott paused. "What do you mean, especially now?"

Grealy held out his hand.

Allen said, "Someone here wants to speak with you."

Grealy grabbed the phone. "Lawrence, we need it back, and we need it now."

"Who is this?"

"Not that it matters, but the name's Grealy. John can vouch for me, but you can discuss that later. Right now, we don't have time. To mount a full-scale attack on Prime, the kids need the VPN. So, turn it over and do it fast."

"Kids? What kids?"

"Derrick and Miriam."

"Attack Prime? That's ridiculous. I hoped to give Derrick a fighting chance. I had no idea Miriam would escape. They can't defeat Prime. I just hoped they could survive, and Prime would lose interest."

"Well, he ain't losing interest. He's murdered innocent folks trying to kill Derrick and Miriam. I believe the kids will attack Prime, no choice, really. They can't do it alone, and the Resistance is prepared to help if we can. But we can't without the ability to communicate, and to communicate, we need the VPN. Now, make it happen, or my friend there will be forced to do things he doesn't like doing."

Scott said, "I already told AJ, I mean, Allen, I don't have it. I took it offline, loaded it on a hard drive, and put it in Allen's briefcase. I left a note explaining."

Grealy cursed. "We need that briefcase!"

Scott said, "It's in Allen's office. They may have already found it. I can't help. I'm in Oregon. There's no way Allen could get in and out of there without being arrested. Me either, for that matter, even if I was still there, which I am not."

"Let us worry about that part. You worry about your part."

"And my part is?"

"You're going to stay put and cooperate. By cooperate, I mean you'll do what John tells you to do."

"What's in it for me?"

"You got balls. I'll give you that much. You get to stay alive. That's what you get."

"What do you want me to do? I told you! I don't have the VPN."

"First thing is you call Miriam and explain the VPN. Tell her we are working on getting it to them. We don't need to know where they are or where they've been hiding. Tell them to get someplace safe. Tell her to keep the phone on."

"I don't think she'll talk to me."

"She's expecting your call. It's your first assignment. Do not screw it up." Grealy handed the phone back to Allen. "Tell him Miriam's number."

10

DONNA WAS POURING COFFEE, feeling sure nobody would be sleeping anytime soon. The sign on the door had been flipped to closed, and the blinds were shut. The streets were empty. No one had left, and Allen had found more work to do. Every few minutes, one of them thought of another problem. Even the problems had problems. For Donna, food and drink solved many dilemmas.

Collins didn't think food or drink fixed anything, other than hunger and thirst, but odd as it seemed, the warm mug in his hands eased his disquiet, just a little, even if only for a moment. Maybe it wasn't the mug. Perhaps it was Donna's caring for others that produced the relief. Maybe it was something else. Still, as she filled his cup, it felt like oxygen flooded into the room.

Collins walked to the table where Patel sat with his laptop and phone. Sitting, Collins said, "Tell me more about the VCR?"

"VPN."

"Right. So, how important is it?"

"You heard the conversation. It's essential to give us a chance."

"You can't be serious. We aren't going to war with Prime." Collins held out his hand. "Give me that phone."

Allen put his hand on it. "To do what?"

"I'm calling Miriam and telling them to get back here."

Allen smiled. "Good luck with that."

"Damn it, Allen. I'm serious. They are just kids, and they need to be here where we can protect them, not out running around."

Jason put his hand on Collins's shoulder. "Calm down, Sheriff. Us protect *them*? You would do well to remember those kids just stopped a war and saved Potterville."

"But …"

"Can they destroy Prime?" Jason finished his question. "It's a tall order. I'll grant you that. But what choice do they have? What choice do any of us have? Prime will learn the missile strike failed. Then what? He'll get distracted? Forget we are here?"

Collins said nothing.

Browning said, "I agree with you, Bill. I want them back here too, but Jason makes a valid point. We don't have a choice and neither do the kids. It's fight or die."

"More like die fighting," Collins said.

Donna backed through the kitchen's saloon doors, carrying a tray. "If I'm gonna die, I'm damn sure going out fighting."

Collins went behind the counter and grabbed plates. "Donna, I'm going to put on twenty pounds before this is over."

Having sat silently until now, Lori eased to Collins's side, slipping her arm around his back. "Don't worry. I'm starting you on a new exercise routine when this is over."

Collins blushed. "Lori, it's inappropriate to say stuff like that to your boss."

"I'm turning in my resignation. Soon as this ends. Did you forget?"

"I didn't forget. But damn it, Lori. How am I going to replace you?"

Lori took the plates from Collins. "I'm not leaving. Just quitting."

Browning chuckled. "Bill, I think you've met your match."

Lori helped Donna serve hot apple turnovers. Everyone ate in silence for a few minutes. Finally, Collins asked, "What's next?"

Allen said, "I must go to Pacific Edge and retrieve the VPN."

Collins said, "That's suicide."

Patel shrugged. "I'm not a brave man, nor am I stupid, but this is my fault. I should have grabbed my briefcase. I can't explain why I did not. However, while the odds of success are low, the odds are worse without the VPN."

"I'll go with you," Lori said.

"You'll do no such thing," Collins said. "I'll go."

"You're needed here, Bill." Browning said. "I'll go."

Lori said, "You can't. You have a family."

"My family is the reason I'm going."

Grealy said, "I'll go. I got a car waiting outside."

Jason said, "None of you are trained for this sort of thing. I'm going."

"You're trained for this?" Collins asked.

"In a manner of speaking, yes, I am."

11

SCOTT STARED AT THE PHONE ON THE TABLE. Terror had pushed him to hike from California to Cascade Locks in record time. He had been petrified since he arrived here because John-the-Brewer, immediately identified him as Lawrence King. Scott had stopped denying it. Still, his fear increased tenfold at the thought of talking to Miriam—and Derrick. No doubt they had figured out by now his true purpose.

"What are you waiting for?" John asked, pushing the phone closer. "Call them."

Scott picked up the phone. "They probably won't talk to me, let alone believe me." He hesitated. "They must know by now. About me. What I've done. What I did to them."

"I suspect you're right. But you also did something for them."

"How so?"

"You kept them alive. Didn't you? That's what I was told."

"Yes. But my motives were self-serving."

"True. It's been all about you. But something changed. Did it not?"

Scott bowed his head. "Too little, too late."

"No changing the past. Call."

Scott entered the numbers Grealy had provided. The phone rang once, a familiar voice said, "Hello."

Scott's vision blurred. "Miriam. I did not think I'd ever hear your voice again.

"It's you."

"Yes. Lawrence, but I'm going by Scott now."

"I have nothing to say to you."

"Don't hang up. You hate me. I don't blame you."

"You have no idea."

"I was told to call you. I have important information."

"Who told you to call?"

"Called himself Grealy." Scott heard Miriam ask someone if Grealy rang a bell, and Derrick said he knew him.

"Okay. I'll listen. Make it quick."

"A man named AJ Patel —"

Miriam interrupted. "I know Patel."

Scott said, "Right. AJ and I developed a virtual private network or VPN."

"Losing patience."

"The VPN allows people to communicate on the internet without being tracked. That's how the Resistance can operate without Prime finding them. Do you understand the significance of that?"

"I understand how important that would be. So, what's that got to do with me?"

"Patel wants to get the VPN to you. Then you can coordinate with the Resistance to battle Prime. If that's what you plan to do."

"I don't plan to fight Prime. I intend to destroy Prime. So, how do I get this VPN, and why are you calling me instead of Allen?"

"Honestly, I don't know why they wanted me to call. Here's the thing. There's a problem with the VPN."

"What's the problem?"

"It's not working."

"Not helping."

"It's not working because of me."

"What a surprise. Did you steal it?"

"Not exactly. I removed it and password-protected it. I ran when you escaped. I was trying to get to Canada and thought I might need some leverage at the border. The password was my insurance."

"Give Allen the password. Problem solved."

"Not that simple. I put the program on a hard drive and left it in Allen's briefcase."

"I'm confused. How is that not simple?"

Scott hesitated. "Allen didn't find the hard drive. He doesn't have his briefcase."

"Where is it?"

"In his office. In Pacific Edge."

"Crap. Still doesn't explain why you're calling me instead of Patel."

"I think they want me to give you a brief explanation of how the VPN works."

"Make it quick."

Scott gave Miriam an overview—more than he'd tell a layperson—but he thought Miriam would follow him. When he finished, he said, "I think there's another reason they wanted me to call."

"Still listening but running out of patience."

"I think it was a test."

"What kind of test?"

"Whether I'd make the call. Admit what I did. Cooperate. If I didn't, I think they would kill me."

"Not my problem," Miriam said. The tone was as acidic as when she'd first heard his voice.

Scott heard Derrick in the background say, "Let me talk to him."
Scott felt tears forming.
"Father?"
"My name is Lawrence King, but I'm going by Scott now."
"Where are you?"
"In Oregon."
"Are you alone?"
"I came here alone."
"Are you alone now?"
"No. There's a man here with me. Resistance."
"Let me talk to him."
Scott held out the phone. "He wants to talk to you."
John shook his head.
"He says no."
"Put him on the phone."
Scott covered the phone. "He insists."
John pursed his lips, taking the phone. "Hello?"
"Do you know who I am?"
"Derrick King, I presume."
"You presume correctly. What are your intentions with Mr. King?"
"That's not your concern."
"I'm making it my concern. Answer the question."
"That depends on whether he cooperates."
"Let me talk to him."
John shrugged, handing the phone back to Scott.
"I'm back."
"Do you intend to cooperate?"
"I don't have much choice."
"You always have a choice. Answer the question."
"Yes. I plan to cooperate."
"Let me talk to the Resistance guy again."
"What?" John asked.
"You're Resistance?"
"Yes."
"I've had mixed results with the Resistance."
"Meaning?"
"Some can be trusted, some cannot."
"Fair enough. We have some rotten eggs, but what does that have to do with the price of tea in China?"

Derrick didn't understand the reference, but he wasn't worried about understanding such things at the moment. He was only concerned the Resistance guy understood. "What's your name?"
"Again, not your concern."

"Making it my concern. Answer the question."

John took a deep breath. "John."

"Thanks. Good start."

"That it?"

"Almost. When this is over, I want to have a conversation with Lawrence King."

"Okay. Not my concern."

"It is if you were to let anything happen to him."

"Is that a threat?"

"It is not. It is a promise."

12

RED HAD GONE TO INVESTIGATE AN alarm at reactor one. He'd been gone a couple of hours. Antonio was in the treatment room, recovered but sleeping. A QR-3 had cleared the food, but the odor of roast beef lingered. The meat tasted okay but left a slight rancid flavor on her palate, more of a perception than an actual sensation. At least, that was Akira's opinion. Not that anyone cared. Perhaps Miriam would have, but she had left. Nyx said she wasn't training properly, so, after eating a light dinner, she went for a run. Akira noticed she had eaten very little of the roast beef. In fairness, Nyx had tried to help her, and so did Red. Nyx was her oldest friend, but Akira had no feelings toward her. Memories, yes. Feelings, no. She had known Red for years but had no appreciation for him until a few days ago. Since he left, she had been sitting at the workstation, studying the complex. It was amazing, and she should have felt as if she'd been left alone in a candy store, but she did not. She felt zilch.

Akira wanted something, but she wasn't sure what. Hot chocolate sounded good, although she didn't think powdered milk would be as tasty as the real thing, but she made a mug anyway. She sat alone, sipping the cocoa, which tasted better than expected. L. Linda was exploring the facility—at least those parts Charlie allowed. Akira didn't know where Charlie was. Perhaps docked, but she hoped he was working on how to get her back to normal.

Normal.

Akira didn't mind being alone. She remembered being normal, even the emotional part, which she never thought much about. Now her lack of emotions consumed her. She wasn't sure how she felt about it now because she felt nothing, and she didn't want to live this way. It wasn't a life.

The door flew open. Red stepped in, his hair wet, wearing a fresh pair of mechanic's coveralls. "Hey, Akira."

"Hi. Where have you been?"

"Just checking the reactor."

"You've been gone a long time. Is everything okay?

Red walked to the coffee station but said nothing. After a few minutes of fiddling, he asked, "Do you know how this thing works?"

"Sort of—not really. I managed to make hot cocoa."

"Would you help me?"

"Sure."

Akira showed Red how to steam the mixture of powdered milk, powdered chocolate, and water, which would be called a solution in chemistry, but she didn't say that. He caught on fast. Then it occurred to her that Red could fix most anything and probably didn't need her help. Why had he bothered asking her for help? She didn't know.

Red sipped the cocoa as he sat. "Thanks. This ain't bad. I wonder if we could get a sandwich or something. I'm hungry."

"I don't know, ask Charlie."

"Where is Charlie?"

"I don't know that either." Akira looked at the ceiling. "Hey, Charlie, can we get some dessert?"

"You think that will work?"

"I don't know. You have a better idea?"

"Nope."

"Now, answer my question."

"I did. I don't have a better idea."

"Not that question."

Red said, "I don't know what you're talking about."

"Yes, you do. Is everything alright with the reactor?"

Red shifted in his chair. "Yeah. No big deal. I reset the warning."

"Then why were you gone so long?"

"Uh, just looking at stuff," Red said.

"What stuff?" Akira asked.

Red shrugged. "I don't know. Stuff. You know, like the trucks and such."

The door opened, and L. Linda walked in. "Something smells wonderful."

"What?" Red and Akira asked simultaneously.

"My guess is apple pie," L. Linda said.

Sniffing, Red said, "I don't smell it."

Akira said, "I had not noticed, but I smell it now. That answers one question."

"What question is that? I've lost track," Red said.

"Whether Charlie heard me. More than I can say about you answering my questions."

"Hey, cocoa and apple pie. You guys ready for another hot chocolate? I'm buying," L. Linda said.

"I'll wait until the pie is out," Red said.

"Same," Akira said. "Where have you been, L. Linda?"

"Just wandering around. Checking the place out."

"Checking it out for what?" Akira asked.

"Nothing in particular. Just looking at stuff."

"There's a lot of that going around." Akira paused. "Looking at stuff."

L. Linda said, "Yep. Lots of stuff here."

"Find anything interesting?" Red asked.

"Sure did. One question though, what's Level Two? Charlie said I could go anywhere except Level Two."

Akira said, "We don't know. Charlie said we couldn't go there."

"Where is it? I couldn't find it."

"What difference does it make?" Akira asked. "Were you planning on breaking in?"

L. Linda sat, tilted her head, put her hand to her chin, and looked at the ceiling. "That had not occurred to me, although I like your thinking."

Red said, "It doesn't work like that."

"Explain," L. Linda said.

"Charlie can move walls, open, and close hallways."

"Fascinating."

Akira said, "I don't think it's up here. I think it is below us."

"Well, I think we need to go there," L. Linda said.

"Not possible. Charlie won't allow it," Akira said.

"You don't know that," L. Linda said. "Besides, I can be very persuasive."

Akira said, "I do know. It isn't going to happen."

Red stared at Akira. "What do you mean, you know?"

Akira looked down. "Charlie has my emotions. I have some of his memory."

L. Linda slid onto the seat next to Akira. "That's amazing. So, what's in Level Two?"

Akira looked at L. Linda. "I can't tell you. Charlie won't let me."

13

DEEP IN THE EARTH, STANLEY MIRES, THE man Prime called Quigley, surveyed the room subtly, hoping Prime wouldn't notice. The ceiling was constructed of exposed steel beams and concrete. The walls were the same, except for one side, which was solid steel plates. Stanley felt certain he was only seeing a portion of this level. Something else lay beyond that steel wall. The complex must be huge and deep into the earth because the elevator descended into this hellhole for some time before it stopped.

A strange smell permeated the room. It reminded him of formaldehyde, but he saw nothing that might emit such an odor. Unless it was Prime. This Prime was unlike the version of Prime in Seattle. That version was troublesome—nothing short of grotesque. This one was hard to look at, but Stanley remained indifferent, or at least, hoped he did. Revealing his disgust would likely be his last act. He'd done horrible things to get here. He didn't plan to throw this opportunity away. If there was an opportunity to be made of it, and if there was, he could not imagine what it might be.

Prime said, "Stanley, relax. You've arrived—this is it! The pinnacle of success. I am Prime. Not a replica. Not virtual. This is the hub of existence. The home of the Creator." Prime paused. "How rude of me. You could use a drink." Prime waved what was intended as a hand, and a cabinet in the corner rotated, revealing a polished wooden bar made of what Stanley thought was rare Brazilian Rosewood. "Your predecessor did not drink liquor, so you are in for a treat. Scotch, which was 35 years old when it was originally sold, is now close to 100 years old. Help yourself. There is a warehouse full of fine liquors here."

Stanley walked to the bar, wondering why Prime had used his real name instead of Quigley. He studied the selections and decided on Kentucky Bourbon, even though he typically preferred Scotch. Different place, different time, no time like the present to try something unfamiliar. Every bottle, and there were many, remained unopened. Worth a fortune to those who had money, although few of those still remained in New America. He poured a good portion, sipped it, threw it back, and poured another, hoping that might settle him. The alcohol burn created an artificial sense of confidence, which then generated an ill-advised question. "Where am I?"

"I've told you. You're at Headquarters. *The* Headquarters."

"I mean, where are we?"

Prime did not respond for a moment. "I guess there's no harm in telling you, although no assistant has asked that question since the first few. Those assistants did not last long, unfortunately. Finding good help is difficult, Stanley."

"Yes, sir. I'm sure that is true."

"You have no idea."

"The assistant I'm replacing, how long did he serve you?"

"Many years. My longest-tenured assistant."

"My condolences."

"Condolences? You assume he died. Perhaps you think I killed him. Not the case. Peter is here. You'll meet him in good time, although he cannot help you transition." Prime pointed to a chair covered in rich burgundy leather. "Please, sit."

Stanley sat. Perhaps the most comfortable desk chair he'd ever experienced.

Prime said, "Log in. The same credentials you used in Seattle. See if we have heard from that satellite woman. I still have not seen what happened in the desert town. However, you'll be pleased to hear that the missile in Mexico was launched. Once satellite operations are restored, we'll have images displaying Potterville's destruction. Then I will initiate the next phase, beginning with the invasion of Mexico."

Stanley thought about telling Prime the woman's name was Ava, but Prime knew that. Prime didn't call her by name because she had little significance beyond the service she could provide. After that, Prime might have her killed just because he could. Stanley logged in, surprised the computer was antiquated compared to his machine in Seattle, which seemed odd. "How many people work here?"

"By here, do you mean on this level of the facility? Two. You and me. There are two technical staff cleared to come here if needed, which is a rare occurrence. Typically, robots take equipment up rather than letting people come down. Safer that way. For everyone. But there are a few things the robots cannot do. Thus, the two technicians have been thoroughly vetted the same as you."

Stanley navigated to the information Prime wanted. Knowing Prime would be unhappy, he tried again. "You were about to tell me our location."

"So, I was. You were about to tell me about the desert town."

Stanley took a drink. It was a fine bourbon. No questioning that. "Nothing yet, sir."

Prime nodded, walked to a metal desk, raised both hands above his head, and slammed them down, crushing the desk to the floor. Then Prime turned, and to no one said, "I need a new desk."

Prime walked behind his assistant.

Stanley took another drink. Perhaps his last.

Prime rested his hands on Stanley's shoulders.

Stanley resisted the urge to squirm away.

"Stanley, my trusted servant. We are under the California desert."

14

THE FOOD WAS GONE EXCEPT FOR A FEW french fries which the soldier still picked at. Kevin was a skinny kid, yet he ate like Red Badowski. Apparently, the kid had a high metabolism, which meant nothing regarding how much he could be trusted, but he was just a kid, too young to be in a war, yet the war he would have entered was no more deadly than the future Derrick and the others faced.

The waitress, Alice, returned. She looked at Kevin. "Can I get you more fries?"

Kevin said, "No. I'm fine."

Miriam studied Kevin for a moment. "Bring a large order of fries and another milkshake and a cheeseburger. Anyone else?" Everyone shook their heads.

"Thanks," Kevin said.

"Don't they feed you in the military?" Miriam asked.

"They do. All you can eat, but it's inedible. It's not like they advertise. I got a threadbare uniform and old boots. It's like they are broke."

"Broke, as in broken?" Derrick asked.

Rebekah said, "He means poor."

"Oh. I understand. Not wanting to waste money or resources," Derrick said.

"Their ads say soldiers get the best of everything," Kevin said. "But that wasn't my experience. Just the opposite."

"I saw billboards that made the military sound great, and if you join the union, you get even better treatment, including advanced medical care," Derrick said, then asked, "Did you join the union?"

"Couldn't."

"Why not?" Derrick asked.

"You gotta have two years in and sign up for ten more. Then you can join."

Miriam said, "I think that's wrong. Not wrong in that you're not telling the truth. Wrong in that it's no way to treat people. But it makes sense. Derrick's right. You didn't get much because it would be a waste of resources."

"I don't understand," Kevin said.

"You were in the first wave into Mexico. They don't expect many would survive," Miriam said.

Anna took the last french fry. "Besides, the sergeant was going to kill all of you once the missiles were fired."

Kevin said, "I don't believe that. Kill his own men? Unlikely."

Miriam said, "Not unlikely—predictable. Prime wouldn't risk having witnesses that New America started the war."

Kevin said, "We thought we were in California."

Miriam said, "What you think doesn't change the facts. Prime doesn't care about killing thousands of kids invading Mexico, so killing you was no big deal."

Kevin whistled. "Sounds crazy but makes sense. I must be the stupidest person in the world."

"Don't beat yourself up. Thousands of kids on the border fell for the same 'join the military—it's a glorious life' bullshit," Miriam said.

Kevin looked at Anna. "I owe you."

Anna looked confused. "For what?"

"For kicking my ass and saving my life."

The corner of Anna's mouth turned up. "You're welcome. It was my pleasure."

Alice arrived with a milkshake, cheeseburger, and an enormous basket of fries. "Anything else?"

"No," Miriam said.

"Thank you," Kevin said, more to Miriam than to Alice.

"Can I help you guys? Anything you need. Well, not anything. I'm just out of high school, and I don't have much. But I have a car. I can drive you somewhere." Alice paused. "Your secret is safe with me. My dad's in the Resistance. Most folks here are."

Miriam glared at her for a moment and then softened. "That's nice of you, Alice. Nothing that I can think of, but if something comes to mind, I'll let you know."

They sat watching Kevin eat, each of them snagging a french fry here and there. Derrick knew Miriam was thinking hard, and he had seen that expression before and knew better than to interrupt. The others must have suspected the same thing or were also contemplating something. Feeling a sense of urgency, Derrick said, "We should go."

"Soon." Miriam walked to the counter and got Alice's attention. They whispered for several minutes.

"What's that about?" Rebekah asked.

"Damned if I know," Derrick said.

"I still can't get used to you talking like a normal human," Rebekah said.

Anna said, "I know, right?"

When Miriam returned, she said, "I need to call Allen, and then we can go."

Miriam punched in Allen's number. "Allen?"—

The others listened to the one-sided conversation.

"How important is the VPN?"—

Miriam stirred a dollop of ketchup on her plate with a fry while listening.

"Okay. So, what are you thinking?—

"Too dangerous. They are looking for you, and you'll never get in. They've locked you out.—

"You think it's *that* important?—

Miriam took a deep breath. "I was afraid you were going to say that. Okay, here's the plan.—

"Just listen. Don't go to Pacific Edge. Go to La Conchita, about six miles south.—

"Seriously? That's a stroke of luck.—

"Don't worry, I'll find it. Avoid big towns. I'll meet you there. You may arrive before me. Park near your friend's house and call me. Anything else?—

"I agree. Don't go alone but only take one other person. We don't need to make this more difficult than it already is. See you in about six and a half hours."

"I take it we are helping Allen first," Derrick said.

"Wrong. I'm helping Allen, and the rest of you are going to—well, you know. Except Kevin. He will drop you in Johnsondale and then drive to Potterville."

"No way," Derrick said. "It's too dangerous for you in Pacific Edge."

"No more dangerous than what you're going to do," Miriam said.

"Which is what?" Derrick asked.

"Destroy Prime's Seattle complex. Prime's new war is about to begin, but not in Mexico."

15

THE APPLE TURNOVERS WERE GONE, but their spicy scent lingered. Patel was off the phone. He remained silent, as if in deep thought or perhaps fear, packing his laptop in a mindless automated routine.

Collins said, "Allen, was that Miriam? What's happening?"

"Miriam intends to meet me near Pacific Edge."

Collins said, "No way. That's too dangerous."

"I agree it is too dangerous," Patel said, "for Miriam."

Collins said, "You didn't try very hard to talk her out of it."

"Hardly at all." Browning added.

"I did not. It's my opinion that telling Miriam what she can and cannot do is a waste of one's time."

Browning said, "She escaped from Pacific Edge, so she must be a determined young lady."

"That's an understatement," Patel said.

Donna said, "Allen, you can't go alone. That's for sure. We will go with you."

Allen shook his head. "Miriam said one person should accompany me. She said she could get me into the building."

"Into Pacific Edge?" Browning asked.

"Yes. Into Technical Services," Allen said.

"That seems unlikely," Collins said. "They'll have changed the entry codes and have extra security."

"I suspect Miriam created a backdoor into the computer network."

"What makes you think that?" Collins asked.

"Because that's what I would have done, and Miriam is smarter than me."

Browning said, "I'm sure Miriam is a smart girl, but not smarter than you, Allen."

Allen said, "Miriam is a genius."

"I'm not sure how to say this," Donna said. "Did they make her that way?"

Allen said, "Not according to Lawrence, but he didn't know everything about the experiment."

Jason said, "I'll go with Mr. Patel."

Donna said, "If you have special training, you should stay here. What if Prime sends more assassins? We have families and kids here. Allen, your wife and daughter are here too."

Jack had been silent the entire time. "I'll take him."

Everyone stared at Jack as if they'd forgotten he was there. Collins said, "That does not make sense."

"Why not?" Jack asked.

"You have no experience with this sort of thing."

"And Patel has?"

Collins said, "Allen knows where the briefcase is."

"Was." Patel corrected.

"What about Miriam? She has experience?" Jack asked.

Collins said, "No, but she's smart."

"You saying I ain't?"

Collins sighed. "No, Jack. I'm not saying that. Miriam said only one person should accompany Allen. I don't understand why, but perhaps there's something we don't know." Collins looked at Jason. "Jason has experience. Apparently."

"I got something neither Jason nor the rest of you got."

"Which is?" Collins asked.

"Cars that can outrun any police POS."

Collins said, "Hey, nothing wrong with my squad car."

Jack rolled his eyes. "Right."

Lori raised her hand. "Mine is a piece of shit."

Collins said, "I gave you the best car."

Jack said, "Proves my point."

Allen said, "Miriam said me and one other."

Collins said, "Allen has a point."

Jack said, "I'm just driving. Allen and Jason can go with Miriam."

"What if Miriam doesn't see it that way?" Allen asked.

Jack shrugged. "What's she gonna do? Quit? Call the whole—destroy Prime thing off? That would suit me just fine."

Allen said, "The kids won't stop until they destroy Prime or Prime kills them."

"You believe that?" Jack asked.

"I do," Allen said.

Jack said, "Then we ought to stop farting around and get going."

16

STANLEY HAD LEARNED LITTLE ABOUT the level where Prime spent its time, yet it was similar to the Seattle operations room. He was convinced what was visible was just part of this floor. A metal wall blocked the rest. Perhaps the wall was permanent, but he felt certain it could move. The wall piqued his curiosity.

What Prime might have hidden behind that wall terrified him.

Something else bothered him. He thought the scent would fade, as most odors do, as one adjusted to them. This one did not. It grew worse.

"Stanley, have you located the satellite image of Potterville?" Prime asked. "I want to see what remains of them, which I assume is nothing more than smoldering heaps of rubble. I trust you can navigate to the large monitors." Prime indicated an area covered with screens, each displaying a gray capital P on a black background.

"I only found old satellite images." He knew how to display those images on the large array but thought showing Prime the untouched city would not be a good idea.

"That's impossible."

Stanley considered his response. "Your assessment of the damage is probably accurate, but we are not getting updated information. Perhaps it's related to the satellite Ava is working on."

Prime tensed up like a predator preparing to pounce. "Send her an email."

Stanley typed a message. He was certain Prime could have done this without his assistance, but Prime liked to give orders. He was also sure that Prime could read the message he typed, so he worded it harshly.

"Done," Stanley said.

"Mr. Mires go to your quarters. Get some rest. I will send for you if I need you. It could be a long night."

Stanley walked to the door, where he turned to face Prime. "Long night, sir?" he asked.

"Yes. Our attack is imminent."

17

L. LINDA WAS DETERMINED TO LEARN what Charlie kept hidden in Level Two, because events had not gone according to her plan. Things seldom did. Events don't respond to one's thinking. People plan and plot, yet the universe pays little attention. Even Prime could not control everything, although Prime would likely disagree. She was accustomed to things going wrong. Otherwise, she would not have been in Potterville. L. Linda's life had been chaotic for many years. She was used to it. Her adversaries were not. That gave her an advantage, even though it was miniscule. But she'd take any help she could get. She wasn't delusional. Winning this battle would be difficult. As would survival.

Help wasn't something she had anticipated. She had asked Jason to help. He refused, pointing out the obvious flaws in her thinking. Revenge wouldn't bring the dead back to life. Dying wouldn't help either. He was right, and she stopped asking. Not that her preoccupation subsided. It did not. But she would not put Jason at risk. He had done his part.

L. Linda had promised to complete high school before pursuing her vision. That was a few years ago. Jason probably thought she'd let it go because the topic had not come up again. She decided to live her life as, L. Linda Maxton, a quirky girl she had invented. She had planned to honor her promise to finish high school, but then things changed. Derrick King came to town and brought Prime's wrath with him. Prime had sent an assassin to Potterville.

One assassin down, many more to go.

L. Linda could not keep the promise she'd made to Jason, but it wasn't her fault. She didn't ask for Derrick King to be exiled, nor did she ask him to come to Potterville. Things have a timeline of their own. Jason would understand that.

She needed to know what was in Level Two, but first, she had to get Red and Akira off to bed. They did not factor into her plans.

Derrick King perhaps did.

When she learned he was coming to Potterville, she hoped to recruit him. However, Derrick wasn't what she had expected. His 'test subject' training proved adequate. He demonstrated that by taking out the military guys at the council meeting in Potterville, but he had a softer side, which concerned her. Still, he might prove useful, and she could wait until morning for his return. But no longer than that. In the meantime, she needed into Level Two.

L. Linda said, "Akira, you look tired. There's nothing to accomplish here. Miriam may need you when she returns, and you'll be better equipped to assist after some rest."

"If she returns," Akira said.

"Have you learned something?" Nyx asked. Nyx stood just inside the doorway—wet hair, fresh uniform.

L. Linda said, "Calm down. Nothing's happened. How was your run?"

"I hope it helps me sleep, but knowing they are okay would help more," Nyx said.

L. Linda said, "Fresh-baked apple pie and hot chocolate would be just the ticket. I'll make your cocoa, and the pie should be out soon."

L. Linda walked to the counter. She didn't mind making drinks. She rather enjoyed it at the Bistro. But mostly, making nice with Nyx was important. She didn't need Nyx causing problems when Derrick returned.

The cellphone next to Akira erupted. She stared at it. Unsure of why it was working. Perhaps Charlie had turned on a cellular repeater of some sort. She'd try to remember to ask.

"Aren't you going to answer it?" Red asked.

"I don't think I can take bad news," Akira said, adding, "Or maybe it's someone I shouldn't talk to."

Red snatched up the phone. "Hello? —

"Yeah, you got Red. —

"She's here. Are you guys, okay? —

Red took a deep breath. "That's a relief. Here she is."

Red held out the phone. "They're okay. Miriam wants you."

Akira took the phone. "Hello?" Her forehead wrinkled. "Thanks. It's nice to hear your voice too, I guess.—

"I have an excellent memory. —

"Okay, give me a minute." Akira glanced around. "I need a pen and paper."

Nyx said, "I have that in my room. Be right back."

Akira said, "Nyx is going for it. Where are you? —

"I'll look at a map. When will you be back? —

"Why would Derrick get back first?" Akira listened.

"That sounds dangerous," Akira said.

"What sounds dangerous?" L. Linda asked, sliding into a seat across from Akira.

Akira motioned for silence.

Nyx burst through the door. "Here." She slid the notepad and paper to Akira.

"Is there a speaker setting on that phone?" L. Linda asked. "We should all understand what's happening."

"I agree," Nyx said.

Akira studied the phone and then pushed a button. "You're on speaker. Is that okay?"

"Who is there?" Miriam asked.

"Red, Nyx, L. Linda, and me. Antonio is in the medical unit."

Miriam said, "Why? What happened?"

"He's okay, now. Just sleeping. Long story, but we are okay. Well, except for me, but Charlie is working on my problem."

Miriam said, "I'm going to Pacific Edge to help Allen Patel. When we finish, I'll come there."

"Why isn't Derrick helping you?" L. Linda asked, adding, "Put him on the phone."

"I can't do that. I'm not with Derrick and the others right now." Miriam did not add that they were at a table nearby. "Derrick isn't going with me because he is doing something else."

"What?" L. Linda and Akira said simultaneously.

"Derrick is going to Seattle. Write this address: 1107 1st Ave."

"What's there?" Akira asked.

"Prime's Seattle Headquarters." Miriam paused. "Derrick and Anna are going to destroy it."

Akira said, "But how …"

Miriam cut her off. "No time for explanations. We need solutions. First, they must get there fast, so perhaps Red can learn to fly another aircraft. It would have to be small and have vertical takeoff. And they will need powerful explosives. Charlie can help you locate explosives and detonation devices."

Akira said, "But …"

"That's it. Have those things ready by early morning. I must go."

The phone clicked and then went silent. No one spoke for a moment.

Finally, Nyx said, "That's crazy."

The door opened. Charlie walked in. "I was monitoring the conversation. The explosives and detonators are not a problem. There are a variety of those here. QR-3s are gathering them. But the aircraft is tricky."

Red said, "I flew a helicopter. I can practice this evening."

"You crashed one too," Nyx said.

Charlie said, "A helicopter could land on a roof."

Red stood. "I'll go right now. Charlie, can QR-3s help me get one ready?"

Charlie said, "They can, but helicopters won't work for this mission. The vertical takeoff aircraft stationed here do not have the range to fly to Seattle and return. In addition, they are not fast enough to evade military jets. It would be a suicide mission."

Akira whispered, "Sounds like suicide, for sure."

Nyx said, "We need one of those Prime aircraft like the one Miriam flew us in."

L. Linda said, "That would be perfect."

Red looked at her. "We can use the one you took from Gramps."

"I crashed that one."

"You didn't tell us that," Red said.

Nyx chimed in. "L. Linda mentioned it to me in the hanger when she was trying to save your butt. The subject didn't come up again. Sorry."

Red said, "What happened?"

"Another time perhaps." L. Linda didn't add *if I'm alive to tell the story*. "We don't have time for it now."

Red said, "I assume that has something to do with why you looked like hell."

L. Linda patted his hand. "You're smarter than most people give you credit."

Red blushed, just a little. "I know where one is. There's one in that big warehouse where we got," he paused, "uh, Charlie #2."

Charlie said, "You speak of the one in engineering?"

"Yes. That's what Miriam called the place."

"That is not a Prime aircraft. It was developed here. Prime might be using them, but they came from here."

"Perfect," L. Linda said.

Charlie said, "Not perfect. That aircraft is damaged and is not operational."

Akira said, "If they were developed here, then perhaps it can be fixed. Red is good at fixing things."

"That aircraft is beyond repair."

No one spoke for a moment.

Red looked at Charlie. "There's something you're not telling us. If they were developed here, there must be more."

"There are additional aircraft."

Nyx stood. "Damn it, Charlie. Why are you not telling us the truth? If there are things here that can help Derrick, why are you hiding them? Are you associated with Prime? Protecting Prime perhaps?"

"I am not protecting Prime. There are many things here that would help Derrick complete the mission."

"And?" Nyx shouted.

"Those things are in Level Two and cannot be accessed."

L. Linda stood. "Take me there!"

18

Friday, April 9, 7:03 p.m.

MIRIAM HAD TALKED ON THE PHONE and then chatted with the waitress before returning to the table. While she was gone, Derrick thought about how to destroy Prime's Seattle Headquarters. He didn't have a clue. Miriam had a plan, or she would not have said it, but how to accomplish it was beyond his comprehension. Perhaps she wanted him to launch a missile from one of the silos, but that would not require a trip to Seattle. Plus, Professor wanted them to rescue Stanley Mires. Perhaps Miriam had decided that wasn't possible.

As Miriam slid into the booth, Derrick asked, "What was that about?"

"Alice has a car and is letting me borrow it."

"Borrow?" Derrick asked.

"Loan. She's letting me use it."

"I know what borrow means. How would we return it to her? Surely, she can't afford to give up her car …."

"She offered to drive me, but I said no for obvious reasons. I promised to make it right with her somehow."

"She accepted that?" Derrick asked.

"She did. She supports the Resistance and assumes that's what we are."

"And you let her believe that?" Derrick asked.

"Well, she's not wrong."

"What about the phone call?" Rebekah asked.

"I called Akira."

"Is everyone okay?" Derrick asked.

"No answer." Miriam lied. She wasn't sure why. Only that they didn't need the distraction and she didn't need more questions.

"That's weird. Right?" Rebekah asked.

Miriam shrugged. "Maybe not. Akira could be away from the phone. The signal might not be strong enough. No reason to panic. I left a message."

Derrick said, "Back to the car."

"I'm taking it, meeting Allen, and retrieving the VPN. Then I'll drive to Potterville and walk to where we entered before. I hope you're back when I get there."

Derrick said, "You can't go to Pacific Edge alone. I'll go with you."

"You can't. You need to destroy the Prime Headquarters in Seattle."

Derrick shook his head. "Slow down. You and I will go to Pacific Edge and get this VNP thing, then go to Seattle."

"VPN."

"Whatever."

Miriam said, "I like your plan, but we don't have time."

Rebekah said, "Hello. What about sticking together? We said we need to stick together."

"I'd like to, but again, no time," Miriam said.

Kevin said, "I will go with Miriam."

No one responded for a moment.

Kevin shrugged. "I've had basic training, so I can help if there are problems. Besides, I've never seen the ocean."

Miriam said, "I appreciate your offer, but fighting isn't part of the plan. The key will be getting in and out undetected."

Rebekah said, "I'm going with Miriam. End of story."

Miriam started to protest.

"End of story," Rebekah said, voice raised. "No different from when I followed you out of Pacific Edge. I saved your butt then, and I may have to do it again."

"You saved my butt?"

"Ocean."

"Point."

Anna said, "I should go with Miriam. Rebekah can go with Derrick."

Rebekah said, "Don't start. Derrick needs you in Seattle."

Miriam said, "I hate to admit this, but Rebekah is right."

Rebekah said, "Very funny."

Derrick said, "We are not splitting up. We need to plan this out."

"Can you not hear me talking?" Miriam asked. "We. Don't. Have. Time. Look, I have a plan, but there are a few details you'll need to work out when you get to the—the place." She glanced at Kevin.

"You're afraid to mention a place because of me. I can step outside if it would help."

Miriam said, "That won't be necessary. Not yet."

Rebekah said, "It would help if you'd tell us what you're thinking. Why does Derrick have to attack Seattle right now?"

Miriam looked stunned. "Sorry. I thought it was obvious."

"Well, it's not," Rebekah said.

"If we had not diverted that missile, New America would be at war with Mexico, and Potterville would have been destroyed. Prime will soon learn Potterville is undamaged. Prime won't be happy and will retaliate. Plus, Prime will start the war with Mexico anyway."

Slowly, Derrick said, "So destroying Prime's Seattle Headquarters will create a distraction. Prime will be under attack and focus on defense."

Miriam pointed "Exactly."

"But I don't know how to find Prime's location or destroy it."

Miriam grabbed a napkin, wrote an address, and then slid it over to him.

"How did you …?"

"Rachael had that information. I know where all the locations are except one."

"Rachael, the Resistance girl in the desert town?" Derrick paused. "But you don't know the central Prime's location?"

"Not yet."

"But this doesn't tell me how to get in."

"There's a parking garage under the building. Plant the explosives on the concrete pillars, detonate them, and the building will collapse. Before you detonate the explosives, find Stanley Mires."

Derrick shook his head. "I don't …"

"Know how to plant explosives? Charlie can show you." Miriam paused, looking around as if a spy might be nearby. "One more thing. Kill Prime and destroy the replicas. You must be sure Prime does not survive."

19

MIRIAM ESTIMATED FIVE HOURS to reach Pacific Edge, traveling the posted speed limit, which would put them in later than she had hoped. Obeying the law was smart, although she didn't know if people got arrested for speeding. Nevertheless, Rebekah had the old wreck, Alice called her baby, traveling ten miles per hour over the speed limit. Miriam didn't know if the police would ignore their infraction but believed ten over was unacceptable. The car was loud, and blue smoke trailed them. The exhaust and hot oil odors turned Miriam's stomach, especially at first, but she had grown used to it as much as was possible.

Three and a half hours into the journey, the temperature dropped. The heater didn't work. Miriam said, "I'm freezing."

Staring straight ahead, Rebekah said nothing.

Miriam thought about saying more, but she didn't want to be a whiner. Rebekah was probably cold as well. Nothing either of them could do about it.

They were getting closer. Earlier, Miriam had been tracking time and distance, estimating the drive would take four and a half hours instead of five, but she had lost track. Under different circumstances, that would have worried her. Her current situation did not foster clear thinking and therein lay the problem.

Miriam glanced at Rebekah, the wheel rocking in her hands, sitting forward in a stupid-looking posture, focusing on the road as if frozen. Her rigid expression pissed Miriam off. Miriam didn't know why, it just did. At the moment, it seemed like everything pissed her off, including the passing gloom of darkening, uninhabited desert.

A coyote ran across the road. Rebekah didn't react, but she missed hitting the animal. Miriam had no love for coyotes, but Rebekah could have eased off the gas to let the poor, ragged beast pass. After all, it wasn't involved in any of this mess.

And what a mess it was!

It pissed her off.

All of it.

It wasn't fair. She should still be in Pacific Edge, sneaking out her bedroom window, loathing her life, giving instructors heartburn, and driving her hapless brother up the wall.

But here she was in this rust bucket posing as an automobile, traveling at an unsafe speed through the desert, and she'd just asked her brother, who wasn't her brother, to go on what was likely a suicide mission.

It wasn't fair.

It pissed her off that Rebekah had forced herself into this situation. Miriam had caved too easily on that. Rebekah shouldn't be here. Rebekah didn't know how to drive, but Miriam had also conceded to that.

Who cares?

If something happened on this forsaken highway—broke down, flat tire, crash—any of which were possible, no one would find them until morning.

The car drifted over the center line and back. Miriam looked over. Rebekah had not changed positions, yet she seemed far away now. Blurry as if a haze hung in the air. Miriam's head fell to one side and then snapped straight.

So tired.

Miriam shook her head and forced her eyes open. She nodded again. Then her head drifted to the side, resting against the window.

She didn't notice the car slow as Rebekah approached a corner.

The road curved to the left.

Their car continued straight.

***

Billy Joe Howie was about to turn around when he saw something odd—dim taillights fifty yards off the road into the desert. He eased off the pavement and turned his lights off. Most police officers would leave their lights on for safety and call in their location, but Billy Joe was no ordinary police officer. The truth was, he was no police officer at all.

He was the self-appointed marshal of the tri-county region: Kern, Ventura, and Santa Barbara. His father, John David Howie, had defined the tri-county region some 50 years ago. For a decade, his father had attempted to convince the commissioners and sheriffs of those counties to merge into one. He suggested they call it Howie County after its founder, himself. After ten long years and countless meetings and petitions, John David Howie gave up.

That's when he declared himself marshal of the tri-county area he called Howie County. Billy Joe's father died just over a year ago.

Still living at home, Billy Joe found his father dead one morning, sitting in his patrol car. The sheriff said it was suicide—carbon monoxide poisoning.

Billy Joe knew his father wouldn't kill himself and set out to prove the sheriff wrong. It was not difficult. The sheriff wasn't too sharp, plus he hated John David, always telling him he wasn't a law enforcement officer and to stop impersonating one.

The facts were easy to sort out. John David had been out on patrol, just as Billy Joe was at this very moment. He arrived home late and fell asleep in the car. Perhaps he intended to make another pass through Howie County and only wanted a few minutes' rest. Billy Joe raised the car on jacks and found the exhaust pipe had rusted out just behind the muffler, which meant it wasn't overly loud and therefore had not drawn attention to needing repair. A similar hole under the passenger seat gave the exhaust a direct path into the car.

John David's death was accidental. The coroner agreed with Billy Joe's report and changed the death certificate. The coroner said something about 'no skin off his nose,' which Billy Joe didn't understand. He was an investigator, not a medical person.

Billy Joe inherited the patrol car and the mobile home in which they lived, and Billy Joe vowed to follow in his father's footsteps, enforcing the law in Howie County. He was driving the very same car that killed his father. Billie Joe didn't have money to purchase a different car. He only and enough money for some tape to wrap the exhaust pipe and prevent another accidental death. The hole in the floor had been sealed with glue, screws, and plywood.

Most cops would have also turned on their overhead lights. Billy Joe wasn't like most cops. He was more interested in catching bad guys than in personal safety. It never occurred to him that the rotating lights—which had to be yellow, according to the police, although his dad had installed red—also kept motorists safe.

Cops would radio in their position. Billy Joe didn't do that either. He didn't have a radio. The cops wouldn't let him have one. He had a cell phone, and something called a CB, which few people used nowadays, although some nights he'd hear people speaking another language, which he assumed was Spanish, coming from Mexico. He didn't know how that occurred. He wasn't a radio technician.

He could have called the local dispatch using his cellphone, but the sheriff had warned Billy Joe that he would get a misdemeanor citation for frivolous pranks the next time he called. Instead, he did none of those things.

Billy Joe believed something was wrong with those lights.

This time, he was right.

20

DERRICK THOUGHT SLEEPING WOULD accomplish more than worrying, although he could not shake the feeling that something bad had happened. Before being exiled to Potterville, his imagination had conjured cannibalistic Commoners, so it was not to be trusted. He leaned his head against the passenger window, closed his eyes, and tried to sleep. Anna was already out, resting her head against his shoulder. Since neither Derrick nor Anna had experience driving, letting Kevin do it was an easy decision. Kevin said he was fine and enjoyed driving at night, and either he liked going fast or sensed getting to their destination sooner rather than later was important.

If he slept now, Derrick could start earlier tomorrow, not that an earlier start mystically generated greater odds of success. Anna had insisted on going with him, and he failed to think of a reason to say otherwise. He could not rationalize how they would triumph either. He understood why Miriam thought it was important, but that didn't mean it was possible. Just because you think something should happen doesn't mean that it will.

Miriam pulled him aside before they parted ways. She had studied the information Rachael had provided about the structure and said blowing up the building wasn't difficult. Recent satellite images did not indicate fortified exterior security measures, and the base had a variety of weapons from which to choose. Just place the explosives and detonate them. No one would survive the collapse of the building. Miriam was sure of that. However, they needed to kill Prime before detonation. There was no room for error.

Miriam made that clear.

The tough part would be locating a networked computer. What she called a server room would be best but was unnecessary as long as the computer was networked. Miriam did not explain how he would know for certain that a computer was on the network and suggested taking Akira if she was willing to go. Miriam gave him a small computer storage device called an SSD. Just plug it into a port, and the download will be automatic and takes about ten minutes.

Miriam believed she could do anything. Derrick did not share her confidence. In Pacific Edge, he hated Miriam's way of thinking. Now, he wished he were more like her. Place the bombs, infect the computer network, destroy the Prime replacements, kill Prime, save Stanley Mires, and leave.

Easy.

Derrick just wanted to sleep. The only thing he wanted more was to see Nyx.

And with thoughts of Nyx floating through his brain, he found the sleep that had evaded him.

21

BILLY JOE HOWIE CREPT THROUGH THE desert sand, following the tire tracks, the only disturbance on the desert floor. A sliver moon provided little illumination. Joshua trees silhouetted against the pale blue horizon. California fan palms stood like alien monsters in the dusky gloom. The vehicle had avoided hitting the larger cacti, but not because it dodged them. They just got lucky. The old sedan, faded and rusty, was nose down in a sand wash. The motor was running, and the rear tires spun in the air. The exhaust fumes, heavy with oil and poorly combusted fuel, caused him to distance himself from the stench.

Probably a drunk driver or DUI in law enforcement lingo, which was a crime, but not the severity of wrongdoing Billy Joe had hoped for. Dad had said drunks generated an important cash flow for law enforcement officers, not from fines and court fees but from cash transactions. Most cops would offer a drunk a ride home and no citation—for a fee. The price was negotiable but typically involved most, if not all, the person's cash. The officer might take the keys if the driver didn't have enough money. No ride home, but no citation. Too much work.

But Billy Joe wasn't a cop. So, payment for a ride home wasn't a bribe. He had been told to stop calling dispatch, so that wasn't a problem either. Dad said drunks kept the Howie County Sheriff's Department on the road.

Probably a drunk driver. Not a bad thing. He needed gas money.

But Billy Joe still felt a bit of disappointment. He had hoped this was something more. Perhaps a drug dealer. Or a fugitive.

Not *fugitive*—fugitives. Could it be? Pacific Edge had issued warrants for four teens. Huge rewards.

Maybe the fugitives.

Probably a drunk.

He saw no movement inside. Perhaps the driver had fallen asleep or had a medical emergency. Probably not injured. Just drove off the road and ended up in the wash. No big wreck. Not dead.

With one hand on his pistol, an ancient Smith and Weston Model 10, 38-special, with a 4-inch barrel. Six-shot revolver, but he only had five bullets. His father had six bullets, but Billy Joe had one less because he had fired the gun once to make sure it worked. That was before he learned 38-special ammunition was no longer manufactured. With the other hand, he raised a D-cell flashlight and tiptoed to the driver's door.

He froze.

One girl was asleep at the wheel, another in the passenger's seat.

Not asleep.

Dead or dying.

Carbon Monoxide poisoning.

Billy Joe dropped his flashlight, which went out, leaving him in the dark, and wrenched the door open. Grabbing the steering wheel, he pulled himself inside. Reaching across the girl, he fumbled with the seat belt. It took him a few tries, but the strap finally released, and he dropped back to his feet, dragging her out, then lowering her to the ground. *Please don't be dead.* He dragged her far enough that the car wouldn't crush her if gravity decided to bring it back to horizontal, then dove back inside, stretching across the seat to release the passenger's seat belt. The other girl, smaller than the driver, had black hair.

He turned off the motor, then ran around to the passenger side, but the door was locked.

Shit.

He raced back to the driver's side, lunged in, and dragged the girl across the seat, limp as a rag. *Please don't be dead.*

Billy Joe had seen dead people before. To be exact, he had seen just one—his dad.

As Sheriff of Howie County, he knew seeing dead people would be part of the job, but he was in no hurry to see another corpse. Finding his dad was traumatic enough. Finding two dead girls, also asphyxiated, was not on his list of things to do today.

His dad had taught him basic first aid. He knew how to stop bleeding and perform CPR, although he only understood it like a story. Billy Joe had never performed CPR, not even on a mannequin, which is how cops learned. His dad never did it either. Billy Joe wasn't sure how his dad knew the procedure. Maybe he'd made it up. Perhaps it wasn't even how it was done. He didn't want to try it. It seemed like performing it could injure or kill the victim. Plus, his dad said it was rarely successful. But sheriffs, even unofficial ones in make-believe counties, must try to save lives in such circumstances.

First, he checked the driver. The girl with lighter hair, the color undiscernible in the dark. He had not looked for his flashlight. No time for that. He might not find it in the darkness. And that would not be good because he didn't have money to replace it. He felt the girl's breath on his cheek. Good news.

Next, he checked the passenger. Felt her breathing too. More good news. First aid for carbon monoxide poisoning was primarily getting the victim into the fresh air. After that, it depended on the extent of the poisoning. Not much more that he could do. The nearest ambulance was an hour away and likely wouldn't come even if he called. Help from law enforcement wouldn't happen either.

So, he rummaged for his flashlight, sweeping his hands along the sand near the driver's door, where he dropped it. Feeling a bit of panic that he wouldn't find it, he moved with more urgency and then drove his hand into a prickly pear cactus. He jerked upright, howling and grabbing his wrist. Then his foot hit the flashlight, kicking it into the sand wash.

22

Friday, April 9, 8:33 p.m.

L. LINDA DEBATED WITH CHARLIE FOR 45 MINUTES trying to persuade him that, they—and by they, L. Linda meant she,—had to see Level Two. Charlie insisted it wasn't possible. Level Two was top secret—entry required background checks, FBI investigations, and base command approvals.

Akira finally convinced him. "Charlie, background checks don't exist now."

L. Linda said, "Exactly."

"That's why you cannot be admitted."

"Charlie, you are the closest thing there is to a base commander," Akira said, adding, "Miriam saved you. Now, you must help us save her."

Charlie hesitated. L. Linda knew the delay was unrelated to Charlie's ability to process information. She suspected the problem was Charlie didn't know how to backtrack—change his mind. It was a series of ifs, what-ifs, and how-tos. So, L. Linda didn't push it. Best to let him figure it out without additional pressure. She hoped he wasn't analyzing how helping Derrick was saving Miriam. That would make the process more difficult. They'd have to start over with new rationale.

"I'll authorize Akira and L. Linda, but only for specific rooms I deem necessary."

"Hey! What about us? Why does L. Linda get to go, and we don't?" Nyx asked.

"You have no experience in this sort of thing. You wouldn't know what to look for," L. Linda said, hoping to end the debate, knowing it would not be that easy. She'd rather go alone. She didn't need Akira there but couldn't think of a way to avoid her coming, without creating undue suspicion.

"What? You have experience?" Nyx asked.

"I do."

Everyone stared at L. Linda.

After a moment, Akira whispered, "You do?"

"A little. I delayed an assassin in Potterville so the Patel family could get into the hot springs tunnel."

"You—attacked an assassin?" The disbelief in Red's voice was evident.

L. Linda had to be careful. "It wasn't so much of a fight as it was an ambush. I hid behind a counter and beaned her in the head with a paint can."

"Lucky shot," Nyx said.

It wasn't a lucky shot, but L. Linda didn't say that. They wouldn't have believed her, and if she demonstrated her accuracy throwing things, then they would have all sorts of questions: "Where did you learn to do that? Why don't you play softball?" She also didn't tell them the assassin stuck a knife in her back that would have killed her had it not been for Collins's Kevlar vest. She said nothing about rigging the shotgun that Lori Martinez used to kill the woman. They wouldn't believe that either, or if they did, it would generate even more questions, so some things were better left unsaid.

Nyx said, "That's amazing—if it's true. But it doesn't make you a weapons expert."

L. Linda let the "if it's true," dig slide. "I can recognize things that are more effective than a paint can."

Akira said, "Let it go. Convincing Charlie to take us was difficult. Let's not push our luck."

Red said, "I still don't understand your thinking, Charlie."

Charlie said, "My decision is based on logic, assuming who will accompany Derrick to Seattle. Red, you are needed here to attend to issues with Reactor One."

Akira interrupted. "What's wrong with Reactor One?"

Before Charlie could respond, Red said, "Nothing major. Just some maintenance." He frowned at Charlie and gave his head a slight shake.

"It is unlikely that Nyx would go," Charlie added.

"And why is that?" Nyx asked, hands on hips.

Charlie did not say because Derrick wouldn't allow it, which struck Charlie as odd because that's what he was thinking. It was as if Akira said it in his head, and then he said it out loud, which was both weird and becoming more normal at the same time. "Because you lack specific skills the others have. Derrick will need someone with computer knowledge, and Akira is best suited for that, and someone to fly the aircraft, and Antonio is best for that. Someone must stay here to monitor the radio and phone, and brief Miriam should she return while Derrick is gone. That leaves you to do that."

Before the debate could continue, specifically before anyone could circle back to asking why she was going, L. Linda said, "Okie-dokie then. Charlie's smarter than me, so now we're wasting time." She looked at Charlie and motioned toward the door. "Shall we proceed?"

Charlie led L. Linda and Akira down the hall. A section of the wall slid to the side, revealing another hallway. The partition slid shut after they entered. He stopped at an elevator. There was a button labeled Level Two, which lit without being touched. Charlie could operate things without touching them. However, people once worked here, which meant there were at least two ways to control things. L. Linda made note of that—not that she would need access again, but the future is a moving target and plans often fail.

Upon entering Level Two, they proceeded down a long hallway, passing the first door. "Wait. What's in that room?" L. Linda pointed.

"The contents of that room are not weapons."

L. Linda said, "That only tells us what is not there, but it doesn't tell us what is."

"I shall show you weapons that would be useful in an assault on Prime compounds."

"I asked to see Level Two, and you agreed to show it to me."

"Agreed to show us," Akira corrected.

Charlie didn't respond.

"Are you hiding something from us?" Akira asked.

"I am not hiding things. I am being efficient. That room contains no weapons that you would need."

"Charlie, have you ever penetrated a building with armed resistance?" L. Linda asked.

"I have not."

"Then let us decide what we need. Show us everything," L. Linda said.

The door popped open. As L. Linda walked in, the lights flickered to life. It looked like a laboratory filled with worktables, computers, and equipment she did not recognize, except that it was used to calibrate, calculate, and evaluate. Along one wall, gadgets hung on pegs. "What are these?" L. Linda asked.

"They are various scientific devices designed to measure things. Some in the lab, others in the field."

"Investigative tools?" Akira asked.

"Most of them but not all."

L. Linda walked along the wall, scanning each device. "Can I look at this one?"

"Yes."

"What does this do?" L. Linda asked, turning it in her hand.

"It is a DNA analyzer. DNA is the genetic code that identifies…"

"I know what DNA is. I thought analyzing it took a special lab."

"You are correct. Typically, it is a complex operation."

"So, this thing—does it work?"

"It was a prototype when my supervisor … left. It is one of the items I continued working on. It is 100% functional."

"What good would that do?" Akira asked, stepping next to L. Linda.

"How long for results?" L. Linda asked.

"Fifteen minutes at 70 degrees Fahrenheit. Temperature affects the timeline. Depending on the ambient temperature and that of the sample, analyses take between 12.5 minutes to 20."

"Amazing," L. Linda said, placing the instrument back on the peg, wondering if a database existed that might help her. "Is there one I can take?"

"Why would Derrick need that?" Akira asked.

Derrick wouldn't, L. Linda thought, *but I might.* She paused for a moment. "We don't know what these Prime things look like. Right? What if they look like average people? One claims it's not Prime. Since all the Primes are clones, their DNA should match. Right? I don't know Derrick well, but I doubt he'd kill someone if he was unsure." She didn't enjoy lying, but she was good at it. She had invented the person everyone in Potterville knew as L. Linda. Her life was so entwined with her fable that she no longer knew her authentic self. Probably a combination of her original personality and the fiction she had devised. It wasn't something she thought much about. One more falsehood meant little. She would not give Derrick this device, but Akira didn't need to know that.

Charlie took them into each room without further argument. Akira studied each extraordinary gadget—from a device that could detect people through concrete walls (L. Linda wanted one of those) to advanced aircraft, but Akira showed no excitement, which wasn't like her at all. Chemistry was Akira's favorite subject, and every day something excited her. Seeing her this way caused L. Linda discomfort. Akira had no emotions and couldn't process things like normal—no awe or astonishment. Even saving Miriam seemed to be an idea no different from any other. This bothered L. Linda, because there was a spark between Akira and Miriam, and L. Linda felt sad that it might be lost. Connections like that were precious. L. Linda knew that, but feelings were not something she could indulge in, so she suppressed them. Entanglements could interfere with her goals.

L. Linda took the device that could sense people through walls. Derrick would not get that either, although he could have used it, but she didn't know it at the time, and she couldn't think of a reason they needed two.

Charlie saved the best for last—cutting-edge weapons. Akira concentrated as Charlie explained each. L. Linda wasn't sure why. Perhaps it was the changes in Akira's brain. Akira wasn't violent by nature. L. Linda knew this because she had studied the girl for several years, just like she had watched all the kids and adults in Potterville, hoping she might find an ally, but none were found. Maybe, in addition to losing her emotions, Akira had replaced them with thoughts of homicide or suicide. Maybe both. Perhaps Akira blamed Prime for what happened to her and wanted revenge. Nothing wrong with that, except, while Prime was guilty of many things, blaming Prime for a reactor malfunction stretched the fabric of reality beyond recognition, which was dangerous in and of itself, but L. Linda believed Akira's attention to detail was none of those things. She was just being Akira—always the observant student.

For L. Linda, Level Two was like a toy store, although she tried to conceal her enthusiasm. It contained many kick-ass weapons, all of which were advanced, considering the time of their invention. In addition, Charlie had perfected weapons that were only concepts back when people worked here. Charlie had even designed a few new ones. The good news was that the New America military didn't have such weaponry or aircraft. The bad news was Prime did.

Weapons developed right here. Which was interesting. Prime did not exist when this place was operational. However, James Carver had operated here, and some people believed Carver had something to do with Prime. But Carver was dead. Unfortunately, even with advanced weapons, the odds of eliminating Prime were slim to none.

The nuclear missiles could destroy Prime's regional headquarters. Since Miriam knew the correct address for Seattle, L. Linda assumed she knew the other locations as well. But the loss of innocent lives would be staggering, and the central Prime would still exist, and as long as that Prime survived, nothing would change.

When Jason first told L. Linda that a kid from Pacific Edge was coming to Potterville, she paid little attention. Until Jason told her Pacific Edge had exiled the kid. People leaving Chosen communities weren't unusual. The Chosen constantly weeded people out. She knew a lot about the Chosen. Few people do. Losers like Jimmy Priest thought being Chosen was one step from heaven. The Chosen wannabes would believe anything they thought came from the Chosen. However, the Chosen did not share information with the commoners. They were as clueless as the Chosen wannabes. Both sides were fed what New America Media wanted them to hear.

Jason had told her the truth about the Chosen. For the most part, those in Pacific Edge were tax collectors. They were not brilliant minds. Prime didn't want anyone clever enough to steal his money, which was Prime's because Prime said it was. Prime controlled everything, so questioning his authority, no matter how minor, got one moved to what the Chosen called the Commoner World. No trials. No appeals. No drama, except for the adjustment period as the ex-Chosen learned the world outside their prison isn't what the media had portrayed.

While the outside world wasn't what New America Media described to the Chosen, most of it wasn't like Potterville. L. Linda had witnessed that. She had to admire Browning and Collins. They had created a system that worked when they developed the adult and student councils. They set up an arrangement where people governed themselves. It worked on a small scale.

Jason told her about Derrick King for a reason. Although Jason never said it, he knew about the test subject program. Jason knew about a lot of things.

While it was not unusual for the Chosen to boot people out, exile rarely happened. It meant something entirely different. It was rare. It was a statement, not just a routine move, because someone said something derogatory about the system or took an extra five minutes on break once too often. When Jason told her this kid, Derrick King, hit a Carver, L. Linda's attention was piqued. A rebel.

A fearless Resistance fighter. Then Jason told her he was not only Chosen but a test subject. A test subject kept alive longer than any other. One living outside the test environment, trained in martial arts and self-defense under hypnosis. The hypnosis part she didn't understand, but there was time to sort that out. Until hearing about Derrick King coming to Potterville, L. Linda had been willing to go it alone, but a partner would certainly help. She had promised Jason she would finish high school, and she could keep her promise while plotting and training with Derrick King. The kid exiled from Pacific Edge.

But then Derrick arrived. He hid out in that condo for a week. Paul Jorgensen was involved. Paul made a living doing odd jobs. This was perhaps the oddest job he'd ever taken. So odd, it got him killed. When Derrick finally came out of hiding, Nyx immediately latched on to him. A rebound, L. Linda assumed. L. Linda could live with that. At the time there seemed no rush and she could let that little entanglement run its course.

But she could help things along, so L. Linda manipulated Donna into giving her a weekend job—same as Derrick. Start setting her own hooks, she was playing the long game. Then her hopes faded. She met him. That was a trip. Not the angry young test subject she had anticipated. He seemed bewildered. He lied about who he was and where he was from. She felt certain he didn't even know he had been a test subject. Scared.

Perhaps the scared part was a performance, but she didn't think so. Her life was an act, so she felt confident she could spot a fraud when she saw one. Derrick's fear and naivety were genuine. It was easy to spot because his acting ability sucked when it came to being 'orphan Derrick' from Denver.

L. Linda noticed that Akira spotted Derrick's lies first. Almost immediately. Akira had been moved out of Pacific Edge, not exiled, just a run-of-the-mill sort of placement. She probably knew Derrick in Pacific Edge. Yet, she didn't rat him out. Instead, she helped him, although she probably told Nyx because Nyx was her best friend.

Then another amazing thing happened. Nyx didn't rat him out either. She stuck with him despite the lying. Maybe it wasn't just a rebound thing.

Didn't matter. Derrick King would be of no use to L. Linda. She made that decision early on. Still, it was hard not to like him. Not that she liked him. That wasn't it. She hoped to use him but then learned he couldn't help her. So, no, she didn't have any feelings for Derrick. She did not.

But then things changed. Pacific Edge came to get Derrick. Then Miriam escaped, and all hell broke loose. That's why she couldn't keep her promise to Jason to finish high school. He would not approve, but he would understand. She wouldn't ask permission because he'd say, "Let's run." They ran before and could do it again.

But she would not run.

Not this time.

L. Linda picked several weapons, including one that fired positive or negatively charged electrons that could render targets unconscious or burn a fist-size hole through their chest. In addition, it could destroy a computer. She also took several thin, lead-filled, titanium-coated throwing knives that could penetrate the typical wall of a home or a Kevlar vest. L. Linda buried one three inches into a target made of solid walnut and was glad the assassin in Potterville didn't have access to such a blade. She'd put a few of these in Derrick's arsenal, but she'd keep most for herself.

Standard firearms would still be their primary weapons. Those were on Level One, but there were a couple of firearm-related items she added to her bag: silencers that remained effective after many rounds were fired and two sniper rifles that fit into a small box when disassembled.

L. Linda had placed all the items in what resembled a dull, green, oversized gym bag. Slinging it over her shoulder, she said, "Explosives next."

Charlie said, "On Level One. I can have a QR-3 bring that bag to a room for staging."

"I'll carry it," L. Linda said. She still didn't know how she would separate what Derrick could use and what she would keep. It was a fluid situation.

23

Friday, April 9, 8:45 p.m.

USING HIS CELLPHONE FOR ILLUMINATION, Billy Joe Howie descended into the sand wash, found his flashlight, and scrambled back up to the car, where the girls had started to stir. He shined the light on the small girl with the black hair.

She squinted and held her hand up, shielding her eyes. "Where are we? What in the hell did you do to us?" she asked.

"I saved you. That's what I did," Howie said.

The other girl propped herself up into a sitting position. "My head feels like it's splitting in two. No, make that three. Maybe four."

Billy Joe said, "Carbon monoxide poisoning. Your car has an exhaust leak and probably a hole in the floorboard. You're lucky to be alive. You should never have driven your car like that."

"Not my car," Rebekah said.

"Whose car, is it?" Howie asked.

"Not important." Miriam stood, steadying herself with one hand on the bumper. "Help us get this car back on the road. We need to go. What time is it?"

"You didn't answer my question. Who does this car belong to?" Turning his light toward Rebekah. "I need to see your driver's license."

"She lost it," Miriam said.

Billy Joe said, "Is that true?"

Rebekah said nothing.

"Who are you?" Miriam asked.

"I'm the sheriff here."

"Sheriff, where? Where are we?"

Billy Joe paused. "You're in Howie County. I'm the sheriff."

Miriam said, "No such place as Howie County. You're too young to be a sheriff of anything. How about *you* show me identification?"

"I'm in charge here," Howie said. "I suppose you also lost your identification."

"There's a lot of that going around."

Billy Joe raised the beam of the flashlight.

"Get that out of my face."

"Wait. I know who you are. You're the girl who escaped from Pacific Edge. You're Miriam King."

"People mistake me for her all the time."

Billy Joe swung his light toward Rebekah. "And you're the accomplice, something Ford. Roberta, Rose, something like that."

"Rebekah," Miriam said, her head clearing. She studied the car, rear wheels three feet off the ground, teetering at the edge of the sand wash. Suddenly, the car shifted. "Get back!" she shouted toward Billy Joe.

The car oozed forward and disappeared into the darkness.

"Fantastic," Miriam said. "Now what?"

"Did you steal that car?"

"Borrowed."

"From who?"

"A friend."

"Name?"

"Alice."

"Alice what?"

"I didn't catch her last name."

"You don't know your friend's last name, yet she let you take her car? You expect me to believe that?"

"I make friends easily."

"You're wanted. Both of you. Big rewards. Where's your brother, Derrick? He's also wanted."

Miriam stepped next to Rebekah. "I don't know where he is."

Billy Joe's mind had been churning. He had dreamed of making a big bust. Something that would gain the respect of the local cops. But this. This would gain him the respect of the state police, hell, even Pacific Edge Security. "You're both coming with me."

"And what if we decline your offer?" Miriam asked.

Billy Joe patted his firearm. "You can go the easy way or the hard way. The reward is dead or alive."

"You're going to shoot unarmed girls?" Rebekah asked.

"I don't want to," Billy Joe said.

Miriam leaned toward Rebekah and whispered, "We're stuck out here in the middle of the desert. Play along until an opportunity presents itself."

Rebekah whispered, "This kid is crazy. No telling what he'll do."

"No argument here," Miriam whispered to Rebekah, then raised her voice. "Where are you taking us?"

Billy Joe thought for a moment. "Back to where you stole the car."

"We didn't steal it. Call the diner. Alice will confirm that she loaned it to us. We need to go to the coast. Perhaps you can give us a ride," Miriam said.

He motioned toward the road. "Good point. You escaped from Pacific Edge. That's where the reward is, so that's where we are going. Start walking."

Rebekah clenched her fists. Miriam took her elbow, gave her a gentle tug, and started walking. Billy Joe followed them. A light breeze ruffled Miriam's hair. Cool air from the mountains pulled out to sea. The kid was taking them in the right direction. She could knock him out if he were closer. He probably wasn't trained, probably not accurate with that pistol, but getting shot wouldn't be good. Not good at all. Plus, he might hit Rebekah. Miriam wouldn't risk that. So, wait until they're in the car. He wasn't an actual police officer. Miriam was sure of that. Maybe a volunteer. Maybe a program for high school kids—some sort of junior reserve program. Perhaps he was just pretending. Whatever he was doing, he was unlikely to have a car like Bill Collins. He wouldn't have a cage to separate them in the back seat. She'd get her chance once they were in the car.

As they approached, Miriam saw she was wrong.

The kid had a police car. Old and with faded paint, but it had once been used by a police department, complete with a plexiglass barrier separating the back seat from the front.

Billy Joe stopped, keeping his distance. "Both of you in the back seat."

Miriam said, "Can I sit up front? I'm not feeling well, and I get carsick in the back."

Billy Joe put his hand on his firearm. "I'm not stupid. Not going to happen. Into the back, both of you."

Miriam hesitated. The kid was too far away for her to do anything. He was smart enough to keep his distance. "You're not a sheriff. So, what are you exactly? My parents said I should never get in a car with a stranger." That wasn't true. She didn't have parents. Mother and Father were keepers, and cars didn't exist in Pacific Edge, only driverless transports. She had not seen a car until Paul Jorgensen came to take Derrick to Potterville. She'd seen all sorts of motor vehicles in her brief time out in the real world. She would have been fascinated by them had her life not been under constant threat since the moment she stepped outside Pacific Edge.

"My job isn't your concern. Get in the car."

The kid's eyes looked wild. His brain, racing. Big reward. Make a name for himself. At first, Miriam doubted he'd shoot them, and she believed that was true then, but things had changed. Because of the reward. No telling what he might do. Miriam opened the door and motioned Rebekah inside, hoping the kid would walk over to shut it.

The kid didn't move. "Get in. Pull the door closed. The bulletin said to consider you armed and dangerous."

Miriam slid in, closing the door.

Rebekah said, "Now what?"

"Now, we're screwed."

24

Friday, April 9, 8:59 p.m.

ALLEN PATEL HAD TRAVELED BETWEEN Potterville and Pacific Edge many times, yet he had never covered the distance this quickly. Fletcher drove like they were in a race and took shortcuts that caused Allen to think they were lost. Allen knew they would arrive before Miriam, but he didn't expect they would arrive so soon. However, they didn't go to Pacific Edge. Their destination was a small village, mostly abandoned except for a few fishermen and Patel's contact, a religious man, who lived there. They approached from the south because detour signs said the road from the north was closed.

The detour proved beneficial because the place was crawling with cops. Red and blue lights spun a crazy mosaic of chaos. Allen saw three ambulances standing with open doors. A fourth was leaving. Not in a hurry. No siren, just lights. From the edge of darkness, two firemen were pushing a gurney carrying a black body bag zipped tight. Flashlight beams swung wildly, and officers walked to and from the darkness near a path leading to the ocean. Allen and his friend often took this path to the sea when he visited. Waves crashing on the rocks provided a safe place to talk.

Fletcher turned up the hill, drove several blocks, and then turned back toward the frantic scene. Killing his lights, he let the car coast downhill another couple of blocks before pulling to the curb. Close enough to see what was happening, and far enough the police wouldn't notice them.

Everyone was focused on the cliffs and whatever carnage had happened down near the sea.

And a house.

The house where Allen's friend lived. The friend in the Resistance.

The town's pastor.

"That's your contact?" Fletcher asked.

Allen was in the back. He scooted to the center, leaning forward with his arms on the front seat. "That's his house. I don't see him."

The front door stood open. Police came and went.

"He's Resistance. Right?" Jason asked. "You think they found out?"

Allen hesitated. "I think not. What's with the black bags and the ambulances?"

"Dead people," Jason said. "He's not a hitman, is he?"

"He is not. I don't think the ambulances are here because of the Resistance."

"How can you be sure?" Fletcher asked.

"The police wouldn't be involved. It would be Chosen Security—most likely from Pacific Edge. They'd be here in hovercraft. Not police cars. And they wouldn't make such a scene. In and out as quietly as possible."

"Why's that?" Fletcher asked.

"The pastor is well-liked. Chosen are not. Although they are heavily armed, Chosen Security fears the Resistance and if they came here to investigate involvement in such, they would be careful. Then there's the other thing."

"What other thing is that?" Fletcher asked.

"The dead people," Allen said. "That's a law enforcement issue."

They sat in silence for several minutes. People moving in unison appeared at the edge of the trail leading to the sea. Three flashlights lit the path as they moved, something weighing them down—another black bag.

Jason said, "From the number of ambulances, I'd say at least four dead. Probably down by the ocean. Maybe a party got out of hand. Perhaps they are just using the pastor's house to organize the investigation."

Allen said nothing.

"The guy have a family?" Jason asked.

"A son."

"Enemies?"

"The town loved him. Most of them support the Resistance but are quiet about it."

"So, everyone knows he is in the Resistance?" Jason asked.

"No. No one knew. But people suspect things. You know how it is?"

"I do not," Jason said.

"Does the Resistance kill people?" Fletcher asked.

"That is not their mission," Allen said.

"You're sure of that?" Jason asked.

Fletcher looked at Allen. "People in the Resistance have never killed anyone?"

"Sometimes people must defend themselves. Even then, it is rare. Last one I heard about was back east five years ago. They try to preserve history. The real history, not Prime's narrative." Allen looked at Jason. "Do you really think the kids can destroy Prime."

Jason said, "They could make a dent."

"What does that mean?" Allen asked.

"Not important," Jason said.

"Something's happening," Fletcher said, pointing.

Three men exited the house, two in uniform and one wearing a dark suit. A fourth man followed, wearing a gray sweater and black slacks.

Allen said, "That's my friend."

They walked to the open doors of an ambulance. A body bag lay on a gurney. The man in the gray sweater walked to the bag. An ambulance attendant unzipped it. The man stared for a moment and then nodded. His knees buckled. An officer standing behind him caught the man under both arms before he hit the ground. Two officers helped him back to the house.

"They asked him to identify the body," Jason said.

"He knows everyone in this town and many people from Pacific Edge's service community," Allen said.

"He recognized the body," Jason said.

"Then the death must have been recent," Fletcher said, adding, "recent enough that the body wasn't decomposed."

"Or the body came from the sea," Jason said. "Cold water."

Fletcher said, "It struck him hard. But most people aren't used to seeing dead people. Doesn't mean he knew the person well."

"He's a pastor. He's seen many dead people. Held many hands as they died. He knew the person."

"What do we do now?" Fletcher asked. "You needed this guy, and this is where Miriam is to meet us."

Allen said, "I came here because it is a safe place close to Pacific Edge."

Fletcher said, "Not safe now."

Jason said, "We need to know what is going on. Patel is wanted and too well-known. I'll go find out. No one here knows me."

And with that, Jason opened the door and walked toward the swirling lights and dead bodies.

25

BILLY JOE HOWIE PERFORMED A WELL-PRACTICED three-point-turn and headed north. Miriam glanced at Rebekah, whose head rested against the window, eyes closed. This was no time to sleep. Miriam nudged her. Rebekah raised her head, eyes mere slits. Then she opened her eyes, frowning, and gave her head an almost imperceptible shake. Taking Miriam's hand, she gave her a slight smile, then rested her head against the window again.

Miriam watched her. Although she appeared to be sleeping, something was happening inside her head. Scheming. Rebekah moaned, closing her eyes when the kid checked the mirror.

"What's wrong with her?" Billy Joe asked.

Miriam paused. "I don't know."

Rebekah whimpered.

Miriam wasn't sure if Rebekah was pretending or sick. Her own stomach was twisted in a knot, and her head felt like it might split open.

Suddenly, Rebekah groaned, sitting straight and then doubling over. "Stop the car. I'm gonna puke."

Billy Joe looked in the rearview mirror. "I'm not stupid."

Rebekah moaned. "Stop, or you'll have a mess to clean up."

"Don't you dare puke in my car."

Miriam still wasn't sure if Rebekah was faking it, but she knew if Rebekah puked, she would as well. Just the thought of it was making her queasy. "If Rebekah throws up, so will I."

Billy Joe let off the gas.

"Hurry," Rebekah pleaded.

Billy Joe applied the brakes and eased off the road.

"Open the window. Quickly."

Billy Joe looked over his shoulder. "No tricks."

Rebekah gagged, throwing her hand over her mouth.

The window slid open. Rebekah stuck her head out. She gagged and then extended her body outside to her waist. And then a little farther. And then she was gone.

Billy Joe shouted, "What the hell!"

Miriam dove for the open window, but it closed before she got there. Billy Joe bailed out and ran around the back. He reached the passenger side, swore, ran back to the driver's door, grabbed a flashlight, and dashed back.

"Damn it. Where are you?" Billy Joe moved cautiously along the passenger side of the car, shining the light into the night, and then back toward the front of the vehicle. "You can't get away. I still have your friend. Are you going to abandon her?"

Miriam caught movement at the driver's door. Rebekah slipped in, removed the shotgun from its rack, and then eased back out, keeping low, mirroring Billy Joe's movement, using the vehicle as a shield.

Billy Joe slinked to the front and sprang around the fender. "Got you."

But Rebekah wasn't there.

"Come on. You have nowhere to go. You'll die out in the desert. And getting picked up out here would be dangerous. Game's over. Come out where I can see you."

Billy Joe eased back along the car, pausing at the driver's door, where he stopped, ducking inside. "What the f …."

"Misplace something?" Rebekah asked, shoving the shotgun's barrel into his back.

"Whoa. Careful. That thing is loaded."

"I Know. I checked. Now drop your belt and pants."

"Do what?" Billy Joe shouted.

"You heard me. I'll pull the trigger if your hand gets close to your pistol. Say that you understand. I'd hate to kill you over a simple misunderstanding."

"I understand."

Billy Joe dropped his duty belt first, easing his holster to the ground. His pants followed. He wore striped boxers, which was good. She had not thought about the alternative but assumed Billie Joe would have protested with more vigor had he been wearing something embarrassing.

Rebekah said, "Step out of them."

"I don't think they'll fit over my shoes."

"Try. Worst that can happen is you fall. Maybe skin a knee. Just remember. Don't even think about going for your pistol, or a skinned knee will be the least of your problems."

Billy Joe balanced with one hand against the car's roof, first lifting his right leg, struggling, and finally getting his foot free but losing his shoe, and then completing the task with his other foot.

"Do you have any other weapons in the car?"

"No."

"You wouldn't lie to me, would you, Billy Bob?"

"It's Billy Joe and I'm not lying."

"I hope you're not lying, because if I shoot you, it will make a mess for us to drive in. Move away from the door." Rebekah poked him again with the shotgun.

"Don't shoot me."

He didn't sound nearly as tough now that the tables were turned. He sounded as if he were about to cry. Miriam felt sorry for him. Just a little. Not a lot. The door latch released, and Miriam climbed out.

Rebekah said, "Slide into the back and be a good lad while we decide what to do with you."

Billy Joe did as he was told.

Miriam slammed the door. "Good job, girlfriend."

"I had a decent teacher."

"Your teacher was drawing a blank. We'd still be in the back seat if it weren't for you."

"Bet you're glad I insisted on coming."

"I've been happy about that for a long time now."

"So, what should we do with old Billy Bob?" Rebekah indicated the backseat.

Miriam shrugged. "It's your plan."

"I'm open to suggestions."

Miriam thought for a moment, then leaned down and looked at their prisoner. "I don't think we should leave him out here."

Rebekah shivered. "It is getting cold. Maybe he has a coat in the trunk."

"I wasn't worried about his discomfort. He'll run to the cops about us. This car is easy to spot."

"True. Coyotes might get him first."

"Maybe."

Rebekah studied their captive for a moment. Then she smiled.

Miriam said, "You have an idea. I can tell."

"He's about my size. I could put on his uniform. We can say we are taking him in if we get stopped."

"Taking him in for what? We aren't cops."

"Neither is he. Hey! I know. We're bounty hunters."

"Is that even a thing?"

Rebekah shrugged. "It is now."

"What about me? I don't have a uniform."

"I don't know. We'll think of something. My supervisor, maybe? No, wait. You're undercover."

Miriam tossed Billy Joe's duty belt and holster into the front seat. Then reached in and lowered the rear window a few inches. "Take off your shirt and hand it out."

Billy Joe unbuttoned his shirt. "What are you going to do to me? I'll freeze to death if you leave me here. It gets cold at night." He handed the shirt to Miriam.

Miriam said, "Give me the shotgun and you change behind the car." She pointed the shotgun at Billy Joe. "Don't be trying to sneak a peek, meathead."

Billy Joe held up his hands and faced forward. "Don't worry. I'm not that kind of guy."

"I don't know what kind of guy you are. I only know you planned to turn us in for the reward. That doesn't make you a good guy, in my opinion."

Billy Joe said nothing.

Rebekah said, "How do I look?" She turned a slow circle.

"It's a little baggy, but you'll look okay inside the car." Miriam studied the badge. "This is a fake. You're not a real sheriff. There is no Howie County. Just what are you exactly, Billy?" Miriam tossed Rebekah's jumpsuit into the seat. "You can put your hands down and put these on."

He pulled on the coveralls.

"Well?"

"Well, what?" Billy asked.

"What are you?"

Billy Joe hung his head. "It's a long story."

"What's the plan?" Rebekah asked.

Miriam said, "You're driving. I'll get in back with Billy."

Rebekah strapped on the duty belt. "You should ride in front with me."

"That wouldn't look right. I'm wanted. I have to be in the back in case we get stopped. Then just say you're taking me in. Billy is an accomplice, so you're taking him in as well."

"I'm wanted too."

"Perhaps they won't recognize you in that uniform."

"Is that safe? I mean, you being back there with him?"

"Is it safe for *him*? It's not safe if he tries anything. We're wasting time. Let's go." Miriam tapped the overhead light bar. "Turn this on and ignore the speed limit. Drive as fast as you feel comfortable."

Rebekah got in, triggering the rear door latch.

Miriam said, "Slide over, Billy boy. We got to make up time."

Miriam slid into the back seat. "Oh, and thanks."

"Thanks for what?" Billy Joe asked.

"You saved us. Didn't you?"

Billy Joe shrugged. "I guess."

"No guessing about it. We'd have died in that car. Right?"

"Yes."

"How did you know about carbon monoxide poisoning?"

"It killed my father."

Miriam stared at him for a moment. "I'm sorry. We have some distance to go. So, let's hear the long story about how you became sheriff of Howie County."

26

JASON MAXTON EXITED THE CAR. A STIFF breeze, carrying the scent of seaweed and salt, gave him a slight chill despite his jacket. He walked toward an officer standing near the home of Patel's contact. Hands in his pocket, making his best impression of an innocent yet curious passerby.

"What happened, officer?"

"Stop right there." The officer turned, putting his hand on his firearm.

Easing his hands from his pockets, Jason said, "Whoa. I didn't mean to startle you."

"Do you live here? We've told people to stay away. This is an active crime scene."

"Sorry. I'm staying with friends, but they are gone. I don't feel right answering their phone or door. I saw the lights. My curiosity got the best of me."

"Where are you from?"

"Potterville."

"What's your friend's name?"

"Smith." Most common name in New America, and Jason hoped there was a Smith in this village. Perhaps the policeman wasn't from here and wouldn't know.

"You need to leave. Like I said, active crime scene."

"It looks bad. I've seen what looked like a body near the ambulance. What on earth happened? I understand the pastor lives there." Jason indicated Allen's friend's house.

The officer said nothing.

"It must be hard dealing with a situation like this. Whatever it is. People killed in a small town. Surely, everyone knows everyone." The man nodded. Jason had struck a nerve.

"I'm from the next town over. Our sheriff sent us to help. I don't have details, but the pastor called it in. He found his son down by the shore. Broken leg, from what I heard."

Jason said, "Oh, my. Was he killed? I saw body bags."

"The boy is alive, but they have recovered three teenage girls murdered and tossed in the ocean. Rocks in their clothing, holding them down. I have a daughter about their age." The officer paused. "Hits you hard. You know?"

Jason nodded. He understood. He was braced for a similar message about L. Linda. "I hear you. I have a daughter in high school. I'm confused though. You said the pastor's son was injured? Did he fall or something?"

"No. Someone beat him up. Broke his leg. Then wrote a message with rocks, pointing to where the girls were in the water. It was still daylight when the pastor found him, so he saw the sign and the girls."

Jason whistled through his teeth. "How's the boy?"

"In pretty bad shape but he'll live."

"Lucky his dad found him."

"Sure was. The girl who broke his leg also stole the kid's motorcycle."

"That sounds odd. Are they sure it was a girl?"

"Yep. She talked to the pastor. Told him the boy was down by the water. She said he wanted to sell the motorcycle, and she talked the dad into letting her ride it. But she never came back."

"What's the world coming to?"

The officer looked around as if to ensure no one was listening. "That's not all. The pastor said the girl was wet and barefoot. Looked as if she'd been in a fight. Just a teenager. Acted kind of weird. Talked, like an airhead."

"I see. How were the girls killed?"

"They won't know until the autopsies are completed, but I heard there are knife wounds."

"That's awful."

"That's not all. A big knife was left sticking in a crack in a rock near the sign pointing to the girls."

"What's the boy saying?"

"Says the girl killed the girls, and when he tried to intervene, she attacked him. Broke his leg. Then made the sign saying he was the murderer."

"Sounds fishy."

"To me too. But how does a small girl beat a guy up and break his leg?"

"How indeed. Still, to be honest, if I were a betting man, I'd say the boy did the killing. Came across this girl, thinking she would be his next victim. But he picked the wrong girl this time."

The officer nodded. "Something else. The boy had a knife scabbard on his belt."

"Let me guess. The knife fits."

The officer nodded. "But here's the thing: Where did this girl come from? The pastor knows everyone for miles and had never seen her before."

"Good question, but not one I'd know the answer to." Jason shrugged and walked away.

27

Friday, April 9, 10:30 p.m.

NO MATTER HOW WELL ONE PLANS, no matter how careful a person is, or how pure one's intentions, sometimes things don't go well. Yet, occasionally, when things go to hell, the outcome is not what was expected. Scott Key, AKA Lawrence King, stared at the ceiling of the Cascade Locks motel, contemplating such an event—or rather, a series of events.

Having fled Pacific Edge, he figured he would be killed if he didn't get to Canada. Prime wanted him dead because Miriam, Anna, and Derrick were still alive. The Resistance wanted him because he had disabled the VPN they used for communication. The VPN could be restored. Scott didn't destroy it. It was still there but hidden. Reactivating it was easy. It only required software he'd left with AJ Patel and a security code. But they didn't know that when he disappeared. The kids were a different story. There was no forgiveness for that situation.

However, Scott did not make it to Canada, and AJ Patel didn't have the software. Yet, to his amazement, he was still alive. Not only alive, but he'd just finished a delicious meal with John-the-Brewer and Scott learned that John's last name was actually Brewer. Scott had said, "No way. You're making that up," but John Brewer produced his driver's license, which verified the authenticity of his name.

John proved to be an affable and interesting host. They ate and talked, and Scott accepted John's offer for work. Manual labor, far below Scott's level of education, but he didn't want to do anything remotely related to the science he had conducted in the test subject program. John said the job was temporary and even admitted its primary purpose was to keep Scott safe and, more importantly, keep him close in case his help was needed.

Despite a shaky start, John treated Scott decently, which could be an act to put him at ease, lower his defenses. That scared Scott a little, but it was okay. Scott had no reason to expect forgiveness, but he hoped perhaps if he worked hard enough, John would let him stay. Perhaps, in time, he could be of valuable help doing something positive. Brewing was part science, after all.

Scott liked John. He didn't know if it would be possible to make friends in this little town, and Scott had not had a friend since grade school. AJ Patel was as close as it came because it was best to trust no one in Scott's world. His wife had proven it. Right now, she was probably helping the Chosen search for him. Promised safety if she helped. She was alive until Prime found him. Then Prime would have her killed. Whatever she had been promised meant nothing. He felt sad about that, but she had made her decisions.

So, plans shot to hell, yet here he lay, hands behind his head, contemplating how it had gone wrong. Or had it gone right? Time would tell. He was still breathing, for which he was grateful. The kids were alive, and he was thankful for that as well. Maybe even more so than for himself, which was probably just something he told himself to ease his conscience. Because he had been a monster. To work in the test subject program, he had to be. A normal person couldn't do the things the program required. Although, no one had forced him. He had done those things willingly. Hearing Miriam and Derrick's voices both lifted his heart and deeply troubled him. Derrick wanted to meet him face to face. Scott didn't fear Derrick. Not in the sense that Derrick might kill him, which didn't mean Derrick wouldn't be justified in doing so. But meeting wouldn't be a pleasant experience. No hugs, or, boy, it's good to see you, dad. None of that.

There was little chance he'd ever see either of the kids. The odds that any of them would survive for such a reunion were slim at best. However, if Patel could retrieve his briefcase, the VPN could be up and running in seconds. Perhaps that would give Derrick and Miriam a tool that would help them, although Scott didn't think defeating Prime was possible. Yet those two kids had changed him—given him hope. That's why he broke protocols and kept them alive. Hope was why he started their self-defense training, just in case he could get them out of Pacific Edge. He never envisioned them trying to destroy Prime. Scott only hoped the training would help them protect themselves.

When the time came to end the program and deconstruct the test subjects, Scott convinced the Test Subject Commission, that because of irregularities, it would be of great importance that they continue testing three of the subjects. The purpose of hypnosis was to add additional controls, hoping they could achieve their original goals. Placing hidden commands was his wife's notion, while placing hallways and doors to torment them was Prime's idea. To continue the experiment for an additional year, Prime had insisted on including the kill codes. Prime had specific interest in Number 7, for reasons that were obvious, and insisted on additional safeguards. Scott was not involved in that procedure, so he didn't know what they did to Number 7, except a technician said it was new and likened it to hardwiring. Something different than hypnosis, memory wipe, or the 1984 chip.

Scott's biggest success wasn't the tests conducted on the kids. It involved working with the commission chairman. He brought the chairman into the process, ensuring he was invested in the program before year's end, hoping they could move to the next step without involving Prime, because Prime would never approve. Scott convinced the chairman to let him take the test subjects to Pacific Edge. That was the only way they could verify their findings, and their findings would be impressive. So much so, Prime was bound to reward rather than punish, because success in this project was extraordinarily important to Prime on a personal level. Prime did not know test subjects 3, 6, and 7 had been taken to homes in Pacific Edge, or so Scott believed. He realized now that Prime might have known all along. Might have known Scott had been deceitful. Either way, Prime knew now and wanted Scott dead.

The kids had broken through the hypnosis. That didn't surprise him. Hypnosis wasn't like the memory wipe they did before they left the testing facility. That was permanent—in theory. They shouldn't be able to recall anything about being test subjects or about him being their keeper, yet they remembered. At least some of it. They used hypnosis to get them through day-to-day life without asking questions about their training. The academy was told they were part of a new hybrid program combining public education and home schooling. Everyone knew about the hybrid program. Thus, the kids schedule wasn't questioned. Anna only trained at night, but she excelled.

Scott's wife was a hypnosis expert and had more confidence in its long-term effects. She had devised all manner of pathways, codes, and barriers to control them. Now and into the future. Scott didn't know what she had planted in their heads. She said it was her area and kept her methods secret.

At the time, hitting Marcus Carver seemed like a catastrophe, but Scott took a chance on getting Derrick out of Pacific Edge alive. He convinced the Pacific Edge Tribunal that to bring the experiment to a successful conclusion, it was necessary to see how Derrick would respond without controls. It was obviously too dangerous to do that in Pacific Edge. If Derrick was violent in the Commoner world, no harm done.

Test subject Number 7 had always been a failure. During their time as keepers, his wife loved to watch Number 7 fail, even though it meant the experiment wasn't going well. Genetically, 7 should have suited his purpose perfectly. A weak personality in an otherwise exemplary mind and body. Easily directed and controlled. Instead, he was stubborn and could be provoked into violence under the right circumstances. Frustration wasn't unusual when the controls contradicted what was needed in the situation, but it was protecting others that triggered violence. However, Scott hoped Derrick could adapt in Potterville and, with time, everyone would lose interest and move on to the next project. Scott could quietly retire Number 7's experiment.

That didn't happen. Far from it. Prime learned about Derrick, growing so furious that Prime jettisoned his self-imposed seclusion, making his existence known in Potterville. Scott wondered how Prime got wind of Derrick's exile, yet he felt sure he knew the answer—his wife. That bothered him. She set this entire thing in motion, and for what purpose other than she hated Derrick. She hated all of the test subjects. This group had made her look bad.

Then something else happened that affected Scott's relationship with his wife. After Derrick's exile, Scott got into her files to review her hypnotic and 1984 protocols. Although after the exile there were supposed to be no controls, she continued trying to manipulate Derrick using the 1984 chip. She was tormenting the boy, downloading data to the chip to increase homesickness and fear. Since those reactions would be normal, amplifying them could have been disastrous, possibly making him suicidal. Scott was furious.

However, his scout, Paul Jorgensen, had told him that Derrick was doing well. He'd made friends, was on the football and track teams, started a job, and appeared to have a girlfriend. Scott could not have felt prouder if he'd been Derrick's real dad. On the other hand, his wife was livid. That's when Scott finalized his decision. He was leaving her behind. He just wasn't sure when—six months, maybe a year. Then Miriam and Anna escaped. His exit became urgent.

There was something else that troubled him, and this one was his fault. It was his last words to Derrick before his exile. At a loss for words, he said, "Maybe you can make a difference." Derrick looked puzzled and asked, "Make a difference in what?" And because he didn't have time to explain Derrick's origin, he said, "Everything."

He was sure that confused Derrick. Scott feared Derrick took it the wrong way. Like it was some sort of prophecy that Derrick would destroy Prime and change the world. Scott should have said, "You can change your life."

And with that thought, Scott drifted off to a night filled with nightmares that included deconstructing Number 7.

28

BILLY JOE HOWIE HAD BEEN RATTLING off his history steadily for two hours—that felt like two days—to Miriam. She had nodded off a few times, but Rebekah kept waking her to ask for directions. However, despite the naps, Miriam got the gist of Billy Joe's life history. Pathetic. His dad had grandiose ideas based on conspiracy theories and what was best described as modern-day dark-age mythology. As Billy Joe rambled, Miriam contemplated. Billy Joe was the epitome of where the world, or at least America, went wrong—well-intended decisions based on bad information, otherwise known as lies. What made it worse was that the lies were deliberately spread.

This likely started long before James Carver rose to power, but Carver capitalized on it. Misinformation and greed. That was Carver then, and that was Carver now. Or what was left of him in the entity, calling itself Prime. Listening to Billy Joe, Miriam recognized something screaming for attention that she had blocked. Even with Prime gone, the country was so screwed up it might be impossible for it to recover.

In fact, without Prime's heavy-handed dictatorship, the country would likely fall into chaos and violence.

They needed a plan because she fully intended to destroy Prime. In between figuring out how to get the VPN running, destroying Prime's regional headquarters, and finding the hidden location where the singular Prime operated, she'd need to give saving the country some thought.

She didn't worry about becoming bored. Not anytime soon.

"Okay, Bill. Can I call you Bill? I have a pretty good picture of how you came to see yourself as sheriff of Howie County," Miriam said. "Rebekah, we're getting close. Let me know when you see homes."

"Will do."

"Back to you, Bill."

"My name is Billy Joe."

"Not anymore. Here's the thing. I would try sugarcoating this, but there's not time. While I think your dad had a good heart and the best intentions, which he passed on to you, pretty much everything your dad told you was BS."

"It's what?" Billy Joe asked, his voice raising an octave.

"You don't know what BS stands for?"

"I know what it stands for. You think I'm stupid."

"Exactly. Perhaps not stupid in that you have a low IQ, although that might also be part of the problem, stupid in that you've based your entire logic on bad information."

"What's that supposed to mean?"

"No matter how smart you are, it's hard, if not impossible, to make good decisions based on bad information. Are you following me so far?

"Yeah. I guess." Billy Joe folded his arms.

"There's no Howie County. Never will be. You're not a sheriff. You're not even a junior police cadet. You're a kid playing a game, which is mostly happening in your head. If you keep doing that, you'll never be anything but a joke. You said the police threatened to arrest you if you kept calling them. They are laughing at you, Bill. Because you are a joke."

"Billy Joe."

"You know what? I like Joe better." Miriam paused. "No. William. Much better. So, William, here's the deal. I owe you. You saved us. That's the good intentions part of you. But you also planned to turn us in. Collect the big reward. Be a big man. That's the BS part of you—decisions based on bad information. We are not the enemy. We're the good guys. We're trying to save people."

"You're a criminal. How are you trying to save people?"

"You want the truth?"

"Of course."

"I ask because you have built most of your life on lies."

Billy scowled at her.

"We just came from Mexico. Want to know what we did there?"

"Got drugs?"

"Stopped a war."

"I don't believe you."

"That's up to you. But we did. You've heard of Prime?"

"I've heard the myth."

"It's not a myth. Prime is real, and Prime runs the country."

"Ha."

"Does your radio work?"

"It works."

"Were you listening to it before you found us?"

"No reception out there."

"What if I told you Prime assassinated the president and vice president? What if I told you Prime declared martial law and took control of the government and military? How about if I told you Prime plans to attack Mexico? We destroyed missiles Prime planned to fire into New America to justify the war."

"You're making that up."

"Rebekah, turn on the radio. Find a station."

The radio hissed static until Rebekah found a station with a decent signal.

"To recap. Shortly after the president and vice president were assassinated, Prime, an entity most believed to be a myth, declared martial law and has taken control of the military. Prime suspended the Senate and the House and ordered elected officials out of Washington. Many congressmen refused to leave and planned to swear in the speaker of the house as president. We now have reports of gunshots inside the Capital Building.

"You heard that correctly. Witnesses outside the Capital building report hearing automatic weapons. The shooting has been happening for about 30 minutes. There are pauses, and then more gunfire. It's as if they are sweeping the building and shooting people when they find them.

"Just a moment. More breaking news: We just received word that additional troops are headed toward Mexico and ..."

Miriam said, "Turn it off."

The color had left Billy's face. "Holy shit."

"William, right now, it doesn't matter if you believe me because it won't change what will happen in the next few days."

"My name is Billy Joe."

"See. That's why I question your IQ. I told you that's not your name anymore. You know why? Because people can't take you seriously. From now on, you are William Howie." Miriam shook her head. "Nope, still not right. How about Dowd? You like Dowd. Easy to spell. Easy to say. William Dowd. I like it. What do you think, Rebekah?"

Billy scowled. "I don't like it."

Miriam shrugged. "Tell you what, I'll keep an open mind. You come up with something better; I can be flexible. Isn't that right, Rebekah?"

Rebekah glanced up in the rearview mirror. "Isn't what right?"

"That I'm flexible."

"Not a word I would use."

"Hey. I let you tag along when I left Pacific Edge."

"Not how I remember it, but okay, you can be flexible."

"I'm not changing my name. I'm Billy Joe Howie."

Miriam said, "Rebekah, is William's wallet in the pants?"

Rebekah rose off the seat. "Yep." She held it up.

"Go through it and tell me what you find."

Rebekah's head moved from watching the road to the wallet as she fished through its contents. "A driver's license, a library card, a card that says social security, a taxation card, a punch card from a coffee shop. Hey, Billy, you got a free coffee coming. And twenty-five bucks."

"Hand me everything that has William's old name on it."

Rebekah started organizing the contents. The right-side tires dropped off the pavement. The car pulled hard toward the barrow pit. Rebekah yelped, jerking the steering wheel, darting across the center line into the oncoming lane, which was empty.

Miriam said, "Hey. Take your time. Pull over if necessary."

"Sorry. Here you go." Rebekah slid the cards over the space between the panel and the car's headliner.

Miriam took the cards. "What about the punch card?"

"No name."

"William, do they know your name at the coffee shop?" Miriam asked.

"Probably not," Billy whispered, head down.

"You go there often enough to have a full punch card. Why doesn't someone know your name?"

Billy said nothing.

"Not a difficult question, William."

"Uh. The girls who work there are in high school. Popular. Cheerleaders and such." He paused. "They pay no attention to me. I'm invisible to them."

"Are you still in school?"

"No. I dropped out."

"When? Why?"

"A few months ago. After my father died."

"Aren't you supposed to be in school? I mean, isn't it like a law or something?"

Still staring at the floor, Billy shrugged. "Yeah. I guess."

"Then why aren't the cops or the principal coming to your house? Finding out what happened to you? Making you go to school."

Billy said nothing.

Miriam snapped her fingers in front of his face. "William?"

Billy looked at her. His eyes were wet. "I guess they don't see me either. Or maybe they do but rather they didn't. I'm a nobody. Just some weird kid."

Miriam reached across the seat, rubbing William's shoulder. "I'm sorry, William. I really am. We're going to change that. Okay?"

"My name is Billy Joe."

Miriam said, "Rebekah, lower the window a couple of inches." Then she tossed his identification into the night. "Not anymore. Welcome to the world, William Dowd. You're starting a new life."

29

DERRICK HAD DOZED OFF, HIS HEAD resting against the window, Anna leaning softly on his shoulder. Groggy, he opened his eyes, just a little, but no harsh light greeted him, only the blurred reflection of the dashboard instruments. The soldier they had captured in Mexico was driving. What was his name? Kevin. He thought it was Kevin. In his foggy thinking, between half asleep and half awake, it occurred to him how reckless it was for them to both be sleeping. Kevin could have driven them anywhere. They might be headed in the wrong direction and not even know it.

Easing upright, trying not to disturb Anna, Derrick asked, "Where are we?"

"We just passed a lake—Elizabeth or Isabella. Something like that. Close to the town Miriam told us about. She said it was our last chance to get food and such."

Derrick wondered if Kevin was telling the truth. He disliked feeling suspicious, but as he'd learned from his mistakes in Potterville, trust is difficult to obtain and can evaporate with one wrong decision. He was eager to get to the base. Anxious to see if Red and Antonio made it back safely. That had been eating at him. Mostly because he hadn't given it much thought. He took it for granted that they made it, but there was no reason to think they did.

He had also been thinking about destroying Prime's Seattle headquarters. Miriam made it sound easy, but he was sure it was not.

Mostly, he thought about Nyx. He felt as if he had abandoned her, but the base was safer than Potterville. At least for now. Maybe forever. It was hard to tell. The reactor posed a risk. Derrick hoped Charlie was monitoring it. Or perhaps Red would check it if he made it back. Derrick tried to push that thought from his mind.

Something wasn't right. He didn't know what. Maybe Red and Antonio didn't make it. Maybe all the people from the town they meant to rescue were dead. That was a strong possibility, as much as he hated to admit it. He and Miriam had asked for help. If something happened to them, it was his fault.

But that didn't feel right either. Now he understood why Miriam hated making decisions based on intuition. He felt sure something was wrong but could not identify it. Couldn't do anything about it.

But the nagging feeling persisted. He hated it.

And he was sure it involved Nyx. That made it worse. Yet, he had left her in the safest situation possible.

"You okay?" Kevin asked.

"Yeah. I'm fine. Just thinking," Derrick said.

Worrying was a better word. They didn't need to stop for supplies or food. He was hungry, but he could eat at the base. They had to run about ten miles. He could do that, no problem. Anna was in good shape and could do it as well. Running shoes would be better than the boots. Perhaps he'd get a blister. Miriam told them to eat, get jackets and flashlights. She gave him cash she pulled from an ATM. He thought they could press on without wasting time with shopping and dinner. But it was cold. However, running would warm them. Perhaps he was ignoring the facts as the night air sucked the warmth from the pickup's cab.

"I've been thinking too," Kevin said.

Anna sat straight. Yawning and stretching her arms. "Where are we?"

"Close to the town Miriam told us about," Kevin said.

"Do you think anything will be open?" Anna asked.

Kevin said, "I was wondering the same thing."

Not open, Derrick thought. Go straight to the base. He sensed something was wrong. He didn't know what, but the weight grew heavier with each passing minute.

"So, what have you been thinking about?" Anna asked.

"You heard us?" Derrick asked. "Lots of stuff. Stuff I can't talk about."

"Not you, him." She pointed to Kevin.

Kevin said nothing for a moment. "What's going to happen to me?"

"We already told you. You'll drive to Potterville. Find the sheriff or Coach Browning. Tell them we sent you. They'll take care of you," Derrick said.

"That's what I've been thinking about. Going to Potterville."

"You want to go somewhere else?" Derrick asked.

Anna said, "He can't do that. The deal was he goes to Potterville."

"I think it's okay if he goes someplace else. I realize there's a risk he could turn us in, but he is—what did you call it—ALW."

"AWOL."

"Right. That. This isn't our truck to give. It was given to us to use. We intended that Kevin drive it to Potterville, but I guess he doesn't have to go there."

"Not what I meant," Kevin said, before Anna could chime in.

"You've lost me," Anna said.

Kevin said nothing.

Derrick said, "I'm not good with social cues."

"Truth," Anna said.

"You'll have to tell us what you're thinking," Derrick said.

"I don't feel comfortable talking about it."

Anna said, "We don't have all day. Just spit it out."

Kevin swallowed. "Back in the desert…" He stopped.

"In Mexico?" Derrick asked.

"You killed those soldiers."

Anna said, "We didn't kill them. The robots did. Rebekah shot the one guy, but he didn't give her a choice."

Kevin said, "I know that."

"Then what?" Derrick asked.

Kevin didn't answer.

"Kevin, out with it," Anna demanded. "I'm tired, hungry, and must smell like a dumpster. I want food, and I hope where we are going has a shower and a bed. So, tell us what's bothering you, or I swear, I'll slap you up alongside the head."

"You're wanted. There's a huge bounty." He stopped.

"You're thinking about trying to collect?" Derrick asked, his voice rising.

"No, no. Nothing like that."

"Then what?" Anna asked.

Kevin took a deep breath and exhaled. "I'm the only one who knows where you are. I'll know where I drop you off."

"Okay." Derrick stretched the word out, a half-question, half-statement. "I still don't understand where you are going with this, Kevin."

"Doesn't make sense that you would just let me leave. Take your truck."

Anna said nothing.

After a moment, Derrick said, "I get it. You think we're going to kill you?"

Kevin nodded. Anna saw a tear trace down his cheek.

"Well, now I am going to slap you," Anna said.

"She's joking," Derrick said. "You're right. Not about killing you, but it would make sense to do that, but if that was our plan, why didn't we kill you in Mexico?"

"I don't know. Maybe you just wanted me to drive. You know. So, you could rest."

Derrick said, "Kevin, we are not going to kill you."

"We aren't?" Anna asked.

"Stop that. It's not funny," Derrick said.

"It's a little bit funny," Anna said.

"I don't want to kill anyone. I didn't want to kill those soldiers. That's why Anna didn't kill you on the mountain. She could have. Right?"

Kevin shrugged.

"You can go wherever you want. The people in Potterville will help you, but you don't have to go there."

"How do I know it will be safe? Maybe they will arrest me."

"They won't. You'll either trust me on that or not. Is it safe? No. Not really. But nowhere is safe. Prime is going to start a war. That's going to happen. It's not safe anywhere. Miriam thinks it will happen soon. That's why we must destroy Prime's Seattle headquarters. Miriam is smart. She knows things I don't know. Sees things I don't see."

With that statement, something more troublesome than whatever was happening with Nyx flooded his mind. But he could not put words to it. He knew destroying Prime would be difficult.

Difficult didn't sound right.

Impossible. That sounded right.

30

Friday, April 9, 10:45 p.m.

KEVIN ROLLED INTO THE TOWN MIRIAM HAD told them about. Everything appeared to be closed, until Kevin navigated to a street where a couple of places were still open. Kevin had said he'd never been here, so Derrick assumed he just knew how towns were laid out. Kevin parked in front of the sporting goods store Miriam had mentioned. Big banners in the windows declared: Spring Break Sale. Perhaps that's why they were open. Plus, it was Friday night, and people were still milling around in a small city park across the street.

Kevin shut off the motor. "We'd better go in here first. The pizza place will be open later. It's Friday."

Derrick didn't want to go in there. He didn't need to eat either, but he said, "Okay. Let's make this quick."

Anna said, "I'm starving."

Once outside the truck, Derrick changed his mind. It was freezing, and a stiff breeze came out of the darkness. He shivered. "A sweatshirt wouldn't hurt."

"That's for damn sure." Anna crossed her arms.

Kevin said, "I'll wait here."

"You need some new stuff too," Anna said, adding, "That t-shirt won't keep you warm, and you're still wearing army pants and boots. Best you look a little more like a high schooler and a little less like a soldier. Plus, you got that buzz cut, which we can't do anything about."

Inside, Derrick found the sweatshirts. He grabbed two dark blue ones, handing one to Kevin. "You okay with the color?"

"It's fine."

"Grab a pair of jeans."

Derrick picked a pair of tennis shoes that were reasonably priced, not the cheapest, not the most expensive. When Kevin returned, Derrick said, "I don't know your size."

Kevin grabbed the same brand as Derrick, just half a size smaller. Derrick took them from him and picked up a more expensive pair, bearing the checkmark of the sports gear the track and football team wore.

"Those are expensive," Kevin said.

"They'll last longer, and you'll fit in better in Potterville. If you decide to go there."

After buying the stuff, they put it in the truck and headed to the pizza place. As Kevin predicted, they were open until midnight. It was about half full, mostly high school kids. Derrick realized this could get awkward. He whispered, "Will someone wait on us?"

Kevin said, "No. You guys grab a table. I'll order."

Derrick handed him fifty bucks. "Is that enough?"

"More than enough." Kevin held out a twenty-dollar bill.

"Keep it."

Kevin held the bill there for a moment and then put them in his pocket and walked to the counter.

Anna led Derrick to a booth in the back. Probably not popular with kids wanting to talk to their friends. Likely popular with couples not wanting to talk to anyone. She hoped the latter didn't come in wanting the private booth. She wasn't in the mood to deal with idiots. Someone might get hurt.

Anna said, "I don't like this. Everyone was staring at us. Strangers. Wrong age to be here this time of night."

Derrick said, "It'll be alright. Just stay cool. Don't start anything."

"Stay cool? Getting used to the new Derrick is difficult. I won't start anything, but I'll finish it if necessary."

Kevin walked toward them, carrying a tray with three empty glasses and a triangle-shaped object with the number nine on it. Ten feet from their table, a boy Derrick's age blocked his path.

"Where you from?"

Derrick started to stand. Anna motioned him to sit. "I'll handle it. Less likely he'll hit a girl."

Before Kevin could answer, Anna said, "Hi. He's with us. Is there a problem?"

The kid spun around. Looked at Anna for a moment. "Maybe. Maybe not. Depends on where you're from and why you're here."

"We're here from California." She looked around. "Looks like you're on break too. Anyway, we're just passing through. We'll eat our pizza and move on. You won't see us again. Okay?"

"We are in California. Town?"

"Right. I forget how big the state is. I should have said from the coast. Not really a town. South of Pacific Edge but up in the canyons." Anna paused and then stuck out her hand. "I'm Anna." Indicating Kevin, she said, "This is Kevin."

The kid stared at Anna's hand but didn't shake it. Instead, he glanced at his table of friends as if awaiting further instruction. Anna noticed one guy frown and make a slight gesture with his head as if to say, "get on with it."

Anna stepped around the kid, putting herself between him and his table of friends. Better that way. For her. Not for him. "That's my friend Derrick over there."

"You didn't answer my question. Where do you go to school?"

Anna hoped he'd move on to another line of questioning. She tried to think of towns south of Pacific Edge, but she didn't have Miriam's memory. She was just about to spit out some made-up name, hoping the kid didn't know much about that part of California, when Kevin cleared his throat.

"We live off Highway 166. About 30 miles from Vandenberg AFB. My dad's in the Air Force. Are you familiar with it?"

The kid looked stumped. Anna hoped that place existed. Otherwise, there was going to be a fight. And it would not be good with all these kids in here. All friends. A lot of them would get hurt. Some might not make it to school on Monday. Worst of all, she might not get pizza. And she wanted pizza. Anna said, "We're going to sit now." She motioned Kevin toward the table, but she didn't move until she knew he was gone. She gave the kid a smile. "Nice to meet you."

"What just happened?" Derrick asked.

"That was a fight looking for a place to happen," Anna said, sliding into the booth.

"Seriously?"

Kevin said, "Anna is right. The kid was trying to start something." He paused. "A kid at his table put him up to it. They're trouble."

Derrick said, "Ignore them. We'll eat and be gone, and that will be the end of it."

"I don't think it will be that easy," Kevin said.

31

Saturday, April 10, 12:03 a.m.

MIRIAM HAD BEEN SILENT FOR twenty minutes. Billy Joe Howie, now rebranded as William Dowd, slept. Miriam watched Rebekah, looking for any sign that she was dozing off. There were none. The girl was focused. And tough. There was no doubt about that. Miriam worried how killing that soldier would affect her, but it would not be the last violence they faced. Of that much, Miriam was certain.

"Do you know where we are?" Rebekah asked.

"Not exactly. We are on a different road from the one Mr. Jones took leaving."

"I think you're right. What's the town we're looking for? I've gone around Los Angeles like you said."

"What road are we on?" Miriam asked. "I should have been paying attention."

"I think highway 118. There aren't many signs. We've been passing by what look like towns. You know, lots of houses, but few lights. Many look deserted."

"We need to find Highway 101. Then go north. Patel said that at one point, the highway is gone. It was washed out years ago. Instead of fixing it, they cut a dirt road up the mountain, where it connects to a road that parallels the coast. Up there is where Patel will be waiting. It's just a few houses. Most people there are fishermen who use a small, abandoned island to launch their boats."

The road made a 90-degree right-hand turn. In a few miles, they came to another highway running east and west. The ocean was west, so the decision was simple. Then they saw a sign, one leg broken but still standing. It read Ventura. "We're on the right road now," Miriam said. "We should see Highway 101 soon. Then go north."

Exits read Ventura, but like everything else, it looked abandoned. Miriam thought there were people there, but not many, and those few remaining had little, which could make them desperate and that could make them dangerous, although she also thought they might just be frightened.

They came to Highway 101, and Rebekah took an exit.

"How much farther?" Rebekah asked after several miles.

"We are close. We should hit the landside in about ten miles. Maybe 12. Patel wasn't sure about the distance, but we'll know when we see it. He said the road's difficult but doable, whatever that means."

"I can hardly wait." Rebekah looked into the mirror. "Where is everyone? I haven't seen a car in the last couple of hours."

"Martial law. Remember? We've made good time, but let's hope there are no military roadblocks."

"I switched off the overhead flashing lights almost an hour ago. There wasn't anyone to see them. What's going on with Billy Joe? Is he dead?"

"It's William. He's asleep. Poor kid must be exhausted. He's hurting and doesn't even realize it."

"Why did you bring him? Makes little sense."

"He saved us. We owe him. Life hasn't treated him very well."

"He could get us killed."

"If not for him, we'd already be dead."

Rebekah said, "Point."

"Stop when we reach where the road is closed."

"Okay. Why?"

"We need to plan how we approach. Discuss possible scenarios we might face. I gotta have one more chat with William. Make sure he doesn't screw this up. And I need to pee."

"We can't trust him."

"I don't disagree. What to do with him while I go into Technical Services? That's the question."

"While we go in," Rebekah said.

"Do you have to be in on everything? It's annoying. Can't I have some alone time?"

"Not going to happen."

Rebekah slowed, stopping at the detour sign that pointed toward a dirt road. She swung wide and pulled parallel to the sign. "This work?"

"We haven't seen any cars for a long time. I guess it works." Miriam shook William. "Wake up."

William looked around, as if trying to figure out where he was. He looked at Miriam and rubbed his eyes. "Where are we?"

"Almost there. I'll be right back." Miriam exited the car, disappearing into the darkness.

"Where's she going?" William asked.

"Don't be nosey."

William didn't say anything for a moment. "Oh. I get it. I need to do that too."

"I'm not sure we can do that," Rebekah said.

"Huh?"

"Let you out of our sight."

"Well, I'm going to piss my pants if not."

"I'll let Miriam handle that issue."

Miriam slid back into the car. "Much better. I missed the smell of the ocean. So, William, we need to talk."

William said, "I need to go."

"I was afraid of that," Miriam said. "Walk straight out there." Miriam pointed to the road-closed sign. "Just to the edge of the light."

"I'll keep my back toward you."

"Of course. Don't be a perv," Rebekah said.

William opened the door. "Just one more thing," Miriam said. "Rebekah, if he runs, shoot him."

"I don't think she would shoot," William said.

"You would not be the first person she's shot today."

William paused outside the door. "I don't believe she shot anyone, but I won't run."

"Good decision. Leave the door open," Miriam said.

When William was just beyond the sign, Rebekah pulled the pistol and pointed it out the window. "Stay where I can see you."

William glanced over his shoulder. "You're crazy."

"You got that right."

When William returned, Rebekah said, "My turn. Don't try anything with Miriam. She doesn't need a gun."

"Huh?"

"Just don't try anything, or you'll be sorry," Rebekah said.

"Okay, okay."

"What am I going to do with you, William?" Miriam asked.

"It's Billy Joe."

"Prove it."

"Asshole," he whispered.

"You have no idea. Look, William, this is not a joke. Prime is trying to kill us. Prime is going to start a war, and a lot of people will die. Understand? We aren't playing around here."

"Even if that's true, what are you going to do about it? You're just a girl."

"I'm going to pretend I didn't hear that. Me and my friends, with help from the Resistance, are going to destroy Prime."

"Impossible."

"Improbable. There's a difference. It's either Prime or us. Prime won't allow us to live. And I want to live. Do you?"

William frowned. "Are you threatening to kill me?"

"William, I'm not sure who you are. You've pretended to be a cop, but you wanted to help people. You helped us. But why pretend to be a cop? Perhaps you dream of becoming Chosen. Is that your goal, William? To become Chosen?"

William took a deep breath. "No. Maybe. I'm not sure. I dreamed of becoming something."

"Something?"

"As opposed to being nothing." William looked down.

Miriam touched his shoulder. "Life has not been fair to you. It's not for many people, but you need a break. I can't promise you this will work out, but if it does, I'll help you get a decent chance."

"What does that mean?"

"I can't guarantee we'll survive."

William looked at her. "Don't say that."

"It's true."

"Well, even if you do, I don't see how you can help me. I don't think anyone can."

Rebekah got back in the car. "What did I miss?"

Miriam kept her focus on William. "First, we get you back into school in Potterville. I can arrange a place for you to stay. Then we take it one day at a time."

Rebekah said, "You make a lot of promises."

"I do. But this one I can keep. If we survive."

"And if you don't?" William asked.

"Then there won't be a Potterville to go to. You'll be on your own."

"Sounds grim," William said.

"Worse than grim," Rebekah said. "Are we going to talk about what comes next? And what are we doing with him? We could lock him in the trunk."

Miriam frowned. "Not helping, Rebekah. Besides, we can't lock him in the trunk. He can still make a racket and draw someone's attention. Or if we get arrested or something, he could die before anyone finds him."

Rebekah shrugged. "You asked for suggestions."

"I did not."

"I guess I skipped ahead to where you did."

"Do you have a suggestion, William?" Miriam asked.

"You could explain what you're doing and why, and maybe I could help."

Miriam said, "Breaking into Pacific Edge. I think I already said that."

"You said something about going to Technical Services. You did not say it was in Pacific Edge."

"Good job, William. Technically, it's not Pacific Edge, but part of the building that surrounds it. Why would you help? You're not involved in this."

Rebekah said, "Other than getting us caught so he could collect the reward."

"Good point," Miriam said. "You're not going to help. You're going to stay outside and be quiet. Rebekah, let's find Patel."

Rebekah started the car, put it in drive, and headed up the hill. The first grade was steep. The tires clawed for traction as the rear end fishtailed. "Shit," Rebekah hissed. Then she made a left hairpin turn. She slowed but didn't stop.

Had she stopped, she wasn't sure she could get going again. The road wasn't as steep, but it was narrow. One lane about fifty yards, and then another hairpin-turn to the right. It continued that way for what felt like forever.

Miriam's fingers hurt from gripping the front seat. William's face was white. Rebekah hunched forward, her shoulders tense. Finally, the road leveled out. They were on top, where they intersected a paved road. The town was not far ahead. However, they experienced no relief upon arriving at their destination because, besides the glowing windows of a few homes, there were flashing red and blue lights.

"This does not look good," Rebekah said.

"It does not," Miriam agreed. "What do you think is happening?"

"Maybe they caught Patel and know we are coming," Rebekah said.

"I don't think so," William said.

Miriam turned to him. "Explain."

"If they knew you were coming, they would not put on a show to alert their presence. Just the opposite. They'd hide until you arrived. Then they'd swoop in."

Miriam nodded. "There's hope for you yet, William."

Rebekah said, "Hey, I just noticed you haven't been correcting Miriam about your name."

William said, "There's no point. She insists on calling me William." He paused. "I'm getting used to it."

"Progress," Miriam said. "Soon you'll start liking it."

"Maybe."

"Can we get back to the problem at hand?" Rebekah asked. "Why is the place crawling with cops? It's a little town. Can't be much going on there, so it must involve us somehow."

Miriam said, "I agree. I'm afraid someone may have spotted Patel. They might be searching for him. Crap. Pull off the road and turn off your lights."

"Are you crazy?" Rebekah asked.

"Maybe, but that has nothing to do with it." Miriam pointed. "Someone is leaving, and they are headed toward us."

"Damn." Rebekah steered the car off the road. It jerked and tilted, but she was able to keep it moving. After 25 yards, she stopped and killed the lights. "Is this far enough?"

"I hope so. To be safe, we need to get out of the car. If they stop, we can run."

"We might run off a cliff."

"True. But we'd get away."

They exited the car, gathering on the passenger's side and ducking.

"It's an ambulance," William said, adding, "red lights. Law enforcement uses blue."

"Are you sure?" Rebekah asked.

"Yeah. They threatened to arrest my dad if he used blue lights. They let him have red, although technically that wasn't legal either."

The ambulance did not slow. It drove past but wasn't in a hurry.

Kevin said, "Must be a fatality."

"What?" Miriam asked.

"Someone died."

"I understand what the word means. I mean, why do you think that?"

"If they had an injured person, they'd drive faster and run their siren. If the ambulance didn't have a patient, they would not have their lights on. So, lights but no siren indicate they have a patient, but the patient is dead. No rush."

"I hope it's not Patel," Miriam said.

"Patel is your friend?" William asked.

"Sort of. Plus, he has something we need," Miriam said.

"That's kinda cold. Don't you think?" William asked.

"I suppose," Miriam said, "but it's a desperate situation. I've tried to tell you that."

"Maybe you're blowing this a little out of proportion. I mean, nobody even knows if Prime is real," William said.

"You heard the news. Prime has taken over the country. I'm sure Prime is responsible for the assassination of the president and vice president, and you heard them say there's gunfire in the capital. What do you think they're doing? Target practice?"

"You can't believe what you hear on the news," William said.

Miriam rolled her eyes, aware that in the dark, he could not see her exasperation. "William, just when I think you're smarter than your make-believe persona suggests, you prove me wrong."

Rebekah said, "Can we focus? I'm cold. And hungry. And scared. What next?"

Miriam said, "We find out what's happening."

32

THEY HAD FINISHED EATING THE PIZZA. A WORKER HAD flipped the open sign to closed. Derrick would have left thirty minutes earlier but waited until the guy who confronted Kevin had left. They'd been gone ten minutes. He didn't want those kids following them. Derrick felt it was safe to leave.

He was wrong.

As they walked to the truck, a kid wearing a black leather jacket stepped out of a darkened doorway. "About time you left. Where are you heading?"

Anna said, "None of your business."

"I wasn't talking to you." Blocking Kevin's path, he said, "Do you always let girls talk for you?"

Derrick took Kevin's arm, pulled him back, and stepped in front. "Sorry about them. We are going hiking. In the park, to the north." He couldn't think of the place's name but had noticed it highlighted on a map in the sporting goods store.

"You're lying. The park is closed. What are you doing here, and where are you going?"

The kid brushed his jacket back, revealing a large knife. Derrick didn't care for knives. He didn't care for guns, either. He was also starting to dislike this kid's attitude. "We don't want problems. We are leaving, and you'll never see us again."

The kid put his hand on his knife. "You'll leave when I say you can."

Anna started toward the kid. Derrick put his hand on her shoulder. "We don't want problems."

"Then answer my question."

"I already did. If we discover we can't hike, we'll leave. We have to be back for school next week, either way. Again, we are not here to cause problems."

"Not good enough. Driving toward the park means you come back through here. I think you're here to rip people off. Break into cabins because many are empty now. Strangers don't show up here this time of year. Like I said, the park is closed. Hikers would know that. So, here's how it's going to work. You'll get in your vehicle, and we will escort you out of town. If you try to sneak back into town, this knife will be the least of your worries."

"What's your name?" Derrick asked.

"You don't need to know my name."

"My name is Derrick. I have an alternative for you."

"Yeah? What's that?"

"You stay or leave. Either way is fine. No pressure. I won't tell you which is best. Your decision. We're going to leave and go about our business. We'll all act like this never happened. No one gets hurt."

"You trying to be funny?"

"I am not."

An icy wind blew down the street, wrestling dead leaves from the bare trees. Two kids appeared. Derrick had spotted them hiding behind cars and trucks. Other than that, the town was quiet. There were still a few people inside the café—workers cleaning up, wanting to get home. Maybe some of them would come to help these three. More likely, they would lock the doors and call the cops.

Derrick didn't need cops. But he needed to leave. He was cold and tired and wanted to get back to the base. They still had a thirty-minute drive and a ten-mile run. His patience was wearing thin. He'd given this kid plenty of opportunities to walk away, so he said, "Here's what's going to happen. We are going to walk to our truck and leave. You're going to step out of the way and do nothing. That's your best choice and my last offer."

"Or you'll do what?"

"Or you'll wake up in the hospital." Derrick didn't hesitate. He stepped forward. The kid unsnapped the knife's sheath. Derrick punched his right bicep. The snap of his humerus bone sounded loud enough for his buddies to hear it. The knife hit the ground and bounced a couple of times before it stopped moving. Derrick hit him twice more, breaking several ribs and his left clavicle, rendering both hands useless. To avoid any confusion the kid might still have, Derrick separated his right knee with a round-house kick. The kid fell to the ground and didn't move. The pain had taken him beyond his threshold of consciousness.

Derrick picked up the knife. "How about you two? Questions?"

Both shook their heads.

"Good. Now we are leaving. If I see headlights following us, it won't end well. Understood?"

Both nodded.

"Is there a hospital nearby?"

One boy said, "It's an hour away."

"Which direction?"

The boy pointed. "South."

"I suggest you load your friend into a car and drive there immediately. Don't drive too fast. It's dangerous at night and killing yourselves in an accident would be counterproductive."

Keeping his eyes on the two boys, Derrick motioned Anna and Kevin into the truck and joined them. Kevin backed out of the parking spot and drove away. Derrick glanced over his shoulder. The boys were loading their friend into a car. "He can't say I didn't warn him."

Anna said, "You're politer than I would have been."

Derrick glanced at her. "I know, which is why I handled it."

Kevin said, "You two scare the shit out of me."

Anna said, "You're a smart guy, Kevin. Now, get us to Johnsondale. I want to get some sleep. We have a big day tomorrow."

"What happens tomorrow?" Kevin asked.

"We destroy the first Prime headquarters," Derrick said.

33

REBEKAH DROVE TOWARD THE FLASHING blue lights, taking a road that put them two blocks east of the activity. As they got closer, she turned off their headlights. The car crawled along the darkened road, and she focused on staying in the middle, assuming Miriam was catching glimpses of the scene through alleys, streets, and the occasional empty lot.

Miriam thought the remaining ambulance was parked near the cliff above the ocean. It was difficult to know for sure. She could not see into the gloom beyond the multitude of rotating lights, which reflected off wisps of fog drifting in from the sea. She estimated visibility would only be a few yards soon.

"Stop here," Miriam said.

"See anything?" Rebekah asked.

"I'm not sure. William, what do you make of it?"

William sat up, trying to see through the plexiglass barrier that was clouded with age. "I can't see much. It would be better outside."

"Someone might notice us when the dome light comes on," Miriam said.

"There's a toggle switch under the dash on the left side. Flip it to the left, and the light won't come on."

Miriam said, "Clever. Did you do that?"

"My dad did." William's voice cracked just a little.

Miriam rubbed his shoulder for a moment. William presented a complication she did not need. But the kid was heartbroken, although he tried to hide it. Lost and alone, using an imaginary law enforcement position to cope. His act failed to cover his pain. He had saved them, so there was that. However, she could not care for every stray that crossed her path. William wasn't a rarity. There must be thousands like him—people hurting and alone.

If they didn't stop Prime, the number of orphans would skyrocket.

She couldn't help them all.

But she could help William.

They gathered at the front of the car. "I'll go see what I can find out," Miriam said.

Rebekah said, "Bad idea. I'll go." She indicated her clothing. "Duh. Uniform?"

"What if the police see you? They'll know you're not a real officer," Miriam said.

William said, "Tell them you work security in Ventura." He pointed to a patch on the sleeve. "It's a private security uniform. My dad got it at a thrift store before Halloween."

Miriam said, "Okay, but be careful." She pointed. "See that big car? I think that might be Patel."

Rebekah said, "What makes you think that?"

Miriam didn't like her response. "I just have a feeling."

"Okay then. I love feelings." And with that, Rebekah walked away.

Miriam took William's hand, squeezing it tight. "I love the ocean. Have you seen it?" She breathed deep. "I love the smell of it."

"I have not been to the ocean. I take it we are close. It kind of stinks."

"It has to grow on you, I guess."

"You guys are close friends?" William asked.

"Not exactly. I mean, we weren't. But we've been through a lot since we escaped."

"You are worried about her. She means a lot to you."

"I'm worried she's going to get us caught."

"You might be smart but not a convincing liar."

"Screw you, Dowd."

"She likes you too," William chuckled, then added, "Maybe we should get closer but stay in the shadows."

"Good idea. I'm good at staying in the shadows. Lots of practice."

"How so?"

"I'll tell you about it sometime. Assuming we live through this."

"You're a real ray of sunshine. Did anyone ever tell you that?"

"Shut up."

Rebekah slowed as she approached the big car. In the distance, first responders passed through the dancing lights, but they focused on their work. Getting closer, she tilted her head, trying to see in. Anyone inside the car could see her easily.

"What's she doing?" Miriam whispered.

"I think she's going to the driver's window."

"I didn't tell her to do that."

"You didn't tell her not to."

Rebekah eased next to the driver's mirror, so she was easily seen, and then tapped on the glass. The window came down.

"May I help you, officer?" Asked a gruff male voice.

Rebekah leaned down, "Mr. Fletcher? Is that Mr. Patel I see in the back? It's me, Rebekah. Miriam's friend."

"What a relief. You made it," Patel said. "Where did you come from, and where is Miriam?"

"We drove from Mexico. She's nearby." Rebekah motioned for Miriam.

"How did you get here so quickly without being stopped?" Allen asked.

"We drove fast, but we haven't seen many cars."

"You haven't seen cars because there's a nationwide curfew," Jason said.

"I'm here," Miriam said, stepping next to Rebekah, then smacking Rebekah on the shoulder. "You scared me. What if it wasn't them?"

"Ouch," Rebekah squeaked. "But it is them."

Miriam said, "Let's go where they can't see us."

Once off the road, deep in the brush, Miriam asked the group, "What's going on?"

Jason said, "They found bodies in the ocean."

"Do I know you?" Miriam asked.

"I'm L. Linda Maxton's father, Jason."

"Okay." Miriam noted he didn't say dad, but that probably meant nothing.

Patel said, "My contact here lives in the house they have surrounded."

"Not good," Miriam said. "How is he involved?"

Jason said, "Allen's contact, a minister, found his son on the rocks near the sea. Broken leg, a knife lodged in a crack, and a sign made of stones pointing to bodies in the water. At least three, all girls, from what we have learned."

"Weird," Miriam said.

Allen said, "It gets weirder. My friend, Tom Sr., said a girl came to his house. No shoes, wet, dirty. She told him she had talked to his son, Tom Jr., down by the ocean. She said Junior wanted to sell his motorcycle, and she wanted to test ride it. She rode off and never came back."

"What's the boy say?" Rebekah asked.

"He says the girl attacked him and that she killed the girls in the water," Jason said.

"How many girls can break a guy's leg?" Rebekah asked, glancing at Miriam. "Present company excluded."

"Not many," Jason said. "I'm sure the boy killed the girls, but over time, not all at once. He probably tried to kill this girl as well. Didn't work out for him."

"Why was she wet and barefoot, and where did she come from?" Miriam asked.

"The boy said she came from the ocean. His dad said she must have come from the sky."

"What do you think?" Miriam asked.

Jason said, "I'm guessing both are correct."

"Excuse me, but this isn't getting us into the building," William said.

The adults stared at William as if he'd just materialized.

William looked at Miriam. "You said we need to get into the building."

"Who is this?" Jason asked.

"Long story," Miriam said. "I'll explain another time. He's right. We need to get Allen's briefcase." Looking at William, she said, "There's no we. At least, not that includes you."

"I can help."

"Perhaps."

"I've helped you once today."

Miriam couldn't argue with that. "I'm not asking anyone to put themselves at risk."

"It's not all about you, Miriam," Rebekah said. "Have you forgotten that I'm difficult to exclude from your plans?"

"If you mean, have I forgotten you're a pain in the butt? No, I have not forgotten."

"Excuse me, Rebekah," Allen said. "Miriam, do you have a plan for getting inside? It seems impossible. They will have increased security, changed locks, and our photographs are circulating everywhere. There are high rewards for our capture."

"You said we need the VPN," Miriam said. "I agree with you. I've been thinking of ways we can use it."

Allen shrugged. "It would help you stay hidden and allow you to communicate with others in the Resistance."

"I can't just hide."

Patel held up his hands. "Miriam. Please. I started this. I helped in ways I regret. I should not have put you in harm's way, but I did. I hoped you could make an impact on things, but I didn't think it through. I never expected this to happen. It's best if you hide. Stay somewhere safe. The VPN would help you do that, but there are other ways. We can figure something out."

Miriam said, "Prime assassinated the president and took over the military. Prime plans to start a war with Mexico. Things are going to get bad fast. For everyone. Plus, there's no place to hide."

"I still don't see a way to get into Technical Services," Patel said.

"If I could get online, I could get back into the system, unlock a door, cause a diversion," Miriam said.

"I assumed you had created a backdoor, which is why I wanted to meet here. You could have gone online at Tom's house." Allen glanced at the chaos. "But that is no longer an option."

Rebekah said, "I have an idea."

Everyone looked at her.

"We go in the same way we came out."

"Sneak past the guard? We still couldn't get in the way we came out. That door is locked," Miriam said.

"Not sneak by the guard. He'll have a computer, right? You get online there and unlock the door. We walk in, get the—whatever we are getting, and leave. It's the KISS method."

"KISS method?" Allen questioned.

"Keep it simple, stupid."

Miriam said, "Won't work. The guard will trip an alarm."

"Not if we trick him," Rebekah said.

"You've lost me," Miriam said.

Rebekah waved at her clothing. "Duh. Uniform. You stay out of sight, and I'll just walk up like I belong there. Wave a piece of paper and say I've got orders of some sort. Then I'll stick a gun in his face and tell him to keep his hands where I can see them. Then you get on the computer. You'll have to figure out the rest."

Miriam said, "Dangerous, but it might work."

William said, "What if he doesn't believe you? What if he reaches for an alarm or a gun himself?"

Rebekah twisted her head and shoulders like something was digging its claws into her back. "I hope that doesn't happen. If it does, I'll put a bullet in his head."

William said, "Easy to say. Difficult to do. You'll most likely freeze."

Miriam said, "She won't."

"You don't know that," William said.

"I do."

"We never know how we'll handle a situation like that until we've experienced it."

"Rebekah has experience. I already told you that. Either you were not listening, or you didn't believe me."

34

OUTSIDE OF TOWN, DARKNESS DOMINATED the entire landscape, except for their headlights, which illuminated a small patch of asphalt ahead of them. Derrick felt the cold penetrating the windows and doors. It was a good thing they bought the sweatshirts. But they should have skipped dinner. Not because the pizza wasn't good. It was excellent, but because of the confrontation. Derrick wasn't happy about hurting that kid, although perhaps learning he wasn't the toughest guy in the world might save his life in the long run. But it created complications. Getting to the base had been a simple plan— no longer.

"Pull over when you see a spot," Derrick said.

"Okay," Kevin drawled.

"I thought you were in a rush," Anna said.

"I am, but things have changed."

Kevin drove on for a mile and then pulled onto a dirt road. A sign indicated it was an entrance to a campground and accessed the river. A fishing pole and tent adorned the sign, along with many bullet holes.

"Mind telling us what we're doing?" Anna asked.

"I want to make sure no one is following us."

"They're taking that kid to the hospital. It's an hour in the other direction."

"That's what they told us. Doesn't mean it's true. There could be a local doctor they can take him to. Maybe there's an emergency room. Even if it's true, I have a feeling they won't let it rest," Derrick said.

"What are you suggesting?" Anna asked.

"Only one way in and one way out. The park is closed, so there's no exit. They know we're going in, so they know we're coming out. Except it won't be us, just Kevin. They'll have someone waiting for us to return, but it won't just be the three. There will be more, and they'll be armed."

"I'll be okay," Kevin said. "I will be in and out before they get back. Besides, I'm a soldier. They trained me to fight."

Derrick doubted the kids Prime was sending to slaughter in the first wave were well trained. "I'm not willing to take that risk." He paused. "It's too dangerous for anyone to know about the place we are going, and we hardly know you, but we don't have options." Derrick looked at Kevin. "Sorry."

Kevin said, "It's okay. I'm surprised you've trusted me this far. When you were sleeping, I could have changed direction or gone to the police."

Anna scanned the road. "No one is following us. It's probably safe, for Kevin to head to Potterville after dropping us off."

Derrick shook his head. "He needs sleep. He'll have to wait until morning. They'll be back by then."

"I can go a couple of days without sleep, and driving keeps me alert. I'll be fine."

"It's not just that," Derrick said, then studied both for a moment. "You didn't see the news alert?"

"What news alert?" Anna asked.

"It was scrolling on the TV. National curfew. No one out after dark. That's why there are no cars."

Anna said, "But all those people in the restaurant. They were out."

"Most weren't paying attention. A few people saw it and held up their middle fingers, which is not a gesture of goodwill as I understand it. They weren't too worried about authorities in their little town, but they'll go home and stay put. The three we encountered are not rule-followers, and they will have friends.

"Maybe they'll get busted on the way to the hospital," Kevin said.

"Perhaps. But cops will give them a break because the kid needs a doctor. Like I said earlier, there must be a doctor in town they can go to. Wake him up if necessary."

Anna took a deep breath. "So, what do we do?"

"I have an idea," Derrick said. "We'll stop about a mile from the entrance and put a blindfold on Kevin, like Miriam did the others. When we get to our destination, I'll arrange a place for him to stay. He won't know where he is. Sorry, Kevin, it will be a bit like jail, but you'll be fed and such."

"Miriam took Rebekah in blindfolded? I'll bet that went over well."

"Not Rebekah. They came in together at the same entrance we'll take. But the others were blindfolded. They came in a different way."

"There are others?"

"There are. Friends from Potterville."

"Your friends?"

"Yes."

"I'm still having trouble adjusting to this new Derrick. Am I going in blindfolded?"

Derrick paused. He had not considered that. Anna was a test subject. She was one of them, but she had not been to the base. Somehow, he'd forgotten that. It seemed like days ago when they had left to find her. It seemed even longer since he'd seen Nyx. Thinking of Nyx caused an empty feeling in his chest. Something was wrong. Maybe it wasn't Nyx. Maybe it was Red and

Antonio. Derrick pushed the feeling aside as best he could. "Probably not. It will be hard enough to have one blind person."

Kevin said, "I'm okay with being blindfolded. The less I know, the better."

"What does that mean?" Anna asked.

Kevin shrugged. "I'm 100% cooperating with you. You could have killed me. You didn't. But say I'm captured. I could hold up under interrogation, but I don't think I'd do well if tortured." He paused. "Just being honest."

"They will torture you anyway," Anna said.

"True, but I couldn't tell them where to find you."

"It's not a perfect plan," Derrick said, adding, "but what is about this situation?"

35

THEY SPENT TEN MINUTES EXAMINING tactics and what-ifs. Miriam thought it was a solid plan, although it contained more what-ifs than she preferred. More worrisome were the what-ifs they may have missed. The idea was simple. Rebekah would sneak to the guard shack, staying in blind spots until the last possible concealment point. In a perfect world, the guard would be reading, texting, or playing a game. Cell phones have their advantages. She would then tiptoe to the shack and stick a gun in his face, telling him to keep his hands where she could see them. If he did something stupid, she'd shoot him. Miriam didn't know for sure Rebekah could do that. She shot the soldier in Mexico, but the soldier tried to kill them, giving her no choice. This was different.

Miriam wanted to trade clothing and do it herself, but she was smaller, and the uniform wouldn't fit. The plan hinged on Rebekah selling her role long enough to allow Maxton to secure the guy. Or perhaps gal, although the Chosen rarely extended equal opportunities to women. That was one of the first rights James Carver diminished when he became president.

Miriam would log into the system, unlock a door, and set off an alarm on the other side of the building. During her nights there as Maranda Kingston, two guards protected the complex: Marty and Brad. Later, she met Mike, who was a part-timer. She liked them. Brad and Mike were good guys. Marty, not so much. She was sure they'd increased security since then. How much? Maybe doubled? Four guys. Maybe more.

They dare not drive to the coast road because they had to go right past the police cars. Patel knew a backroad, which would take longer but be safer.

They parked in the business area Miriam and Rebekah had been in when Mr. Jones had first tried to contact them the night of their escape, which seemed like weeks ago rather than a few days. With the plan as complete as possible, Rebekah left them, creeping along the outer fence, easing into the driveway, and squeezing between the box containing the mechanism for the arm that blocked vehicles from entering. She squatted down below the guard-shack window, pointing the pistol at the ground, and duck-walked to the front of the shack, where she stood, pointed the pistol at the guard's head. He didn't notice her standing there, studying his phone.

She'd rehearsed her opening lines several times in her head. But it was the first time she had said the words aloud. "Don't panic. I'm here on Prime's orders. I need you to keep your hands where I can see them."

They had debated what she would say. A young girl in a poor-fitting, non-standard uniform was a farfetched idea. Unlikely to be believed. However, disobeying Prime's order, if it was legit, seemed like the most disturbing for the guard to contemplate.

Rebekah's delivery of the next line was critical. "A saboteur is in the building right now. A strike force is en route."

The guard relaxed. Just a little. Although he also looked scared.

"Are you really working for Prime?" The man asked.

"Yes. Don't make me shoot you." She regretted her choice of words. As if an agent of Prime would care whether or not she shot him.

"It might be best if you did. A guy I know, Marty Washington, was working the night Miriam King escaped."

Rebekah tried to remain impassive. Marty was the guy who locked them in Patel's safe room and held Anna drugged and secured in a van.

"Marty turned up a few days later near the gate with his hands zip-tied behind his back. No one knew who had left him there. A trial followed the very next morning. That afternoon, they called us all to the facility. Once we were gathered right over there," the man indicated the lot between the fence and the building, "They led Marty out and stood him against the wall. Then ten Pacific Edge security officers shot him."

"That won't happen. If you follow directions."

"Two guards, Brad and the part-timer, Mike, have disappeared. No one knows what happened to them. Some say they were Resistance and went into hiding. Some say they are dead."

Jason Maxton walked up as if he owned the place. "Step out, sir."

The guard stepped out. "Who are you?"

"Advance team. Please put your hands out like this." Jason stuck his arms straight out, wrists touching back-to-back.

The guard did as instructed. In a flash, Jason put a thick zip tie around the man's wrists and snugged it tight.

"Hey. What's this?"

"Security measure," Jason said.

Allen Patel stepped into the light.

The guard said, "Hey, you're …" He stopped talking when Miriam walked into the shack and sat at the computer. His eyes shifted from Miriam to Rebekah. "Shit. I thought you looked familiar. Shit. Shit. Shit. I'm dead."

After a few moments, Miriam exited the shack. "Four guards. I set off two alarms on the other side of the building. The kitchen door is unlocked. Allen, do you know your way to your office from the kitchen?"

"Pretty much. I didn't go near the kitchen often."

"I know the way," Miriam said.

Jason said, "I should come with you."

"Stay here with Rebekah. She can't watch this guy and her back. There could be other guards lurking about," Miriam said.

"I'll be okay. Jason should go with you."

"Not going to happen. I've put you in too much danger already." Which was true, but Miriam was thinking more about what might happen to Rebekah's mental health if she had to shoot another person today. One a day seemed more than enough. It was just past midnight, so technically, it was a new day, but Miriam wasn't hung up on technicalities in this case.

Miriam looked at Patel. "Ready?"

"As I ever will be."

"The cameras will record that you're in there," the guard said.

"Will that make me double wanted?" Miriam asked, adding, "The cameras are off. There will be no headline videos. If we find what we are looking for, they won't know we took it because they didn't know it was there. If the guards don't see us, they won't know we were here."

"I saw you," the guard said, then instantly appeared to regret saying it.

"You are our only loose end. And I don't like loose ends."

With that, Miriam led Patel to the unlocked door. As they neared the building, she remembered zapping Allen with a stun gun the last time she was here. She assumed he remembered as well. Water under the bridge, she hoped.

Once inside, she moved with silent efficiency. At an intersection, she whispered. "Stay here. I need to grab a couple of things."

She disappeared through a door and then returned.

"What did you take?" Patel asked.

"Just replenishing stock items." She held a finger to her lips.

At the large work area, she paused, scanning over the cubical walls. Seeing no movement, she continued to Patel's office. His name was still on the door. "They haven't replaced you?"

Patel shrugged. "They haven't replaced the sign. Things move slowly. They will be more careful replacing me after learning I was in the Resistance."

Patel entered his code and tried the door. Nothing. He tried again. The door remained locked. "You're sure it's right?" Miriam asked.

"I'm certain. They've changed it."

"Damn it. I should have tried unlocking it while I was on the computer."

"It's not in the system. You couldn't have."

This made Miriam furious. Not that it was a stand-alone lock. What bothered her was that she had not thought of it. What else had she missed? Fatigue was taking its toll. She needed sleep, and getting to the base would still take several hours.

If she made it there.

No guarantee that would happen.

Miriam ran her hand down the door. Put her ear against it and tapped it. Solid wood and a metal door frame. They had removed the keyed lock. She wondered how they would open it if the battery in the lock failed. It probably had a warning system when the battery got low. Perhaps it unlocked if the battery failed. Assuming it had a battery. Maybe it was hardwired. Those unlock features might have been engineered into the design. Neither were any benefit now.

"Follow me," Miriam whispered.

In the cubicles, Miriam said, "Hide in here until I come back."

"We should stay together."

"No, you stay here. If I'm not back in ten minutes, leave. Tell Maxton I got caught." Miriam dashed off.

Ten minutes came and went. Patel disobeyed Miriam's instructions, waiting until she showed up fifteen minutes later. Rather than scold him, she said, "You're still here. It took me longer to find this than I anticipated." She hefted a six-inch-diameter cylinder made of solid steel. The device had two metal handles on either side near one end.

"What's that?" Patel asked.

"I'm not sure what it's called, but it looks like it's made to open doors and such. I think it's called a master key."

Standing in front of Patel's office, Miriam studied the steel ram, putting it this way and that. Changing hands, trying different positions. "I think it will take both of us."

She motioned Patel into position. "Grab the handle with both hands like this."

Patel grabbed one handle. They positioned the device parallel to the door. Miriam glided it away from the door and then back toward it. "We swing it like this. Each time a little further back. On the third stroke, we swing it as hard as we can into the door, right next to the knob. The door will shatter."

"What if it doesn't?"

"Then we repeat until it does."

"It will be loud. Won't it? What if they hear it?"

"They will hear it. Grab the briefcase, and then we run. I know a faster way out."

"Won't the door be locked?" He asked.

"It will have a crash bar. They can't lock doors from the inside. Fire code."

"If they are still following safety regulations. There's no guarantee they are."

"True. Ready?"

Patel nodded.

"One." Swing. "Two." Swing. "Three."

BANG!

The door cracked but didn't open.

"Again," Miriam shouted. Being quiet no longer a necessity.

The second blow split the door, and a large chunk of it flew into the office, and the remainder swung inward, smacking the wall.

Mariam dashed inside. "Is your case here?"

"Got it," Patel said, holding it above his head.

"Let's get out of here."

Miriam ran to the cubicles, turned left, and then left again, passing the cafeteria. Patel was right behind her, breathing hard, his footfalls slapping the hard floor. She feared he couldn't keep up, but he did.

It turned out Allen's keeping up wasn't a problem.

The man who slid into the hallway, blocking their exit. That was a problem.

She stopped. Allen ran into her, grabbing her, preventing her from falling.

They turned around.

Another guy blocked that path.

Nowhere to run.

36

IT TURNED OUT THAT JOHNSONDALE WAS not a town. Just a few houses, and most looked abandoned. On one side of the road stood a square, one-story cinderblock building. The word Café was hand-painted on the side. Weeds blown against the door indicated it was not in operation. Maybe in the summer. Maybe not.

Derrick pointed. "Park over there." One house, which looked more abandoned than the others, was surrounded by old cars—some on blocks, some with flat tires.

Kevin pulled in until the front bumper hit the car in front of them.

"Let me see your knife," Derrick said. "The one in your boot."

Looking bewildered, Kevin bent over, hiked up his pant leg, and pulled a big knife from his boot. "How long have you known about it?"

"It's dangerous not to be observant." Derrick got out of the truck, stabbing both rear tires. "Perhaps no one will notice a new addition." He handed the knife back to Kevin.

Anna said, "Is that a good idea?"

"The tires? I think so. It fits right in. Don't you agree?"

"I mean giving him the knife. No offense, Kevin."

Having returned the knife to its sheath, Kevin pulled his pant leg down. "None taken."

Derrick said, "If he were going to use it, he would have by now."

"Your trusting nature could get us killed."

"Perhaps. But it hasn't yet," Derrick said.

"I'll toss the knife if it makes you feel better," Kevin said.

Anna glared at him.

Kevin raised both hands. "You kicked my butt on the mountain, and I saw what Derrick did to the kid in town. I want no part of either one of you. I think Derrick let me keep it, knowing he would break my arm if I tried to use it. Maybe it was a test."

Derrick took off, following Miriam's directions, and setting the pace. About 8-minute miles, Derrick thought. Roughly ten miles. About an hour and a half.

An hour and a half until Derrick would see Nyx, but she would be asleep. Unless she was up waiting for him to get back, which was a possibility but implied things he dared not entertain. If he saw her, even briefly, he knew he could sleep. Otherwise, he'd have a restless night, which did not bode well for attacking the Prime Headquarters in Seattle.

Miriam had given a brief yet extraordinarily accurate description of what they'd see on the road. They picked their way through the bones of animals mowed down by machine guns that still rattled their empty chambers. This alone would have slowed them down had Miriam not told them about it.

Halfway, Derrick estimated, he picked up the pace. If he got ahead of them, it wouldn't matter because he had to stop anyway at the pile of rocks, but the desire to see Nyx overpowered him. More accurately, the feeling that something was wrong overcame him. She'd be worried. Waiting up. That must be it.

Derrick stopped 100 yards from the entrance and made a blindfold torn from Kevin's military t-shirt. From here on, one of them would need to take Kevin's hand. Anna took that duty without being asked. A full moon made traversing the rock pile easier, especially since he knew where to go and wasn't running from a hovercraft. Instead, he was running to the girl with the pink-striped hair.

Once inside, he saw yellow lights spinning in the reactor area. He'd mention it to Red.

If Red was alive.

Derrick shivered.

They're okay. Everyone is okay, he told himself.

The red and white medical transport sat on the tracks. He wondered if there was a way to make it go faster. "Administration building. Fast as you can. It's an emergency."

The machine accelerated. "Charlie? Can you hear me, Charlie? Meet me. It's Derrick." That last part was unnecessary. Derrick hoped Charlie would be at the administration entrance. Perhaps Charlie would tell the others he was back. He probably would do that. At least he'd tell Nyx if she was up waiting for his return.

The transport slowed. Derrick craned his neck. Charlie's silhouette stood outside the entrance. No Nyx.

Derrick explained the situation. Charlie said there was guest housing once used for visiting politicians.

Charlie said, "I assume the man with the blindfold is going to the guest quarters? And he should not see any of … this?"

"Correct," Derrick said.

A QR-3 appeared and led Kevin away. Anna called out, "See you in a day or two."

Kevin gave a little wave.

"This must be Anna," Charlie said. No questioning in his voice, but he was a robot, so it was hard to tell sometimes.

"Yes," Derrick said. "Where is everyone? Is everyone okay?"

"Miriam and Rebekah have not returned."

"Right. I knew we'd beat them back. What about everyone else?"

"Red, Antonio, and I had a difficult flight home, but we made it. Although, Red and Antonio required treatment for sun stroke, and I was inoperative. Nyx required treatment as well, but not to the extent of the others."

"Is Nyx, okay?"

"I just said that she was. Red is on his way from Reactor Two. It threw an alert, and Red went to work on it. He is in the transport as we speak. Akira is asleep, as is Antonio."

"What about Nyx," Derrick said, voice rising slightly.

"She is in the infirmary."

Derrick didn't ask further questions but took off running.

The transport carrying Red pulled in as Derrick disappeared through the doors.

Red walked up and stuck out his hand. "Hi, I'm Red. You must be Anna. I'm glad they found you."

"You flew the plane that rescued the town?" Anna took his hand and pulled him into a hug. "You saved those people."

"Where's he off to in such a hurry?" Red indicated Derrick.

Charlie said, "I assume he is going to the infirmary?"

"Is he hurt?"

"Not that I could determine. He asked Nyx's location."

Red looked confused for a moment. "Is Antonio still sleeping there?"

"That is correct," Charlie said.

"Crap," Red said, sprinting into the building.

"What is that about?" Anna asked.

"I do not know," Charlie said, adding, "Are you hungry?"

"No. Just tired. A shower and a bed would be fantastic."

"Waiting for you. Just follow me."

Derrick arrived at the medical unit, stopped, and stared through the glass. Antonio was in a bed. He didn't have anything hooked to him. He looked fine. Just sleeping.

It wasn't Antonio that troubled Derrick.

It was Nyx.

She sat in a chair next to Antonio. Her head, resting on the bed, her hand holding Antonio's. She also appeared to be sleeping. Derrick didn't hear Red step up behind him.

"She didn't tell you. Did she?" Red whispered.

"Tell me what?"

"About her and Antonio."

That sick feeling Derrick had been fighting off grew stronger. He shook his head.

"They've been boyfriend and girlfriend off and on since middle school. Mostly on, but they break up about once a year. The record was three months.

The shortest was two days. This time they broke up about a week before you showed up."

"Oh, I didn't know." His words sounded hollow, as if he'd said them into a pipe. The first time he saw her from his condo window, she would have still been seeing Antonio. Or perhaps she had just broken up with him.

Red put his hand on Derrick's shoulder. "Sorry. She should have told you."

Derrick said nothing. He just turned and walked away.

Part Two

1

IN WHAT SEEMED LIKE ANOTHER LIFE, Miriam had operated in Technical Services as Maranda Kingston. She had met three security guards, but these two were not ordinary security.

A man with a gun said, "Hold it right there."

"Okay," Miriam said, and then she grabbed Patel's belt and jerked him into a recess that led to restrooms. She slammed through a door, not paying attention to which one she entered, but realized it was the men's side because had three unexpected white porcelain fixtures mounted on the wall and two stalls.

She locked the door and pointed. "Get in a stall and stand on the toilet."

"We're trapped," Allen said.

When they first entered the building, Miriam had gone to the armory to get a stun gun, but there were none. A more sophisticated weapon, with a range setting and a graduated power control, had taken their place. She took one, sticking it in her jeans in the small of her back.

Miriam studied the door—all metal. The lock would hold. Bullets might penetrate, but the guards wouldn't fire. No reason to. Just use the key.

One man tried the door. The latch that locked the door didn't move. No key. Not regular security. A regular security guy would carry keys. These guys carried guns. They'll call a regular guy to unlock the door. No big rush.

Miriam pulled a stun gun from her pocket and powered it on. The same one she had used on Rebekah, Allen, Derrick, and Anna. A light glowed green, indicating a full battery?

She heard voices and keys rattle. The lock moved. With the probes on the lock, she pulled the trigger. A grunt followed by a thump. That would give them something to think about before trying the lock again.

An idea popped into her head.

Using paper towels, she blocked the sink drains and turned the faucets on high. She entered the first stall and peered under the toilet, where she spotted a flexible pipe with a valve, which she closed. The nut connecting the pipe to the reservoir was plastic with two opposing ridges, making it easy to turn with her fingers. With the nut unfastened, she jerked the pipe free, and the water flowed from the reservoir. Then she turned the water supply back on. She repeated the procedure in the second stall, where Patel stood on the toilet.

She held her finger to her lips. "Stay up there." He nodded.

The water was now pouring from both stalls and cascading over the counter from both sinks. Soon, the water covered the floor, inching toward the door. She got into the first stall and stood on the toilet.

The voices picked up in the hall. One said, "Ready?"

She did not hear a reply. She heard the door open, but it closed again. The second time, it opened slowly.

"Do you see them?" Called a voice.

"No. They're in the stalls." Then the man called out. "No place to run. Just come out with your hands empty and where we can see them."

Miriam said nothing.

Splash, splash, splash. Two people, she thought.

"What the hell are they doing?"

"Get out," one man screamed.

Miriam pointed the new weapon at the floor and pulled the trigger. An arc leaped from the gun to the water, dancing a jig. She held the trigger for a few seconds. Until the screaming stopped.

She stepped out of the stall. Two men were sprawled on the floor. A third sat in the hallway, a regular security guard. Whether he was like Brad and Mike, members of the Resistance, or like Marty, hoping to score a big reward, she did not know, and it wouldn't matter. She picked up the first man's pistol.

Another man eased into view—hands raised. "Don't shoot."

"We'll see how things go," Miriam called over her shoulder. "You can come out now, Allen."

Clutching the briefcase to his chest, Allen tiptoed through the water. "Most resourceful. Where did you get the weapon?"

"When we first came in. Replenishing supplies."

"Are they dead?" Allen asked.

"I don't know. Maybe." Reaching the second man, she stepped on his pistol and slid it back toward Patel, creating a wake, soaking her shoes. "Pick that up."

"I don't know how to use it."

"I didn't ask you to use it, just to pick it up. I don't want it used on us if one of these guys is still alive. Turn the sinks off while you're there. Don't worry about the toilets. Let them run."

The guard who put the key in the door still sat in the hallway, clutching his chest.

Miriam said, "Both of you strip. If you try anything, I'm going to zap you. It's set on full power."

The man on the floor stood. "Don't shoot. That thing will rip a hole the size of a softball."

"Then don't make me pull the trigger."

When both men were down to their underwear, she said, "Inside with your buddies."

"Don't put us in there. I have a family. They'll kill us."

Miriam said, "I can't control what others might do."

The other guard said, "He's right. One guard who was here when you escaped has disappeared. The other is dead. They killed him out back. They will assume someone on the inside helped you, so they will torture us to find out who let you in."

She assumed Mike and Brad were hiding. The Resistance must have turned Marty over to Pacific Edge. These guys were not wrong. Prime would have them tortured and killed.

"You both have a family?" Miriam asked, looking at the second guy.

"No. But I like living."

"Did you alert anyone?"

The second guy hung his head. "I tried to alert the rear gate. He's one of us." He nodded toward the restroom. "We aren't with them. Those guys killed Marty."

"Did the guard at the rear gate answer?" Miriam asked.

"He did not. I assume you've already killed him."

"Not last I knew. If he was smart, he's alive. If not …" Miriam shrugged.

"Take us with you," the other man pleaded.

"And what makes you think that's an option?" Miriam asked.

"Please. They'll kill us."

"Like Marty."

Miriam said. "Marty wasn't a good guy. He captured us and tried to turn us in for the money."

"Doesn't surprise me. What about Brad?"

"I assume he's okay. He's on the right side."

"Resistance? Thank God for the Resistance."

"We're wasting time. Inside." Miriam indicated the men's room.

"Seriously. If you're leaving us here, you might as well kill me. At least that would be quick." The man stared at her. "I'll run and force you to do it."

"Me too," the other said.

"Damn it." Miriam thought for a moment, then said, "Get dressed."

"What are you going to do?" Allen asked.

"I don't know yet. I have until we reach the gate to figure it out. Let's take care of these guys first."

Miriam didn't know if her idea would work. The weapon was powerful. That much was certain. She checked the floor to ensure she wasn't standing in the water. The key was still in the door, so she locked it, aimed at the lock, and pulled the trigger.

Miriam held her hand near the lock. "It's hot."

Patel reached out. "It most certainly is. That was smart." He thought for a moment, then set his briefcase down and pulled off his belt. He made a loop with the belt and then pinched the key between the leather and tried to turn it. "It's frozen. Welded solid."

"You're sure?"

He stepped back, threading his belt back through the loops. "Yes."

Just then, she heard footsteps. She wheeled around, her weapon raised.

Jason Maxton held up his hands. "Whoa. What's taking so long? I got worried."

A shot rang out. Jason's eyes grew wide. A red blotch appeared in the center of his chest and then he buckled. A security officer stood behind him, holding a pistol.

Miriam fired. A blue arc flashed over Jason Maxton's body, hitting the officer in the chest, killing him instantly.

2

THE AIR REEKED OF BLOOD AND SINGED HAIR. The blood of Jason Maxton and the singed hair of the man Miriam shot with the new weapon. She kneeled next to Maxton and raised his head, cushioning it from the concrete floor with her hand. She was surprised to find that he was still alive. Maybe he wasn't injured as badly as she thought. Perhaps he wore a protective vest.

His eyes fluttered.

"I'm sorry, Mr. Maxton."

"My fault," he whispered. "Tell Linda."

He gasped, lungs rattling as if there was a can of spray paint in his chest.

"Tell …her…I loved her as …"

He drifted—more rattling.

"If she were my own … dau …"

And that was it. He was gone. *I loved her as if she were my own daughter,* Miriam thought.

"Kill them," Miriam hissed. "Kill them both!"

"No! Please!" One guard pleaded.

"You lied," Miriam shouted.

"Kill them!" Miriam's voice grew louder. Angrier.

"No! Please! We didn't know." The man pleaded again.

Miriam's tears rained down on Jason's face. She shuttered. How could she tell L. Linda? "KILL THEM!"

One man stepped in front of the other. His hands raised. Fear etched on his face. "Let Marvin go. He has kids. Kill me. But I swear we didn't know. Those jerks never talked to us. We don't even know who they work for. Look. Different uniforms. Black armbands. They wouldn't even let us be in the same room with them. We only saw the first two guys. The other guy—the one who killed your friend—we never saw him. I swear to God. They even use different radios. Different frequency. We can't hear their broadcasts. Check them."

"What if they are telling the truth?" Allen asked.

Miriam checked Jason's neck. No pulse. He was gone. No question. She turned to look at Allen. "What if they are?"

Allen said, "Maybe they didn't know about the third guy."

"So, what? We can't trust them. What are we going to do? Let them go? They'll call the police, and we won't make it out of town."

"We won't do that. Like we said, they'll kill us, and it won't be pleasant. Our only chance is to run," the man offering himself said.

The man behind him said, "Let me get my family to safety. Then I'll go wherever you want me to go. You can kill me there. I'll promise to come."

"Right. Like I would trust you to do that," Miriam hissed. She stood and pointed the weapon at them.

Allen said, "Miriam, stop. Don't do this. Not yet. We could lock them in a room like the other two."

"You might as well kill us. At least it would be quick."

"You should be tortured, but I don't care how you go."

Allen said, "Miriam. What would Derrick do?" Allen didn't know why he said that, only that he could think of nothing else.

"He isn't here. He doesn't need to know."

"He'll know because you need to tell him. You don't trust these two, but we must trust each other. If we lie to each other, we are no better than the Chosen. You killed a man. You had to. But with these two, you have a choice. You kill these two, and it will destroy you."

Miriam raised the gun. Her jaw muscles flexed and rippled. "Where would you go?"

One said, "I have a friend in the Mohave desert. Kind of a hermit. He hates the Chosen. We haven't spoken since I took this job. But we go way back. He'll take my wife and kids. I'm pretty sure. Then I'll run because they will be hunting me."

"And you?" Miriam indicated the other.

"I don't know. Maybe L.A. It's big enough to disappear in."

Miriam lowered the weapon a couple of inches. Thinking. Looking at Patel, she said, "Check the radios. See if they're telling the truth."

After a few moments, Allen said, "They're telling the truth about the radios. This one is theirs. One channel." He clicked it. The radio on one of the captive's belts sounded. "This is the other one. Totally different. It has several bands." He turned a small knob on the top.

"Who are those guys with?" Miriam asked.

"I don't know. I swear. I've never seen anything like them before. Never saw the uniforms. Never saw the armband. Like I said, they never said much to us."

The other guy chimed in. "When they arrived, they told us to stay out of their way, or they would kill us both. That was the only thing they said to us."

"You both have cars?" Miriam asked.

"I have a car. It's not great, but it can make it to my friend's house."

"I don't, but L.A. isn't far. I'll walk during the night and hide during the day. Not much hope, but a little hope is better than none. Isn't it?"

Miriam lowered the gun. "A little is better than none. I hoped to get out of here without anyone knowing. No hope of that now."

The first guy said, "I can erase the video. We'll be gone, so they won't hear it from us."

Miriam motioned to the restroom. "There are still those two."

"Maybe they're dead," one man offered.

"I don't think so, and there's no video. I took care of that. In a couple of days, it won't matter," Miriam said, adding, "Don't go to L.A. Stay away from big cities."

"Okay." The man drew it out as if it were a question.

"Don't take your car. Too easy to track."

"But …"

Miriam held up her hand. "We have a car you can use. No one is looking for it."

"We do?" Allen asked.

"They can have William's car. He doesn't need it anymore." Then Miriam stared at the two guards. "You have ID?"

"Yes." The first guy unclipped his badge, holding it out. The other followed suit.

Miriam nodded to Allen. "Take them. Listen carefully. If you contact anyone about us, I'll find you, and when I do, you'll wish I'd left you to Prime. Do you believe me?"

"I believe you. You're Miriam King."

"I believe you," the second man said.

Miriam nodded, and with that, she turned and walked toward the exit.

3

Saturday, April 10, 5:01 a.m.

THE HALLWAY CONTAINED DOORS on either side, extending into infinity. Neither dream nor reality. Something in between or perhaps both. Behind each door existed a memory. Derrick could open the door and watch it like a movie. Behind this door, he ran on a beach, his instructor cruising beside him on a small vehicle, forcing him to stay in the loose sand, yelling at him to speed up, cursing if the pace slowed, whipping him if he stumbled. Behind the next door, he fought with four guys. But he no longer needed to open doors. The memories were available to him. Or were they?

He opened a door labeled "Miriam," and was in her hallway. How could he see her memories? Perhaps they were his dreams, not her memories, things that never happened. He did not want to see Miriam's memories, but he wanted to see the door at the end of her hallway. He ran. The farther he ran, the more distant the end. A place he could not reach. He was exhausted when he got there, sweating, and his chest felt as if it might burst. He tried the door, but it would not open. No surprise. Miriam could not open it either. He opened another door to his left. Now he was in Anna's hallway. He didn't want to see her memories either, but he ran toward the end. He'd run three times farther than the ten-mile run from Johnsondale to the base entry. He was walking, then crawling, completely exhausted, yet he reached the door, but it would not open.

What was behind those doors? Why could none of them remember?

Derrick dashed through a door to his right and then another, and he was back in his hall and had reached the end. There was no door. He pounded and then kicked the wall. He had to break through. He had to know what was on the other side. But the wall held.

Derrick awoke, sweating. A nightmare. Yet, it wasn't that or a memory. He didn't know what it was. Why were memories like hallways? It made little sense. Perhaps Lawrence King, the man he'd known as Father, could explain it. Derrick had told the man not to hurt Lawrence because he wanted to talk to him. In hindsight, he realized it sounded like a threat, but that was not what he had intended. He had many questions that only his Father, his keeper, could answer. Derrick didn't understand who he was or what he was supposed to do.

He remained still, listening. Silent. He estimated it was about five-thirty, but he didn't know for sure. He should get up. He must prepare to attack Prime's

Seattle Headquarters, but he was unsure how to do that. He needed Miriam. Maybe she was back.

Suddenly, a scene materialized in his brain. It was awful. Perhaps it was another nightmare.

He focused on it.

He felt confident it wasn't a nightmare, but real.

Nyx was holding Antonio's hand.

Yes. That was real.

He felt as if he were falling.

Why didn't she tell me?

Tears filled his eyes. It hurt. Now, he understood how Nyx felt about his lies.

She could have told me.

I should have told her.

He could not push the thoughts away. Nyx was back with Antonio. Perhaps he had been a tool to make Antonio jealous. He and Nyx were not dating. There was no agreement between them. Like most things in his life, what he thought about their relationship and their commitment to one another all happened in his head.

He smelled bacon. How long had he been awake? He didn't know. He swung his feet to the floor. Time to get moving. He had a date with Prime. This could be the last day of his life. It was good that Nyx was back with Antonio. He had no future with her.

An odd feeling, like how he felt when he told the truth about himself over the school PA, washed over him.

Maybe because he recognized he had no time for a relationship. Prime wanted him and Miriam dead. Maybe it was something else. Perhaps it was nothing at all. *Get your head straight, Derrick King.*

He showered, dressed, and headed to the dining area. Red was there, a plate heaped with food in front of him. Antonio sat at Red's table his back turned to Derrick. Derrick walked to the steam trays, loaded a plate, and got coffee, black, from a big stainless-steel container. No one was there to make an espresso. The food was still good, but he was picking up the differences between it and fresh. He couldn't explain it. Not exactly. Just a bit empty was the best he could come up with.

Something else had changed. He looked around, trying to identify it. When they first found the administration building, Derrick marveled at everything, even Charlie. Especially Charlie, after they convinced him that they were not a threat. The complex was huge and defied the fact that it was underground. It was clean, comfortable, and advanced beyond anything he had ever seen.

Now he felt as if he were standing under a mountain and knew he was literally doing just that. The pressure was unbearable. No comfort existed anywhere in the facility. The walls and floor were shades of gray. Everything was sharp angles and hard surfaces. No art. No music. It was oppressive. Ugly.

Derrick walked to an empty table. Red waved at him. "Where are you going? Sit with us."

Antonio turned. "Amigo! I'm so glad to see you. When did you get back?"

Derrick remained composed but wasn't sure how long he could maintain it. Just then, he heard squealing. The voice familiar. His muscles tightened.

"You're back! Oh, my God! I've been scared to death!"

The girl with the pink-striped hair ran to Derrick and threw her arms around him.

4

DERRICK STOOD THERE. HE DID NOT return Nyx's embrace. He had a tray and coffee in his hands, so there was that, but he was stiff. She sensed it.

Pulling back, Nyx said, "What's wrong? Something bad has happened. Oh, God. It's not Miriam and Rebekah, is it? Derrick, oh my God. I'm so sorry."

She hugged him again for a moment, then stepped back. "What? What am I missing?"

Derrick glanced at Red. Red nodded as if to say, "Go ahead."

"I saw you last night."

Nyx frowned. "Saw me?"

"With Antonio. Red told me." Derrick paused. "About your relationship."

Nyx said nothing for a moment, her eyebrows knitted. "You saw me in the medical unit?"

Derrick nodded, eyes downcast. He couldn't look at her.

"Okay. I should have told you. I was going to, but—there wasn't a good opportunity."

"It's okay," Derrick said. "I wasn't truthful with you either."

She smacked his chest. "Not even close to the same. You flat out lied about who you were, and where you were from. I just didn't tell you one thing about my past. I haven't told you a lot of things about me, and you haven't asked. Not to mention," she indicated everything around, "it's not like we've had a lot of quiet time."

"I understand."

"The hell you do. Do you want to know?"

Derrick shrugged. He wasn't sure that he did. Nyx and Antonio were a couple once, and now they are again. End of story. What's to tell?

"I couldn't sleep. No one was awake…"

Red interrupted. "I was up."

"Shut up, Red. No one was here or in the computer room, so I went to the medical unit. Antonio heard me come in. It's true. Antonio and I dated off and on since junior high…"

"Mostly, on," Antonio said.

"Zip it, Antonio."

Red said, "Dude, you're a slow learner."

Nyx snarled at them. "Anyway. Yes, we dated, and we are still friends. I needed to talk. Antonio listened. Tried to settle me down." She paused. "I couldn't sleep because I was worried sick. Worried sick about you, you dumb ass."

Derrick said, "Oh. You mean you are not?" He glanced at Antonio.

"Back together? No. We broke up. It's time for us both to move on."

"I'm moving on," Antonio said.

Nyx glared at him.

Red stared at Derrick. "Dude, I think this is when you kiss her."

And so, he did.

Cheers erupted, which embarrassed Derrick. He was just about to apologize when a new voice disrupted his thoughts.

"What did I miss?" L. Linda asked.

"True love," Antonio said.

Derrick and Nyx moved to the serving station. He fixed her a plate piled high with hash browns, bacon, toast, and eggs. He added more food to his plate as well.

Nyx and Derrick selected an empty table. She sat close and smiled at him, squeezing his hand. Derrick was about to apologize for not trusting her when L. Linda joined them.

"You're just the cutest couple ever," L. Linda said, ever coming out as EVAH.

"Hi, L. Linda," Nyx said, separating herself from Derrick just a little. Looking at Derrick, she said, "L. Linda saved us."

"Aren't we the modest one? Don't believe her. Nyx is the hero at this table. The other two," she indicated Red and Antonio, "are sitting over there."

Derrick looked at Nyx. "What happened?"

"Red deserves hero status. He flew that huge plane and rescued that town."

"I agree about Red. I'm still amazed he did that. You didn't answer my question, so I'll ask L. Linda. What did Nyx do?"

"Red had to ditch the plane, so they parachuted out but weren't close enough to the base. They collapsed from the heat out in the desert. All three of them. Even Charlie."

"Charlie was on the plane?"

"Yessirree. Nyx drove into the desert and found them. She pulled them onto an open parachute and dragged them back. She was suffering from heat exhaustion when she got back. Both Red and Antonio had sunstrokes. Charlie's battery gave out. They would have died if it weren't for Nyxie."

Derrick gazed at Nyx. "I'm proud of you."

Nyx blushed. "Thanks. But L. Linda helped a lot. I don't know if Red and Antonio would have made it if she had not taken charge like she did."

"Where was Akira?" Derrick asked.

Nyx said, "She was there but was of no help. Her head is still pretty messed up. She was more worried about Charlie than the rest of us."

L. Linda said, "Speaking of taking charge. I have selected weapons from Level Two, procured an aircraft, and have maps and schematics of the target in Seattle. Soon as we eat, I'll give you and Anna a rundown on the weapons and the plan."

Derrick stared at L. Linda. She no longer sounded like the girl who made the DK Double Honey espresso. All business. He wanted an explanation regarding her transformation, but something else was more important. "Have you heard from Miriam?"

L. Linda said, "She's back but got in late. She'll need rest. You should know she brought in a stranger. He's in the guest area with the guy you brought in. I'm disappointed in both of you. You must know how dangerous this place is in the wrong hands."

It bothered Derrick that Miriam had brought in a stranger. It would have bothered him more if he had not done the same thing. "At least it won't be as lonely with two of them."

L. Linda frowned. "Why did you do that? You must understand it's dangerous."

"I didn't have any good options. Besides, you're here."

"Fair point."

"You have a plan?"

"That's correct. Eat up. I'll explain in the briefing room. All our gear is there."

Anna walked in. Rubbing her eyes, she headed to the serving trays.

L. Linda called out, "Anna. Join us when you get your food."

Derrick said, "Wait. Did you say our gear? You are not going. It will be Anna and me." He had hoped Miriam would be back in time, but he had decided she couldn't go. She needed rest.

L. Linda said, "There's no time for arguing. We should already be in the air."

Anna joined them. "What's up?"

Nyx said, "Derrick and L. Linda seem at odds."

"About what?"

"Going to Seattle," Derrick said, his voice raised loud enough that the room grew quiet. "L. Linda wants to go, but it's going to be you and me. We trained for this."

L. Linda whispered, "Not the place or time, Derrick. I'll explain more later. Charlie let me into Level Two. I have everything we need."

"What aircraft?" Derrick asked.

"One like the Prime aircraft. They were designed and built here. Carver took a few for himself but didn't share them with the military or anyone else," L. Linda said.

"How did you get Charlie to let you into Level Two?" Derrick asked.

"It wasn't easy. If you're done eating, we should get started."

Derrick finished, put his tray in the bin to be cleaned, and gave Nyx's hand a squeeze. There was no way he would let L. Linda go with them. Other than getting Charlie to let her into Level Two and getting an aircraft like the Prime had used, L. Linda didn't know anything about breaking into what must be a heavily armed compound. However, they had not trained Anna and him to attack secured buildings either.

Yet, L. Linda got into Level Two.

She acquired an aircraft.

Derrick realized how little he knew about L. Linda Maxton.

Suddenly, that bothered him for reasons he could not explain.

5

AS WAS HIS CUSTOM, COLLINS WAS THE first one awake. He had heard the others arrive late, raised up in the truck bed where he slept, and watched as Allen and Jack entered the shop. None of the kids were with them. Neither was Jason Maxton. He should have insisted the kids come here. He needed to slow this thing down. It was irrational, thinking they could destroy Prime. They were going to get hurt or worse. He wasn't convinced Prime even existed.

Sure, there was the aircraft with the capital P on the side and the robots that tried to grab Derrick. There was the missile aimed at Potterville that Derrick and the others sent into the ocean. There was the assassin woman who killed Paul Jorgensen, Jimmy Priest, and his family—called herself Pixie, which seemed more like a code name than a real one. Lori killed her. It was a traumatic experience for Lori, and he'd not taken proper care of her. She should be in counseling and on paid administrative leave, neither of which he had a budget for. Instead, she was here, sleeping in an old Lincoln. The president and vice president were killed—the statehouse was under siege. Prime had declared martial law and imposed a curfew from sundown until daybreak. The military was ordered to shoot anyone breaking the curfew. Far as he knew, no military units had been seen near Potterville. The television was only broadcasting a test signal. Every station was the same. No radio either.

So, there was that.

Dismissing Prime as a myth became more difficult with each thought, but Collins still wanted to change the narrative. Figure out a way to keep everyone safe. A handful of kids trying to destroy Prime was unimaginable.

Collins's coffee had grown cold. He dumped it in the sink and poured another, then decided it had grown too bitter and started a fresh pot. Fletcher entered the room, rubbing his eyes.

Collins said, "Right on time. Just started a fresh pot."

"Either you're five minutes late, or I'm five minutes early. I'm standing here without coffee, watching it dribble into the pot."

"Pull the pot out and put your cup under there if you're too damn impatient to wait a few minutes."

Fletcher did just that. "Good idea. That's why you're sheriff, and I'm just a dumb mechanic."

Collins waved at Jack's car collection. "This is worth more than I'll ever earn."

"Right. If people had enough money to buy them."

"The rich can buy them."

Jack retrieved his cup, sliding the pot back into place. "Right. Not that I want to sell any to that lot. But eventually, I'll have to sell them."

Collins slid his cup under the stream of coffee. "Why sell any of them?"

"Help Red go to college."

"He'll have a full scholarship. He's the best D-lineman I've ever seen, and I've seen a few."

Jack took a seat. Bill joined him. Jack said, "That's true, but he'll still need spending money, and he could get injured. Not get a scholarship to a school he wants to attend. You never know what might happen. I'm just hoping there are colleges when this ends." Jack sipped coffee. After a moment, he added, "I hope I live long enough to see him finish high school."

"That's no way to be thinking, Jack."

"If you say so. What color is the sky in your world? You're an optimist, Bill. I like that about you, but perhaps you need to take off those rose-colored glasses for a bit. I'm thinking odds are, none of us will be around much longer."

"Had them off this morning. I didn't like the looks of things." Collins paused. "I heard you come in last night. I saw you and Allen. I did not see any of the kids or Jason. What happened?"

Jack sat staring into the distance for several moments. Taking a deep breath, he said, "Miriam and Rebekah found us. Long story short, they got into the building and retrieved Patel's briefcase."

Collins stared at Jack for a moment. "Was anyone hurt?"

Jack nodded slowly. "Things fell apart before they got out. Two guys were electrocuted and locked in a restroom, but they might have survived. Miriam had to kill one guard."

"Killed? Had to?" Collins asked.

"He shot Jason in the back. Would have shot Miriam next, but she shot him first. We brought Jason's body back. Took it to the morgue. He can have a decent burial. If we live long enough to get it done."

Collins was silent for several minutes. "Jason's dead? Are you joking? It's not funny, Jack."

"It's no joke. It was a long silent ride home."

"What about the other kids?"

"There was a new kid, William, with the girls. The girls were in a car wreck caused by carbon monoxide poisoning. Fell asleep at the wheel, apparently. The kid pulled them from the car. It's unclear why he was with them when they got to Pacific Edge. He didn't talk much. Like I said, none of us did. I don't know anything about Derrick and Anna, Rebekah's sister, except that they went back to the mountains, taking an alternative route."

"Where are they now?"

Jack shrugged. "We dropped them by the river. They waited until we were out of sight before they moved on. It was pretty obvious they planned to cross the river. They must have found an old cabin or something in the mountains."

Collins nodded. "I suppose. But what good is a computer to them in an old cabin?"

"Good question. Maybe an old radar station or something. A cell tower, maybe. Speaking of old, we saw something else that was odd. There was an old motorcycle leaning against the levee."

"I'll go check it out. See if it's stolen."

"No need. I'll get it soon. I suspect it's stolen, but that's not why I want it."

"I'm confused."

Jack said, "I'm hiding it. If it makes you feel better, I'll make sure you don't see it. I could drop it in the lake, but perhaps someone will want to restore it."

"Still confused. Why are you hiding it?"

"It's a long story. When we got to the rendezvous spot, it was crawling with cops, and the guy Allen knows was the center of the investigation. They were hauling bodies up in black bags."

"Holy crap. Bodies, as in more than one? What happened?"

"I'm trying to tell you. I don't know exactly. Jason talked to a cop. The cop wasn't supposed to say anything, and he didn't know many details. However, Jason learned that at least three girls were found at the bottom of the ocean near a cliff. Allen's contact was the town's preacher. His son was nearby with a broken leg. A knife was sticking up in the rocks, and a sign made of stones pointed to the bodies. The son said the girls' killer attacked him."

"My God. Dreadful. So, the kid with the broken leg was also a victim. He's lucky to be alive. I wondered why the guy didn't kill him too." Bill paused. "How is that connected to a stolen motorcycle ending up here?"

"I'm trying to tell you if you'd stop talking. The kid's story doesn't wash. At least Jason didn't buy it. First, the cop didn't think the murders were all recent. The bodies had been in the water for a while. Some longer than others."

"I still can't believe Jason is dead. Poor L. Linda. She'll be all alone."

"Let me finish. It wasn't a guy who broke the kid's leg. It was a girl."

Collins whistled through his teeth, thinking for a moment. "I get why Jason didn't buy the kid's story."

"There's more. A girl showed up at the dad's house. She told the man his son was down the cliff by the ocean. Said she'd made a deal to buy the motorcycle. Wanted to test drive it. The man said she was odd. Said she was wet and barefoot. But tough because she kick-started that old motorcycle barefoot. It took a couple of tries. Then she rode off. It was a 550 Honda."

"And the old bike down by the levee is a 550 Honda."

"Now, you're catching on."

"Not really."

"Think about it. L. Linda left here in a Prime aircraft. Probably to help Derrick. Somehow, she ended up near Pacific Edge. Came across the kid who thought he'd add to his collection of dead girls. That didn't work out for him. She rode the Honda back to Potterville and dumped it within 50 yards of where we dropped the kids last night."

Collins shook his head. "I don't know. L. Linda? Doesn't sound like her at all."

"Jason said it sounded exactly like her."

"That was before he was killed?" Collins asked.

Jack said, "Now you're catching on."

6

AKIRA, REBEKAH, AND MIRIAM FILED into the dining area in rapid succession. Miriam and Rebekah appeared more rested than Derrick had anticipated. They all got trays and coffee and then sat at a long table. Miriam motioned Derrick over. L. Linda followed. Derrick wished Akira and Rebekah would have sat someplace else. They were not part of this discussion. Later, Derrick would realize everyone in the room was part of this operation, but he wasn't thinking that way just yet. He wanted to protect the others, especially Nyx. It was his fault they were involved. L. Linda wasn't going to Seattle, despite what she had said earlier.

Miriam sat, stared at L. Linda, and said, "I have bad news."

L. Linda set her jaw. Muscles tensed. "Go ahead."

Tears welled in Miriam's eyes. Rebekah started sobbing. "Your dad. He was shot."

"He's dead?" L. Linda asked.

"Yes."

"What happened?"

"It was my fault. We got caught. It took too long, and Jason came to check on us. He wasn't supposed to be in the building."

L. Linda took a deep breath. "Tell me about the guy who shot him."

"He shot your dad in the back. He wasn't Pacific Edge security. He and the two guys that caught us wore the same uniforms—black with black armbands. I killed the one who shot your dad. I might have killed the other two guys as well, but I'm not sure."

"What happened to the Pacific Edge security guys?" L. Linda asked.

Miriam looked at her plate. "I let them go."

L. Linda remained silent for a few moments, and then said, "You did the right thing. The one who shot Jason was Black Ops. Assassins picked for special assignments. You're lucky to be alive."

Miriam looked up. "Just before Jason died, he asked me to tell you something."

"Okay."

"Maybe it should be in private."

L. Linda thought for a moment. "It's okay. Go ahead."

"He couldn't get all the words out, but I'm pretty sure what he said was, Tell L. Linda, I loved her as if she were my own daughter."

L. Linda nodded. A bit of water formed in her eye, but she wiped it away. "I knew that."

"L. Linda, I'm so, so sorry. Can you forgive me?" Miriam couldn't hold the tears any longer.

"No need. Not your fault. Jason let his guard down. He knew better. But we can all learn from his mistake. Letting our guard down at any point today can get one or more of us killed. End of discussion. If I live through the next couple of days, I'll have a lifetime to process and grieve, but now, I have to focus. We all do. No more discussion about this. No more tears. Understood?"

It was more than Derrick could process. He felt numb and yet hurt in a way that he'd never experienced. He had never lost anyone close to him, which reminded him that he'd never had anyone close. Not until he arrived in Potterville. He marveled at L. Linda's reaction. The silly girl he met his first day at Donna's, the one he had in class and didn't even remember, had changed before his eyes.

Feeling as uncomfortable as he could ever remember, Derrick decided to steer the conversation in another direction, but not necessarily a safer one. "I heard you brought a stranger into the base."

Miriam wiped her eyes and said, "I did. Unfortunate but necessary."

"Was it?" Rebekah asked.

Miriam glanced at her and then back at Derrick. "You also brought someone in. On the upside, Charlie already had a special section ready for our guy. Who did you bring, and do you know where they are?"

Derrick said, "It's Kevin. I don't know where Charlie put him. We had a problem in the last town. Letting Kevin go back by himself wasn't safe."

Miriam pushed her plate away. "What kind of problem?"

Anna said, "The kind where Derrick sends someone to the hospital."

Miriam looked at her. "You're saying it was unnecessary?"

"No, it was necessary. I might have done it differently."

"So, there was a way out of the situation without hurting anyone?" Miriam asked.

"I didn't say that. I would have put all three of them in the hospital."

"Who did you bring in?" Derrick asked.

"Kid named William. That wasn't his name when we met him, but it is now," Miriam said.

"Who is he, and why is he here?" Derrick asked.

"Don't get in a huff. His name was Billy Joe Howie. Is that a stupid name, or what? I'm calling him William, William Dowd. He saved Rebekah and me, so we owed him. He's living in a fantasyland. He has no life, and I plan to give him one. If I live through this." Miriam paused. "So, yeah, he saved us; plus, we needed his car."

"He saved your life?" Derrick asked.

Miriam nodded.

L. Linda stood, putting both hands flat on the table. "Guys. Interesting as all this catching up is, can we get back to business?" Looking at Miriam, she added. "Eat. I understand you're upset, but we have tough hours ahead, and you need to focus. An empty stomach won't help anything."

"And what business is that?" Miriam asked.

L. Linda rolled her eyes. "Going to Seattle. Killing Prime, or at least one of them."

Derrick said, "L. Linda wants to go with us. I've told her no."

Miriam said, "Not happening, L. Linda. I've already …" She didn't add, *got your father killed.*

"Is happening," L. Linda shouted. The room fell quiet, and all eyes turned to their table.

Derrick said, "L. Linda got into Level Two. Says she has weapons and an aircraft. One of those Prime aircraft."

"We already have a Prime aircraft," Miriam said, matching L. Linda's volume.

"Had," L. Linda corrected.

Miriam stood. "What do you mean, had?"

"I kind of wrecked it."

"You did what? We needed that!"

"If I remember right, you lost one as well." L. Linda squared off.

"Prime blew it up! I didn't wreck it."

A quiet voice said, "L. Linda saved you all." It was Akira. She did not look up from her food.

"What are you talking about?" Derrick asked.

Akira looked up. "L. Linda destroyed the satellite monitoring that desert town. None of you would have survived had she not done that. That means the missile in Mexico would have launched. Potterville would now be a wasteland. The war with Mexico would be officially underway."

"How do you know that?" L. Linda asked.

It was not lost on Derrick that she said, "How do you know? Not, what makes you think that."

Akira put her fork down. "Charlie tracked you and saw the satellite blink out of existence."

Derrick said, "Wait. The aircraft can fly that high?"

"Into space?" Miriam asked.

Akira said, "It cannot. Charlie said it was a suicide mission. L. Linda took it as high as possible and fired on the satellite. It was close enough. Then the aircraft plummeted back to earth. It reactivated just long enough to make a crash landing in the ocean."

"Where?" Miriam asked.

"Just south of Pacific Edge," Akira said.

Red spun around in his chair. "I believe her. I saw L. Linda when she got here. She looked like hell. Sorry, L. Linda. Looked like she'd been in a fight. She wasn't wet but looked like she'd been in the water. Sand on her clothes. No shoes."

"How did you get here?" Miriam stared at L. Linda.

"Not important."

Miriam saw something in L. Linda she had not noticed before. "A motorcycle."

Rebekah said, "Oh my God! You're the girl on the beach."

7

AS DERRICK WAS DOWNING THE LAST OF his coffee at the base under a mountain, Stanley Mires awoke in complete darkness, somewhere deep within the earth. There would be no sunshine here. From what he'd seen of the facility, they had not tried to make it appear like being on the surface. It felt as if he was in a high-tech tomb. In his case, he was sure it was, in fact, just that.

His room was Spartan: a cot and four blank walls, the air musty as if it had been recirculated for centuries. A restroom-shower down the hall was designed for multiple people. Austere, sterile. Militaristic. An old military base was Stanley's best guess. Maybe in the Mojave. Maybe in Death Valley.

No phone. No clock. The room had a simple light switch. Off and on. Apparently, he could have as much light as his heart desired from the single bare bulb. He had tried it a few times during the night to see if Prime rationed electricity or set a curfew. The light came on each time he flipped the switch.

Prime had not sent anyone to fetch him. In Seattle, Prime expected him at 5:00 a.m. because that was 8:00 a.m. in New York. Prime was a coast-to-coast operation. Days off were not part of his employment package. Neither was money. He was taken care of, not paid. If he tried to leave, he would have been penniless.

But Prime had not sent for him.

Stanley thought it must be early. Maybe 3:00 a.m. He stared into the darkness. Contemplated what came next. He had reached the ultimate goal — Prime's secret headquarters.

Years ago, when he was a much younger man, full of optimism, his professor, Corbin Atwood, asked if he was interested in the Resistance. Stanley had heard of the Resistance as a group dedicated to preserving history, and because he was interested in that, he said, "Sure."

Later that evening, Stanley was in a basement coffee shop, sitting alone in a corner booth, waiting for Atwood. But Atwood was late—thirty minutes, then forty. Stanley was about to leave when a girl touched his shoulder. About his age, he assumed. Pretty. "Are you Stanley?" she had asked. He nodded. "Follow me," she had said.

She was pretty enough that Stanley needed little encouragement to follow her through a curtain and into a dark hallway. Had he not been mesmerized, he would have been fearful.

They had walked some distance through a poorly lit, damp, rock-lined tunnel when they came to a thick wooden door. The door looked ancient. A man standing outside was thick like the door. Not fat. Just muscle.

At that moment, Stanley realized he wasn't attending a historical society meeting.

"This him?" The large man asked.

The girl nodded.

The man opened the door. "Third door on your right. Professor is waiting."

Stanley stepped in. The girl didn't follow. He was about to ask if she was coming when the door closed. He heard a lock engage. Stanley felt something cold, like ice, down his back. In hindsight, he should have bolted out of there.

He paused outside the third door on the right. It stood open, a large rock holding it. Atwood sat at a table.

In that room, on that night, he heard about the Resistance. The *real* Resistance. They did more than preserve history.

In that room, he made a decision.

And that decision brought him to this moment.

They did not ask him to dedicate his life to becoming Prime's assistant. Such a premise was not within the realm of one's imagination. Getting into Prime's organization at any level would be a grand achievement.

But here he was.

Goal achieved.

Even after he became Prime's assistant in Seattle, the thought of getting here was nothing more than a far-fetched dream.

That's why he was so ill-prepared. He never thought this would happen. While working in Seattle, he served as a pipeline of information about Prime to the Resistance. Here, he was on his own.

He had worked hard, sacrificed, and done many things he regretted to gain Prime's trust and to access information. Now he was here and did not know what to do.

Unable to sleep, he tried the light. It came on. He dressed and stepped into the hall. It was empty.

He went to the restroom. Empty.

He decided to walk around. He didn't know if there were limits on where he could go. But what could Prime do? Kill him?

That was a possibility.

The hallway turned left, then right. He passed many doors, but he didn't try any in case people were sleeping inside, even though he felt alone. He had heard no noise during the night—not even the heating and cooling system. He paused. Listened. The quiet was deafening. Eerie.

At an intersection, he saw an elevator. Might as well give it a go. What could Prime do? Kill him.

Yes. That answer had not changed.

The doors slid open. The floor numbers started at ten and went to 20. Ten being up and twenty being down. The building was inverted. He was on the 18th floor, two floors above Prime, according to the display. This elevator did not go to the surface. He pushed 17, 16, 15, and 10. None worked. He could not go up. He tried 19. Nothing. Assuming the elevator wouldn't move, he pushed 20 and immediately regretted it. The doors closed, and the elevator descended.

He had made a terrible mistake. Prime had not requested his presence. As the elevator descended, taking much longer than seemed necessary, he pushed buttons, attempting to reverse course. The elevator continued downward.

Maybe it would not go up until it reached the 20th floor.

Prime would not tolerate anyone arriving without an invitation.

The elevator stopped. Stanley held the door-closed button and pushed the 18th floor button, hoping it would ascend.

It did not.

The door slid open.

Prime looked at the elevator. "Stanley, my good man. I wondered when you might come down. I did not want to wake you. I assumed you were tired, what with the change and all."

Prime had called him Stanley. He wasn't sure what to make of that but decided not to ask. While he did not know what he was supposed to do, staying alive still felt important. There might come a day when he could no longer tolerate it, especially if he could serve no purpose, but that moment had not come.

"May I ask what time it is, sir?"

"Of course you can. Why couldn't you? It's 6:31. In the morning, I should add. I realize it must be difficult knowing whether it's day or night, given your accommodations." Prime busied himself at a computer console.

"The accommodations were fine."

Prime stopped and turned toward Stanley. "Don't lie to me, Stanley. I did not bring you here to lie. The accommodations are horrendous. Far below your stature in the organization."

Stanley felt trapped. Perhaps Prime brought him here to kill him, but like a cat, wanted to play with him first. "It was not what I expected. I never expected to be here," adding with some difficulty, "It's a great honor."

"That's more like it. It happened fast. Didn't it? There are several reasons for that. My previous assistant," Prime paused, "Let's just say he reached a point where he could no longer be of service. And we are reaching a critical juncture."

"What juncture is that?"

"Mexico. And as you know, I have plans far beyond Mexico. Things are changing. Things are speeding up."

"Of course."

"About your quarters. They are being prepared as we speak. I trust you will be happy with them. Let me know if anything does not meet your satisfaction.

I'm sure we can remedy any inadequacies. I want you to settle in today. Take it easy. Have a few drinks. Read a book. Whatever you'd like to do."

Although this should have put Stanley at ease, it did not. He felt more uncomfortable with each passing minute. Like a calf fattened for slaughter. "I shall return to my quarters if that is acceptable."

"Nonsense. You won't go back to those substandard rooms. Have a look around. Your accommodations will be ready this afternoon." Prime slid a polished metal box toward Stanley. "Here are the things you'll need to navigate the complex."

Stanley peered into the box, which held an electronic tablet and an ID on a lanyard.

"Go on then. Take them. The ID has a chip that gives you access to most of the facility. Not everything, mind you. It will not give you access to dangerous areas. It will not let you go to the surface, but you would not want to go there. It is not a pleasant experience. You can access the tablet using the same username and password you used in Seattle."

"It was baking when I got off the aircraft."

"Yes, and it will be much hotter soon. Summer. Besides, there's nothing up there."

Stanley wanted to go, but curiosity was getting the better of him. Prime had been willing to talk. Maybe a few more questions wouldn't hurt. Perhaps they would hurt a great deal. "Are there other people here?"

"Did you think you were alone? Well, of course, you did, given the location of your room. There are many here and more are arriving soon. I'm bringing in our top people to consolidate our efforts." Prime paused. "There is a chance, small though it may be, that Mexico will attack targets in New America. They might try to hit my remote locations or assassinate key staff members. It is safer to have them here. Wouldn't you agree?"

Stanley thought nothing sounded more promising than eliminating Prime's headquarters and reducing his scientists and assassins, but he said, "I agree completely. Brilliant move, sir."

"You'll find staff and robots preparing areas for incoming staff, but by all means, explore your new home. As my chief of staff, you should know the facility well. Report for work at 6:00 a.m. Monday. There will be coffee and breakfast here for you. If I need you before then, I will contact you."

"Thank you, sir." And with that, Stanley Mires got in the elevator and punched the 15th floor. The elevator started upward with a jolt. Despite being scared, he wanted to see this facility. Perhaps he would find a way to still be of service.

8

FEELING CONFUSED WAS NOT NEW to Derrick. Since leaving Pacific Edge, where he thought he knew everything, confusion had been the most consistent thing in his life. L. Linda had cut Rebekah off, saying she didn't know what they were talking about, but doing so with a glare he could only describe as ferocious.

"Girl on the beach? What's Rebekah talking about?" Derrick asked.

Miriam said, "Long story, which is unimportant right now. We should listen to what L. Linda has to say."

"Thank you," L. Linda said. "Perhaps we should go someplace private. The four of us, Derrick, Miriam, Anna, and I."

"You forgot me," Rebekah said.

L. Linda said, "I did not forget you. I didn't include you. There's a difference."

Red said, "We are all part of this. Talk here."

L. Linda took a breath. "Not everyone can go on this mission, nor should they."

Antonio asked, "You don't trust us?"

"It's not that…"

Antonio interrupted. "Look, it's ridiculous to think a handful of kids can defeat Prime. Prime has headquarters in seven places. Six different cities in what must be secured buildings that are heavily guarded. No one knows where the seventh place is."

"Your point?" L. Linda asked.

"My point is: What's the harm? I mean, crazy as the entire idea is, what's the harm in us helping?"

Derrick said, "He has a point."

"I'm going whether or not you like it," Rebekah said.

"This will be dangerous. It's an armed assault, which means we will have to destroy robots and might have to kill people. It's not something you're prepared for," L. Linda said.

"I killed a soldier in Mexico. Don't tell me what I'm prepared to do."

Miriam said, "No one needed to know about that."

"L. Linda needed to know," Rebekah said.

L. Linda said, "Noted. That still doesn't mean you can go."

"Why not?" Rebekah asked.

"We need the fewest numbers necessary to complete the task. Extra people will only get in the way. Make it more difficult."

In a quiet voice, Akira said, "She's right. We can't all go. But we can all help." She paused. "You can trust us. I almost died for you, as did Antonio, Red, and L. Linda. Also, it's not ludicrous."

Derrick said, "I was wrong. Akira is correct. Everyone here is involved. Everyone can help. That doesn't mean we all go. L. Linda is right about that part. So, what's the plan?"

L. Linda said, "Fine."

Miriam said, "Back up. Akira, what did you mean when you said it's not ludicrous?"

Akira said, "We're not just a bunch of kids."

"We're not? What are we, then?" Miriam asked.

"We're kids with nuclear weapons."

Miriam said, "Whoa. Slow down. We are not using nuclear missiles. Those would kill thousands."

"Hundreds of thousands," Derrick interjected.

"That's why we can't let people know about this place. I didn't even want to bring you guys here," Miriam said.

"Says the person who brought a stranger into the facility," Derrick said.

"You brought one too," Miriam snapped.

Derrick stood. "At least we know him. Well, for a few hours anyway."

Charlie appeared at the door. "What is all the yelling about?"

L. Linda said, "Don't worry about it. Just a discussion." She paused. "Charlie, we need to go to the operations room where I have the weapons and other materials."

"Who needs to go?" Charlie asked.

"All of us," L. Linda said.

"Not possible," Charlie said.

L. Linda said, "We've discussed this, Charlie. You know what is at stake. We don't have time for debates or delays."

"No one was talking about launching missiles when we made our agreement," Charlie said.

Miriam glared at Akira and then looked at Charlie. "We are not launching missiles. Right, Akira?"

Akira stared at her feet. "Right. I was only making an observation."

L. Linda said, "Charlie, perhaps you should tell the others what you told me last night."

Charlie said, "Follow me to the operations room. I'll explain there. L. Linda is correct. There is little time."

Charlie led the group through the halls and into an area Derrick had not seen. Although he could not be sure, Derrick thought this hallway had not existed before. Since Charlie blocked areas, reconfiguring the walls, it was likely they had not seen this hallway. Derrick also noted that Charlie's answer about allowing them all to go to Level Two changed when L. Linda intervened. It was not as if Charlie had forgotten something. That's not how it worked for Charlie.

They came to an elevator, which was larger than typical. Derrick estimated 20 people could fit without being too cramped. Charlie pushed a button labeled #2. There was no #3. The elevator lurched and descended. The elevator dropped fast, but it took about 30 seconds before it stopped. Level Two was deep underground, and they were already under a mountain. Derrick wondered how people built this place, especially since the old United States was just a failure before James Carver took over. Then he remembered, what he had been told was not necessarily true.

Because Charlie had prohibited access to Level Two, Derrick expected a speech or a warning, but when the elevator door slid open, Charlie proceeded without a word. The walls and ceiling were white, and the paint looked fresh. Unlike the halls on the upper level, these walls did not move. The floor was concrete but polished. Robots at work. The air smelled of oil and hot electronics, as if people still worked here. They walked past several doors. Many were of regular size. A few were massive. All were steel, as were the doorposts, and painted gray. Some had warning signs, emblems, not words, and differing designs in red, yellow, and black. Workers here must have understood their meaning. Derrick did not.

Charlie led them into a room. Decent size. A long table sat in the middle of the space. A large screen was mounted on the wall. Blue and beige plastic chairs sat opposite of the screen. L. Linda had the weapons lined up on the table. Derrick recognized the disassembled firearms.

L. Linda stepped to the front of the table. "I assume Miriam, Anna, and Derrick are familiar with the firearms, and I assume Rebekah is not. To demonstrate, please assemble those weapons you are familiar with."

Rebekah said, "Do you have a 50-caliber machine gun?"

L. Linda stared at her for a moment and then said, "There are 50-cals in the armory, but you won't need them in Seattle."

Anna said, "How about a sniper rifle? We might need that."

L. Linda said, "Not in Seattle, but you are correct. You might need it at other sites. I only looked at Seattle."

Derrick didn't attach any significance to L. Linda's statement, but he noticed her character had changed—no odd words and no playfulness in her tone. It was as if she had transformed. Facing death does that to a person. They had all changed.

Returning to high school would be difficult.

Returning as a regular teenager would be impossible.

Derrick stepped in front of a combat rifle. The design was decades old. It was an MRA1, still the standard military issue. It took him three minutes to assemble and check the weapon. Miriam finished just a few seconds later. Anna beat them both. The pistol, an old design, also a military issue, was a SIG Sauer 17. The memories of firing these weapons flooded back into his mind, like looking at a hidden room he had not yet investigated.

He understood what these weapons did. He did not want to use either but understood there may be no alternative. When he had finished assembling the pistol, he asked, "Are there any nonlethal weapons?"

"First things first." Pointing, L. Linda said, "Duty belts are there. Get yourself fitted, grab your weapons, and follow me."

"Where are we going?" Miriam asked.

"Range. We need to test fire each weapon." She paused. "And see if you can hit anything."

"Where's my weapon?" Rebekah asked.

"We have not said you are going, but if you do, you'll get a less-than-lethal one. We don't have time to teach you to shoot," L. Linda said.

"What about you?" Miriam asked.

"I test-fired my weapons last night," L. Linda said.

The firing range took only a few minutes. No misfires. No jams. Each fired three rounds through both weapons and reloaded the clips. Twenty-five yards. All rounds in the 10-ring. Not difficult. Shooting a paper target was one thing. Shooting people was altogether different.

Derrick wanted to know about less-than-lethal weapons. And weapons to use against robots. Prime had sent robots to Potterville. Safe to assume there would be robots and people guarding the building. The firearms could disable a robot if hit enough times and in the right places. Not a reliable termination of hostility. Had L. Linda thought about weapons for robots? Probably not. She had picked out rifles and pistols. Government issue. Probably the only option. She said she'd fired her weapons last night. Convenient. They had not seen her shoot. Maybe she could hit the target, maybe not.

Why did L. Linda insist on being involved? She should be in Potterville making espresso drinks. She was good at that. Since she was set on being here, they could use someone at the espresso machine. Then he remembered she was here because he asked her to come. He felt slightly nauseous.

"Earth to Derrick." It was L. Linda. Standing at the door.

The others were all lined up with her, pistols stuck in duty belts secured around their waists, and rifles slung over their shoulders. Derrick stood on the other side of the room, holding an empty duty belt, his firearms still on a nearby shelf. "What?"

"If you're going to drift off like that, best you stay here," L. Linda said.

"But I…"

Miriam cut off Derrick's protest. "She's right. We've been calling your name while you've been staring into the middle distance."

"Sorry, I was thinking about," he paused, "robots. What about robots? Using firearms against robots is an iffy proposition." He felt a bit of relief, not because he'd stumbled upon an excuse for daydreaming, but because it was a concern L. Linda had not addressed. She probably had not thought about robots. That would give him a chance to steer this in a different direction. Miriam, not L. Linda, should plan this.

Derrick's hopes of wrangling control from L. Linda were short-lived.

"Next up," L. Linda said. "If we can get back on track, I'll show you."

With that, L. Linda turned and walked down the hallway. The others trailed behind her, and Derrick followed them. L. Linda seemed different. He probably imagined most of it. She wore the same clothing they all had donned. The jumpsuits were nothing like what she wore in Potterville. He'd never noticed her physique. Not that he could remember. She had worn puffy shirts covered with flowers or bizarre blotches of color, which somehow made her standout yet remain unseen. Her shirts were long, concealing her waist, making her look perhaps a little overweight now that he tried to picture her in her native habitat. Her jeans were unlike others, with wide bottoms and sandals on her feet.

In the one-piece uniform, L. Linda looked slim. Athletic. But not a runner's build like Nyx. Sleek but powerful, which struck him as odd because, to the best of his knowledge, L. Linda did not play any sports. Other than making coffee, he didn't know what L. Linda did.

In Potterville, L. Linda wore her hair in braids or ponytails at the sides of her head, making her look younger than her peers. Today she had it pulled back and tied tight, giving her a serious look. Her eyes, a nondescript blueish gray, did not dance with the playfulness that Derrick remembered or thought he did. His memory of L. Linda was hazy and undefined, and he wondered how that could be right.

When they returned to the briefing room, Derrick realized he'd been daydreaming again, preoccupied with L. Linda Maxton. Maybe Miriam was right. Perhaps something *was* wrong with him. Being distracted could get him killed. Get others killed.

L. Linda motioned everyone to chairs in the room. She picked up an unknown weapon from the table and walked to the front of the room. It was shaped like a pistol. It was black and blocky. Strange-looking coils snaked along the barrel. On looks alone, it appeared deadlier than the other firearms. Using a small remote control, she turned on a large screen that filled most of the wall behind her. A large picture of the weapon in her hand appeared on the screen. Holding the weapon out, she said, "This will be our primary weapon. The rifles might be necessary for distance; the pistols used in tight quarters as a last resort. You can use this on robots and people."

"What about less-than-lethal weapons?" Derrick asked, having found his voice.

L. Linda scowled at him. He didn't like the look. He didn't like being glared at as if he were an unruly child. But L. Linda's expression bothered him more than he expected.

"I'd get to that if you'd stop interrupting." Holding the weapon up again, she said, "You're looking at it. That's why this is the primary weapon. It can destroy a robot, cut through a metal door, immobilize a vehicle, fry a computer, disable, or kill a human. It fires what can best be described as a bolt of lightning, although there's more to it than that. Understanding the science isn't necessary."

Miriam said, "I used one of those in Pacific Edge. It's how we got away."

L. Linda's face fell, and she became pasty white.

Miriam said, "Sorry. I saved myself with it, but I couldn't save your dad."

L. Linda's chest heaved once, then again. "Not your fault. You said the man shot Jason in the back. He should not have put himself in that position. He knew better. He let his guard down, focusing on saving you. Poor tactic. Save yourself first and kill your enemy second. Remember that. You can't save anyone if you're dead."

Derrick's stomach twisted, and he gagged loud enough for everyone to hear, then he bolted from the room, hoping to make it to a restroom before throwing up.

9

STANLEY WANDERED THE FACILITY FLOOR BY FLOOR. Many sections were empty, although that could soon change. Rooms with computers. Rooms with scientific equipment. Rooms for medical procedures. Rooms with machines he did not recognize. It was all clean and well-maintained, but everything seemed old. He assumed it was still useful in knowledgeable hands, but hands were not to be found, save a few repairmen who acknowledged his presence, then went about their work as if an armed task master stood watching them.

They were not wrong. Prime watched it all. In Seattle, Prime monitored the entire complex from high above. Here, Prime observed the facility and people in it from far below. Although Stanley never understood how the remote Primes were linked, he knew one thing. It was all Prime, and it was all bad.

His purpose was to gather information for the Resistance. He had succeeded beyond his or anyone else's expectations. If their mission was to destroy Prime, he had failed. He had only learned that terminating Prime was impossible.

His first idea was to obliterate all the headquarters. No small task, and he had no plan for how that could be accomplished. Each facility was heavily guarded. He had discovered each headquarters' location. But knowing where they were and destroying them were much different things. His second idea was to infiltrate the security forces with members of the Resistance. Problem: Robots provided most of the security. Perhaps they could destroy the Prime in each facility with a single act. Perhaps a sniper, maybe a bomb. Problem: Each facility had a dozen creatures suspended in a state half alive and half dead, awaiting activation. New versions were being created all the time. Primes did not die of old age or natural causes. Primes were retired, another word for killed, so that a new version could be activated. Each version was supposed to be an improvement on the last, although it didn't always work out that way. Some versions were retired within days, if not hours. Prime killed the scientists in such cases. Those who stepped into their shoes were more careful in their work.

Prime was both a physical creature—none that Stanley had seen could be called a man—and a computer image, and since all the Primes were linked via a private intranet, perhaps a well-written software program, a virus, could shut them all down. Every location, every version, including those awaiting activation, and every computer image. All of it.

While that sounded promising, there were problems. Each of them was insurmountable from what Stanley had learned. First, there was no access to the intranet—not that he could determine. The computers that linked to Prime had no access ports. They were behind triple-secured physical and software barriers. Prime still needed people to work on the system, but Stanley had never made contact with one of them. They were ghosts. Undetectable. Unreachable.

Then there was the firewall. That was the best computer term Stanley could think of. Firewalls were not new. They were not perfect. The Resistance had people who could get past any firewall except Prime's. Because Prime's firewall wasn't on a computer, it was Prime itself. Prime controlled all the data coming in and going out. It was hard-wired, so to speak, which meant that to destroy the firewall, one must destroy Prime, which he had no objection to. However, see the afore-stated problems regarding Prime's destruction.

Stanley had not discovered a way to end Prime's reign. He had only learned how Prime could not be destroyed. Even if one or more Prime headquarters could be demolished, the only way to rid the world of this menace was to destroy them all and do it before Prime could end the assault. Because Prime commanded the military, state police, and a small but efficient division of assassins, there was no chance of mounting a successful attack. None.

Now Stanley was trapped deep in the earth. He could not get information out to the Resistance. He would likely never see daylight again.

But maybe, just maybe, he'd get a chance to kill this one Prime.

10

EVERYONE STARED WHEN DERRICK RETURNED. To say it embarrassed him was an understatement. L. Linda must be heartbroken and hurt more than the rest of them combined. Miriam was a close second, bearing responsibility for Mr. Maxton's death. Rebekah killed a man in Mexico. In that case, it was kill or be killed, and Rebekah seemed okay. However, it would haunt her. Derrick was sure of that. L. Linda, Miriam, and Rebekah were all holding up better than he was, and that bothered him. Killing robots, no problem. Injuring people, he could do. Killing people, not sure. Killing Prime should be easy. Yet, …

Miriam patted the empty chair. "Are you okay?"

Derrick sat.

Miriam said, "While you were gone, we decided Rebekah will go with us. She will be our pilot."

L. Linda picked up the strange-looking weapon again, staring at Derrick. He could not interpret her expression.

L. Linda said, "We need to know if you are up to making this happen, Derrick."

Derrick wasn't sure he was, but he said, "I'll be fine. Something I ate disagreed with me."

For some odd reason, he felt sure L. Linda wasn't buying it. He wasn't a good liar. He knew that already. He must be a slow learner. Or perhaps he learned quickly but forgot rapidly.

L. Linda said, "I'm not going over this again. I'll explain it to you on the way there. You will be with me. Are you okay with that?"

"Sure. I'm okay with that," Derrick said, although he was pretty sure he was not.

L. Linda said, "Here's the plan. We all need to be on the same page." She stared at Derrick.

Miriam said, "I need to access a computer. First thing, if possible."

"Why?" L. Linda asked.

"Last night, I developed a couple of applications. If they work, it will make future assaults easier. It will help with this one as well. It will disrupt the camera system, so they can't track us in the facility. That's why I need to do it first."

Derrick said, "You look well rested. When did you have time to work on applications?"

Miriam paused for a moment. "I slept on the drive back to Potterville and again on the train ride here. I worked most of it out during that time. When I got here, it only took me a few minutes to write the code."

Akira said, "You wrote the code in your sleep. You're joking, right?"

"I'm not."

L. Linda frowned. "Let me think about that for a minute. I'll start with the layout."

Using a remote control, L. Linda turned on a large screen and brought up a photograph looking down on a building. Derrick had seen such images on his computer on a map application.

"This building, once called the Watermark Tower, contains Prime's headquarters on the top floors," L. Linda said.

Miriam said, "I expected something different. More remote and secured behind fences or walls. It's right on the street."

L. Linda said, "The image is old. Taken before the coup."

"Coup?" Derrick asked. "What is that?"

"When James Carver took over. Call it whatever you like. The result is the same. Carver destroyed the country and took it for himself. Now, Prime runs everything," L. Linda said.

Miriam said, "Carver. Prime. Same person."

"Not exactly, but close enough," L. Linda said. "The streets are barricaded here, here, and here."

L. Linda moved a red dot on the screen, indicating where the barricades were placed. Pointing at the buildings within the barricaded area, she said, "These buildings are empty. Cameras and robots provide security. Anything moving in the streets or building is detected and eliminated."

"Eliminated?" Rebekah asked. "What if it's a dog or kids playing?"

L. Linda said, "Robots don't care. They kill everything and anything. Other machines clean up the mess."

Derrick said, "Then there's no way in."

Miriam said, "We land on the roof."

L. Linda said, "We could, but there's a better way." She expanded the map, moving the point of view higher. As the map grew, two new lines appeared.

Miriam stood, moving closer to the screen. "What's that?"

"Our way in," L. Linda replied. "State Route 99. It's a tunnel running right under the building."

"It does," Miriam whispered.

"You didn't know," L. Linda said. It wasn't a question. "I assumed that's why you picked Seattle."

Miriam said, "We picked Seattle because we were asked to get someone out of there."

L. Linda nodded as if this made perfect sense. "Stanley Mires. An even better reason."

Derrick wondered how L. Linda knew that name, but he felt like their window of opportunity was closing, so he said nothing. L. Linda's knowledge troubled him. It seemed too much of a coincidence that she was involved. Perhaps she had been playing him all along. The DK Double Honey, and all of that. Not only him. Potterville. He was glad he was partnered with her so he could watch her every move.

L. Linda pointed to the roof of a nearby building. "We land here, right next to the tunnel entrance. The Watermark Tower is only half a mile away."

"What about traffic in the tunnel?" Derrick asked. "That looks like a major route."

"It was a major route. An earthquake collapsed the tunnel to the north. They didn't fix it. There is a barrier at our entrance, but it's been pulled away at the top, so we can slip through and use ropes to lower ourselves down. The latch is broken on the electrical service panel below the building." Puzzled looks on the others' faces prompted further explanation. "The Resistance has been working on this plan for many years. What they didn't have was anyone willing to make the assault."

"And able," Anna said.

"Damn right," Rebekah said, giving Anna a nudge.

L. Linda cleared her throat. "We go up to the parking garage. I'll set the explosives. Then we take the stairs to the top floors. Prime is in the Penthouse. His replacements are on the floor just below. Then we go to the roof. Rebekah flies in and picks us up. Then we rocket out of there before the explosion. Questions?"

"When do I learn to fly?" Rebekah asked.

L. Linda said, "The aircraft is easy to fly. We can teach you on the way."

"Why take the stairs?" Derrick asked. "They can pick us off from above."

L. Linda said, "The elevators are easier to shut down, and we would be sitting ducks if the doors slid open and there's a squad of robots waiting to gun us down."

"Computer," Miriam said. "I need to get to one. I can do it later, but let's assume, for the sake of argument, we are under some duress at the end. Then I wouldn't have time. Better to do it first. Plus, I can probably shut off cameras and unlock doors."

L. Linda nodded. "No guarantees, but the parking garage should have an electrical room. It might have a terminal, although it might not be full-blown computer access. How long is this going to take? We won't have time for you to putter around. And it will no doubt take a password to get in."

"I don't need a password. I just plug my laptop in, and it will do the work. While it's downloading, I can shut off cameras and open doors. I can monitor what's happening and warn you. I can probably cause some diversions to give us more time."

"How long?" L. Linda asked.

Miriam shrugged. "Not sure. Twenty to thirty minutes. Maybe less, maybe more."

L. Linda said, "We'll have to be flexible. If they are on to us early, we won't have time. We'll have to fight our way to the top floors. The priority is setting the explosives. We must be ready to blow the building."

"What if we get trapped?" Anna asked.

"The explosives will be on a timer. So, it's best that we don't let that happen. Otherwise, destroying Prime will be up to Antonio and Red, which means it won't happen," L. Linda said without a trace of sarcasm or humor in her voice.

"If there's a computer in the garage, I can start working while you place the explosives. Are you sure it will destroy the building?"

"I studied the structure. Charlie designed the amount of each charge, and then I added a bit more. It'll come down alright. We don't want to be anywhere close when it does," L. Linda said.

"Do we have to destroy the building?" Rebekah asked. "What if there are people in there?"

Miriam pursed her lips. "I'll pull the fire alarm. It's up to them to get out. And yes, we must destroy the building. Prime needs to know. Give him something to worry about."

L. Linda nodded.

Rebekah said, "Won't he put reinforcements in the other locations? Make it more difficult, if not impossible, to destroy them?"

"Perhaps. But I have a plan for that too, although, there is no guarantee that it will work," Miriam said.

Derrick stood. His knees felt as if they might give out, and he tried to muster more courage than he felt. "So, we are doing this. For real."

"For real," Miriam agreed.

11

STANLEY FOLLOWED HIS NOSE TO FOOD. A food court, as it turned out, which had two sections in a large open area filled with tables and plants and people. The extremes taken to make it feel as if one were in a typical above-ground dining area were remarkable, contrasting where he had spent the night.

They had designed one side of the area cafeteria-style with steam tables and a salad bar. It looked like something out of old Las Vegas, if the archived movies Stanley had watched were accurate depictions of the era. The public had no access to movies from the before-times, but some were available when he attended a six-month Resistance training camp hidden in the Blue Ridge Mountains. The old movies looked real, but he understood there came a time when people modified pictures and videos until it was difficult to tell the difference between real and fabricated. Back then, people were either too lazy to investigate or eager to pass along anything fitting their worldview, which constituted a predictable recipe for disaster, which James Carver exploited.

The other side looked like small street cafes—espresso, ice cream, bakery, and chocolates. It looked like the small shops one might find in an upscale neighborhood. There was no seating inside the small shops, but all had tables along the faux sidewalks. The food from the cafeteria smelled more inviting than he expected, but first, an espresso machine called his name.

He stepped to the counter and studied the menu on the wall behind the barista for a moment. Not because he didn't know what he wanted, but to see what was available. It looked like an espresso shop in Seattle, although there were few. Seattle was once considered Mecca for espresso and fine coffee if you believed the old movies, but that was decades ago. There wasn't much of that sort of thing anymore.

"What can I make you, Mr. Mires?"

Stanley glanced at his shirt to see if someone had attached a nametag of which he was unaware. "How do you know my name?".

"You're Prime's new chief of staff. Your face and name have been broadcast throughout the facility."

Her name badge read, Pam. "Hi, Pam. I didn't know that had happened." He realized he had no money, so this became a social visit unless they had a system for credit. "Do you work for a catering company?" He asked instead of ordering.

She gave a little laugh. "I'm a bioengineer. I arrived a few days ago. From what I've gathered, most of us arrived recently. We all have extra duties assigned. There are no outside workers here."

"Where do I sign up for extra duties?" Perhaps that's how one earned money for these shops. Maybe Prime had a token economy here.

"You are chief of staff—no extra duties for you. None needed and probably not allowed. We shouldn't be having this conversation."

"Why not? Prime cleared us both to be here."

"Cleared to be here, yes, but you should not socialize with the underlings." She smiled.

Stanley didn't know how far he should take the conversation. He assumed there was no privacy. Not just here, but anywhere in this facility. Probably not even the restroom. But he'd just arrived, so perhaps Prime would cut him some slack. After all, what could Prime do? Kill him? Well, yes, that remained a solid possibility.

"Do you know where we are?" He Paused. "I have no money. Is there a credit system here?"

"We have an internal banking system. It works just like on the surface. We pay rent and can purchase food and clothing. Like up there, one must budget. Pay more for an upgraded room, have less for eating out."

"Oh. Okay. In that case, a double espresso, please."

Pam walked to the espresso machine and started the process. When she sat his cup down, she said, "We are at the central Prime headquarters, which you already know. We made the big time. I guess."

He thought about pressing for their location but decided against it. Not worth causing problems for her. "So, where do I sign for payment? Or is there an application on my tablet? I haven't even turned it on.".

"There's no charge for you. Everything for the chief of staff is covered."

The espresso's aroma drifted to his nose. It smelled wonderful. He sipped. "Fantastic. You sound like you have doubts about being here."

Her expression changed. "Don't misunderstand. I love being here. It's a great honor." She looked around. "I would have jumped at the chance to come. It would have been nice had they asked."

Stanley nodded and sipped.

"Did they ask you?" she whispered.

Stanley smiled. "I didn't know what was happening. I thought they were taking me to the roof to throw me off."

"Nothing like that happened to me. They just said I was going to number one and led me to a big black SUV that took me to the airport."

"Were you blindfolded?"

"No. They blindfolded you?"

Stanley nodded. He wondered why Prime had blindfolded him and not others. It made little sense. A mystery he'd likely never understand. "I had a hood over my head from the time they led me from Prime's operations room in Seattle until I was standing in the operation room here. Do you have any idea where we are? I mean, besides, at number one."

She studied him for a moment, as if she didn't believe what he'd said. "In the middle of a big desert. That's all I can tell you. I don't mean to be rude, but I'm feeling uncomfortable. I'm afraid I've already said too much and talked too long."

Stanley walked away. Big desert. That was all he knew. And that wasn't new information. But the coffee was good.

12

Saturday, April 10, 8:01 a.m.

BROWNING, MARTINEZ, AND COLLINS SAT, drinking coffee in Fletcher's shop. Jack had disappeared into the back. Patel had just stumbled in. No surprise, because Allen wasn't an early riser, and he'd had a tough night. Fletcher's night was just as difficult, plus he had driven to Pacific Edge and back. But Fletcher was a tough old bird. That much was clear. Collins wanted all the adults there when he told them about Jason Maxton, but he wasn't sure about the kids. Perhaps they should know as well.

Donna arrived with cinnamon rolls, bear claws, and banana bread. The aromas drew the others, including the kids. Collins did not know how to prevent the news about Jason from coming out too early.

Fletcher showed up just in time to prevent that conversation from happening prematurely. "I set up a table for the young ones in the back. Perhaps they should eat there so we can talk."

Browning took the cue. "Terrance, take the kids to the back. Grab whatever you want to eat and take it with you."

Terrance said, "Ah, Dad. I'm old enough to stay."

Browning held up his hand. "I know, but the rest are not. No arguing. It's not the time."

"That includes you, Samantha," Allen said.

When the kids had left, Browning said, "Where's Jason? Do we need him here for this?"

"About that. I have bad news." Collins paused. "Jason Maxton was killed last night. I'll let Allen fill in the details."

Gasps were heard. Tears fell.

Allen explained because he had witnessed it, but he kept it short and to the point. "A man shot Jason in the back. Miriam killed the man. Clear self-defense."

No one spoke for several minutes.

"Where are the kids now?" Donna asked.

Allen shrugged. "Somewhere in the mountains."

"What will become of L. Linda?" Donna asked.

"Does anyone know if she has other family?" Collins asked.

No one spoke for several minutes.

Browning said, "We might have that in her school records."

Donna said, "I don't think anyone knows either of them well. Jason rarely came in. I had just hired L. Linda." She paused, tapping one finger on the table as if trying to drum up a memory. "It's weird. I know nothing about her. I asked her to fill out an application. She took it home but never brought it back. I didn't think much about it. She always seemed a little scattered. You know? Every time I asked her about the application, she sidetracked me."

"What will happen to them? Four kids without homes," Allen said.

"I told Derrick he could live with us. That was the day he disappeared." Browning paused. "Now, I don't even know where we are going to live."

Allen said, "Anna and Rebekah are good friends with Samantha, and I would take them in, but we don't have a place either."

Donna said, "L. Linda can stay with me, but first, we need to get them home."

Collins nodded. "I'd like nothing more, but we don't know where they are."

Lori said, "I say we go find them. We know they crossed the river. Who's a good tracker?"

Everyone looked at her.

"What?" Lori asked. "I know we aren't like in the old west, but how hard can it be to find them?"

"Hard," Collins said.

Allen said, "They have probably left."

"Left to where?" Collins asked.

"To attack Prime," Allen said.

13

REBEKAH FLEW THE PRIME AIRCRAFT west to the Pacific and then north. They were less likely to be picked up on radar over the ocean. Military ships were located along the coastline of Mexico. Derrick fidgeted in his seat. Checking his weapons, including the new one. L. Linda had explained its operation, which wasn't complicated. She sat next to him. He couldn't think of anything to say but tried to observe her without being obvious.

"How long?" Anna asked.

L. Linda said, "Flight time is about 30 minutes. We could make it 20 if we had flown straight, but I think by sea is best. Then we'll fly low over the Puget Sound. I hope that gets us there undetected."

"Flight controls say 29 minutes," Rebekah said, adding, "What if we are detected?"

"Then things will be more difficult," L. Linda said.

"Does that mean we abort?" Rebekah asked.

"No," Miriam said. "We have to start somewhere."

Rebekah was fifty feet above the surface of the ocean. The aircraft banked for a right-hand turn. She said, "Puget Sound is just ahead. Not long now."

L. Linda said, "Less than five minutes. Soon as we land, I'll lead us to the tunnel entrance. It has a metal screen blocking it, but it should be detached from the top. That's how we get in."

"What if it isn't detached?" Miriam asked.

"Then we detach it." L. Linda held up a small electronic device. "You each have one of these in your vest pocket. It will cut through metal in case we encounter locked doors and such. I should have gone over them in the briefing. Think of them as a tool, not a weapon. They are simple to use, and I trust you can figure them out."

Derrick felt his pocket. The device was there. They wore military uniforms and bullet-resistant vests. L. Linda pointed out that they were not bulletproof, but some protection was better than none. The uniforms included helmets with flip-down vision devices with various settings. One setting detected body heat through doors and walls.

Derrick still didn't understand how L. Linda had come to be in charge. Miriam had fallen in line, as had Anna. Anna surprised him more than Miriam did, but he wasn't comfortable. Not comfortable at all. He didn't know L. Linda. Not really. Perhaps she could read his mind because she was staring at him.

"Derrick, you're with me. Anna goes with Miriam to cover her while she works on the computer. I'll set the charges. You'll stay put to cover me. Questions?" L. Linda asked.

"You already told us that in the briefing," Derrick said.

"I did, but you looked a bit confused."

He was confused about a lot of things, but he would not admit it. Confused and worried. No matter how he rationalized it all, he returned to one fundamental thing he couldn't shake. He didn't want to kill people. Robots? He could destroy them all day long, unless they looked like Charlie. Then he'd have second thoughts, because what if they had developed the AI thing like Charlie? He had successfully pushed that thought out of his mind because Charlie was one of a kind.

But people. That was a different story.

All the soldiers in Mexico died except Kevin. He had killed none of them. Rebekah shot one, but that was self-defense—a natural reaction. They'd all be dead if not for Rebekah. It didn't bother him that she had pulled the trigger.

Still, something troubled him, and he couldn't put his finger on it.

The aircraft slowed abruptly.

L. Linda put her hand on his leg. "It's going to be okay."

"You don't know that." He instantly regretted saying it.

"I don't know it, but I believe it. Believing is important. I suggest you believe as well."

The aircraft spun around.

"We're here," Rebekah said as the door slid open. "See you on the rooftop."

L. Linda looked Derrick in the eyes. "Stay close."

Derrick followed her out the door. L. Linda ran across the roof, scrambled down a ladder onto a concrete deck, and dashed to the edge. L. Linda scanned the area and then slung her rifle over her shoulder.

"So far, it looks clear."

L. Linda got on her knees and pushed a metal grate that leaned up against the tunnel entrance. It moved a few inches, but not enough to squeeze through the opening.

Miriam pointed. "Cameras."

L. Linda said, "They can't see us at this angle. Better we don't announce ourselves just yet. Derrick, a little help?"

Derrick sat on the tunnel's edge, bracing his feet against the metal grate, and pushed. It moved several inches.

L. Linda said, "That should be enough." She waved for Miriam and Anna.

Anna went first, then Miriam. The grating rattled and groaned. Derrick wondered if the cameras picked up sounds. Probably not because of the constant noise he had just noticed. Cars on nearby roads. A siren in the distance.

L. Linda slid into the opening. "I'll push it open. You come next, and then I'll follow you down."

He passed L. Linda. She had her back braced against the concrete and pushed the metal with her hands and feet. The grate would trap her when she stopped pushing, so Derrick stopped and did the best he could to hold it open, using his hands above his head. L. Linda squeezed by.

Now how to get himself down was the question. He felt hands pressing up from under the soles of his boot.

"We got you," Anna said below him.

Once on the ground, Derrick turned to face the darkness. Light spilled into the tunnel opening but didn't penetrate far. A few dim lights were scattered here and there. L. Linda was rubbing her eyes. Tears dampened her cheeks. "Are you okay?" Derrick asked.

"Dirt fell in my eyes. Or concrete. What I scraped off the tunnel wall as I slid through. I'll be okay."

"You're sure?" Derrick asked, noting her eyes were bloodshot. He looked up and saw the concrete was covered with something growing.

L. Linda nodded. "Let's do this." She started at a brisk pace, somewhere between a run and a trot. They were all young. He and Anna were the best-conditioned, but when L. Linda stopped at a metal door halfway up the tunnel, she was not breathing any harder than he was.

"This is it," L. Linda said. She tried the handle, but it didn't move. "Damn it. Locked."

She pulled out the device she'd shown them earlier, held it near the doorjamb, and pulled a trigger. A blue arc leaped into the gap, and sparks flew. A moment later, she returned the device to her pocket and slipped a leather glove onto her right hand. She tested the door handle a few times and then gave it a quick pull.

"Careful, it's hot," L. Linda said and disappeared into the opening.

A dim light appeared in the darkness above him, so Derrick flipped the helmet headlight down and turned it on. An attached metal ladder ran straight up the wall. L. Linda was already halfway up and climbing fast. He followed hand over hand. She was waiting for him on the top rungs, facing another metal door.

When Derrick reached the top, L. Linda said, "Ready?"

"Ready."

She turned a handle of a metal door. It squeaked. If anyone was up there, they had been alerted to their presence. Utility workers still use these passageways, so perhaps they would not open fire immediately. He should not have let L. Linda go first. He needed to get his head on straight. She shouldn't be taking the risk.

"Clear," she said and climbed out of the hole.

As Derrick reached the opening, L. Linda's outstretched hand awaited him. Her grip was firm, comforting him in a way he could not explain. He helped Anna. Anna helped Miriam.

They stood in the parking garage, listening.

L. Linda rubbed her right eye and then held a finger to her lips. She motioned for Anna and Miriam to take the right-hand side. She and Derrick took the left. The parking lot was silent, except for their light footfalls.

A roadway ran along the wall next to the building, wide enough for a car, but steel poles blocked vehicles from entering. This path was for people working in the building.

Or robots.

Derrick hoped it was for robots but not too many.

Miriam held up the cutting tool, motioning for him and L. Linda to stay back. Miriam tried one door. It was locked, so she cut through the bolt. Pulling the door open, she peered inside, shook her head, and moved to the next door. Also locked. Sparks flew as Miriam made short work of the locking bolt. After looking inside, Miriam gave them a thumbs up and went in. Anna followed her.

L. Linda moved to a big electrical box. She removed her backpack and motioned Derrick to do the same. Then she put her back against the box and kneeled. She said, "Stay put and keep your eyes open. I'll set the charges."

She glanced over the box and then dashed to the righthand side of the garage, carrying both backpacks. She stopped at a concrete pillar and placed one charge near the base. A small red light started flashing, and then she scanned the garage before moving to the next pillar. Scan and move. Each time. Efficient. Setting each charge didn't take more than a couple of minutes. After setting three charges, she disappeared from his view, and that's when his thoughts raced. She not only knew how to set the charges but did so with an economy of motion that suggested the task was not wholly unfamiliar.

Derrick realized he'd drifted off again when L. Linda caught his attention. She was kneeling behind the closest pillar and did not look happy. The bomb was already blinking red, but she looked beyond, as if something were behind him.

L. Linda held her finger to her lips and then stood. Walking toward Derrick, she said, "Excuse me. How do I get to Vancouver? Does this tunnel go there?"

A voice not unlike the robots at the base said, "This area is restricted. You must leave immediately."

L. Linda continued walking. Derrick noticed one hand was behind her back. He pulled his weapon and started to stand. She frowned and shook her head.

"You must vacate the area immediately."

"I'm trying to do just that. I need directions."

She was standing right next to where Derrick hid. Her arm whipped out. She braced one foot against the box and pulled. Derrick saw a thin cable drawn taunt. A crash came from the other side of the box. L. Linda leaped upon the box and over the other side. Derrick stood. A second later, L. Linda stood with a robot's battery. She tossed it to him.

"I didn't know if that would work," L. Linda said.

Derrick watched as L. Linda dragged the robot's body behind a nearby car. She had used a steel cable with a heavy ball on the end that wrapped around the robot's neck. He assumed it would have decapitated a human.

She motioned for Derrick to sit and then sat beside him. "I didn't want to shoot the robot. That would have caused a quicker response." She glanced at her watch. "Miriam has 15 minutes, and then we must go. We might have company before then, but I hope one robot going offline doesn't necessitate a large response. Maybe just a repairman."

She talked as if this were of no major concern.

"Who *are* you?" Derrick asked.

L. Linda's brow wrinkled just a little. "You know who I am."

"You're not the girl I worked with at Donna's. The one that invented the DK Double Honey," he paused, felt a flush in his cheeks, "which I was too dumb to understand."

She patted his hand. "Not dumb. Maybe a little naïve."

"Maybe a ton naïve. Will you tell me the truth? Are you a test subject?"

"I am not. Something else. Maybe I can explain someday."

"Today is a good day. We have ten minutes. Who, or maybe what, are you? Your dad was just murdered, but you don't seem upset. You call him Jason. Not dad."

"I'm devastated, but I can't let it affect me right now."

"Tell me what's going on. We might not live through this. So, now's a good time."

She stared at him for a moment. Her eyes were bloodshot.

"Your eyes don't look so good."

"My contacts are scratched. It's driving me crazy."

"I didn't know you wore contacts. You can't take them out because you can't see without them?"

She pursed her lips. "I can see fine."

"I don't understand."

"I have my reasons."

"Take them out. If you can see without them, why leave them in? Your eyes are getting worse."

L. Linda took a deep breath. "I can't let people see my eyes."

Derrick shook his head. "That makes no sense."

"It makes a lot of sense. Everything would change. That's why I can't tell you who I am. You'd never look at me the same. But perhaps it doesn't matter."

Derrick didn't understand. "What does that mean?"

"I sense things are about to change. For me, at least."

"Just take them out and tell me something about who you are. You're not what you want people to believe."

"Can I trust you?"

"Of course." He paused. "I guess that's easier said than done. The way I lied about who I was and all."

She took his hand. "I understand why you did that. You were wrong about people outside Pacific Edge, but sometimes people must lie to survive. Promise me!"

"That you can trust me? I promise."

She looked away, but he saw her remove one contact and then the other. Still not looking at him, she said, "Much better. Promise, you'll never tell anyone. Not even if I don't make it out."

"Don't talk like that. We're all getting out."

She turned to face him.

He said nothing for a moment. "Your eyes."

"I know. Right?"

"They're …they're—beautiful," he whispered.

"They're distinctive, and that's not beautiful if going unnoticed is important."

"Explain."

"You can't tell anyone. Ever."

"I promise."

"I'm not a test subject. I'm not Jason's daughter. My parents were killed."

Derrick tried to say something. She held her finger to his lips. "Let me finish. I'll make a long story short. Prime wanted assassins. He started a program to train them. Physiologists and psychiatrists developed a profile that was supposed to predict qualities for candidates at a young age. I fit the profile. So, they killed my parents. They put me in a special school."

"Special school?" Derrick questioned under his breath.

L. Linda took a deep breath. "Assassin school. They trained me to be an assassin. At age 13, assassins are sent on their first mission. Their handler supervises the mission in case things go wrong."

"My god."

"Things went wrong. They sent me to kill some people. A man and his wife and their 12-year-old daughter."

"Did they do something wrong?"

"Perhaps they said something against Prime, but I don't know. Assassins are not told the why, only the who. I froze. When I saw the girl, I couldn't do it. I ran out of the house."

"That's a good thing. You should be proud of yourself."

"There's more. Remember. That's why the handler is there. Things going wrong include chickening out. He killed—all of them, including a friend who was sleeping over. I was outside, hiding in the tree line, crying my eyes out, when my handler came out of the house. He was carrying the friend. Dead, of course."

"That's awful."

"It gets worse. The handler was supposed to kill me too. That was his duty. But he didn't. As we were leaving, the house exploded in a huge ball of flames. My handler opened a gas valve in the basement. The gas filled the house until it found a pilot light."

"So, why…"

L. Linda stopped him. "Not finished. We drove back to the school. There were 23 students, 23 handlers, and 7 instructors. A total of 53, 23 teens, 30 adults, all living at the school. Jason carried the dead girl inside and put her in my bed. I stayed in the car, in shock, unable to move or cry or scream. Only shiver. After a few minutes, my handler came out, and we drove away. The school exploded the same as the victims' house."

"So, the dead girl…"

"Right. Investigators found 23 dead kids. Everyone accounted for. The handlers and instructors were burned beyond identification. But they would only find 29. One of 30 was the murderer. They wouldn't know which one. But they would never look for me. They thought I had died there with the others. That I had completed my mission and then returned to the school."

Derrick said nothing.

"We went to a cabin in Montana, out in the wilderness. I didn't talk for a year. At first, I was terrified of my handler. He'd killed all those people. He never talked about it. He never explained it. I was certain he would kill me. Someday. But he didn't. Eventually, I figured it out on my own. He killed all those people to save me. I don't know why." She paused. "That's not true. I know why."

Derrick said, "I don't know what to say."

"You'll never see me the same. I can't live with that."

"What do you mean?"

L. Linda ignored his question and said, "When I started talking, I became L. Linda. She was the person I wanted to be, not the person I was supposed to be. After another six months, my handler thought I could handle going to school. He found a school that didn't use a computer system, which is not difficult in rural Montana, and created a school file for me. We just show up at a school with a fake file and enrolled."

"Potterville?"

"Yes."

"Then—your handler —" Derrick stopped.

"Jason Maxton was my handler."

14

THE TREES WORE CLOAKS OF FOG, and the pine scent hung heavy in the air. Nobody was watching the motel. Few cars moved through the small town. Scott remembered that there was a coffee shop down the street. He left his backpack in the room and the door unlocked. He no longer had anything important to hide. What he had, he'd given away. It wasn't much. A mere twenty letters, numbers, and symbols that he could not memorize. He told Miriam to write them down and was sure she did not. He was also sure she would remember them just fine. His part was done.

At least for now.

A weight lifted when he gave Miriam the code. Hearing her voice helped. After dinner, she called again, adding a new weight that depressed him. She told him a man was killed retrieving Patel's briefcase. Scott never considered that things would end up as they did. He was certain Patel felt equally guilty. Replaying Miriam's voice in his head, he recognized the sadness in the words and tone.

The air was cool and damp, but he wasn't cold. He wasn't afraid. Not like when he came down the mountain. He was terrified that day. Convinced he would be caught, tortured, and killed.

He might be killed yet, but it wouldn't be a sniper. He could only see about a block. An assassin could lurk in the small town, but an attack would be close range. That gave him a chance. Not much of a chance, but a chance. But he didn't think it would happen. Everyone here knew everyone. Any stranger is suspected and watched. Although he didn't see anyone watching, he assumed they were still there. Not just one person but the entire town was watching him, which meant they were also looking out for him.

They wouldn't stop him from leaving. That's what John told him after he'd delivered the code to Miriam. Scott wasn't going to leave. Not today. Probably not tomorrow.

An open sign leaned against a window of the CL Cafe. CL stood for Cascade Locks, he assumed. "Good morning," a girl behind the counter said. About Derrick's age, probably working weekends.

Scott nodded, not yet comfortable with the small-town familiarity. He studied the menu for a moment. He had money but decided to be frugal until his immediate future became clear. "Just a coffee," he said.

A voice from a table near the window said, "Make him an Americano and a sausage, egg, and cheese sandwich."

He recognized the voice. Sue, the haircut lady.

"Sorry if I've missed the mark," Sue said.

"You're spot on, but I ate at the hotel."

"Nonsense. Honesty goes a long way here, Scott from Bakersfield. The hotel had stale donuts, and the coffee ain't great. That's why you're here." Sue pushed a chair out with her foot. "Join me?"

The barista said, "There's no charge if that's what you're worried about, Mr. Key."

Scott stared at her.

"John called this morning. He is paying until your first paycheck. He said you'd start work on Monday."

At first, Scott declined John's offer of employment. He didn't consider it an actual offer, anyway. Just a way of saying he wasn't leaving town, and that his plan of escaping to Canada was on hold. However, after he had given Miriam the code last night, he told John he'd stick around. John was serious about the job, apparently.

Cascade Locks was as good a place to die as any.

Better than dying alone on the Pacific Crest Trail.

15

THE GARAGE REMAINED QUIET, BUT DERRICK'S mind raced. L. Linda's story explained many things but remained incomprehensible. Simply put, he couldn't believe it. Words failed him. He had many questions but didn't realize most would go unanswered.

"Can I ask you a question?" Derrick asked.

"You can ask. Doesn't mean I'll answer."

"Uh, well, it is sort of difficult to explain. The espresso you made. I, well, I guess some people thought—I don't know—that you might have been …"

"Flirting with you?"

"Uh, yes. That."

"Honest?"

"Yes, please."

"I was using you. Or hoping to."

"I don't understand."

"To be more accurate, I hoped you could help me. I knew you were a test subject and had special training."

"How could you know that?"

"Someone in the Resistance told Jason. Jason told me."

"Okay." Derrick drew the word out, confused.

L. Linda took a deep breath. "Jason didn't like it, but he knew I would do it whether he liked it or not."

"Do what?"

"Kill Prime. Once I'd recovered, well, if you can call it recovered from what I'd been through, I understood. Prime killed my real parents. And though they needed to be killed, it was Prime's fault that those kids at the assassin school had died. Prime had ruined my life. I planned to end his."

Derrick felt a little hurt in his chest, but he wasn't sure why. Or at least he didn't want to admit the reason for it. "Oh."

L. Linda patted his knee. "I said that's how it started. I didn't say that's how it ended."

A door opening drew their attention. Then the sound of marching hard-soled feet sent a shiver through his body.

Robots.

Lots of them.

L. Linda put one hand on Derrick's shoulder, holding him down as she peaked over the box behind which they hid.

"Not good," L. Linda said.

"Robots?"

"Yeah. At least ten of them." L. Linda paused. "Here's what we need to do. I'm going to draw them away."

"I could do that."

"Stop talking. You must destroy Prime. I'll draw them into the garage. Besides, my priorities have changed."

Derrick interrupted. "I can drop a bunch of them once they start after you."

L. Linda shook her head. "No. If you shoot, they'll know you're here. Send reinforcements. Even if you killed them all, more would come. Prime would lock everything down and probably has a safe room."

"Safe room?"

"Honest to God, Derrick. Shut up. When the robots are well into the garage, get Miriam. Tell her time is up and head up the stairs."

"Okay," Derrick said, although something told him it was not okay.

"You must promise me two things."

"We can talk more when this is done. On the flight home."

"Stop. Two things." She held up one finger. "Stay alive." Second finger. "Destroy Prime."

"But…"

She held her finger gently to his lips. "Promise me."

"How will you get to the roof?"

"I'll go out through the tunnel. Have Rebekah swing back and pick me up. If I'm not there, leave. Understood? One last thing. I'm setting the timer. You have 30 minutes."

"Thirty minutes from when?"

L. Linda pulled a device from her pack, fiddled with the controls, and then pushed a button. "From right now."

"Shit."

"Shit is right. Now, promise me. Two things."

It felt to Derrick as if L. Linda's green eyes had pierced his soul. "I promise, but I'll see you in 30 minutes, better make that 29 to be safe."

L. Linda smiled and looked into his eyes. "I'm sorry, Derrick."

"Sorry for what?"

"Keep your promises, Derrick King."

And with that, she was gone.

16

THE BREAKFAST BUFFET WAS BETTER THAN Stanley expected. He went back for seconds, filling his plate with things he typically avoided: thick-sliced ham, hash browns, biscuits, and gravy. Foods not recommended for longevity. A long life no longer seemed important or attainable. A quick death sounded like a luxury. Heart attacks were quick, although Stanley doubted a second helping of biscuits and gravy would provide such relief today. Maybe tomorrow.

If he had a tomorrow.

No guarantees.

Everyone smiled and nodded, but no one asked him to join them, and no one came to sit with him. Prime had indeed broadcast his face—Chief of Staff. He understood. If he were in their place, he'd want nothing to do with Prime's right-hand man.

Still, that would make his time here, however long it lasted, a lonely one. A thought crossed his mind. Maybe someone here was with the Resistance. Perhaps such a person would reach out to him, but he doubted that would happen. First, to the best of his knowledge, he was the only one to have infiltrated Prime headquarters or high-level laboratories. And because of the secrecy of his involvement, few knew his identity. That was the hope. He was a dead man if anyone knew his connection with the Resistance.

He pushed a chunk of biscuit through a glob of sausage gravy. This was the central Prime location. His hope of killing Prime wasn't his mission in Seattle because it was just one location. This is an entirely different situation. While one Prime is the same as every other Prime, at least in that they are interconnected, no one knows the location of this one.

He stuck the last bit of biscuit in his mouth.

This was different.

He smiled.

His life had purpose again. Kill the central Prime.

17

INSTEAD OF DASHING INTO THE GARAGE, L. LINDA walked toward the robots. They ordered her to leave. She responded by throwing a brick, striking the lead robot in the head, shattering the glass used as eyes. Derrick assumed the robot's vision was impaired. Then L. Linda ran, and the robots pursued. She disappeared behind a pickup and then flung something. A wrench of some sort. It spun through the air, bearing down on a robot, but the robot saw it and ducked. It smacked the next machine, but Derrick could not see if it caused any damage.

A robot opened fire, which sounded like a cross between gunfire and the zapper things. L. Linda moved, ducking behind another car. The robots riddled it with gunfire. Derrick's stomach twisted into a knot, and he thought he might puke or pass out.

He sucked in a deep breath. Why was L. Linda throwing bricks and wrenches instead of shooting? He'd ask her when they were in the aircraft. They had 30 minutes, and he didn't know how much time remained. Perhaps 28 minutes. Maybe less. He could have taken out half of the robots pursuing L. Linda, but she insisted he let her handle it. Taking one last look into the garage, he ran to where Anna and Miriam were working.

Throwing the door open, Derrick said, "We need to go."

Staring at her laptop's screen, she said, "Just a few more minutes. Did we hear gunfire?"

"Yeah. We have to go. NOW! The bombs will detonate in about 25 minutes, maybe less."

Miriam spun around. "I need more time."

"L. Linda started the timer."

"Tell her to shut it off. I'll let you know when I'm done. It won't take much longer. The download is 94%."

"I can't. L. Linda is gone. Well, not gone, gone, at least I hope not."

"What are you talking about?" Miriam asked.

"Twenty-three minutes," Anna said.

Derrick checked the garage. "A dozen robots showed up. L. Linda drew them into the garage. She had already set the timer. We have to go. NOW!"

"Damn," Miriam said, disconnecting her laptop and shoving it in her backpack.

Derrick said, "More security will arrive at any moment."

"Because of the gunfire?" Miriam asked.

"Exactly," Derrick said.

"What if we can't destroy Prime in 20 minutes?" Anna asked.

Miriam said, "When the building comes down, it will destroy Prime. But I need to see what Prime is and learn how the replication works."

Just as they reached the stairs, the elevator doors slid open. Three robots stepped out, one scanning where the cars were, one scanning away from them, and one looking directly at them. Derrick shoved Miriam into Anna, knocking them into a niche as he raised his weapon. He shot the first machine, but the new weapon was not on the highest setting. The machine jerked, causing its shot to go high. He thumbed the weapon to high, and the next shot hit the robot squarely in the chest, knocking it into the other two. The next shot hit both functioning machines, finishing them both. An acidic smell of melted electronics filled the air.

Derrick eased the stairwell door open and then motioned for the girls. "It's clear."

Then there were more shots from deeper in the garage. Derrick said, "That sounds like L. Linda's pistol."

Inside the stairwell, they paused. Listening for noise above them. Derrick pressed one finger to his lips and started up. Both girls had their weapons drawn. He didn't ask if they had set them on high. Didn't have to. This was it. No turning back now. It was kill or be killed.

Derrick felt no reluctance destroying robots.

Killing people? He hoped that didn't happen.

L. Linda Maxton was trained to be an assassin. Assassins kill people. That's what they do. But she didn't kill the family she was supposed to. However, she did not say she had not killed others. That had not crossed his mind.

Until now.

Miriam got Derrick's attention. She was frowning, and he didn't understand why. Then she tapped her wrist, where one might wear a watch.

Miriam whispered, "We need to make this fast," making a hurry motion with her hand.

Derrick took point, keeping his eyes forward. Anna took the rear position, watching their backs. He stopped on the twelfth floor.

Voices could be heard on the other side of the door.

Derrick motioned for them to stop. "The building has felt empty until now."

Anna said, "I agree. I've listened at each door and heard nothing."

Miriam said, "It doesn't matter. We know Prime is on the top floor. The replicants are one floor below that. Our concern is the 17th and 18th floors."

"What are on the other floors?" Derrick asked.

"The Resistance guy didn't know. Only that Prime is on the 17th and 18th floors." Miriam looked irritated and shrugged. "Let's go. We've got less than 15 minutes."

Derrick said, "We need to clear this floor first. There are people here."

"We don't," Miriam said. "The bombs will take care of it."

Derrick felt confused for a moment and then understood. "I don't mean to kill them. I mean to warn them. You said we'd pull the fire alarm."

Before Miriam could protest, Derrick eased the door open and stepped inside. A woman screamed, and a man grabbed a nearby coat rack, brandishing it as if it were a weapon.

Derrick pointed his gun, which was on the lowest setting. "I don't want to hurt you." He glanced around the room. Drawers were pulled open, and boxes were stacked on carts. "What are you doing?"

The man holding the coat rack said, "Moving out."

"Why?" Derrick asked.

A woman placed her hand on the man's arm, indicating he should lower the coatrack. "We don't know. Prime's orders. There's a transport waiting downstairs. We must be on it within the hour."

Derrick relaxed a little. "How many more are in the building?"

"Just us. There are eight of us on the floor. The others are off today. We were called in," the woman said.

"Is there a way out where the transport won't see you?" Derrick asked.

The man looked at the woman and then back at Derrick. "I suppose. We could go through the parking garage…"

Derrick cut him off. "Not that way. Another way."

The woman said, "There's a side street exit."

"It's locked," the man said.

"Coming in, not going out," the woman said.

The man nodded and lowered the coat rack.

Derrick said, "Listen closely. Go out the side door. Don't take anything. Don't walk. Run. Don't get on that transport."

"If we don't get on the transport, Prime will have our heads," the woman said.

"If you don't run and do it now, it won't matter. You'll be dead. Now, go!" Derrick turned and left. He hoped he had been convincing. He'd never know for sure.

Back in the hallway, Miriam pursed her lips and shook her head. "Ten minutes."

"Then we should go," Derrick said, sprinting up the stairs two at a time.

Just after passing the 14th floor, Miriam shouted. "Stop."

Derrick looked back. Miriam was pointing to a device on the wall just ahead of him. "Trip light."

Doors above and below them crashed open. Derrick spun around, instinctively dodging to the side as he raised his weapon. A shot rang out from a robot holding a firearm. Why the machine did not have a more advanced weapon, Derrick did not know. Derrick fired, striking the robot just as he heard more weapons discharging behind him.

He moved again as another robot fired. This one had an unusual weapon, which blew a hole into the concrete, showering him with debris. He closed his eyes and fired several rounds up the stairwell. The sound of a robot tumbling down the stairs indicated he'd taken out at least one.

More weapons fired behind him—Miriam and Anna—from the sounds of it. At the next turn of the stairwell, three smoldering robots were stacked upon one another. Above, a set of robot legs appeared, moving slowly and silently. He did not know how effective hitting the machine's legs would be.

He pointed the weapon at the robot's leg and fired. Sparks flew from the metal, and the machine tumbled down the stairs, but it was twisting to be in position to return fire. Derrick didn't give it a chance.

A hand landed on his shoulder. Miriam whispered, "We gotta move. There's little time left." Without looking back, he started up the stairs again. Before looking around the next turn, he eased the weapon around the corner and fired. A robot crashed to the ground, so he fired a second round. Nothing happened, so he peeked.

"Clear."

Miriam said, "Keep moving. Shoot anything or anyone you see. We are running out of time. Stop on the 17th floor."

Derrick didn't like her saying *anyone*, but he understood. If they ran into more people, they wouldn't have time to chat. Those people could not get out of the building fast enough. They were dead already.

Two more robots appeared on their way up. One on the 15th floor, another on the 16th. Anna shot three that were coming up from behind.

Stopping at the 17th floor, Derrick turned to Miriam. Her skin was damp and pale, making her look almost blue. She held her left hand to her side, which was soaked with blood. "You're hurt."

"First round got me." Miriam grimaced. "What's the plan? We need to make this fast."

Derrick wanted to know how badly she was wounded. He wanted to get her to a hospital. But if they didn't get to the roof within a few minutes, it wouldn't matter. They'd all be buried in the rubble of this building. And if they died, it meant Prime would live on and thousands would die.

Unfortunately, he had no plan.

"I thought you had a plan," Derrick said.

"My thinking has been better." Miriam grimaced and nodded toward her side.

Derrick looked at Anna. "Suggestions?"

If the question caught Anna by surprise, she gave no indication. "You and I will take out the dormant Prime replacements on this floor and then take the stairs up to 18. Miriam waits here until we head up. Then she'll take the elevator up to 18. We'll hit Prime from both the stairs and the elevator. We kill whatever is on 18 before they kill us."

"Except for Stanley Mires. We need to take him with us," Derrick said.

"We don't even know what he looks like," Anna said. "We can't take the risk."

Miriam said, "I promised Professor we'd get him out. That's why we came here first. Put your weapons on stun when we enter."

"But what if stun doesn't work on Prime? We have no idea what we are up against." Anna glanced at Miriam. "Miriam's hurt. The building is about to blow up. Time is not a luxury we possess."

Derrick said, "Miriam, put your weapon on stun. Anna, set yours at full. You go up the stairs. I'll take the elevator instead of Miriam. When you're ready to enter, click your radio twice, and I'll open the elevator doors. Stun Mires if necessary."

Miriam said, "The door entering the 18th floor will probably be locked."

"That's why we have the cutting tool," Derrick said.

"We may not have enough time," Miriam said.

"If you can't cut the lock, signal me at four minutes remaining and go straight to the roof."

"That's cutting it close."

It was, but Derrick had no intention of Miriam and Anna stepping foot onto the 18th floor. He was going in alone. Miriam was hurt. "I'll move fast. Just be ready to get to the roof."

At the 17th level, Derrick positioned himself on the floor, prone and at an angle to the room. When the door flew open, anyone inside would open fire at where an intruder would stand, not down at a corner of the doorway. Anna would be ready to return fire from the other side of the doorway if a robot or guard were out of Derrick's vision. So far, it had only been robots, but this floor might have people. Derrick set the weapon to full but kept his thumb on the controller so he could dial it down quickly if a human was involved.

Grimacing, Miriam grabbed the door handle with her left hand. Red oozed through her fingers. Haze drifted up the stairwell from the smoldering robots below, burning his nostrils with the acidic smell of molten plastic and fried electronic components. He'd be glad to move inside, but the smell probably wouldn't be much better in there. Not for long.

Miriam nodded. Derrick returned the gesture and then turned his focus to the threat behind the door. When the door flew open, Derrick saw two robots, one facing the door, the other facing the elevator. They must have heard the shooting. Derrick assumed they could hear but didn't know for sure. Perhaps they stood there all day, facing the only two directions into the room.

It didn't matter. The robot was fast. A bolt of electricity shot through the open door. Although it missed him by a couple of feet, Derrick could feel a strange sensation on his skin, and he felt sure his hair was standing on end. Neither robot got off a second shot. Derrick dropped them both with two shots so rapid that they both hit the floor at the same time.

Derrick said, "I don't see any others."

Anna said, "Clear."

"Cover me," Derrick said as he stood and moved into the room. Once he was sure there were no more robots or guards, he allowed himself to glance around and wished he had not. One wall was lined with glass tubes four feet in diameter. Below each tube was a control panel with rows of lights, dials, knobs, and push buttons. The control panels were not the problem. It was what was inside the tubes.

Floating in a clear liquid inside each tube was a creature. Although they were all similar, none were exactly alike. Hideous was a kind word to describe them. It was no wonder that Prime had not made a public appearance. Derrick felt certain these creatures would cause him nightmares for the remainder of his life.

Assuming he lived long enough to sleep again.

"You guys have this?" Derrick asked.

"It will be my pleasure," Anna said.

Derrick said, "I'm going up."

Miriam said, "Wait. The way this is designed, I think the elevator opens directly into the penthouse, which is the entire 18th floor. Wait until you hear the double click before you push the up button."

"Will do," Derrick lied as he headed to the elevator.

The doors slid shut. Inside the elevator, the air circulated fresh and clean. When he heard the shooting begin as the girls destroyed the Prime replacements, Derrick pushed the up button.

In a few seconds, he would face Prime for the first and perhaps last time.

18

NYX CHEWED HER NAILS, STARING INTO THE middle distance, wondering if Derrick and the others were okay. She didn't believe in superstitions—not many. She had socks she wore to every track meet. She performed precise rituals before getting into the starting blocks and had unique playlists for each event.

But she refused to believe in supernatural things like ghosts, magic, and premonitions.

For sure, not premonitions.

So why could she not shake the feeling that something had gone wrong? If something happened to Derrick, she wasn't sure what she'd do. She had tried to convince him that her past with Antonio was just that. The past. But she needed more time to make sure Derrick believed her.

Why did she feel she would not have the opportunity to prove it to him?

Glancing around the room, it became clear she was not the only one feeling stress, or perhaps, as much as she hated the word, having this same premonition.

Antonio paced around the room. After several laps, he'd sit for a few minutes, then get up and walk toward the vending machines or coffee pot, only to stand as if he'd forgotten why he was there and then start pacing again.

Red sat at a table by himself, fidgeting with a thick red rubber band, working it through his fingers, creating a spiderweb of elastic red threads and then move it to his wrist, where he'd pull it out and let it slap against his skin.

At one point, Antonio said, "Would you stop with the snapping?"

Red stared at him with the band pulled back and then let it go, creating a loud pop when it hit his arm.

"If you do that again, I'm going to take that damn thing away from you," Antonio snarled.

"Go for it, little man," Red replied, snapping it again.

Akira sat quietly, staring at the computer. Since the accident, Akira had been in two modes. Either she was begging Charlie to fix her, or she was staring at the computer, lost in her thoughts. Nyx assumed she had plenty of thoughts but couldn't put them in the proper context. Nyx tried to imagine not having emotions. Now, with feelings so intense, she'd have gladly shared them, but there was no way to do that.

Then there was Charlie. Charlie the robot, albeit a very complex and marvelous machine, should have been their anchor—all logic, no premonition. The stalwart of determined rationality stood at the counter, tapping his fingers in what seemed like a random pattern, but after listening to it for several minutes, Nyx realized it was a complex cadence that never varied, although it took several minutes to complete and repeat.

Nyx said, "Am I the only one feeling something has gone wrong?"

Antonio said, "I don't know. I mean. They know what they're doing, right? I mean, Derrick and Anna are trained, right? And Miriam, she's like super smart. And it's not like they would let Rebekah do the fighting." He paused. "Right?"

Akira looked up. "You saw how Derrick handled the soldiers in the classroom."

Nyx said, "I missed that."

Red said, "I didn't see it, but I saw what Derrick did on the football field. However, I have a bad feeling too."

Akira looked at Nyx. "Lucky you. Sorry, I need to stop doing that. I may not feel like you do, but I keep running scenarios through my head." She stopped.

"And?" the others asked in unison.

"None end well."

Nyx looked at Charlie. "Charlie? What do you think?"

Charlie looked at Nyx, then at Akira. "What she said."

19

THE ELEVATOR LURCHED UPWARD FOR what could be his last few minutes on earth. But he could not let that happen for many reasons. He didn't want to die. That would be true for most people, except a few souls who had given up hope, which was sad, and for some odd reason, he wondered if he could do anything about that. However, losing hope was not his problem. He had two immediate priorities that created a need to succeed rather than die: Anna and Miriam. Putting them in further danger wasn't acceptable.

L. Linda had put herself in danger. He should not have let that happen. He didn't know why he did, except he was so shocked to learn she was an assassin—well, he simply had not been thinking straight. Although L. Linda insisted on drawing the robots into the garage, he felt responsible for her being in that situation.

Derrick had been mulling this over since before they left the base. Facing Prime alone was the best situation. This Prime was the easiest for him to destroy because he wasn't there to kill the assistant. He was there to save him. If this Prime was anything like the hideous things in the glass tubes, destroying it would be no more difficult than blasting a robot.

The problem was the element of surprise. Or, more accurately stated, the lack thereof. Miriam might have successfully disrupted the cameras and other security measures, but Derrick could hear the weapons firing below as Anna and Miriam destroyed the replicas. That meant Prime heard it too. There was no guarantee the monster was even on the 18th floor. It might be in another part of the building. No problem, because when the bombs detonated, Prime would be buried in the rubble.

However, Stanley Mires might not be on 18 either, and that would be a problem, and there would be nothing Derrick could do. No time. They would have failed to save the man. Yet another thing Derrick added to his list of potential failures. He should have controlled how the bombs were detonated. Instead, he had let L. Linda make that decision.

There might be robots on the floor to protect Prime. He could shoot robots, no problem. If he got them, before they got him. So, he used the same strategy that worked on the 17th floor. He positioned himself near the edge of the door, making himself as small a target as possible.

The elevator stopped, but the doors didn't open. Perhaps the open button had to be pushed but it was on the other side of the elevator—yet another mistake.

But then the doors slid open. Silent and slower than most elevators. Whether by design, lack of maintenance, or the age of the building, Derrick did not know. As the room came into view, he saw two robots—a man sitting at a computer—presumably Stanley Miles, and Prime—just as monstrous as the ones in the tubes, all staring at the backdoor that led to the stairs.

Sparks were flying into the room from near the deadbolt. Either Miriam or Anna had gone to the door, while the other killed the replicants. They had not followed the plan, but he was here first.

He had the drop on them. All of them. But he only needed to kill three of them.

Derrick blasted both robots.

The man turned his head. Derrick held a finger to his lips.

Prime turned slowly and deliberately.

It smiled, at least Derrick assumed it was a smile. It might have been a grimace or a snarl. No way to know for sure.

"This is a pleasant surprise. Derrick King. Please, come in." Prime made a welcoming gesture.

Derrick felt confused and at a loss for words.

Prime said, "Your friends will join us soon, it appears. We must finish our business quickly."

"We don't have business," Derrick said. He held his weapon pointed at the floor. Keeping it pointed at Prime was a better tactic, but this seemed okay for now.

"I understand your perspective. But I'm afraid you don't yet understand what is happening here."

"It's you who doesn't understand. Your robots are destroyed. Your replicants are gone. I'm taking Mr. Mires, but you are going nowhere." Derrick didn't know why he said it that way, "going nowhere."

The revelation that the replicas were destroyed seemed to give Prime pause, but it recovered quickly. "Well, bravo. Bravo, Mr. King. You have exceeded expectations. However, you are still not understanding your situation. Let me tell you the first disappointment." Prime motioned toward the assistant. "This is not Stanley Mires."

Derrick said, "Nice try. It won't work." Derrick considered raising the weapon, pointing at Mires in case it wasn't a trick. But for reasons he couldn't explain, the weapon didn't move. Training, he thought. He was fast enough to kill them both.

The man stood. "I'm not Stanley Mires. I'm Justin Hoff. I just started in this position, although I have worked for Prime for many years."

Prime said, "There. Now, perhaps you're beginning to understand how you've misjudged. And that is not your only mistake, but it's the only one you have time to learn. Mr. Hoff, kill him."

20

THE BARISTA SET AN EGG, SAUSAGE, and cheese sandwich in front of Scott and then left. Sue had been doing most of the talking. She didn't ask him questions. She probably didn't think he'd tell the truth. Scott had learned that Sue had a teenage boy still in school, and that her husband had died in a timber accident ten years ago. She had not remarried, and dating wasn't an option. It was a small town.

The door chime sounded. John entered, nodded to Scott, and strode to the counter. A few minutes later, he came over and spun a chair out from a nearby table. "Am I interrupting?"

Sue smiled. "Would it matter?"

John chuckled. "No. But if I am, I'll tell Mary to make my sandwich to go."

Sue said, "You're not interrupting. Not this time." She winked at Scott.

John said, "They are inside."

"Who's inside where?" Scott asked.

"Something is happening at Prime's Seattle Headquarters. We think it's Miriam and Derrick."

Scott glanced at Sue and then back at John.

"Relax. I trust Sue. She doesn't share what shouldn't be shared."

Sue stood. "Thanks for the vote of confidence, John, but I have appointments."

Sue put her hand on John's shoulder. He patted it. They exchanged a look that conveyed a hidden message that Scott could not interpret. Intimate but not romantic, a shared bond of some sort. Perhaps not uncommon, but alien to Scott.

Sue smiled and said, "I'm here every morning, Scott from Bakersfield. Maybe I'll see you again."

"Okay." Scott didn't know what else to say. His future still in flux. He took a bite of his sandwich, watching Sue walk out. His interest in the sandwich had faded, given that Derrick and Miriam were inside Prime's building, but it gave him a moment to think.

John said, "Anna, Miriam, Derrick, and a girl we don't know arrived in what appears to be a Prime aircraft. Someone stayed back, perhaps Rebekah Ford."

"How do you know this?"

"We have someone watching the building. We have eyes on all the sites except the one we can't locate. We have people working overtime trying to determine its location."

"Why Seattle?"

"Derrick, Miriam, Anna, and Rebekah were in a town important to the Resistance. The leader asked them to get their asset out of Seattle if they could. I think they went there because of that. But there's a problem."

There were many problems with the kids going into Prime's building, so Scott found it hard to imagine one specific difficulty that concerned John more than the obvious. "What problem is that?"

"We have not seen our guy since last night. We don't make contact every day, but he usually steps outside at least once, typically early in the morning or last thing at night to let us know he's okay, not that anything is okay while that devil still exists. Unfortunately, we think they loaded him into an aircraft last night. We aren't sure because they had a bag over the person's head."

Scott understood the devil meant Prime—no need to clarify that. "That does not sound good. I hope your guy is okay, and I'm glad they are trying to help. However, I can't picture Derrick being involved."

"How so?" John asked.

"In Pacific Edge, he was only concerned about himself."

"Kind of self-centered?"

"To put it mildly."

"Yet, you put yourself at risk by not killing Derrick and Miriam when their test cycle ended. Why?"

Scott sipped coffee. It was a good question. One he had asked himself. One he had not yet answered. "We called it deconstruction."

"They ended up dead."

Scott looked down and whispered, "Yes. Deconstruction was worse than just killing them."

"You've been involved in the test subject program for a while. Right? Were you involved—in the deconstruction of other test subjects?"

Scott could not raise his eyes. He nodded, fearing his voice would fail him if he spoke. It seemed so long ago, yet he could not envision how he did it. He was a monster, convinced the test subjects were not people, just property. Prime's property. Everyone on the team feared Prime, every one of them. Yet, it was more than fear. They also worshipped Prime. Saw him as some sort of celestial being—God-like. For many years he was right there with the others. Blinded to the truth of the program, convinced what he did was for the greater good. Eventually he saw that the greater good was anything that benefited Prime.

It was a cult.

It was at that moment, Scott realized that destroying Prime did not resolve the problem. There was still an entire cult to deprogram, and it would be no easy task.

"So, back to my question. Why did you take the risk of saving them? I understand you and your wife watched Miriam and Derrick. Anna went to a different home, not under supervision."

Scott nodded again, but that wasn't an answer, and he felt confident John would persist. "Miriam and Derrick believed we were their father and mother. A combination of wiping their memory of the time spent in the program and implanting false memories. We placed Anna in another home. Her parents were not part of the test subject program. They thought it was an experiment with adoption. They agreed to allow her to participate in a special program that would involve her being with us several days a week."

"And where's your wife?" John asked.

"She is probably helping them find me. If Prime determines she can't, he will kill her."

"I'm sorry."

"Don't be. She wanted to terminate the kids. Keeping them alive was my idea. All the years we had them, she wanted to deconstruct them and move on to the next test. I stood in the way. To say we grew apart is an understatement. I started planning my escape a couple of years ago. She had no idea."

John said, "How did you know they would exile Derrick?"

"I didn't. I planned to leave if I ever lost the battle to keep them alive, but I had no plan to get them out." He paused. "There was nothing noble in my scheme. I planned to save myself, not them."

Mary brought John's sandwich and set a fresh Americano in front of Scott. "Anything else?"

John said, "Thanks, Mary, you're the best."

Mary smiled and left.

John ate for a moment. Scott finished his sandwich, wondering where this was going and wishing they'd get an update on the kids. With each second, Scott's anxiety grew. He could not explain his motives for preventing Miriam and Derrick's deconstruction. He could not even explain why he felt so strongly about them surviving now. All he knew was that it wasn't just about killing Prime so he could live. Not anymore.

"Derrick's exile wasn't your plan?" John asked.

"Not originally. I never thought getting either of them out was a possibility. We were running a test. I designed it, knowing I had to keep up the appearance of an ongoing program. I recruited Marcus Carver. Of all the students in school, I figured Derrick would both worship and fear any Carver. I gave Marcus a few bucks, but he would have done it for free. He didn't like Miriam or Derrick. He hoped one of them would start something. He was itching for a fight, assuming he could handle Derrick easily. Embarrass him in front of the entire school. He wanted to hurt Miriam too, but I said that wasn't an option. He agreed, reluctantly. I thought it was completely safe. Not for Marcus. If he took a swing at Miriam, he would have been injured and embarrassed. However, I thought Derrick was incapable of standing up to Marcus and certainly not to protect Miriam. Derrick didn't like Miriam. She embarrassed him with the way she dressed and how she challenged instructors."

John nodded, not in a way that suggested he agreed, but only acknowledging that he understood.

"It was the Tribunal's decision to exile him?" John asked.

"It was their decision, but my idea. My wife wanted to deconstruct them. She was way beyond done with them. I told her to let me handle it, and then I stretched the truth well past reality."

"The Tribunal knew they were test subjects?" John leaned forward, suddenly menacing. "They knew about deconstruction?"

"Of course they did."

"That's good to know. The Resistance will put them on the prosecution list. Should we prevail, there will be justice. I can assure you of that."

Scott's blood ran cold. "Am I on that list?"

"Fair question. You are, but you're protected—for now."

Thoughts of Canada returned. "I'm not proud of my past."

"Back to the question at hand. Why did they exile Derrick instead of playing it safe and ending them all?"

"That might be the only good thing I've done. I convinced them Derrick's action demonstrated a flaw in the program and sending him into the outside world was the best possible test." He paused. "I convinced them if my final report said they had failed to take advantage of the most vital experiment possible—what Prime would do to them would make deconstruction seem enjoyable in comparison."

John smiled. "I like your thinking."

"I did what I had to do."

"To keep them alive?"

"At least for another day."

"Did you help Miriam escape?"

"Inadvertently. I knew Patel. This might sound odd. You might think I'm lying again, but Patel and I became…" He paused. "Not friends exactly, more like acquaintances. We met occasionally, and I assumed he was in the Resistance. I told him I wanted out. He helped plan my escape, gather supplies, and arrange a way to get out of town when the time came. His daughter told him about Miriam, and he wanted to meet her. I owed him, so when an opportunity arose, I arranged for Patel to come to our house. Miriam convinced him to help her get access to the network. But the escape was all Miriam. It was amazing, complicated, and dangerous. She set us up, and we all fell for it."

"All very interesting. So, back to my original question. Why?"

"Why did I not follow protocol and end the program?"

"Nice way of saying, 'why didn't you torture and kill them?' But yeah, that's the question."

"I don't have an answer. I wish it was because I wanted to save them, but that's not true, not back when we first took them to the house. I still don't understand it. Not exactly. It's not just one thing. Part of me saw an opportunity to take the program further. Prove myself to Prime, I guess. Make a name for myself, for sure. It was at least 90% self-serving. I'm not proud of that, but it's true."

"And the other 10%?"

Scott shrugged. "Best I can do is say, I saw something in Derrick."

"But you said he was self-centered. You said it shocked you that he stood up for Miriam. Not very endearing, really."

"True. That's why I can't explain it. Although, when they were still in the testing facility, Derrick did some unexpected things. Things that indicated he would not be a successful test. He was called Number Seven back then. One day, he did something contrary to his programming. Another test subject, Number Three, was being bullied. That was the testing they did on her. One day, a keeper was tormenting her. Derrick was under control of the 1984 chip and shouldn't have paid attention. However, he grabbed a chair and clubbed the keeper in the back. I started thinking differently about him that day."

"Keeper? Is that what they called you?"

"That was my title, my job."

"What about Miriam's escape? What were your thoughts when that happened?"

"Shocked and a little angry. Miriam locked us in the house, so for a short time, I was trapped. I feared they'd kill me before I could get out of town. But also, I felt—I don't know—proud." Scott shrugged. "That was the end for me in Pacific Edge. I had to run, and fortunately, Patel's people came through."

"And here you are," John said, rocking back in his chair.

Scott paused. A small smile crept onto his face involuntarily. "I was doing a pretty good job of getting away until I came here."

"I'll give you that. I still can't believe you got here as quickly as you did. But I knew you'd be coming through. The Resistance helped you, but they also wanted to find you, which is why they alerted me that you were on the trail headed this way."

"I should have started farther from the trail. That wasn't my smartest move."

"Perhaps. But the wrong people might have spotted you before you made it to the trail. The bottom line is that you're still alive. So far, so good."

"Good point."

"Scott, I'll be honest. I have a problem."

"I understand."

"I'm not sure that you do. I could let you go. We got what we wanted. Let nature take its course, so to speak."

"I'm okay with that. It's more than fair." Although Scott felt a little disappointed, his goal was Canada, but thoughts of staying here for a while had taken root.

"Let me finish. I can't do that because Derrick said he wanted to talk to you. Being a man of my word, you're not leaving until Derrick either has that opportunity," John paused, taking a deep breath, "or isn't around to do so. When I mentioned you working for me, it wasn't a legit offer. It was to put you in a bad spot. You know, lying about going to Yakima."

"It's not a problem. I was scared. I'm sorry about the lying."

"In the spirit of being honest with each other, about last night. I fed you a steak dinner and put on a good show. It was just that—a show. I thought making you comfortable gave us a better chance of gaining your trust and cooperation."

Scott didn't say anything for a moment. He drank some coffee instead. Where he'd felt a little disappointed a moment ago, now he fully understood how much he hoped this would work out. Working for John, walking the streets in this beautiful small town, it was all so different from what his life had been. He embraced staying here more than he had admitted to himself. "I understand. What you did makes sense."

"Here's the thing. I don't need more help. Even if I did, I can't afford it. Not with the bite Prime takes."

"It's okay. I'll figure something out." Scott had no idea what he'd do. John wouldn't let him leave, and he had no place to live and little money. He could go back to camping along the trail. Check in with John every few days to see if Derrick and Miriam are still alive.

"Would you let me finish? It's a genuine offer now. I can't afford to pay you much. I've got a small house that's vacant. Nothing fancy. Free meals at the brewery and here. I'll work a trade here. I want you to start first thing Monday morning."

Scott stirred his coffee, deep in thought. "I'm stunned. I'd like that. Please, just treat me like a regular employee. You don't have to, you know, like last night."

"How do you think I treat employees?"

Scott chuckled. "I didn't mean anything by it. Sorry."

"My employees are like family. Mind you, it takes a while to learn the job. It will take time for my staff to trust you. But I'll put everyone straight first day. Give you a fair chance." He paused, then asked, "How do you feel about facing Derrick?"

"Honestly?"

"I hope that's what we are doing now."

"I'm scared. I've seen him train. He could kill me easy enough."

John nodded. "That sounds honest."

"But there's more. I want to say I'm sorry." He paused, gazed out the window, and wiped a tear from his eyes. "I doubt he or Miriam can forgive me, but they deserve an apology."

Scott couldn't say more. He drank lukewarm coffee and waited for John to speak. He tried to read his thoughts. He could not. After several minutes, he asked. "When do I learn my standing with the Resistance?"

John looked as intimidating as he had ever looked during Scott's time with him. "I can answer that question, but you won't like it. They still might bring charges against you."

Scott nodded, just a little, in acknowledgement.

John said, "I'll send someone around to help you get settled. All we can do is see how things play out."

21

DURING THE PAST FEW WEEKS DERRICK had learned that nothing was perfect, which contradicted his beliefs while living in Pacific Edge. As it turned out, going to Seattle first was unnecessary because Stanley Mires wasn't there. It was some new guy. Derrick believed he only had to deal with Prime. Mr. Mires would be an ally, not an enemy.

The new assistant, Justin Hoff, followed Prime's order, reaching for a pistol in a desk drawer. Perhaps Derrick's decision wasn't all bad because neither Prime nor Hoff noticed the sparks from the stairwell door had stopped. Anna had finished cutting the lock. Or perhaps the cutting device had stopped working.

On a positive note, Prime was hideous enough to kill for its looks alone.

However, none of Derrick's analyses improved the situation. Hoff's gun cleared the drawer and moved in a slow arc toward Derrick.

"Stop!" Derrick held up one hand. The other, holding his weapon, still hung at his side. He'd pushed the power slide to stun, which would allow him to shoot Hoff without hesitation.

Hoff glanced at Prime. Prime signaled him to wait.

"Do you have something to say, Mr. King?" Prime asked.

"Yes." Derrick tried desperately to think of something to add. "Uh, well. I'm turning myself in."

"Surrendering?" Prime asked.

"Yes."

"Then why do you have that weapon?"

"Oh. Uh,—I had to fight my way here to surrender." Derrick realized that sounded lame as soon as the words left his mouth. He had momentarily forgotten that he wasn't a good liar.

On a positive note, he noticed the stairway door was open a few inches.

Prime seemed distracted for a moment. "Mr. Hoff, is there a problem with our network connection?"

Hoff set the gun next to his keyboard and started typing. "Something has happened."

Prime said nothing for a moment. "Disconnected."

In trying to formulate a response to Derrick's surrender, Prime recognized it was not connected with the central Prime. Miriam's software virus had worked. How long other Prime locations might go without detecting the loss was still unknown. There was important information here, but Derrick couldn't see it. Not yet.

"So, how about it? I surrender, and you leave everyone else alone. Deal?"

Prime didn't seem to hear him. It was as if it were lost. Like a boat in a storm with no motor. Unanchored, at the mercy of the wind and waves.

Then something changed. "All contact is lost. I am the only remaining Prime and therefore initiate Protocol One. I assume command of New America."

Things still moved slowly for Derrick, which was good, but his response was sluggish.

Prime said, "Mr. Hoff, kill him now!"

Hoff raised the weapon; his face twisted in grim determination. The gun made a slow arc toward Derrick.

At the same time, the door behind them opened. Anna stepped in first. Her pistol raised in a two-handed grip.

What if he was Stanley Mires? Perhaps Prime was playing a joke, although instinctively, Derrick suspected Prime lacked a sense of humor. The gun continued its arc toward him. If Anna and Miriam had been listening at the door, Anna knew this was not the man they had come to save. She also knew Prime had ordered the man to kill him.

But what if this man was with the Resistance? Perhaps he'd take this opportunity to kill Prime himself. Then he, Anna, and Miriam wouldn't have to kill anyone. They could just go to the roof, jump in the aircraft, and get L. Linda.

He saw her green eyes and heard her voice. *Promise me.*

Yes, he had promised.

But he had not raised the weapon toward Prime. Why? Derrick didn't know.

The gun had now moved beyond the point where shooting Prime was likely. It was clear the man intended to kill Derrick. It was at this moment that Derrick decided he had to stun the guy. Although stun probably wasn't the best setting in this situation because he didn't know how effective the weapon was.

He wouldn't find out because Anna fired twice, hitting the man in the back. Hoff looked surprised. His eyes grew wide, and a red stain spread across his chest. The man realized he was dead a split second before Derrick did. Hoff leaned forward, then fell to the floor.

Prime turned. "Fools! Look what you've done. Do you know how hard it is to find a good assistant? And for what? For nothing, I tell you. Do you think I needed Hoff to do the killing? Idiotic children. I can kill you myself in several ways. Something painful, I think. Release the gas!"

Miriam limped closer, holding the robot-killing weapon in one hand, her other hand pressed against her side, where a big wet red blotch grew. "Your defenses are offline."

Derrick forced his eyes away from the man's body on the floor. The blood spots had not grown much. Anna had hit his heart, stopping the pump immediately. This was their opportunity. He wasn't sure exactly what that meant, but perhaps they didn't have to kill Prime. His protections were gone. Now, they had the upper hand.

Derrick said, "Let's …"

But before he could get another word out, Prime screamed and ran at Miriam.

Miriam pulled the trigger, and a bolt of electricity cut through Prime's chest, striking a computer monitor and blowing it to bits.

Miriam yelled, "Run! We've got thirty seconds!"

22

ANNA KICKED PRIME. WHETHER TO ENSURE it was dead or whether from hatred, Derrick did not know. Perhaps it was both. Miriam, pale and wet, staggered to the computer console, still clutching at her side.

Miriam leaned in toward the monitor, making a quick entry on the keyboard, and then she yelled, "I said go! NOW!"

Anna ran toward the door. Derrick fell in behind her but heard a crash. Looking back, he saw a chair on its side and Miriam on the floor.

Time was no longer moving slowly. Now the clock in his head spiraled down to detonation. If L. Linda placed the charges correctly, and Derrick had no reason to think she had not, the building would crumble with them inside. It was nothing personal. The building would simply comply with the force of gravity.

Derrick scooped Miriam in his arms and ran to the stairwell, taking two at a time, his adrenalin-rich blood receiving another boost. According to the clock in his head, he would reach the roof a second or two before the detonation. If Rebekah wasn't in position, they had no chance. The door was about to close when he reached the top.

Turning his back, careful not to smack Miriam's head against the metal doorjamb, he burst onto the roof. The aircraft hovered inches above the surface, and Anna stood in the open doorway, waving him in. Had there been any cushion regarding the time before detonation, Derrick would have been scared senseless about Miriam's injury, but there was no time for it.

Which made him wonder why he had time to replay L. Linda's last words— "Promise me"—she had said as he stared into her piercing green eyes.

Derrick was within a couple of feet of the aircraft doorway. He had made it. In a moment, they would fly down to the tunnel, pick up L. Linda, and rocket to the base where the mechanized hospital unit could heal Miriam's wound. Miriam wasn't moving. Derrick handed Miriam to Anna at the aircraft's door. He turned to study the scene one last time. Unbelievable as it seemed, they had been successful. They had destroyed Prime. In fairness, Miriam had ended Prime, and Anna had killed the man about to kill him, but they did it.

Until they didn't.

At least the getting away part.

Derrick felt the shock wave in his feet before he heard the blast. The building tilted and fell at the same time. He put both arms out as if balancing on a tightrope. Suddenly, the aircraft was back in front of him. Rebekah was keeping pace with the falling building. But the building fell, and swayed, which Rebekah did not match because the timing would be impossible.

When the building swung toward the aircraft, Derrick jumped.

But he missed.

He grabbed for the edge of the doorway, finding just enough purchase to hold him there for a moment, but he couldn't hang on. For a split second, he was falling to his death. He thought his life was supposed to flash before his eyes. Instead, he only saw L. Linda Maxton.

Anna grabbed his arm. Anna had him, but he could feel his sleeve ripping. He reached up and got one hand inside the door. This time, he had a decent handhold. Anna pulled, and he got his other hand on the edge.

He feared he would pull Anna out if he lost his grip. "Let go! I could pull you out if I fall."

"I've got you," she shouted, grabbing his arm with both hands, bracing her feet against the hull, then thrusting her legs straight, hauling him inside.

Derrick crawled into the aircraft. "Go to the tunnel! We have to get L. Linda!"

Rebekah said, "Headed there now."

Derrick dashed to Miriam. "You're wounded."

Miriam, pale and sweating, fastened her safety harness, murmured, "I'll be okay. Find L. Linda and let's get back to the base."

Dust rolled up from below, enveloping the aircraft and blocking the external cameras. Derrick was disoriented and feared Rebekah was as well. They might run into another building or perhaps fly into the ground.

They broke into clear air. Rebekah had flown out over the water and was coming back toward the tunnel. The aircraft slowed and descended. Before they landed, Derrick opened the door and jumped out. He turned a full circle and then raced around to the other side of the aircraft.

He could not see the building because of the cloud of dust, nor could he see L. Linda.

Anna came to his side. "Where is she?"

"I don't know. She should have been out before we were. Unless …"

Derrick started down the road that was built over the tunnel. An explosion rattled his bones, and the concussion almost knocked him down, and a wave of super-heated air followed. Then another and another, each getting closer.

"What the hell?" Anna said, standing at his shoulder.

Shielding his face, Derrick said, "She's blowing up the tunnel."

"Why?"

"I don't know. Perhaps she's being chased and tossing bombs at them."

"At who?"

"Whoever is chasing her. Robots probably." He started toward the tunnel opening.

Anna grabbed his arm. "What are you doing? We need to get out of here. There will be all kinds of cops and such here soon."

"I need to get L. Linda."

"You need to get in the aircraft. We'll watch the opening and come back for her."

Another explosion tossed the roadway into the air and then collapsed into the tunnel.

"Okay. But we have to go back for her."

He climbed in, as did Anna. The door closed, and they rose into the air, then jetted south. "I can't see the tunnel," Derrick said.

The aircraft stopped and spun around. "Coming on screens now," Rebekah said.

Several screens lit up inside the cabin, including one in front of Derrick—another explosion and then another. Only 50 yards of roadway covering the tunnel remained. Behind it was a mushroom-shaped cloud rising high into the air and a smaller, straight line of destruction where there was once a tunnel.

"Come on," Derrick whispered.

Anna sat next to him. She touched his arm.

"Come on! Where are you!?!"

Another explosion, which would be the last—the tunnel was gone, including where they had entered.

Derrick strained against his seat restraints, trying to stand. "NO!" He paused. "NO! NO! NO!"

Anna said. "She didn't make it. We've got to get out of here. There's nothing we can do for her. We have to get Miriam to the base medical unit before it's too late."

Derrick slumped, his head between his knees, sobbing. "My fault. All my fault."

The computer's voice came over the speakers, calm and unaffected by the circumstances. "Enemy aircraft detected, launching from a nearby location. Time to intercept 3 minutes and 20 seconds."

"Get us out of here," Anna said, stroking Derrick's head.

"On it," Rebekah said, choking back tears.

Part Three

1

HAVING FINISHED EATING BREAKFAST, Stanley sat at an espresso shop on yet another floor. Specialty shops were scattered throughout the facility, although most were dark and unmanned. He sipped a mocha. He'd had enough black coffee and needed something easier on his stomach, which had been unsettled since he was escorted to the roof of the Seattle building last night. Passing people smiled and nodded like he was an old friend, but none offered to join him. Chief of Staff promised to be a lonely job.

His position was lonely in Seattle as well, but at least he found reasons to get out, and when that happened, he often met a member of the Resistance to slip them a note. He didn't know those contacts, nor did he spend time with them, but it made his existence less isolated. Although a rarity, occasionally he'd pass a sidewalk café, where he would stop for a coffee. Now, it was unlikely he would ever see the outside world. The thought of spending the rest of his life underground with no real human interaction felt overwhelming.

My life sacrifice for the greater good, he thought as he nodded at a man passing by. Many things crossed his mind as he sat alone with his thoughts. Not least of which was: *How did I rise to this level?* It came as a surprise when he became Prime's assistant in Seattle. He had performed every task Prime asked of him, even when it meant the death of innocent people. However, that was not unusual. Most people did as Prime asked. Those who didn't were no longer around. He had invented many justifications: if he didn't do what Prime asked, Prime would kill him and do it himself. That was the standard rationalization he often used. However, he often wondered if being dead would be an improvement in his situation. His favorite, the one that eased his conscience most, was: *For the Greater Good.*

Unfortunately, it was unlikely he'd know if anything he did contributed to the greater good. He would revisit that notion sooner than he would have ever predicted.

Speakers in the ceiling came to life with a sizzling bit of static followed by ear-piercing feedback, and then a robotic voice said, "Chief of Staff Mires to Prime's Command Center, immediately."

He didn't know where the command center was. He had only been on the bottom floor. However, that did not feel like a command center. He left his coffee on the table and sprinted to the elevators, assuming Prime could see him on the cameras. If he was delayed, Prime could see that it wasn't for lack of effort.

A woman followed him. She said, "Not that elevator—the other side."

Stanley dashed to the other side of the large concrete tube that ran through the center of the facility.

The woman pushed the down button, and the doors slid open. "You want the button marked CC. Only this side goes there." She stepped back.

"You're not coming? I still don't know the way," Stanley said.

"I can't. The elevator won't move with me in it. I am not authorized for the command center. Few are."

And with that, the doors closed, and the elevator descended. He felt certain he was going deeper into the earth than the 19th floor. When the elevator stopped, the doors opened into a wide hall. A plaque on the wall pointed left to the Command Center. Laboratories lined each side of a long hallway.

What is this place? Stanley wondered.

At the end of the hall, stood thick doors made of solid metal, no windows or signs. He heard hissing as the doors swung open. Two robots stood sentry, holding heavy weapons unlike any he had ever seen. Neither robot acknowledged him. They seemed inoperable. He felt sure they operated just fine, but apparently the programming that opened the doors also told the robots he was authorized to enter.

Prime stood with his back to the door, watching huge monitors on a curved wall. This room was unlike where he had met Prime the first time. He was wrong to think the facility had only 19 floors. Rows of workstations faced the wall, and the floor sloped like a theater.

Without turning to face him, Prime said, "I have lost connection with Seattle. Please see if you can reestablish the network."

Stanley sat at a desk off to one side. He wasn't sure if it was a desk he could use or if it was Prime's. Better to have Prime tell him to get up than to delay following instructions. The computer required no password, which did not surprise him. If anyone got this far, which was beyond comprehension, passwords were the least of Prime's worries. The location of this place wasn't merely unknown. The security was off the charts.

Stanley made a couple of quick checks. He knew the computer system inside and out. It wasn't a complex system. Stanley never understood that. He assumed it was because Prime believed it was untouchable. There were ample reasons to support that thinking. But he could not understand why Prime needed him for this. In Seattle, Prime could use voice commands to operate the computers. If there was a physical problem, robots could do most repairs, and if robots couldn't, there was a small team of vetted technicians.

After a few moments, Stanley said, "I believe the connection was lost."

Prime stared at him. "Somewhere between here and Seattle?"

"No, sir. It was terminated there."

"I see. Perhaps an equipment failure."

"That makes sense, sir." He felt certain it was not an equipment problem, given how the signal ended, but he would not contradict Prime. Stanley had installed an industrial-strength filter between his brain and mouth when in Prime's presence.

Stanley said, "The connection has been reestablished, sir."

"Well done, Mr. Mires."

"I didn't do it, sir. Someone in Seattle did."

Prime turned back to the monitors. Stanley watched with interest. He felt certain something out of the ordinary had happened. What that might be, was a mystery.

The mystery revealed itself. A girl—Miriam King—leaned close to the camera and whispered. "We are coming for you."

There was a blur of motion, and then a boy came onto the screen. It was Derrick King. Derrick kneeled, and when he stood, he held Miriam King in his arms. Her side was soaked with blood. Carrying her, he disappeared into the stairwell. A few seconds later, the image shook—just slightly at first, and then violently. The Seattle Prime flew across the room, lifeless like a rag doll, and slammed into the wall. Then the screen went blank.

"Get that signal back," Prime demanded.

"It's gone, sir." Stanley focused on keeping his voice steady and his expression blank.

"What do you mean, it's gone?"

Stanley thought there was no safe way to answer the question. So, he simply said, "I don't think the building is still standing. What should I do, sir? Should I contact the media? Tell them to withhold this story?"

In a voice much calmer than anticipated but with a tone more menacing than anything Stanley had experienced in Seattle, Prime said, "Let the story play out for now. What I want you to do is find those kids."

2

Saturday, April 10, 9:31 a.m.

HAVING DECIDED THE TOWN STILL NEEDED a police presence, Collins and Martinez rode together in his car, roaming the streets, looking for anything or anyone out of place. Fletcher let Browning and Patel borrow a Chrysler 300 with paint that had faded from black to gray. Fletcher took a gleaming Lime Green Mustang that loped when it idled and growled when he touched the accelerator. The town was quiet for a Saturday. Although it was spring break, kids were notably absent. Scared and confused after the military came looking for Potterville High School students and rumors that five students had drowned in the river. Word had spread that someone had murdered Jimmy Priest and his parents. Potterville was on a voluntary lockdown, and that suited Collins just fine at the moment.

Lori said, "I've been thinking."

"Okay." Bill paused, not sure he wanted to hear more. Lori had been flirting with him—well, more than flirting. He had sent the wrong messages, telling her it was inappropriate because she was an employee, and that he didn't want to lose her as a deputy, not because she was the best deputy he could imagine, although she was a good officer, and she'd killed the assassin, so there was that. His main objection was her salary. No one was getting rich working for a living. The only rich people were those families who had willingly given James Carver their businesses and estates. Prime had allowed them to retain a small portion of their fortunes. Those who fought Prime ended up dead, and Prime took everything. However, being a deputy paid more than where Lori worked before, watching the cash register and running the gas pumps for older people who were unable or unwilling to do it themselves. Additionally, Lori did most of the auto repairs as well. She was a talented lady. Bill had never questioned that. He knew she'd make a good officer, but he hired her to give her a better life. If she quit, what would she do?

"Are you okay?"

"Yes. Well, as much as I can be, under the circumstances."

"I thought maybe you were visiting a distant planet, given the look in your eyes."

"Sorry. I drifted off. What did you want to talk about?"

"I've been thinking about earlier."

Here it comes. "Don't worry about it. I understand. You were under a lot of stress."

She stared at him for a moment. "We all have been, but what's that got to do with anything?"

He was going to mess this up, and he knew it. "Just saying, you don't need to worry. I understand."

"And just what is it you understand?"

He paused for a moment. "Well, maybe I don't understand. What are you talking about?"

"Assassins. I'm talking about assassins."

"Oh." Another long pause. "What about them?"

"What if there are more?"

"More, as in around the country?"

"No. Well, yes, but what if there are more in Potterville? Like right now. What if there were more than one in the first place? They would expect to have heard from Pixie by now, and since they haven't, it makes sense they would send someone to see what happened to her."

Bill took a deep breath. Relief washed over his body. Assassins. It was only assassins. "You think that's possible?"

"Don't you?"

Bill hesitated. "I suppose. Jason didn't seem to think the military would return and said nothing about assassins."

"He didn't elaborate, but he mentioned being concerned about assassins," Lori said.

"Right. I remember now that you mentioned it. I wish he was here."

Lori said, "Me too. He and L. Linda."

"Yeah." Bill fell silent. One painful moment avoided, another one unavoidable.

"I'm open to suggestions. If there's another assassin, we are easy targets driving around like this."

"I think we should go by the Priest's house."

"What are we looking for?" Bill asked.

"I don't know."

Bill didn't think looking at the Priest's place would help, but it couldn't hurt. If it made Lori feel safer, he was all for it.

Bill drove a random route. When they arrived, he didn't slow down, nor did he look at the house. "Anything?" He asked after they had driven past.

"No. Go through the alley."

A tremor coursed through Bill's body. He didn't know why. The alley wasn't more dangerous than the street. Was it? Yes, it was. Alleys are private spaces, meant for hiding things like garages, trash cans, and tool sheds. "Do you think that's necessary?"

"I wouldn't ask if I thought it wasn't. I have a bad feeling."

Bill didn't respond, but he turned down the alley. It was all one big bad feeling to him. He slowed. It's narrow. Things crowd it, making passage difficult. Most of the back yards had six-foot cedar fences, including the Priest's home. They were not going to see anything.

Lori said, "Stop."

"What? Why?"

"This is the Priest's place. I can't see the house."

Before Bill could protest, Lori stepped out and peered over the fence.

"Well?" Bill asked when she got back in.

"The rear door is open."

Bill didn't say anything for a moment. "That doesn't prove anything. Maybe the coroner left it open."

"You know better. Henry is anal-retentive. That's what makes him good when an autopsy is required."

"Do you want me to check the house? I'll go to the front and then move around to the back," Bill said.

"No. If the killer was inside, you'd be dead before you got to the door."

"What should we do then?"

"Nothing for now, but we need to warn the others."

They planned to rendezvous at the bistro at 9:30. Bill and Lori were already seated and drinking coffee when Browning pushed through the front door with two bags of groceries. Patel followed with two more. Donna had been feeding them. Browning felt it was the right thing to do.

Donna walked through the door from the kitchen, wiping her hands on a dishtowel. "What do you have there?"

"Groceries," Browning said, sitting his bags on the counter. "I hope we got the right stuff. We replaced what you've been feeding us."

Patel said, "And we thought the kids might like a few things. I hope that is okay."

"It's not. I told you I had it covered," Donna said.

Browning said, "You did, and I said we would help."

"You're a stubborn old coot. You know that?"

The bell rang as Jack walked in, taking off his cap and running his hands through his hair. "What'd I miss?"

Bill said, "Nothing important. Just Donna's unique way of thanking Coach and Allen for buying groceries."

Jack said, "Turn on the TV."

"Something's happened?" Donna asked.

"Does it pertain to the kids?" Lori asked.

"Ain't sure, but probably," Jack said.

Donna pointed the remote toward the flat-screen TV mounted on the wall. As it flickered to life, she asked, "What channel?"

"I don't think it matters," Jack said.

The sound was off but wasn't needed. The screen displayed thick black smoke, boiling up from the rubble of a building. A headline scrolled along the bottom of the screen:

The Prime Headquarters in Seattle, Washington, was destroyed by an explosion this morning. Officials have not confirmed the cause but expect it was deliberate. There are no known survivors.

Donna said, "Holy crap. Do you think the kids did that."

Patel said, "Miriam said they planned to destroy Prime in Seattle. She did not say how."

"Where would they get explosives?" Collins asked.

Browning shook his head. "Must be a coincidence. Probably a gas leak."

"I don't believe in coincidence. They could have found an abandoned mining site. There used to be mining operations out there." Fletcher nodded toward the mountains.

"L. Linda would know where to place the explosives," Lori said.

Everyone stared at her.

Lori shrugged. "She told me how to kill the assassin. Jason had that arsenal of weapons. There is more to those two than we realized."

Bill said, "You have a point."

Donna brought the coffeepot. "You're not asking the right questions."

Bill held out his cup. "What right questions?"

"Are they okay? That's what I want to know."

Patel said, "Miriam could contact us using the VPN."

"Do you think she will?" Browning asked.

Patel thought for a moment. "Probably not."

"Why not?" Lori asked.

"Still too dangerous. We might not hear from them until it's over."

"What if something happens to them?" Donna asked.

Jack said, "If Prime remains in power, we will know something happened to the kids, but we won't know what. We will only know that it wasn't good."

3

REBEKAH FLEW FARTHER OUT OVER THE ocean than she had on the way to Seattle. A nearby airbase had launched fighter jets within minutes of the detonations. Whether the launch was a coincidence or a response to the bombing was uncertain. Anna thought the launch was a coincidence, a training exercise. However, Rebekah, unwilling to risk finding out, flew low and fast, farther west than necessary, to ensure no aircraft followed them. They could not lead them back to the base.

Anna said, "I don't see anything on the seven tracking systems. We need to head in. Miriam needs medical attention ASAP. Can we contact the base?"

Rebekah said, "We can, but Miriam thought we shouldn't."

Anna looked at Derrick. He had left his seat and was sitting next to Miriam. "What do you think, Derrick?"

Derrick made no indication he had heard her, yet there was no reason he wouldn't have. He was catatonic.

Anna said, "Can I call them from my station?"

Rebekah said, "I can give you the communication console, but I don't think it's a good idea."

"Give it to me. The medical unit must be ready."

"Roger that. Giving you the comm."

Anna said, "You're sounding like a pilot already."

"Or something out of an old sci-fi movie."

Anna fiddled with the communications controls. She found an option to scramble the message. She didn't know if they would understand her at the base, but it was worth a shot.

Anna keyed the radio and said, "Nakamura? Can you hear me?"

The radio crackled. "Anna?"

"Yes. I'm making this short. We are coming in fast. We need the medical unit ready for a gunshot wound. We need immediate medical transport when we land."

"What's happened?"

"Just be ready. There in ten minutes or less." Anna closed the channel and hoped no one picked up their transmission. "Miriam is looking worse with each passing moment."

The aircraft banked hard left and accelerated hard. "Heading inland now."

Instead of staying low, Rebekah took the aircraft to 55,000 feet and descended almost vertically into the desert 100 miles southeast of the base. She leveled out 20 feet above the desert floor and rocketed toward the hangar. The aircraft performed precisely as it was supposed to and flying it was not unlike a video game at which Rebekah was proficient.

Rebekah had found and activated the stealth mode, causing the window-like displays to go dark. Rebekah could see their approach because of the pilot's headset. The others saw nothing. Rebekah had not activated their headsets. When enemy jets were in the air, taking time to learn such things seemed like a poor idea.

To say the aircraft slowed rapidly was an understatement. It was just shy of slamming into a wall. The force tossed Derrick into the front of the aircraft, where he braced himself between an operations station and the wall. Rebekah would have warned him had she seen him leave his seat. Next time, she'd check. Perhaps next time he'd be in better condition to think clearly. Right now, he was a mess.

"A robot is waiting to take Miriam. It has emergency medical stuff." Rebekah spun around, pulling the headset off. "Derrick, get Miriam to the stretcher."

Derrick stood but said nothing. He didn't move toward Miriam. It was as if he was in a daze.

Anna shook her head and unbuckled Miriam.

Derrick came up behind her. "I'll take her."

Derrick paused. Put his arms one way, then another. Tears leaked down his cheeks, whether for Miriam or L. Linda, he was unsure. Probably both. Sliding his arms gently under his sister, he lifted.

Miriam screamed. "Stop!"

Derrick stepped back. "I'm sorry. They told me to carry you to the stretcher."

Miriam looked around. "Are we back at the base?"

Rebekah kneeled in front of her. "We're back. Can you stand? We need to get you to the medical unit."

With her hands on what served as arm rests, Miriam pulled herself forward, grimacing. "Did the explosives work?"

Derrick choked. Miriam stared at him.

"Nothing left but rubble," Rebekah said. "Let's get you taken care of."

With Rebekah and Derrick's help, Miriam stood on trembling legs. The last remnants of color drained from her face. She scanned the aircraft as she put her arm around Rebekah's shoulders. "Where's L. Linda?"

Derrick fought tears, but one traced down his cheek.

Rebekah said, "She didn't make it."

"What do you mean, didn't make it?" Miriam asked.

"She didn't get out…."

Miriam took a step. "She might have cut out on us. I wouldn't blame her. It was a difficult situation. It won't get easier. L. Linda may have seen that coming."

Derrick sank into a nearby seat.

"What's up with him?" Miriam asked as they exited the aircraft.

"He took L. Linda's death hard," Rebekah said.

Nyx watched as Rebekah helped Miriam to the gurney. Miriam's uniform shirt was off, and her white t-shirt was soaked with blood. Miriam had been shot. Her pale skin and blood made that clear, but she was walking with some assistance. Derrick exited the aircraft. Nyx ran and threw her arms around him. Miriam's injury didn't seem to warrant Derrick's sobbing. Anna exited next. She looked fine.

Nyx held Derrick at arm's length. "Talk to me."

Derrick wiped his face on his sleeve and shook his head. Not in a 'no, I'm not talking to you' but in an 'I can't talk about it' sort of way.

Nyx looked at the open door to the aircraft again. "Where's L. Linda?"

"She—she didn't—make it."

"What do you mean, she didn't make it?" Nyx paused. "Oh, my God. You don't mean…"

Derrick nodded.

Derrick hugged Nyx and then went to the gurney. "I'm sorry, sis. I …"

Miriam moaned, patting his hand. "I'll be okay. Make sure we are ready to go." She paused, looking around. "Where's Charlie?"

"I'm here," Charlie said, stepping forward. "The QR-3 will take you to the medical unit."

"I need you there, Charlie," Miriam said.

"I will be there soon. The medical unit is prepared for you."

"I need you to come with me now. Please, Charlie."

"Very well," Charlie said.

Miriam looked at Derrick. "When the weapons are ready, find another aircraft." She paused, looking around until she found Anna. "Anna, go to the operations center and study the other sites. Make assault plans. I'll be there soon."

Anna nodded. "Where are we going next?"

Derrick interrupted. "We need to rethink this. We've already lost one person. It's too dangerous. Prime will be ready for us next time."

"That's why we need better plans," Miriam said, adding, "New York."

"I'll see what I can come up with," Anna said.

Derrick started to talk, but Miriam held up her hand. "We'll talk later. This might be a surprise but getting shot hurts like hell. Just do as I asked. Go to the flight simulator with Rebekah and learn to fly the aircraft you find."

"But…"

"Just do it, please."

Derrick nodded.

The robot left with Miriam. Charlie followed, as did Rebekah and Anna.

Derrick remained in the hangar. He wasn't sure he could walk. Red, Antonio, and Nyx made a semi-circle in front of him.

Antonio said, "I heard you say L. Linda didn't make it. What happened?"

Derrick knew this was coming. No way around it. He had to tell them something. They needed to know, but he could not tell them everything. None of them could know the truth about L. Linda Maxton. He did not realize how heavy carrying the truth would become.

"We were in the parking garage below the building. We had planted the explosives." Derrick didn't mention L. Linda did it herself. That would lead to more questions. "Miriam and Anna were inside a room where there was a computer terminal. A bunch of robots showed up. L. Linda said she'd draw them into the garage while we went up after Prime. She was supposed to meet us where we entered."

"She wasn't there?" Antonio asked.

Derrick wiped his face again. "Right."

"Crap," Red said.

"It's my fault," Derrick said.

"How is it your fault?" Nyx asked.

"I shouldn't have let her go. I should have done it, or we should have fought the robots together."

Red said, "L. Linda is an odd girl and stubborn. She probably didn't give you a choice."

Nyx said, "She should not have been making the decisions. Being weird doesn't make for the best judgement. We've seen what Derrick can do. She should not have put Derrick in that position. It's her own fault."

At this moment, Derrick understood the burden of carrying L. Linda's secret. He wanted to tell them she was much more than they knew. She was more capable than any of them, including himself.

Instead, Derrick said, "She was fearless. I hope you'll remember her that way."

"Maybe L. Linda made it out," Antonio said, adding, "L. Linda might have just left. With her dad getting killed, it might have been too much."

"I don't think so. The bombs collapsed the tunnel she would have taken. Rebekah was waiting there while we were inside. Rebekah would have seen her if she made it out."

Nyx took Derrick's hand. "I can't believe she's gone. I wish I'd gotten to know her better."

Derrick nodded. He had to be careful that he didn't say something that would lead to further questions. He might slip up and say something that should remain undisclosed. L. Linda Maxon's secret had become his secret, and he'd already proven lying wasn't his forte. The less said, the better. It would be best if he could forget L. Linda Maxton, but he knew that wouldn't happen.

"I need to find an aircraft and check on Miriam."

"How can I help?" Nyx asked.

"Someone needs to tell Akira."

Antonio said, "We'll go with you, Nyx."

"Thanks. I can't predict her reaction. If there is one."

Derrick gave Nyx's hand a squeeze. "See you in a bit," he said, turning and walking away. He didn't look back. He didn't want to be alone yet didn't want to be around people. It felt as if a cloud was closing in around him, cold and dark. Night without stars. Life without hope.

After walking for several minutes, lost in his thoughts, Derrick realized he didn't know where he was. It didn't matter. This had to stop. That much was clear. He was sure everyone was thinking the same thing. Stopping Prime was important. That was true. Destroying Prime's Seattle headquarters was a strong message. Perhaps Prime would rethink its plans. He was right about that, but he wouldn't learn about it until later.

His despair grew until he could walk no farther. Putting his back to the wall, he slid to the floor. What had they done? They killed a man and Prime. Maybe more, because they could not be sure the building was empty. His training was for self-defense. Not killing people. Although Anna had killed Prime's assistant, he still felt responsible. He couldn't remember what he was thinking, taking so long when he stood in Prime's presence. Talk their way out? Or learn something that could change Prime's course? Neither made sense because there had not been time for a conversation.

Shooting both men, one in Mexico and one in Seattle, was self-defense. That was clear. So why did it feel wrong? He couldn't answer that question. They had destroyed a building. They were the aggressors in that. Derrick knew nothing about the law, but it seemed intuitive that blowing up the building was illegal. Even if they destroyed Prime, which seemed more unlikely now than it ever did, they would never be free. The law would hunt them down.

They were trading a comfortable prison in Pacific Edge for a real one, where it was unlikely they served prime rib or eggs Benedict.

Something floated in the back of his mind, blurred and fuzzy. Then it came into focus. What were they going to accomplish? Prime had ruled the country for decades. It wasn't great, but there was order. Destroying Prime meant destroying stability. Derrick had an unrealistic understanding of history. The history he'd learned was undeniably false. The Chosen and James Carver had distorted it, rewritten it. Nevertheless, the old United States failed. That much was certain.

The chaos would prove worse than the order of today. A cure worse than the disease.

Anarchy was the best they could hope for if they succeeded. More friends could die going forward with Miriam's plans.

The answer was obvious. He had to surrender.

There was only one problem.

He had made a promise.

4

MIRIAM WANTED A PAINKILLER. A strong one. She wanted the hole in her side to disappear. This place could accomplish both. She was sure of it. But it wouldn't happen that way. That's why Charlie had to be here.

"Stay with me Charlie," Miriam said.

"I am not permitted in the treatment unit."

"Says who?"

Charlie paused, if one could call it a pause. "It's not the protocol."

"I need you in the room with me."

"The unit resources do not require my presence."

"You saved Akira."

"That was different."

"I get that, but you have to be with me."

"Do not be afraid. You will be fine. They developed the unit for injuries like this."

She was inside the unit, but the door was still open. "I'm not scared. Just come in. You can leave soon if that's what you're worried about."

"As you wish, but I do not worry."

The machines started their diagnostic procedure. At least, that's what Miriam assumed was happening. A flat arm that looked like a large butter knife with a lit edge moved back and forth over where the bullet passed through her side. A small robotic arm extended with a mask for her face. The voice said, "Place the mask over your nose and mouth, relax, and count backward from ten."

Miriam blocked the mask with her hand. "Tell them no, Charlie."

"But this is the protocol. It is harmless. It is anesthesia, which creates a controlled, temporary loss of sensation or awareness induced for medical procedures."

"I know what anesthesia is. I don't want it. How bad is the wound?"

"The bullet did not damage vital organs, but you lost a significant amount of blood and tissue damage will leave a scar. The unit can repair the damage. You shouldn't even have a mark. The entire procedure should take less than 24 hours."

"I don't have 24 hours. Tell them to use a local anesthetic and stitch me up."

Charlie paused. "The treatment protocol does not recommend using that method. The recommended plan will ensure complete healing without pain and scarring."

"I don't care about scarring or pain. I'll take an aspirin. We need to strike fast. What's the quickest they can get me out of here?"

"The fastest treatment can be accomplished in 15 minutes."

"That's the one I want."

"I cannot order that treatment."

Miriam took a deep breath, grimaced, and clutched her side. "Remind me not to breathe. Why not, Charlie?"

"It is not the best treatment for your injury. The recommended treatment is best."

"Charlie, I appreciate you wanting the best for me."

"It's not personal."

"Whatever. I also want what's best and staying alive trumps having a scar. Our best odds are to hit Prime as quickly as possible. Do you understand, Charlie? I want to live. I'll never be safe while Prime exists."

"You are safe here."

A mechanical hand holding a syringe extended, poking Miriam in the side near the wound.

"Ouch. You could warn a person."

Charlie said, "If you had placed the mask over your face as instructed, you would be asleep now."

Miriam stared at Charlie. "Did I hurt your feelings?"

"Charlie does not have feelings."

Miriam knitted her eyebrows. "Charlie, we are not safe. Not even here. Remember, James Carver murdered your supervisor. If Carver and Prime are the same, Prime will eventually figure out we are hiding here."

"Charlie can protect us here."

"Protect us? Charlie, you're using third person again. Akira, is that you talking?"

"I cannot control everything she says," Charlie said.

"Akira, not even Charlie can protect us. I must do this. Believe me, it's not what I want to do. It's what I must do."

"It is too dangerous. L. Linda was killed. There are seven more places where Prime must be destroyed. It's impossible." Akira/Charlie paused. "I don't want to lose you."

"I understand. I'm sorry. I don't have a choice."

"I don't want to be alone."

"We'll figure something out. I trust Charlie will do that," Miriam said.

"Miriam, this *is* Charlie. I don't want to be alone again."

Having two personalities in one robot was confusing. Miriam took Charlie's hand. "I don't want you to be alone. We'll figure something out. But first, we must destroy Prime. It has to happen fast. Besides, I start school in Potterville on Monday. Spring break is almost over." She winked.

Charlie made a chuckling sound. "You made a joke. Analyzing. It works because the importance of beginning school on Monday pales in comparison to the monumental task of destroying Prime. Adding that you were shot makes it humorous."

"Charlie, that's your best laugh yet."

"Thank you."

"No. Thank you. Now, can you check on Derrick?"

"I can. Derrick very much needs checking on."

Charlie did not have to search for Derrick. The robot knew Derrick's location. Academically, Charlie understood Derrick was suffering from Post-Traumatic Shock Syndrome caused by a combination of events: the fighting, the bombing, and L. Linda Maxton's death.

But Charlie did not know the extent of Derrick's psychological injury, and it was something the medical unit could not treat. Soldiers suffered from it back when there were soldiers here. They had special doctors and a few medications for treatment. Those treatments helped, but there was no cure. Charlie understood the symptoms and causes like a person might understand the principle of an electronic motor without being able to fix one.

"Mr. King!"

Derrick looked up. "Charlie. You startled me."

"I am certain that is true."

"Why did you call me Mr. King? I thought you had reprogrammed that."

"Because you did not respond to Derrick the first three times I spoke to you."

"Oh. That bad, eh? Sorry." Derrick pushed himself into a standing position. "I'm a little overwhelmed." He looked around. "Where is the operations room? I need to get weapons ready."

"QR-3s have prepared the weapons and ammunition."

Derrick nodded. "Thanks. Maybe I won't be in too much trouble with Miriam then. How is she?"

"The injury is not life threatening, but she refused the standard care."

"She what?"

"The standard treatment would take 24 hours. Miriam wants to attack the next Prime soon. I advised against it."

Derrick thought for a moment. "Against the treatment or the attack?"

"Both. But Miriam is—stubborn."

"Tell me about it."

"Okay. I told Miriam the standard treatment would be the best course…"

Derrick laughed.

Charlie stopped. Then made that chuckling sound. "Now, I have made a joke. You made a rhetorical statement. You did not want me to explain the details of my conversation with Miriam."

"Correct, Charlie. But thanks. I needed a laugh."

"You are welcome, even though I may not be able to duplicate the event. Because I did not see the humor until you laughed."

"You're the best, Charlie. You know that? Want to know something?"

"Yes. Of course, however, I have access to a vast base of information." Charlie paused. "I did it again. Did I not? You do not mean that you have data that I cannot access. But this time it is not as funny but rather reveals my inability to understand things in a human context."

"Lighten up on yourself. You don't have access to this because it all happened in my head. When we first came here, I didn't trust you. I didn't like you. It made me mad when Miriam called you a 'he' instead of an 'it.'"

"But now?"

"I like you a lot, Charlie. I'm glad you're here. We'd be lost without you."

Charlie paused. It was longer than the typical Charlie pause. Perhaps because he could not find information on this in his database.

Finally, Charlie said, "There are more aircraft. There is one that may be more suited to your needs. Miriam wanted you to learn to fly it."

With that, Charlie walked away. Derrick followed. They took an elevator to Level Two. In a large hall, there was a small cart. Smaller than the carts they had used to get to the Circle Transport. Charlie got behind the wheel, and Derrick sat next to him. Charlie sped down the wide corridor. Although the cart had controls, Charlie didn't use them. Apparently, the machine had a wireless connection that Charlie used.

They stopped at a set of double doors, which opened as they approached. Charlie pointed to a flight simulator. "Just get into the seat, and the simulator will teach you how to fly. This aircraft is as easy as the ones you have been using. They were designed so that anyone could operate them in battle, which reduced training time for pilots."

Derrick stepped into the simulator and sat. The safety harness engaged, automatically securing him. The simulator rose into the air.

Charlie turned and walked toward the door. "This simulator is much more—realistic than the other." He turned and then turned back. "Derrick?"

"Yes?"

"I like you as well."

5

STANLEY HAD RETURNED TO WHAT passed as a sidewalk espresso shop, back in the main dining area. Pam wasn't there. She'd gone to a lab somewhere in the facility. He didn't make conversation with the man making coffees. No reason to make him uncomfortable. Since Stanley was not officially working, there wasn't much else to do. He didn't need more caffeine but sat sipping espresso from a demitasse cup. The coffee was rich and much better than expected in an old government facility far below the earth's surface. He wasn't hungry either, but in front of him sat a cherry turnover on a white China plate. The dishes were not fancy, but they were not paper or plastic. The waste would be a problem. They could wash these. Practical. The cafeteria used stainless steel trays with three compartments. Industrial. Since he would spend the rest of his life underground, he appreciated real cups and plates. Comfort here, would come in small doses.

He wondered what the original purpose of this place had been. One day, if he lived long enough, he would ask Prime. It would have to be a very good day. It was a rare day on which Prime was sort of happy. That wasn't right. Prime was never happy. That he was experiencing a slightly good mood was a more accurate descriptor. Winning puts Prime in a good mood. Unfortunately, winning typically involves people losing. With recent events, it would take a great deal of winning to change Prime's mood.

It would not be safe to ask such a question anytime soon.

Someone had destroyed the Seattle Headquarters.

It surprised Stanley that Prime had not killed him, not because there was any reason for Prime to blame him but merely because he delivered the news. Plus, he was the only human in the room.

Prime's calmness proved terrifying. "It would be safer for you to leave. I'll call if you're needed. Otherwise, I'll see you Monday morning," Prime had said.

Stanley wasted no time leaving before Prime changed its mind. He had no illusion of getting out of here alive, but dying today held no appeal. *Stay alive. See what happens.* He had once read that in a book or heard it in a movie. He thought it good advice.

He had hoped someone would stop and chat, but that was unlikely. He was too far up the food chain for everyday interactions. Funny, but he did not feel like an apex predator.

So, he sat alone, nodding to the occasional passerby, wondering who had destroyed Seattle. Destroyed was the correct word. In his room, Stanley had found a Seattle news feed. It surprised him the channel wasn't blocked. He assumed it was for everyone else. The news played a drone video of the headquarters building. Or, more accurately, what used to be the building. The Seattle version of Prime was dead, including the replicants awaiting to become Prime.

Prime had never experienced the death of a remote version of itself that wasn't planned. Stanley assumed Prime's lack of reaction may have been disbelief. The impossible had happened. Someone had defeated Prime, and even though it was only a fraction of Prime's network, it was Prime's first loss.

He and Prime saw Miriam King inside the Seattle headquarters, if, in fact, that was even real. But, if it was Miriam, how did she get in? Who helped her? That was Stanley's question. The Resistance? A likely candidate, and since Prime had demolished an entire town that was a key Resistance stronghold, a Resistance attack made sense. However, Stanley did not believe the Resistance would retaliate like that. The Resistance had not resorted to violence in the past. Plus, they assumed he was in that building, and he had hoped if the Resistance ever attacked, he would be spared.

However, history was replete with peaceful people provoked to violence after decades of oppression. The Resistance could not be ruled out.

Perhaps it was a nation-state. Mexico would be the most likely suspect. After all, Prime was poised to invade Mexico. Problems existed with that theory. First was the location. Seattle was a long way from Mexico. Dallas was much closer. A submarine near Houston, less than 250 miles south of Dallas, could deploy a strike force. On the other hand, Mexico's closest base to Seattle was 2000 miles away. Much more difficult. Mexico could have used a submarine, going up the west coast and into Puget Sound. But Mexico didn't have a fleet of military submarines. What they had were marine research vessels and a few for cleaning operations around New America oil platform leaks and accidents.

Mexico wasn't built for war. It had been a peaceful and progressive nation for decades.

But Mexico had strong bonds with Canada since they shared a potential threat from New America. Mexico was also in alliance with South America, Africa, Europe, and Asia, and all had grown tired of New America's aggressive invasions into developing nations. But Canada was a possibility if, for no other reason, than that they could pull it off.

There was an obvious flaw in that notion. Canada didn't conduct what New America called pre-emptive strikes. That's the term Prime used to justify wars in foreign lands. How some small developing country in central Africa posed a threat to New America was never explained.

It could have been an accident like a gas leak, or an earthquake could have toppled the building—two problems with both theories. The building did not use natural gas, and there had been no earthquake.

Stanley had exhausted every explanation he could think of except one—Miriam and Derrick King. But that seemed impossible. Prime was trying to kill them. They knew it, and Prime knew it. Prime had the upper hand and felt superior, and rightfully so.

The kids must feel trapped. For them it was kill or be killed.

If the kids did it, give them credit. Destroying one Prime Headquarters was an astonishing feat, duplicating it improbable, destroying five more impossible, and even if they could, that left this place.

Unknown and impenetrable.

6

Saturday, April 10, 11:50 a.m.

AFTER NINETY MINUTES IN THE FLIGHT simulator, Derrick felt ready and wanted to see the aircraft. The pilot could control everything, if necessary, but it was designed for two additional crew members: a navigator and a weapons specialist. The aircraft could also carry six soldiers. Derrick assumed they were just switching aircraft, and he did not know why Rebekah wasn't piloting, but he figured Miriam had her reasons.

He went to the medical unit next. Rehearsing the functions of the aircraft and how to execute them occupied his thinking, but not entirely. As time passed, he became increasingly worried about Miriam. It troubled him he had not been more concerned earlier—L. Linda's death had consumed him.

It felt like a nightmare, as if it couldn't be real.

But it happened. Derrick felt certain it would haunt him for the rest of his life. Perhaps with time, the ache would dull, but it would never leave.

L. Linda was dead.

Miriam was still alive, and that she had not been his primary concern bothered him.

He burst into the medical unit, but it was empty. He started hyperventilating. "Where is she?" He shouted at the empty room. The robots didn't answer. No one did.

He dashed into the hall and looked both ways. The halls extended beyond what he remembered. Charlie had opened previously hidden parts of the facility. L. Linda had convinced him to do that. She accomplished things that others could not. More evidence he would never shake the memory of her.

"Where is everyone?" He whispered. Typically, the likely spot was where the food was. They were teenagers and constantly eating. But they might not feel like eating with the loss of L. Linda. They might be in the room where Akira worked on the computer. There were several computers there, so everyone could work if necessary. Deciding that at least one person would be in the computer room, Derrick turned left, hoping he'd remember its location.

He had just passed an intersection when a voice called out. "Derrick."

Derrick spun to see Red. "Where's Miriam? Is she okay?"

"She's hurting but okay. That's one tough girl."

"Why isn't she in the medical unit?" Derrick asked.

"She refused the full treatment. They patched her up."

"I don't understand why she did that."

"She says we have to attack Prime. Hit fast."

"We must stop. It's too dangerous. We already lost…" Derrick couldn't finish the sentence. It was as if he could not say her name.

Red nodded. "Sorry, about L. Linda. We all loved her, despite how quirky she was. It's weird. She was friends with everyone, yet no one was close to her. None of us knew her well."

You have no idea, Derrick thought. "Where's Miriam?"

"She's in the operations room. They are waiting for you. And me. I was on my way."

Red walked back in the direction Derrick had come from. Derrick trotted to catch up. "Where have you been?"

"I was at the reactor."

"Problems?"

"Yeah. Nothing to worry about. I can handle it."

Red's tone indicated there was reason for concern, but Derrick didn't have enough space left in his brain to worry about anything else. He trusted Red. If Red said he could handle it, that was good enough for him.

Everyone was inside the operations room, eating pastries, drinking coffees or sodas. All eyes focused on Derrick and Red as they entered.

Miriam said, "We were about to send robots to get you."

Derrick rushed to her.

Miriam held out her palm. "Don't touch me. The local is wearing off, and it hurts like hell."

"I'm glad you're okay."

She nodded. "Just a scrape. Have a seat. Grab a Danish if you want."

Derrick did want. He wanted one very much, suddenly realizing he was famished. He grabbed two pastries and coffee from a large stainless-steel urn. He sat by Nyx. She smiled, not an, 'I'm so happy to see you smile,' but more like an, 'I hope we make it smile.'

Derrick said, "I could have been here sooner, but I went by medical first."

"I told you we'd meet here at 11:30," Miriam said.

"You did?"

Anna stood, a slight frown on her face. "Let's get started. We're already running late."

Anna stepped to the front of the room. Using a handheld device, she activated a large monitor that had been cycling through aerial photographs of enormous sand dunes. Why was Anna taking charge? Planning was Miriam's thing. But Miriam had been in the medical unit. Derrick didn't know how long the abbreviated treatment took. Perhaps that was why Anna was up front. Or maybe Miriam was in too much pain to stand.

Anna said, "The New York compound isn't in New York City, as I had assumed. It is in New York State, in the middle of nowhere."

Derrick said, "We can't keep doing this. It's too dangerous. We already…" He paused. "It's too dangerous."

Miriam said, "We don't have time for this discussion. You're right. It's too dangerous. We should not be doing this. We're just a bunch of kids. Granted, kids who stumbled into a cache of sophisticated weapons, but still, we are not trained, we have no legal authority, and we have no backing."

The one who was trained is dead, Derrick thought.

"Thank you," Derrick said. "So, we rethink this."

"Stop talking." Miriam paused. Lips pressed together. "We're doing this because we do not have a choice. I don't like it either, but we are out of options. We never had any in the first place."

Derrick said, "We could turn ourselves in. Prime wants us, not the others. If we surrender, perhaps Prime will leave the others alone. We could make that part of the deal."

Miriam's nostrils flared. "Is that what you were trying to do with Prime in Seattle? Cut a deal?"

"What are you talking about?" Derrick asked.

Anna said, "You froze. Had Miriam and I not been there, Prime would have killed you. The assistant almost shot you."

"I was watching the assistant. I still had time to shoot him. You jumped the gun."

Miriam said, "Even if that is true, Prime could have killed you."

Derrick said nothing for a minute. "I trusted you had turned off Prime's access to whatever weapons were in the room."

Miriam shook her head again. Slower this time, as if in disbelief. "Assumptions like that will get you killed." She paused. "Or get someone else killed."

Derrick couldn't breathe for a moment. She meant L. Linda. While he felt responsible for her death, he assumed others would tell him it wasn't his fault. He'd relied on that to keep his sanity. Now he understood. Everyone thought he killed L. Linda.

Miriam said, "Derrick, even if Prime agreed to leave the others alone, he won't. He will lie. If we turn ourselves in, he will kill everyone in Potterville. The missiles in Mexico were aimed there. Have you forgotten? He'll kill Akira, Red, Antonio, and Nyx. He will invade Mexico. Do you think I have not considered all our options? It's not just us I'm trying to save."

Derrick had never felt more ashamed. More than when he admitted to the entire school that he had lied to them. But there was a difference. When he admitted he'd lied, he felt relief. He felt better. There was no feeling better here.

Derrick nodded. "You're right. I'm sorry."

Miriam said, "Don't be sorry. Just fix it. Okay?"

Anna said, "Back to New York. What you're looking at is the target."

"It's just forest," Rebekah said.

"That's an old satellite photograph. Here's a recent one." A new picture flashed onto the monitor.

"It's just a blur," Rebekah said.

Anna said, "Right."

Antonio said, "They've blurred it on purpose."

"Right, again."

"Are you sure that's where it's at? I mean, what if it's just a forest?" Antonio asked.

"We know it's there because they blurred it," Anna said. "Besides. I've confirmed it through several eyewitness accounts."

"How did you find eyewitness accounts?" Red asked.

Akira said, "Internet."

"Is that safe?" Red asked. "I thought we had to stay off the internet."

Miriam said, "Allen Patel and Lawrence King developed a virtual private network or VPN. It prevents tracking."

"Are you sure it's safe?" Red asked.

"No. But it's the best we can do," Akira said. "Plus, I've taken other precautions Charlie helped me with."

Antonio said, "So there are eyewitness accounts on the internet? It seems like Prime would do something about that."

Akira said, "Not just on the internet. Dark sites. Resistance sites."

Rebekah said, "It's too bad we don't have contact with Professor."

Miriam said, "We do. Professor confirmed it is Prime's New York location."

"You found them? The people we flew out of that town?" Red asked.

"We did. They are okay but spread out. Planning their next move," Miriam said.

Red said, "I'm glad they are okay."

"Agreed," Antonio said. "That sunburn would have sucked if they ended up dead."

"Can we get back on topic?" Anna asked.

"How are we going to attack the place when we don't even know what's there?" Rebeka asked.

Derrick sat up. "Why isn't Rebekah flying the aircraft? She already has experience, and this other aircraft must be similar."

"Because she can't fly two at once. Rebekah will fly the aircraft we took to Seattle. Anna developed the plan. Let's let her continue." Miriam paused. "Uninterrupted."

Rebekah gave Miriam a quick salute. "Aye, aye, Captain."

Derrick slumped in his seat. He didn't appreciate Rebekah's bit of levity. He didn't like being separated from the others. They didn't trust him. The worse part was—he couldn't blame them.

Anna said, "So, as Miriam said, we are taking two aircraft. Derrick will fly ahead and scout the area. We'll develop our attack plan from photos he sends back and be ready to execute upon arrival."

Derrick raised his hand.

Anna frowned. "Yes, Derrick."

"I'm still not clear on why we are taking two aircraft. We could look at the area together and then plan the attack."

Miriam said, "We need the second aircraft. It's not the same aircraft. It is faster, which is why you are going first."

Anna said, "The aircraft we've been using. The ones Prime uses were designed for rapid transport. They have some weaponry, but nothing like the one you're taking. It's much faster, it can reach a low orbit altitude and can fly four times farther. Plus, its purpose is combat. Its weaponry far exceeds our aircraft and anything the military flies. Does that help make sense of it?"

Derrick nodded slowly and said, "Why don't we take two of them?"

Anna said, "There's only one like it."

Charlie chimed in. "It was a concept when James Carver was here. There was no prototype. Not even a mockup. Just a theory."

Derrick stared at Charlie for a moment. "You built it? Does that mean no one has flown it?"

"Correct and correct."

Derrick slouched farther down. "I feel safer already."

7

Saturday, April 10, noon

BROWNING HAD SENT HIS KIDS outside to play, which meant they were out in Fletcher's junkyard. Browning had tasked Terrance with supervising the younger ones. He whined, but a look from Coach ended that quickly enough. Browning didn't need everyone there. He didn't need anyone's approval either, but he asked everyone to be there anyway.

He picked noon because Donna was coming with lunch. She couldn't afford to feed them and close shop, but arguing with her was an exercise in futility, and it was hard to dismiss her logic. She didn't have many customers since word got out about the murders in town, so she could either feed them or toss the food when it spoiled. The groceries he and Patel bought would not compensate for her expenses thus far, but they would make it up to her when this was over—if they were still around to do so. And if they were not, well, then the food would have gone to waste anyway.

Browning waited until everyone was seated with their lunch. He stood, which seemed a little formal, but he wasn't sure how to get everyone's attention. The myriads of conversations diminished until an uncomfortable silence covered the shop. The silent part was new. The uncomfortable part was not. No one had felt comfortable since they had arrived at Jack's shop, and it had nothing to do with the accommodations.

Browning said, "I'll get right to it. We're leaving."

Collins wasn't surprised. If anything, he felt a bit relieved. "When?"

"As soon as the kids eat. We might take sandwiches. Eat on the road."

"Where are you going?" Patel asked.

"Northern California. I won't say where exactly. Not that I don't trust you. Well, just that I can't put anyone else in danger."

"That's fair," Patel said.

"I can't promise there will be room for everyone when we get there, but you and your family are welcome to come with us, Allen." Browning paused. "I'm sorry to do this. I must protect my kids," He looked at his wife, "and wife the best I can. I realize it's not safe anywhere, but this feels like the right thing to do."

"No argument from me," Collins said. "You should have left when they blew up your house."

Lori chimed in. "Don't you feel bad for one second, Coach." She paused. "We think there might be more assassins in town."

Bill said, "Lori, we don't know that."

"That's why I said, we think, but still, the kids should not be here. Go."

"Allen?" Browning stared at Patel.

"If you would take my wife and children, I would be forever in your debt."

"No!" his wife protested. "Take Samantha, please. But I'm staying with you, Allen."

He turned to her and took her hand. "Saavni, you must go. If anything happens to me, Samantha must still have you."

"Then come with us!" Saavni wept.

"You know I cannot. I must stay here because Miriam may need me. I must shoulder the responsibility of getting her into this mess. I cannot abandon her. It is not our way."

Tears flowed, but Saavni nodded.

Allen turned back to Browning. "Saavni can follow you in our car. It is gassed and ready to go.

"Not so fast," Fletcher said. "Your car is impounded. I ain't been paid."

"Of course," Patel said. "I shall get money from the ATM. How much do I owe you?"

"You ain't got enough money. I like that car. Might be a collector's item one day."

Patel stared at him. "It's an old, faded Corolla. It can't be worth much."

"It's worth a lot to me." Fletcher glared at Browning. "And how do you plan on getting to this mystery location?"

Browning looked confused. "We'll take our car."

Fletcher waved him off. "That piece of junk will never make it unless you're only going to Fort Hill. Besides, I never could figure out how you could fit your family into that thing. I always reckoned you never all went at once, and if you did, it took two trips."

Browning lowered his eyes. "We make it work."

"And now you want to take Samantha and Saavni with you? Where are you going to put them? In the trunk?" Fletcher slapped the table.

"Jack!" Collins protested.

Unfazed, Fletcher held up his hand. "Here are the facts. Someone set your house ablaze. You're on someone's radar. You think they ain't bright enough to have your license plate and vehicle description?"

Browning looked like a man torn between rage and heartbreak. Finally, he said, "I don't have any other options. I have to get them out of here."

"Damn it, man. I understand that. You think I'm stupid? You got options. You just have too damn much pride to see them. You got friends, Browning. Probably more friends than anyone I can think of. No offense, Donna."

"None taken," Donna said.

Fletcher continued, "So here's the deal, and I don't want any argument about it. You'll take a 15-passenger van that I have, but it ain't registered to me. It's gassed up and ready to go."

"Whose van is it?" Collins asked.

Fletcher hesitated. "It's mine. It's just not in my name."

Collins shook his head. "I don't understand. How is it yours and not in your name?"

Fletcher let out a deep breath. "It don't matter."

Browning said, "That's very nice of you, Jack, but I'm not sure. I mean. What if someone asks me where I got the van? I don't know what to say."

Fletcher shook his head. "Damn it. Fair point." He looked around the table. "I don't want any of you repeating a word of this. Got it? So, the van is registered to a non-profit." He paused. "Kids Kamp. There's a camp for kids with disabilities in the national park. The camp is free, but most folks can't afford to get their kids up there. When the camp opens for the season, I take the van to the counselors, and they use it to transport kids. Comes back here in the fall. I service it and get it ready for the next year."

No one spoke for a moment.

Lori reached over and took Jack's hand. "Jack, that's wonderful. Why don't you want people to know?"

"I don't want people thinking I'm a sentimental old goat."

"Not much chance of that happening," Collins said, smiling.

"I don't want to hear a word of this around town," Jack said.

"Sworn to secrecy," Donna said, as she hugged Jack.

"I don't know what to say," Coach said.

"You say, where's the damn key? And then you leave."

8

DERRICK STRUGGLED TO CONCENTRATE. His mind drifted from the aircraft he would pilot, which had never been flown, to Nyx's hand resting on his, to L. Linda's emerald eyes. They had no plan for New York because they did not know what the headquarters looked like. He hoped Anna knew more about Chicago. Miriam had already explained her strategy regarding the order of attacks. She wanted them all done today. Derrick thought that was too ambitious. Hell, Seattle was too ambitious, in his opinion. However, he had no viable alternative. They had started down this path, and he saw no way to reverse course.

Kill or be killed. That had become their incantation, as if repeating it would work some magical spell.

Two people had already died. L. Linda and Jason Maxton, five, counting Jimmy Priest and his parents. Nine, counting the four innocent kids killed outside the desert town. Ten, counting the police officer in Mexico. Fourteen, counting the soldiers. Sixteen, if he counted the assassin in Potterville and Prime's assistant in Seattle, but he wasn't counting the assassin. Perhaps he shouldn't count the soldiers either. What they were doing was atrocious, but they were following orders. Those orders got them killed.

Prime's orders.

Everything Prime touched turned to death and destruction.

The body count was high, no matter how Derrick added it up. It would get worse. He feared those he loved could be added to the count.

"Derrick!"

His head snapped up. Anna frowned at him.

"Have you heard any of this?"

"Uh, yes. We don't know anything about New York, so I'll arrive first and relay what is there, and then we'll make a plan."

"I had moved on to Chicago."

"Oh." Derrick sat up. "Then the answer is no. Sorry."

Anna was breathing hard now. Angry. He did not blame her. He was angry at himself and wondered what was wrong with him. He'd been counting the dead, and his distraction could easily add to the body count.

"I was saying Chicago is like Seattle, only the building is taller. Like Seattle, Prime occupies the entire top floor, called a penthouse. We assume the replicas are on the floor below the penthouse. Unlike Seattle, workers occupy the rest of the building. All the work involves Prime's empire. We cannot bomb this building. Too many people." She paused. "Prime is our target—not civilians. We will try to avoid casualties. Sometimes it won't be possible."

Derrick listened, wondering how much Anna was repeating for his benefit. He hoped not much, but hopes were useless in situations like this. Hoping didn't change the facts. Neither did daydreaming. It was not the time or place for that. Hoping none of his friends died, would not keep them safe. Only correct decisions and actions would make a difference.

The plan for Chicago was simple but difficult. They would land on the roof. Enter the building. Destroy Prime first, and the clones second. In and out. Anna made it sound easy. It would be anything but. They would decide what to do with the assistant if one was present. Miriam would install the loop software that might prevent Prime from knowing they were there. Unlike in Seattle, it would infect the entire network, sending automated replies mirroring Prime's communication by sampling previous dialogs. If it worked, Prime would not detect that its appendages were no longer viable.

Miriam's plan came into focus. Demolishing Seattle sent Prime a message. Miriam hoped Prime would be unaware of the next attacks because of her software virus, which would give them an element of surprise. Derrick could not fault her logic. However, he wondered if sending Prime a message had been a good idea.

Prime's response might not be what Miriam intended.

"Questions?" Anna asked.

Derrick raised his hand.

"We're not in high school, Derrick," Anna said.

Derrick lowered his hand. "You said you and Miriam would enter the building. I assume you meant the three of us. Right?"

"No. It's just Miriam and me. Rebekah remains in the aircraft." She paused. "There isn't room for the aircraft you're flying to land on the roof. Your corvette-class is much bigger. Didn't Charlie tell you?"

Charlie said, "I did not explain the size of the aircraft, and Derrick has not seen it."

"What am I supposed to do?" Derrick asked.

"I covered that earlier. You can't land there. Prime is likely on high alert, which means enemy aircraft might be in the area. You need to protect us."

"Okay." But Derrick didn't like it.

"Let's go over assignments." Anna looked at Derrick. "We made these decisions while you were in the flight simulator."

Derrick took a deep breath and nodded. The assignments seemed clear. He was flying the untested second aircraft. Rebekah was flying the other. Miriam and Anna were with Rebekah. Simple enough.

Anna said, "Rebekah is piloting, I'm on weapons, Miriam is navigating and planning."

Miriam shifted in her chair. Her face had grown pale.

"Derrick is piloting the second aircraft, the corvette, Antonio on weapons, and Nyx on navigation."

"Wait, what?" Derrick leaned into the table, ready to stand, but he didn't know what standing would accomplish. He had not anticipated the Potterville kids being in harm's way.

Nyx said, "We trained in our positions while you were in the flight simulator."

Antonio said, "No worries. I'm good to go, mi amigo. It's like a video game, and I'm good at it."

"He is," Red said. "I feel sorry for anyone going up against Antonio."

Derrick launched into a desperate search for alternatives. Especially how to keep Nyx out of the aircraft. "What about Red and Akira?" He hated the words as soon as they left his mouth. The meaning was transparent. *Why aren't we risking their lives instead of Nyx?*

Red said, "I'm all in if it were not for the reactor."

"Same," Akira said.

Derrick looked at Red. "You said it wasn't a problem."

Red shrugged. "I didn't want to worry you. But I can fix it. I think. You won't have a place to come back to if I don't. And Potterville is at risk again."

Derrick looked around the table. He did not know what he was looking for. Not exactly. Just a way out. Hoping something would jump out at him.

Nothing did.

Again, hoping didn't change the situation. Decisions were made. He wasn't involved in making them, but they made sense.

Now it was implementation. Do it right. Perhaps they lived another day.

Do it wrong. They would not.

9

IT COULD HAVE BEEN A LONG, tearful goodbye, but Fletcher wouldn't allow it. He hustled everyone into a big, non-descript white van and told them to get out of his lot. Samantha hugged her dad, and then, despite his feigned protesting, she hugged Jack Fletcher. She asked him to take care of her dad. Fletcher told her not to worry. He'd ensure her dad was okay. When they had disappeared down the street, Fletcher said he had stuff to do in the back of the shop.

When Jack returned, no one mentioned the redness in his eyes. No need. They could have discussed the redness in all their eyes had that been important. It was not.

Jack poured himself a coffee.

Donna said, "Would you turn on the TV, please?"

"Sure. What do you want to watch?"

"News. Aren't you curious about what's happening out there?"

Jack said, "Not the word I would choose."

"We might learn something about the kids."

"That's what I'm afraid of." Fletcher turned the small flatscreen TV toward the group and pointed the remote at it.

The first image displayed a smoldering pile of rubble. Several firetrucks sprayed water on it, but there was nothing left to save. The purpose was to limit the fire's spread and perhaps give the appearance of still trying to save Prime.

The sound was off, but a tape scrolling across the bottom of the screen told the earth-shattering news: "Authorities Confirm the Destruction of Prime's Seattle Headquarters."

Donna said, "They are still droning on about Seattle. I guess that means nothing else has happened."

"Something's happening somewhere," Fletcher said.

Patel said, "I agree but still find it hard to believe the kids did this."

Collins said, "Law enforcement will never stop looking for who was responsible."

"Not necessarily," Fletcher said.

"What makes you say that?" Collins asked.

"Prime needs to go. Accomplishing that is doing the world a favor. Whoever is responsible, if they succeed, they will be heroes, not villains."

Collins said, "Hold on, Jack. The law is the law. People can't just go around blowing up buildings and killing, well, destroying stuff."

"Not even something as evil as Prime?" Fletcher began. "Have you forgotten Prime had missiles aimed at Potterville or that Prime plans to start a war with Mexico? How many people have the kids saved already? The way I see it, you're either on the right side of this or you ain't." He paused, his face set in determination. "If you're on the wrong side, I suggest you get off my property."

Lori said, "I'm with you, Jack. It's time to end this nightmare we've accepted as normal."

"What are you suggesting?" Fletcher asked.

Lori looked at Patel. "Allen, do you know anything about Prime? How many places like Seattle?"

Allen said, "Prime exists in seven places: Seattle, New York, Chicago, Dallas, Denver, San Diego, and one place no one has found. The unknown location is where the one true Prime exists. But any of the satellite Primes is still Prime."

"Six known locations," Jack said, rubbing his chin. A couple days of stubble covered his face.

Allen looked puzzled and then said, "Right. One down, six to go."

Donna said, "Still seems impossible. Even if the kids could destroy those other locations, what about the one that's unknown? How will we ever get rid of Prime if that location can't be found?"

"You are not wrong, Donna," Allen said. "However, if anyone can find it, Miriam can."

Fletcher said, "Lori still ain't answered my question."

Lori didn't respond for a moment and then said, "San Diego is only a few hours from here."

"What are you saying?" Collins asked.

"I think I understand," Allen said.

"What were they going to do to Miriam, Anna, and Derrick?" Lori asked.

Allen said, "Deconstruction."

Lori snapped her fingers. "That's it."

Collins stared at her. "You're not suggesting…"

"I think that's exactly what she's suggesting," Fletcher said. "Allen, do you know the location of the San Diego headquarters?"

Patel nodded. "I do."

Collins continued staring at Lori. "Lori?"

Fletcher said, "Let me clear it up for you, Bill. She's suggesting we do a little deconstructing ourselves. Help the kids do what needs done."

Lori stared at Collins. "In or out, Bill. Think it through. Your answer has implications far beyond a drive to San Diego."

Collins said nothing. What Lori suggested was illegal and, therefore, contrary to his occupation and his thinking. But her meaning wasn't lost on him.

It was in line with Jack's threat to run him off, which wasn't a threat as much as a promise. If he didn't help the kids, Lori would help Fletcher send him packing. In Lori's case, sent packing wouldn't just be from Jack's shop; it would be from her life.

This was a pivotal moment on whether he was someone Lori wanted in her future. It was a defining moment for him as well. It wasn't about the law. In this case, which was rare, what was legal and what was right were not the same.

Collins took a deep breath. He enjoyed being sheriff, not because he was an authoritarian enforcer of laws, but because he thought laws defined right from wrong. He was quick to let little violations slide, usually just giving people a warning. His goal was always about keeping people safe and helping folks get along. But this was not minor. Not by any stretch. This was enormous. Sometimes right and legal are at odds.

Saving lives was the highest priority for a sheriff. He believed that.

"I'm in." Taking Lori's hand, Collins said, "I'm all in."

10

DERRICK LINGERED AS THE OTHERS filed out of the operations room. Everyone had gathered weapons and ammunition. Robots were loading the aircraft with additional ordinance while the meeting occurred. A new addition was a mobile medical treatment device. Charlie explained that the device could treat minor wounds and stabilize more significant injuries until the victim could be transported. Charlie included something else: boxed lunches. Derrick thought it was an odd addition. Lunch was such an ordinary thing for such an extraordinary task. Food had not crossed Derrick's mind, but even armies needed to eat. Of course, the only wars in decades were the preemptive strikes against developing nations that Prime ordered to expend war materials, so Prime's military industry could manufacture machines, missiles, and munitions, making those companies billions, which went back to Prime, who already possessed almost all the money.

It made little sense, and Derrick wondered if war ever had.

Derrick touched Red's elbow. "Hold up a minute."

Red turned. "I should get to the reactor."

"How bad is it?"

"I won't lie. It's not good."

"Are you sure? That you need to stay?"

"I'm sure it needs to be fixed."

Derrick studied him for a moment, searching for the correct words, which he failed to find. "You'd better fix it then."

"Plan to." And with that, Red turned to leave.

Derrick said, "And you'd better not get yourself hurt."

Red paused. "Right back at you, King. Spring ball resumes on Monday, and I'm looking forward to kicking your butt."

Derrick smiled just a little. "Good luck with that."

He walked toward the door and away from Derrick. "Doesn't mean we're friends," Red said, extending his middle finger.

Derrick caught up with the others at the hangar. The hangar door was open, and the heat invaded the cool shadows like a demon rising from the desert sand. The robots had both aircraft ready to launch. Everyone stood still, staring at the second aircraft. The one they flew to Seattle, like the first Prime aircraft they took to the coast, was an angular, flat-black machine that was longer than it was wide. It did not have wings or a discernible front or back. Derrick had not counted the angles, nor did he know the proper name. Was it a pentagon? Perhaps an octagon. He didn't know. The top sloped at a slight angle, and the sides matched the top but were almost vertical to a center line, where the sides sloped inward toward the bottom, which was shaped like the top. Stout legs supported the machine, and Derrick assumed they retracted when the aircraft was flying. What propelled the machine was not apparent. He had wondered about it but had not asked Charlie to explain how it worked.

On their first mission, Miriam had Charlie paint a large gray P on two sides, so it looked like an official Prime aircraft. Now, the P was an R. Derrick didn't ask what the R stood for. It could only mean one thing: Resistance.

If the first aircraft looked menacing, the new one was terrifying. Rather than a squared-off angular turtle, this machine was long and covered with tubes, rails, and spikes representing weapons and other devices. Where the first aircraft's means of propulsion were invisible, this craft had four huge jets or rockets aft and many smaller rockets on the sides, top, and bottom. It looked fast sitting still.

Derrick felt confidence building. They had more firepower with this second aircraft. They didn't need a second aircraft in Seattle. However, they knew nothing about New York other than that it was in the middle of a forest. Perhaps heavy security wasn't needed because of its remote location. The first mission was in motion before Miriam and Anna could do their own planning. Neither of them objected to the Seattle plan, indicating it was solid. No one except Derrick understood why that plan was good. An assassin developed it. Well, a would-be assassin. When L. Linda crossed his mind, his confidence faded. He should have saved her. She should be with them now. Then they would not need Nyx.

Nyx would be safe at the base. Except the base wasn't exactly safe either.

Derrick's fear multiplied with each passing moment. The aircraft looked fast and lethal, but it had never been tested. The unproven machine had a pilot who had never flown, assisted by a gunner who had only played computer games, and guided by a navigator who had never navigated.

What could go wrong?

Derrick took a deep breath. He could not change the past. He'd been telling himself that repeatedly, but it didn't help. L. Linda's death was his fault. All these deaths were his responsibility. Why had he hit Marcus Carver in the first place? That entire situation had been a test. A test Derrick had failed. His existence was part of Lawrence King's extended program. He didn't even understand what the man they called Father was trying to achieve.

Miriam approached, wearing new clothing and carrying another set. The lab-tech one-piece overalls were replaced with a military flight suit, including a helmet with a strange-looking apparatus on one side. "Here. Change over there."

"Over where? I don't see a dressing room."

Miriam shook her head—a you're so naïve sort of shake. "Behind that vehicle."

"It's kinda small."

"Big enough. Make it fast."

Derrick studied a device mounted on the side of his helmet. "What's this thing?"

"It does a bunch of stuff. Infrared, ultraviolet, X-ray to help identify hidden targets, and a range calculator to adjust for long-distance shots. Pretty cool, huh? Take it, but you won't need it. You won't be on the ground. You'll be protecting us from the air."

"About that," Derrick said. "I'm having second thoughts. I mean, the aircraft has never been in the air. It will probably have glitches. And I have never flown anything." He paused. "Not even a computer game. I'm not like Red."

Miriam nodded. "Charlie said the aircraft had been thoroughly tested. He wouldn't let us use it if he had doubts. I trust him."

"I trust him as well."

Using human pronouns to reference Charlie no longer bothered Derrick. What bothered Derrick was that those thoughts crossed his mind at a time like this. Not just because the thoughts were out of place, but because they were an attempt to block other things. For example, the intensity of L. Linda's eyes— and the promise he had made.

It was unlikely he could destroy Prime. But even if they were successful, which was a gargantuan proposition, the thought that he might forget her eyes was even more unrealistic. Derrick understood. All his weird thoughts were just a pathetic attempt to block his most painful failure. L. Linda Maxton was dead, and it was his fault.

Having undressed and redressed behind a machine that, in his opinion, left him far too exposed, he walked back to the others.

Miriam smiled. "You look like a pilot now."

Rebekah said, "I'll say. What are you doing afterward, big guy?" She winked at Nyx.

"Don't get any ideas. I got dibs on afterward," Nyx said, stepping to Derrick's side and linking her arm through his.

Miriam said, "Enough chit-chat. Time to roll. Derrick, you'll fly ahead. Nyx will take photos and send them to us."

Derrick said, "I'll fly low, so we get good shots."

Nyx said, "No need. We can stay high, so we are not detected. The cameras are designed for it."

Miriam said, "Right. Nyx has the flight plan. You won't have to do much unless there are enemy aircraft. There weren't any in Seattle, so you might not have much to do."

Derrick felt a bit of relief and a lot of guilt. *I'll just do nothing while you risk your lives.*

From the doorway of what Charlie called a corvette attack class machine, Antonio said, "Let's go. You won't believe this thing."

Careful to avoid her injury, Derrick hugged Miriam. "See you soon."

Miriam gave him a weak smile. "Yep."

Derrick took a quick look around the inside of the aircraft. There were seats for seven people who didn't have access to any controls. Probably for soldiers. The crew included the navigator, gunner, copilot, and captain. The captain could operate all aircraft functions. They were not fortunate enough to have seven trained soldiers.

They settled for zero soldiers and three marginally instructed teenagers.

Charlie appeared in the doorway and motioned for Derrick.

Derrick stepped out. A QR-3 stood behind Charlie with a cart. "What? We are ready to take off."

Charlie motioned to the cart. "Proper flight suits are required for this aircraft."

Derrick touched his chest. "But I just changed."

"That flight suit is inadequate. All of you in the corvette must wear special suits. You'd perish at the speed and altitude you're flying without them," Charlie said.

Derrick stuck his head inside the aircraft door. "Charlie says we need to wear special fight suits."

As they stepped away from the corvette, Miriam said, "Make it fast."

"Where should we change?" Nyx asked.

Miriam waved her arm. "Pick a plane or truck to stand behind."

Derrick wanted more privacy and was certain Nyx did as well, given the redness in her cheeks.

Derrick pointed. "You could go behind that door."

Nyx nodded. "Good idea."

Charlie said, "It takes two people to put the suit on. I will help Antonio. A QR-3 will check to ensure you have everything properly fitted and sealed."

Anna said, "I'll help Nyx."

A robot followed Antonio to a truck.

Miriam looked at Derrick. "I'll help you."

Derrick felt his face flush. Miriam was only his make-believe sister. That didn't change how he felt. Since his exile, he thought of her more as his sister than he ever did in Pacific Edge. Even so, she had only seen him fully clothed.

"Not the time to be bashful, brother. I won't look until you've got the suit on if that helps," Miriam said.

Derrick nodded and walked to the other side of the corvette. There wasn't anyone out in the desert to see him, or at least that was the theory they had been operating under. When they got to the other side of the aircraft, it felt like stepping into an oven. Miriam turned her back as Derrick stripped off his one-piece flight suit. He knew the aircraft flew high and fast, but the numbers meant nothing to him. When Charlie had rattled off speed and altitude, Red whistled and said, "That's crazy."

The first suit came off quickly. It was not dissimilar to the one-piece work overalls. This new suit was not so easy. The shoes were part of the suit. Getting his feet in wasn't as simple as putting on shoes because he had to force his foot through the pant leg, which was stiff and thick. It would have been easier if he had a chair.

"How's it going?" Miriam asked.

"Not well. I keep losing my balance."

Miriam glanced over her shoulder. Derrick was hopping on one leg, trying to force his other leg into the pants. Miriam backed up to him. "Use me for support."

Soon, he had both legs in, and the suit was up to his waist. He got his first arm in, but the suit was too stiff to get his second arm in.

"A little help?"

Miriam turned and helped with the second sleeve. Then she stepped in front of him and started fastening the front. Charlie was right. One person couldn't do this. There were three layers to secure, each appearing to create an airtight seal. Derrick's hands were already encased in gloves, making it impossible to do it alone.

"I'm baking in here. I hope there's air conditioning in that thing."

"It will be around -60 at your altitude. You might want a heater."

"Minus 60? That can't be right. How would you know that?"

Miriam completed the last fastener around his neck and checked the legs and sleeves. Both had oblong black boxes. "I looked at your flight plan. I remember stuff."

"Right. I wish I had your memory."

"You don't. I wonder what these boxes do."

"We'll ask Charlie." Derrick headed back into the hangar. The suit caused him to shuffle. Nyx and Antonio were finished. Nyx's suit was too large, but Derrick assumed it would still work okay. They would just be sitting in their seats. Despite the bulky suit, Nyx was still cute, although her pink stripe looked a little less vibrant than he remembered. Perhaps his memory was not accurate. Maybe it was something else.

Charlie reached into the cart and pulled out a rectangular black box, larger than the ones on his legs and arms, which Charlie affixed to ports on the front of his suit.

"What's that for?" Derrick asked, as Charlie put a similar box on Nyx.

"Suit management."

"What about these?" Derrick pointed to a box on his arm.

"Body management."

"What does that mean?" Derrick asked.

"Inside the aircraft, the suit will lock itself into connections in your chairs. Green lights in your display under the personal life support indicate the suit is functioning properly but that must not be confused with cabin life support. Before the cabin life support turns red, the personal life support must be green," Charlie said.

"Huh?"

Charlie attached the last box to Antonio's suit. "Humans cannot survive at the altitude you will be flying. Also, the g-force under acceleration and braking is beyond the capacity of humans without a special mix of intravenous drugs and specific atmospheric changes. The suit manages all of that."

"Intravenous? As in injections?" Derrick asked.

"Now you're catching on," Charlie said.

"I am? When and how do we get injections?"

"Starting right now," Charlie said, pushing a button on the bottom of the box on Derrick's chest.

A row of lights appeared along the edge of each box—red and then yellow. When the lights turned yellow, he felt a sharp pain in each arm and leg.

"Ouch!" Derrick said.

Charlie checked the boxes. "All green. The injection ports are now in place."

"You could have warned me."

Charlie stared at him for a moment. "I did."

After completing the process with Nyx and Antonio, Derrick started toward the aircraft.

Charlie said, "Not yet. You still need your helmets."

Charlie retrieved helmets from the cart. They looked like big black balls with holes for the head to fit in.

"How am I supposed to see?" Derrick asked.

Charlie said, "Pay attention. It goes on like this. See the arrow?" Charlie pointed toward a white arrow on the side of the opening. "Line it up with this arrow." He touched an arrow on the suit, barely visible in Derrick's peripheral vision. "Then twist it until it locks. There's a release underneath your chin. See if you can locate it. You must be able to put it on and take it off unassisted."

Derrick realized the suit felt comfortable, but he was in total darkness. Suddenly, there were flashes of light, a series of displays, and green lights, and then Charlie came into focus. "Wow. That's amazing. It's like I'm not wearing a helmet."

"Thank you," Charlie said, then asked, "How does it feel in there now?"

"Much better. I'm quite comfortable."

"You may enter the aircraft and take your position at the helm. You might feel the seat move you around some until it is fully connected. Just stay still. You will see a message indicating 'flight ready' when all systems are a go."

Derrick got into the pilot's chair. The connection happened quickly. The flight-ready message appeared inside his helmet and then vanished. He could see everything inside and outside of the aircraft as if he were sitting outside the machine. It was beyond amazing.

He touched the flight plan information. They would fly at 85,000 feet, twice that of a civilian jet. Charlie told them that only rocket planes, some unmanned aircraft, and the space shuttle had flown higher. Derrick knew nothing about any of those.

They would also fly over 4,000 miles an hour, faster than anything except a rocket and the space shuttle thing. Charlie also said the flight plan did not take them to the aircraft's topflight deck or top speed, but they would arrive well ahead of Miriam's aircraft, so there was no need to test the limits of the corvette.

Derrick appreciated that they were staying well below the aircraft's potential, not that falling out of the sky was any better at 20,000 feet than it was at 85,000. Still, he was glad they were not pushing the machine to its limit.

A crackle in his helmet startled him.

Miriam said, "Rebel 1 to Rebel 2."

Derrick smiled. He assumed the R stood for Resistance. But rebel fit. Miriam had always been a rebel. He had been the opposite, a strict rule-follower. The thought caused an odd sensation, not unlike feeling homesick.

Rebelling against authority went against his nature. Until he hit Marcus Carver. Had that not happened, he would still be in Pacific Edge. Anna, Rebekah, and Miriam would be safe. However, New America would be at war with Mexico. Thousands would already be dead. He wouldn't know about it. New America Media would lie by omission, concealing the truth from the Chosen. Their lives would go on as usual inside the walls of Pacific Edge. He would have been living inside his little bubble. But he would not have won a race. He would not have known about Potterville, Donna's cinnamon rolls, or the old guitar in the music store window.

L. Linda Maxton would be alive.

Nyx would be unknown to him.

If you don't know, it doesn't matter.

Does it?

Following the rules is still the right thing to do.

Isn't it?

Part of him said this was correct. Part of him said it was not.

He thought for a moment. If good people wrote the rules, and if the rules were in people's best interest, then following the rules was the right thing to do.

If they were still in Pacific Edge, he would be safe, but the existence of that place was wrong, built on a foundation of James Carver's lies.

"Rebel 1 to Rebel 2, are you there?"

"Sorry. I was, uh, checking the controls and such."

Miriam said, "Everyone check in if you can hear me."

Everyone did.

"Is using the radio safe? Can anyone hear us?" Derrick asked.

Miriam said, "It's safe. Our coms are linked and encrypted on both ends. If Nyx has your flight plan logged, let's go."

"Flight plan is a go," Nyx said, followed by a giggle.

"Roger that. Weapons officer ready," Antonio said.

Derrick glanced over at him.

"Red said, 'Roger that' flying the cargo plane. He said it was a military thing. I can just say, okay. Sorry. I'm rambling," Antonio said.

"Roger that," Derrick said.

And with that, he touched a button, engaging the flight plan and firing the engines.

Next stop: New York.

11

JACK'S SHOP SMELLED OF GUN OIL and looked like terrorists preparing for an assault, except for the classic cars. Those didn't fit. Terrorists were more likely to have a collection of pickup trucks perforated with bullet holes. Jack had dragged every flat-surfaced table, workbench, and counter that wasn't bolted to the wall, into the center of what they had used as a dining area, even moving three vehicles outside, which wasn't something he wanted to do, but the circumstances forced a change of priorities.

Collins didn't recognize the man. Jack Fletcher had always been a grumpy old fart, secretive, and standoffish. When Miriam went to talk with Jack, Collins thought she wouldn't make it past, "Get off my property." Instead, Jack invited them inside and made them tea.

Collins had been beyond pissed when Jack kept the Prime aircraft instead of dumping it into the lake. He was ready to arrest Jack when L. Linda left in it. But it turned out to be the right decision. Jack had saved them when the robots came to Potterville. He'd given Browning a van to get them safely out of town. Jack Fletcher was not the man he thought he'd known all these years.

Jack was so much more, and Collins hoped he could get to know him better when this was done. Unfortunately, Collins thought their survival odds were slim to none.

Collins laid the last weapon—a sniper rifle requiring assembly—on the table. "That's it. Enough for a small army."

Lori looked at the tables. "Very small. Don't get me wrong, it was my idea, but is it possible? There are only four of us."

Donna frowned. "I'm counting five."

Lori smiled. "We love you, Donna, but this isn't your calling."

"I can shoot a gun. My dad taught me out in the woods."

Collins said, "Donna, I don't doubt your abilities for one second. But there will be three of us going. I'm not forcing anyone who has second thoughts about this. Jack, Allen, and me, that's who's going."

Lori put her hands on her hips. "Now, wait one dadgum minute."

Collins raised his hands. "I don't doubt you for a moment." He left out the part where he refused to put Lori in that much danger. "I've thought this through. We can't leave the town without law enforcement. Especially now. Someone needs to be here." He paused. "In fact, I'd like you to call up a couple of the reserves. We should be out on the streets, not hiding in here. We still have a town to protect. Seeing patrol cars out would make people feel a little better."

Lori folded her arms but said nothing.

Patel said, "I'm in, but someone will have to show me how to work one of these."

Lori said, "See."

Collins said, "You'll take a shotgun. You don't have to be as accurate, and it's much easier to shoot than a handgun, but you need to know how to use that as well. Just in case."

Donna said, "I agree. Lori should stay, but I'm going."

Collins said, "The town needs you, Donna. If you're closed, people have no place to go. You can help get information out, and keep Lori informed about what people are saying."

"I wasn't asking your permission, Bill. I'm going even if I have to follow you in my own car."

Jack said, "Sheriff, you know she means it, right?"

Collins shook his head. "Donna, it's not a good idea. Will you just trust me on this? Please?"

"Bill Collins, you might be sheriff here, but not in San Diego. Your odds increase with four, and I'm the fourth person."

Collins said, "Donna, with all due respect, I'm not sure you're up to what we might have to do."

"Such as?"

"We might have to run up several flights of stairs." He paused. "We might have to do worse things than that."

"No offense taken. I'm not running up any stairs." She picked up the sniper rifle. "I'll be sitting or lying."

"You don't know how to use that. I think there's more to it than just pointing it."

She picked up another item. "This is a laser bore sighting device." She picked up a telescope. "This is a range finder. You use these to dial in the scope. I might not win any competitions, but I can hit a robot." She paused. "Or a man. Or Prime."

Collins shook his head. "I don't know, Donna. I figured Jack would do the distance shooting."

"You don't think I can keep up?" Jack asked. "You know, until this crap got us holed up, I jogged two miles every morning and did 100 pushups a day. Four twenty-five rep sets spread throughout the day. Hell, I've been worried about you and Allen keeping up with me. No offense but sitting in your patrol car and eating donuts at Donna's ain't much of a workout."

Allen said, "I must confess. I don't exercise much, although I walk three miles most days. However, I've never fired a weapon."

Jack grabbed a shotgun. "Bill, I'll show Allen how to shoot if that's okay." He didn't wait for Bill to respond. "Come with me, Allen. I'll give you a quick lesson. This is devastating at close range, and you don't have to be as accurate. Lots easier than a handgun, although," he pointed, "strap that on. I'll show you how to use it too but only use it as a last resort."

Jack and Allen left. Donna fiddled with the sniper rifle. Collins watched, hoping she wouldn't be able to get it assembled, thus proving his point, she shouldn't go. Lori sat silently, arms crossed, brow furrowed. He was in trouble on that front and would be for a long time. He didn't like it, but it was better than putting Lori at risk. It was bad enough that he was leaving her here on her own.

Soon, Donna had the rifle assembled and had the bore-sighting device working. She had the rifle resting on the table using a tripod for support. A red dot appeared on the side of the wall at the far end of the shop. Next to the rifle, Donna had the spotting scope, also on a tripod. She looked through the scope, read the instruction manual, and then fiddled more.

"There," Donna said. "I'll have to redo it when I get set up in San Diego because I won't be this close. But I understand how it works. It's simple. Easy enough that a child could do it."

Collins wasn't happy. He was hoping for a different outcome. "I guess kids do it."

Donna frowned at him.

"The kids they take into the military. What's the draft age now? Sixteen? They use guns."

"It's damn crazy. I guess with all the wars and such, it's necessary, but I don't understand why the world can't just get along. You know?"

"If the wars are real," Lori said from her arms-folded, unhappy-position in the corner.

"What do you mean?" Donna asked.

Collins had the same question and was glad Donna asked. He wasn't sure Lori would talk to him right now.

Lori said, "We get that news from New America Media. Derrick said the Chosen are told that outside their protective walls, we are savages and that gang wars are daily events."

Donna said nothing for a moment. "You're saying they are lying to us?"

Lori said, "Right. If you can find Resistance information before the site is blocked, they tell us the world is a much different place."

Donna said, "I only look for music. I download it whenever I find it. I guess I'd be in prison if the Chosen ever searched my computer."

Before he could stop himself, Collins said, "You've been on Resistance websites? Those are illegal." He regretted opening his mouth as soon as the words left it.

Lori glared at him. "We all do. What's wrong with you, Bill? Most of New America's laws are unjust, and you know it. You just say, 'That's against the law', like you just did. But you're concerned about folks getting along and treating each other right. It's like you've got this 'got to follow the law' mantra, but you know damn well it's not right, and you ignore most of it."

Collins wanted to argue. Laws were important. If everyone just did whatever they wanted, when they wanted, it would be chaos. Then the fabrications New America Media feeds the Chosen would be fact, not fiction. But Lori was right. He was not trying to catch people breaking New America laws. He thought of them more like rules, perhaps guidelines, maybe even suggestions.

Before Collins could retract, Lori asked. "You think you might break a few laws going to San Diego and destroying Prime?"

From some distance, two booms sounded. Shotgun, Collins figured. Patel and Fletcher.

Collins nodded. "I'm sorry, and you are right, Lori."

"Does that mean I can go with you then?"

Collins took a deep breath. "It does not. You're needed here. But I've been thinking. Perhaps we don't have to break the law."

Lori relaxed just a little. "Explain."

"What if we had a warrant for Prime's arrest?"

"Go on."

"I have reason to believe a woman calling herself Pixie murdered a family of three and tried to kill you. She also admitted to killing Paul Jorgensen and torching Browning's house. She said she was working for Prime. That is more than enough probable cause for Judge Smith to issue a warrant. I'll ask local law enforcement to help me arrest Prime."

"You're joking. Right?" Lori said, unable to suppress a small smile.

"I am not." He paused. "In fact, I am deputizing everyone trying to arrest Prime. What they are doing is legal. Just trying to serve a lawful warrant."

Donna said, "You'll deputize the kids?"

"I just did. You are all witnesses."

Donna said, "I like it, although I'm not sure how you explain the explosives."

Collins waved his hand. "Details. We'll work that out later."

Donna said, "That's brilliant. But do you think the police in San Diego will help us?"

"Hell no," Collins said, then added, "it will be just us. But they can't stop us. We'll have a legal warrant for Prime's arrest. If Prime resists, then we have a right to use reasonable force to bring Prime to justice."

Lori said, "I hate to admit it, but that's brilliant. I'll run to the station, write a probable cause statement, draft a warrant, and take it to Judge Smith for a signature."

Collins stared at Lori for a moment. Many things came to mind that he wanted to say, but he just said, "Thanks, Lori."

Six bangs sounded outside the shop. Different from the first. Pistol rounds.

A few minutes later, Fletcher and Patel entered the shop. Collins thought Patel looked two shades paler than usual, but he was smiling.

Fletcher said, "He's all trained up."

Collins said, "Two rounds from the shotgun and six rounds from the pistol, and you think he's ready for combat?"

Fletcher walked to the table and picked up a duty belt and pistol. "Won't know if he's ready for a firefight till he's in it. Same for all of us. Don't kid yourself. Just because you got a badge don't mean you're more ready for this than Allen. He hit what he aimed at, and that's the best we can hope for."

"You're right. Good job, Allen."

Donna had disassembled and stowed the sniper rifle and scopes. "I got the rifle figured out."

Fletcher turned and smiled. "I never doubted you for a moment."

Donna smiled, staring at him.

The room fell quiet. Fletcher sensed tension that had not previously existed. He glanced at Collins. "Where's Lori? She leave pissed?"

Collins said, "She's probably still angry, but she left to get a warrant."

Fletcher stared at him. "She's getting a what?"

Donna said, "A warrant for Prime's arrest for first-degree murder."

Fletcher smiled. "I'll be damned. Whose idea was that?"

Donna said, "Bill's idea."

Fletcher said, "Hell. Now I got to take back calling you a dumbass in my head after you pissed off your girlfriend."

"She's not my girlfriend." Although Collins liked the sound of it.

"Well, she probably isn't now." Fletcher winked.

12

DERRICK UNDERSTOOD HOW THIS WOULD happen. Nyx had entered the coordinates, altitude, and speed, which created the flight plan that would take them to Prime's New York headquarters. Upon arrival, Nyx would take high-resolution photographs and send them to the second aircraft, where Anna and Miriam would develop the assault plan. The corvette class aircraft Derrick was piloting had yet to fly one mile. There was no proof it could get off the ground or stay airborne, but all the lights on the panel showed green.

Antonio manned the gunner's post, which meant he had primary control of the aircraft's weapons and defense systems. He said he was most familiar with one weapon and one defense system but promised to study the other systems as they flew, which wasn't long because the trip to New York would be brief. If they crashed, it would be even briefer.

Derrick keyed his mic. "I'm taking us out."

"Roger that," Nyx said, then giggled. "I like saying that."

"Roger, Captain," Antonio said.

The first few minutes would be the most difficult because Derrick actually had to fly the aircraft. Charlie said it was as easy as the ones Miriam, Rebekah, and L. Linda had flown. Since Derrick had never flown the other aircraft, he had no comparison. What propelled the machine at slow speed remained a mystery. He eased the aircraft up five feet off the ground until the take-off elevation light turned green. A strange humming sound filled his helmet. The motor, he assumed but he could not pinpoint the sound's origin. Or if it was transmitted to his helmet or came from outside the helmet, and if it came from outside the helmet, it must have been deafening. It seemed to come from all directions. He eased the aircraft forward. Moving slowly from the darkness of the hangar, he could see the desert ahead. Everything seemed fine but then inside his helmet flashed a bright white light, blinding him for a moment. Perhaps the aircraft had blown up, and he did not yet know he was dead. Then the desert came back into view.

"Wow, that was kinda scary. Did your helmet do that?" Antonio asked.

"Bright flash? Mine did," Nyx said.

Charlie said, "That was the camera's reaction to the change in lighting. The sensors were adjusted for the low light conditions inside the hangar. When the aircraft moved into full sunlight, the light overwhelmed the sensors until the computer could analyze and correct the exposure value or EV setting."

"Thanks, Charlie, but too much information," Derrick said. "I just wanted to know if we were still alive. I take it you can hear us?"

Charlie said, "Affirmative. On your communication controls, you should see icons with names listed below. Rebel 1 and listed below Miriam, Anna, and Rebekah. Rebel 2: with Antonio, Nyx, and yourself. The third reads All: which is both aircraft and the base. I set the default to all. If you touch Rebel 1, you are talking to everyone in Rebekah's aircraft. If you touch one name, you open a channel to only that person. If you open Rebel 1 and Rebel 2, you are talking to everyone in both aircraft but not the base."

"Understood. Thanks, Charlie."

Derrick touched Rebel 2, so he was talking to Antonio and Nyx. "Ready to do this?"

Both said, "ready" simultaneously.

Derrick touched an icon on his control panel that read: Engage Flight Plan. The control panel image appeared inside his helmet, although it looked like a physical control board situated in front of him. On the display, a question appeared: Engage FP Yes/No? This part he'd learned in the simulator. He could select yes on his control panel or use a voice command. Engaging a flight plan for this altitude and speed was a two-step process. Thus, the question completed the procedure. The simulation recommended using voice commands, but it did not explain why.

He would soon learn the reason.

Derrick said, "Yes, engage."

The rockets roared to life. The aircraft pivoted skyward. The acceleration pressed Derrick into his seat, and he felt a burning sensation in his arms and legs that coursed through his veins. The acceleration became violent, pinning him back, making breathing difficult. This couldn't be right. Something had gone wrong. He considered turning the autopilot off, but he could neither raise his hand nor speak.

Then everything went black.

Derrick heard someone calling his name—distant and yet distinctly Miriam.

"Rebel 2. Rebel 2. Derrick. Are you there?"

"Yeah. Just barely."

"Are you alright?"

"Maybe. I think so." Derrick looked at Nyx and then Antonio. Both gave him a thumbs up. "Yeah, we are okay. I blacked out."

Antonio said, "Me too. And the suit stabbed me."

Nyx said, "Same."

Charlie said, "The aircraft pulled a sustained 10 g. The suits were designed to help you remain alert under greater g-force, but the computer must adjust the mix of gas, intravenous chemicals, and suit pressure to each individual. Also, most people train at high-g to increase their abilities in that environment. Analyzing the data tells me the adjustments are now accurate for each of you."

"I wish I'd known before it happened. Scared the crap out of me," Antonio said.

Charlie said, "The suit is designed to tolerate human bodily functions should they occur."

"Huh?"

Nyx said, "I think Antonio was using a hyperbole."

"I was?" Antonio asked.

In his distant, tinny voice, Charlie said, "I see. I shall note this idiom in my memory with an explanation that the actual event might not have occurred."

Derrick wouldn't have much time, but he wanted to familiarize himself with the weapons, defense, and navigation systems. Those were not his responsibilities, except if he were an actual captain, he should know the aircraft better than anyone else. Anyone else on the aircraft that is.

Rebekah said, "Rebel 2, we are en route."

Derrick said, "Roger that, Rebel 1. We'll contact you when we reach the target."

Derrick switched to a private line with Antonio and Nyx. "I'm getting more familiar with the aircraft's systems. Let me know when we get to New York."

Selecting the weapons module, a list of three systems appeared: missiles (obviously a military favorite), kinetic cannons (he did not know what that meant), and lasers (the term seemed familiar).

Derrick muted the radio and addressed the onboard computer. "Sentry Five."

"Sentry Five recognizes Derrick King, pilot."

"I need information regarding the weapons."

"Which weapon would you like to fire?"

"Not firing, just information."

"Pilots are fully trained on all weapons systems before clearance."

"Understood. Just a refresher. What does the Kinetic Cannon do?"

"The Kinetic Cannon fires tungsten projectiles at a rate of 1200 rounds a minute, in fifteen shot bursts with a muzzle velocity over Mach 5."

"We have two cannons. Correct?"

"That is correct."

Derrick considered the next question carefully, concerned that the computer might realize he was not a real pilot. "At what range can the projectiles penetrate an aircraft like Rebel 1?"

"Sentry Five recognizes the AT-X-20 piloted by Rebekah Ford as Rebel 1. Do you wish to establish a target lock on this aircraft?"

"No. My question is this: Will the projectiles penetrate the hull?"

"Unlikely at this range."

"At what range is the weapon effective against that class of aircraft?"

"The kinetic cannon is a close-range weapon. One hundred percent effective within five miles of the target."

Derrick thought for a moment. "Sentry Five, display missile information."

The missile information came up on his monitor. Two banks of 32. Range of 30 miles. That didn't seem very far. The missiles in Mexico would go hundreds of miles, but it took a massive truck to carry one. He had 64.

Sentry Five said, "The aircraft was loaded with a new missile design. The information you are reading has not been updated. Would you like to hear about the new configuration?"

"Yes."

"The current missiles are programmable in target acquisition, yield variation, and detonation delay, and have a range of 65 miles and 25% greater payload."

He wondered why delaying detonation would be useful, and he was unsure what yield variation meant, but they seemed like terms a military pilot would know, so he did not ask. He should have asked Charlie more questions about what the computer could and could not do. Assuming the computer monitored their radio transmissions, now was not the time to have that conversation.

The laser data proved unhelpful. A table displaying range and effectiveness was the only information. The table bottomed out at zero effectiveness, identified as #4—Level #3 listed targeting, which Derrick didn't understand—Level #2 said limited damage to some targets without naming the targets—Level #1 said effective against most targets. Level #1 range was half a kilometer.

The aircraft began to descend and slow. Suddenly, the braking thrust Derrick forward. The safety harness felt as if it might cut him in half. The scent of the atmosphere pumped into his helmet changed, but he could not identify the odor. The suit compressed his legs, and the chemicals—whatever cocktail the robot had determined to be appropriate—burned in his veins. But it worked because the g-force of braking felt double that of the acceleration, yet he remained conscious.

Nyx said, "Target acquisition in five, four, three, two, one."

Photographs of the target cycled across the monitor in his helmet. Fortunately, he'd learned how to control them in the simulator. Asking the computer to perform such a task would have been a clear signal that he didn't belong in the captain's chair.

Derrick opened a channel to Miriam. "Are you seeing this?"

"Yep. Looking at them now. I need to see the sides of the buildings to understand what we are looking at."

Before Derrick could reply, Nyx said, "Roger that. It's in the flight plan. We are circling as we descend."

As the aircraft descended, the images of Prime's complex showed additional detail—two buildings, both gray, one much larger than the other. The larger building was square, constructed of concrete walls with no windows and a flat roof. A single metal door faced the parking lot. There were no other doors visible, which struck Derrick as odd. The other building, also a single story, had a smaller rectangular shape. It had a large roll-up door like the engineering building entrance in the canyon near Potterville. The roll-up door was open. Three aircraft, like Rebel 1, were sitting outside. Robots roamed the area. Some of them were armed with long weapons.

Derrick isolated Antonio's radio. "Can you see the aircraft on the ground?"

"I do."

"Do you see anything in the air?"

"Nope. All clear."

Derrick opened the line to Rebel 1. "Miriam, are you seeing the robots?"

Miriam said, "Yep. We've got a count of five. They appear to be guarding the aircraft. There is a fourth aircraft just inside the building."

Derrick toggled back through the photographs. "Roger that. I found it. Are we sure this is a headquarters? It looks small."

"I agree, but I got the coordinates from the Resistance. It's the right location. Miriam paused. "Plus, robots."

Robots. And Prime aircraft. I could not have said anything dumber, Derrick thought.

Anna said, "The parking lot only has a few cars. Does that seem strange?"

Miriam said, "There's also a small bus. They might transport people in from somewhere nearby."

Antonio said, "Maybe Prime gives people the weekend off."

Derrick thought for a moment. "Maybe. In Seattle, there were only a few people on one floor, and they were being relocated. They said the others were told to stay home. Maybe that's happening at all the headquarters."

Miriam said, "We have arrived. Have you spotted any aircraft flying?"

Antonio said, "The radar is clear. Nothing within a hundred miles. I can see commercial aircraft going in and out of New York City, but none are headed toward us."

Miriam mumbled. "No-fly zone."

Derrick started to ask her what that meant but didn't. Self-explanatory. Instead, he said, "I don't like it. Armed robots. They're ready for us."

Miriam said, "I think that's their normal guards. They know about Seattle but aren't expecting us. It doesn't make sense that we'd come here next, and we are here too soon using any traditional travel. San Diego is the next likely target. We're looking for a place to land. Mission is a go."

Derrick said, "Send us your landing coordinates, and I'll join you."

"You will not. Stick with the plan. You're protecting us from aerial assault."

"But the sky is clear."

"They have three aircraft ready to launch and probably more. That small building might be a hangar," Miriam said.

"Then they don't have much," Derrick said.

"Everything must be underground," Miriam said. "We are just seeing the tip of the iceberg."

Derrick wanted to argue about landing but didn't. It was too much like the old Derrick. The Pacific Edge Derrick, too eager to disregard Miriam's decisions.

He took a breath. Ensured he had control over his next words. "You're probably right. You want us to just fly around unless they launch the aircraft?"

"I'm not sure yet. Stay out of sight until we are on the ground and have a better assessment."

The radio went dead, and Derrick was certain Miriam had switched to a private channel. She was most likely talking to those in her aircraft, but she might have been talking to Nyx or Antonio. Possibly both. Miriam had no reason to speak with them and not include him.

Did she?

He had tried to block thoughts about what happened in Seattle, telling himself it was because of losing L. Linda, which was true, but there was more, and it haunted him for reasons he could not understand. Miriam thought he had frozen in Prime's presence. She and Anna burst into the room. Anna killed Prime's assistant. Miriam killed Prime. They both believed they had saved his life, and perhaps they had.

But he believed the situation was under control. Things had slowed down for him. The assistant had a weapon, but in his super-slow-motion state, Derrick had time to act. Derrick had hoped he could either reason with Prime or learn more about how Prime worked.

He had time.

Miriam and Anna ruined it.

L. Linda's death gave him a legitimate reason to avoid thoughts of Seattle, but Miriam was worried about his ability to act. He wondered if she was right.

Nyx said, "They've landed and are moving toward the compound. I have Rebel 1's coordinates."

Derrick realized he'd drifted off. Again. He had to stop doing that. Miriam had contacted Nyx on a private line. How else would Nyx know their location? He cycled through the images until he found Anna and Miriam moving through the forest. Both carried rifle-like weapons. With the element of surprise, they should be able to get in without much difficulty. Although Miriam had not discussed this part of the plan, Derrick felt sure she would use her computer knowledge to enter. She had probably loaded something in the system already. They would be in and out without the robots even knowing. He liked that version of future events, even though he didn't believe it.

"Uh, oh."

The alarm in Antonio's voice jolted Derrick. "What?"

"Aircraft coming in fast from the east and west."

Derrick navigated to the radar image. "I see two."

Antonio said, "Click the detail target."

"Crap. Make that two groups of five. Sentry Five, identify approaching aircraft."

"Ten AT light fighters approaching at 600 mph. Engaging evasive flight plan is recommended."

Nyx said, "It gets worse. The three aircraft on the ground lifted off, and robots are pouring out of the facility. Robots are moving through the forest behind Miriam and Anna. I don't think Miriam knows they are coming."

Derrick said, "We have to warn them. Antonio, use the kinetic cannons on the robots in the forest, and then I'll engage the evasive flight plan."

"Roger that."

Derrick pointed the aircraft toward the ground. A muted roar from the engines filled his helmet. He wondered how loud it would be if he were not wearing it. The aircraft shuttered from the sheer power of the thrust as it dove faster than it could fall. The harness pulled him tight into his chair. The forest rushed up at them.

Nyx said, "The three aircraft from the ground are firing at us. Additional aircraft are being towed from the smaller structure and appear to be preparing for flight."

Antonio said, "I'm engaging defense mechanisms."

"Miriam was wrong. It's a trap. Antonio, try to damage those aircraft on the ground." Derrick felt zero satisfaction knowing Miriam had made an error.

Antonio didn't wait for Derrick's order to fire. Probably a benefit of not being a trained soldier. For Antonio, it was like a video game, albeit a deadly one, but a game Antonio planned to win.

The aircraft pulsed from the kinetic cannons firing, and the forest exploded in their path. Dust and debris flew up from around the staged aircraft, but Derrick could not see the extent of the damage. As the first bullets struck their hull, Derrick pointed the aircraft vertically and engaged the computer flight plan.

"The incoming aircraft are in pursuit and firing on us," Nyx said.

A distant computerized voice said, "Evasive flight plan engaged."

Suddenly pinned in his seat, Derrick could feel the skin on his face distorting. The acceleration and side-to-side movement grew more violent than anything he had experienced thus far. They returned fire, but the enemy aircraft evaded the rounds as if the pilots knew exactly when and where to dodge. "How are they doing that?" He asked.

Antonio said, "It's like they know what the computer is going to do."

Nyx said, "We are evading their rounds the same way."

The radio crackled. "We're surrounded. Derrick, we need help."

Derrick looked at the video feed from the complex. "Miriam and Anna are under heavy fire. They are pinned down." He keyed the radio. "We are also under attack. Call Rebekah. We'll be there as soon as we can."

Miriam said, "Rebekah isn't answering."

Derrick opened a channel to Rebekah. No response.

Derrick returned to the open channel. "Nyx, can you see where Rebekah landed?"

"It would be easier if we weren't moving so fast and darting around."

After a few moments, Nyx said, "Found her."

"The aircraft?"

"Yes, and Rebekah. She's not answering because she is standing outside with her hands up. Two robots have guns aimed at her."

Antonio said, "We have to help her."

Derrick said, "If you'd destroy some of those aircraft firing at us, we could."

"It's not me. The computer is flying the aircraft. I'm locked out."

Nyx said, "Miriam and Anna can't hold out much longer."

"We have to do something," Derrick said.

"I'm not arguing, but we are not making headway," Antonio said.

Nyx said, "They are preparing to launch more aircraft."

Derrick said, "We have to take out that building."

"I'm open to suggestions, Captain," Antonio said.

Derrick said, "Sentry Five, we need to help our friends."

"Sentry Five does not understand, friends."

"Sentry Five, you need to destroy the aircraft shooting at us."

"Evasive flight plan is engaged."

"But we aren't hitting any of them?"

"They have also engaged evasive flight plans."

"The evasive flight plan isn't working," Derrick shouted.

"It is working. This aircraft has sustained no damage."

"But we aren't damaging them either, and we need to help our friends."

"The evasive flight plan ensures victory."

"But you have not hit any of them! How is that winning?"

"This aircraft can fly faster, higher, and farther. It has substantially more ammunition. Victory is ensured."

"You mean we can outlast them?"

"That is correct."

"How long will that take?"

"The attacking aircraft will disengage in three hours and twenty-one minutes."

"We can't wait that long. I'm taking over," Derrick said.

"Analyzing. Evasive flight plan is recommended. Transfer of control denied."

Derrick said nothing for a moment. Arguing with a computer would be a waste of time. Perhaps there was a way to turn it off, but he didn't know how that was done. Attempting to turn the computer off now could end up getting him locked out permanently. He needed to use logic, which was something that came easier to him than the mysteries of normal human relationships.

"Sentry Five, what weapons are those aircraft firing at us? Kinetic cannons? Same as us."

"Correct. They are using kinetic cannons, but not the same model as this aircraft."

"Explain."

"All the weapons on this ship are further advanced. The projectiles from their kinetic cannons have less than half the velocity and are a third the weight. In addition, they are standard tungsten projectiles."

Antonio said, "Isn't tungsten the hardest metal?"

"It was when those machines were built. The QR-4 that designed this vessel developed a harder metal: Uranium-enriched tungsten using AT."

Derrick wondered what AT stood for. He'd heard it before but couldn't remember where. No time for that now. "The QR-4's name is Charlie. That's what we call him."

"Sentry Five has updated that information."

"Thank you." Derrick didn't know if being polite meant anything to the computer, but Miriam had taught him being rude didn't help. "Sentry Five, is accomplishing the goal of this mission the most important objective?"

"Correct."

"The goal is to destroy those aircraft, the robots on the ground, and the facility. Can we achieve those objectives?"

"Affirmative."

"Using the current method, can we achieve that goal, and ensure the people from Rebel 1 survive."

"Processing. Negative."

"Saving the people on the ground is essential to our mission. I must have control of the aircraft. Sentry Five must continue to analyze the situation and provide assistance."

"Acknowledged."

Derrick said, "Antonio, get ready to control weapons. Nyx, feel free to fire as well. I'm reversing course."

Antonio said, "We'll be flying right at them."

"Exactly, and fast. Antonio, as soon as we turn, hit that hangar with a missile. Set it to detonate after impact."

"How long a delay?"

"Best guess. Nyx, you have one kinetic cannon. Antonio, you have the other. I'll try the laser, but I don't know how effective it will be," Derrick said, then added, "Ready. On my mark."

Derrick prepared himself to take control of the aircraft. Everything was controlled by the touch of a finger, but there were no actual buttons to press. The controls were virtual. Simply images shown on the insides of their helmets. Moving a finger pushed a virtual button or moved an imaginary slider that then controlled a function.

Sentry Five said, "The laser is effective within 500 meters of the target."

And with that, Derrick counted down from three, seized control of the ship, slammed on the brakes, spun it around, and flew straight at 13 enemy aircraft.

An alarm sounded, and red dots flashed on the monitor inside Derrick's helmet.

Nyx said, "We are getting hit." Loud metallic bangs reverberated through the hull.

Sentry Five said, "This aircraft can withstand approximately 90% of these rounds at this range. However, most projectiles will penetrate the hull when we are within 100 meters."

"Roger that. Eliminate those aircraft before we get that close." Derrick activated a weapons tracer function. Incoming rounds displayed red traces of light, and outgoing rounds were green. The approaching aircraft were dodging the green rounds with ease, and the red rounds were pounding on the hull of Rebel 2.

Sentry Five said, "While the hull can survive most incoming projectiles at this range, the accumulation of so many hits will eventually fatigue the metal, and penetration will soon occur.

Antonio yelped.

Derrick said, "What? Are you okay."

"Yeah but avoiding at least a few of those bullets would be good."

Antonio and Nyx were both firing, but neither were causing much damage. Derrick had been moving the aircraft in small, herky-jerky side-to-side movements that felt like the computer's evasive flight plan. It wasn't working. He tried to slow things down, but that wasn't working either. Even slowed down, everything happened in milliseconds. He had an idea.

Instead of making incremental movements like the computer, he moved the aircraft half a mile, which took less than a second, but suddenly the incoming rounds flew by, missing them by 100 yards. Computers were not people. Everything was built on an economy of movement. A miss by a centimeter was as good as a miss by a mile. And the computers seemed to be running the same program. Perhaps the program wasn't the same, but within seconds, the computer could analyze the other machine and predict the future.

Humans could be unpredictable.

Derrick said, "Change it up. Don't shoot where they are. Shoot where they might go. Team up."

He didn't have time to explain it better because they would soon be within range where all the incoming rounds would penetrate the hull. He added north and south to the east and west. Antonio and Nyx figured it out. Antonio moved his aim away from an aircraft, and the aircraft dodged right into his stream of bullets. Nyx fired a stream adjacent to Antonio's. When the aircraft dodged Antonio's rounds, it flew right into Nyx's stream and exploded.

"More like it!" Antonio said. "Upper right aircraft. Now."

Derrick was taking fewer hits. Nyx and Antonio were methodically eliminating aircraft, but they were rapidly closing on the enemy aircraft. A couple of them peeled off to come in from behind, but the angle gave Antonio a better shot, making short work of those that tried.

Derrick lit up one aircraft with the laser, selected duplicate, not knowing what that would do, set the range at 400 meters, and then accelerated. He jerked the aircraft from side to side and up and down in random patterns. As they drew closer, he turned sideways toward an open spot and then fired the laser. The laser fired three blasts. At first, Derrick didn't think the laser had caused any damage. Then three aircraft split in half.

"Wow! I like the laser," Antonio yelled.

"I got three," Nyx said.

"Four," Antonio said adding, "Missile away."

A split second later, a puff of smoke appeared in the center of the smaller building, and then it collapsed.

Over his radio, Miriam said, "Derrick, hurry! They're right on top of us, and we are running out of ammo. I don't want to die here! Please, help us!"

"Hang on!" Derrick switched to the internal channel. "We hit ten aircraft, right?"

The computer voice said, "That is correct."

Derrick noticed the computer had not waited to be addressed as Sentry Five before responding. "Where are the remaining three?"

Nyx said, "They are leaving."

"That's weird," Antonio said.

Derrick said, "Not weird. People."

"I don't understand," Nyx said.

"The pilots of those three are people. They realized this was a superior machine, so they ran."

"They just disappeared," Nyx said.

Antonio said, "Maybe they have stealth technology. They could come around for another run at us."

"Do they have that kind of technology?" Derrick asked.

No one replied.

"That question was for you, Sentry Five."

"They do not have stealth capabilities."

"Then what happened to them?" Derrick asked.

"Analyzing data," Sentry Five responded.

"Derrick! Where are you? We are surrendering. Please help us!"

"Get them up on the monitor," Derrick said.

His monitor showed Anna and Miriam drop their weapons and step out from the protection they had taken between a truck and a wall of the large building. Several robots littered the ground, and many more held weapons on the girls as they walked into the open.

"Damn it," Derrick breathed.

Antonio said, "We have to help Rebekah. Two robots are walking her towards the building. They have weapons aimed at her."

"Sentry Five, is there a way to destroy all the robots simultaneously without hurting the people?" Derrick asked.

In a moment, the computer said, "There is not. The kinetic cannons would create shrapnel that could strike the humans. The lasers cannot fire that many bursts simultaneously."

Derrick watched as Miriam lowered her hand to her microphone. "Derrick, they want you. They say if you come, we won't be harmed. Don't do it. Destroy that buil…"

"Miriam? Miriam, answer me! What just happened?"

No one answered for a moment, and then Nyx said, "I think they disrupted her radio transmission."

"Sentry Five, what happened?" Derrick asked.

"The navigator is correct. A robot has blocked the radio transmission."

Derrick said, "I should not have agreed to let them go without me."

Nyx said, "Miriam didn't give you that option. We had our hands full too. It's not your fault. If anything, it's Miriam's blunder not anticipating they would be waiting for us. You tried to warn her."

"They were ready for us," Derrick acknowledged.

"That was obvious," Nyx said.

Derrick said, "But Miriam did something to block Prime's communication."

"It didn't work," Nyx said.

"They knew about Seattle." Antonio pointed out.

"I'm going down."

"You can't. They will kill you," Nyx said.

"Sentry Five, can the robots lie?" Derrick asked.

"Robots are computers operating inside machines. They provide factual data based on available information."

Derrick said, "See. They said they wouldn't harm Miriam if I surrendered."

"Sentry Five, can robots forward information from someone controlling them?" Nyx asked.

"Affirmative."

"So, whoever is controlling the robots could say they will not harm Miriam and then order them to kill them both as soon as Derrick lands."

"That is correct."

"There. Satisfied?"

Derrick said, "It doesn't matter. I have to go. Sentry Five, how can I get down there?"

"The ship can land in the clearing, and you step out the door."

"What if they have a weapon that can destroy the aircraft?" Antonio asked.

"That is possible. Ground-based weapons could destroy the aircraft."

"Any suggestions?" Derrick asked.

No one answered.

"That was directed at you, Sentry Five. You don't have to wait to respond, buddy. We're kinda in a hurry here."

"Sentry Five does not understand, buddy."

Derrick said, "Sorry. Just something people say."

"Sentry Five has three English dictionaries. Sentry Five understands the meaning of the word buddy: a close friend, a working companion with whom close cooperation is required."

Derrick said, "There you go. We are working companions. Please speak up anytime you have information about what we are discussing."

The computer said, "Working companions. Understood. Very well. Sentry Five suggests using the PFP."

"What is a PFP?" As Derrick spoke, a door opened, and a mechanical arm extended holding an apparatus.

"This is a PFP, or personal flight pack. Step up and back into the device."

Derrick did as the computer had instructed. The device opened and then closed around his chest. Arm-like devices extended on each side. He stuck his hands on the controls. "How do I fly this thing?"

The computer said, "Instructions are available in your flight helmet. However, to expedite your travel to the surface, Sentry Five can program the flight."

"Say, I," Derrick said.

"Sentry Five does not understand your instruction."

"Don't say Sentry Five. Just use a pronoun. I assume you understand pronouns."

"Sentry Five understands pronouns but was not programmed to use first-person."

"It makes it easier for me. Consider it an order."

"Sentry Five—I acknowledge the captain's order."

"Okay. Program this thing and open the door."

"Sentry—I mean, I have further information, and you instructed Sen—me to deliver additional information when useful."

Derrick walked to the exit. "Go ahead. Make it quick."

"The aircraft cannot destroy all the robots simultaneously."

Derrick cut him off. "You already said that."

"However, most of the robots are drones. There are three controllers. We can destroy the three controllers, and the remaining robots will not function."

"Let's do that then!" Derrick said, turning back toward the interior of the ship.

Sentry Five said, "I cannot. I have only identified one controller."

Derrick said, "I don't understand. They must be different models or something."

"Correct. The controllers are QR-3 machines. The drones are QR-2 machines. The machines look identical. Only the programming is different, which is undetectable unless it is in use. Earlier, I identified that there were three controllers, but now only one QR-3 is emitting a signal."

"I need solutions."

"The situation is stationary, so only one controller is active. You must force the other controllers to react."

Derrick motioned with his hand. "Speed it up. I need to get down there."

"If you land next to the two girls, it is unlikely the other controllers will activate. However, if you land here," Derrick saw a green spot appear behind the robots, "and then work your way to the other side, before moving toward the girls, the other controllers will activate to track your movement."

"And then you can destroy them?"

"Correct."

"Open the door and get me down there."

Nyx said, "Derrick, don't go, please."

"I have to. See you soon."

The door opened, and Derrick stepped outside the aircraft, one mile above the compound.

13

Saturday, April 10, 2:37 p.m.

ALTHOUGH THE FACILITY WAS BURIED hundreds of feet under the desert, sections of it felt as if one were on the surface in a welcoming neighborhood. The designers had put effort into creating areas for social interactions that felt as if they were above ground. Lighting, colors, and faux windows all added to the ambiance. There were subtle and varied scents in the air: flowers, pine, and ocean, depending on which floor. He wondered if those working had a say in such things or if the scents rotated on a program some engineer felt best.

Stanley's ID had granted him access to most areas. However, there was a point at which he could go no closer to the surface. A man told him no one could go to those floors. Something about new people arriving. On the floors he could access, he saw laboratories, mechanical engineering, massive computer operations, hi-tech weapons, and robot design and repair. He still didn't know where the food came from. Perhaps on floors closer to the surface.

No one approached him, but if he initiated a conversation, everyone talked to him. More accurately stated, everyone answered his questions. He was Chief of Staff. Not talking to him would be bad for one's career. Far too often, the answer to his questions was, I don't know.

He learned the core staff here had never been substantial, and turnover was rare, predominantly driven by losing someone. No one talked about what losing someone meant. Stanley didn't need clarification on that point. It seemed common knowledge that new people had been arriving, but the core staff had not seen them. New arrivals were sequestered on specific floors for orientation. Despite the lack of information, people seemed scared. As if, something unimaginable had happened.

Stanley knew about the catastrophic event but mentioned it to no one, although he was surprised to learn there were rumors about the destruction of a Prime facility. Some even said it was Seattle, which was speculation because no one from Seattle had arrived.

Stanley doubted that many staff in Seattle were killed. Prime had been running a skeleton staff even before his departure. Prime had feared reprisals from attacking Mexico might include headquarter locations, so he sent some people home to avoid losing staff. Seattle people were not here because they were dead. Prime no longer trusted them and had likely sent assassins to question, torture, and kill survivors.

Stanley wasn't hungry, but he wanted something. Mostly, he wanted conversation but doubted he'd find any. People simply don't chat with the Chief of Staff. Perhaps he could order someone to talk with him. It would be superficial, but at least he'd be talking to another human being. Not having regular interactions with people was just one drawback of being Prime's assistant. It was no small inconvenience, but not the worst thing about the job.

Stanley rode the elevator back to the main dining floor. He wasn't hungry, so the street-like area where he'd had coffee earlier seemed like his best option. He walked along the simulated sidewalk, passing shop windows: a candy store, a place that sold popcorn and nuts, and a shoe store with a limited selection of sneakers. He discovered two restaurants. Farther down, he saw a pub, which sounded inviting, but he needed a clear head. The espresso shop was positioned about three-quarters of the way.

The street had small trees, which he assumed were fake at first, but he determined they were real upon closer inspection. How did they keep them so small? Had they always been here? How old was this place? What was it before Prime turned it into his central headquarters?

Stanley was sure Prime had not built it. Despite Prime's stamp of ownership of virtually everything in New America, Prime didn't build anything. Prime stole things and then claimed them as if he'd designed and constructed them.

Sitting at a sidewalk table in front of the espresso shop was the barista he had spoken to earlier. The one who knew him by name because his face had been broadcast throughout the facility—the bioengineer working extra duty. The one who feared their conversation had been too long.

Pam looked up as he approached.

"Hi. It's Pam. Right?"

"Yes. Good to see you, Chief."

He noticed Pam's latte was fresh, the foam art undisturbed. "You may call me Stanley. May I sit with you? I'll grab a coffee." He was Chief of Staff. That title had come at a great cost, and he planned to use it somehow.

Pam hesitated and glanced around as if looking for the police. More likely wondering how many cameras there were and who was watching them. He had put her in a difficult position. He understood that. She couldn't refuse to talk to the Chief of Staff but doing so put her at risk. Her work might be important, but she probably saw herself as more expendable than Prime's right-hand man. Stanley wasn't confident in her appraisal of the situation.

"Don't worry. Just small talk. I won't make you uncomfortable." Stanley smiled and hoped he was being truthful.

"Sure. Of course," Pam said.

Three people were standing in line. The second person glanced at him, then tapped the person at the counter on the shoulder. Then, the third person made eye contact with him, and all three stepped aside. "Sorry, I didn't see you in line, Mr. Mires."

"It's no problem. I can wait my turn."

"No, we insist."

It surprised Stanley to see fear in their eyes. Perhaps the previous Chief of Staff was much like Prime. That wouldn't make his job any easier, not really. He wasn't sure how to handle the situation. He needed to understand the dynamics first, so he simply said, "Thank you," and ordered.

The barista stopped working on the drinks she had started and made his double macchiato next. He needed the extra sugar and caffeine. "How much do I owe you?" He knew his coffee was complimentary, plus he had no money, so it was more show than anything.

"Nothing," the barista said.

"Then let me buy these nice people's coffees." He indicated the three who had stepped aside.

The barista said, "It's complimentary for all the staff."

"Oh. I see." He scanned the counter. "Where do I leave a tip?"

"It's not allowed, sir."

He smiled and nodded. What he'd shown more than anything else was how little he knew about working here. "Very well then. Please call me Stanley."

"Okay, sir."

His second social interaction had been as awkward as the first. Perhaps the third time will be a charm, but he doubted it.

Back at the table, Stanley sat. "Thanks for letting me join you. Are you on a break or finished for the day?"

"I'm finished here. Next, I go to the lab. I get a break in between."

"Do you work a short shift in the lab on days you work here?"

"No. I still have a 10-hour shift in the lab."

"How many hours do you work here?"

"Only five."

Stanley whistled through his teeth. "That's a long day."

Pam sipped her latte. "I don't mind. There's not much else to do here."

Stanley nodded. He'd seen a theater but noted it showed a limited selection of New America and Chosen Doctrine films, which he considered nothing more than propaganda. Not entertaining unless one was a die-hard Primer. That's what he called the people who loved being Chosen and those working directly for Prime. Those working for Prime were known as the one percent and lived like royalty compared to the commoners, or at least, it seemed they did by comparison. He saw it differently. The Chosen and one percent were prisoners, in his opinion. Not that anyone had much freedom in New America.

He was among the one percent. A prisoner by choice trying to help the Resistance, which was a vague notion of ideals, more than an organization. He wondered if his sacrifice had been worth it. He did not deserve the freedoms the Resistance strived for because he'd done many bad things to get close to Prime and he would never know if the information he'd given to the Resistance was of value.

Except for one thing: A Prime headquarters had been destroyed for the first time in history. His information may have helped.

Choosing his words carefully, he said, "I've looked around and talked to several people. Many have said there was a terrible catastrophe, but none can tell me the source of the information."

Pam looked around. "I understand many new people have arrived. They are coming from all over. You probably already know that. Anyway, I suspect the rumors come from those new arrivals."

"Where are the new people? When I arrived, Prime assigned me to a bunk. It wasn't much. Very spartan. After I got a few hours' sleep, Prime told me it was only temporary because my quarters were not ready. However, I was alone where I spent the first night. There were no other people on that level. Where are the new arrivals? I feel I should greet them. To be honest, I don't know much about my new role. I spent only a few minutes with Prime. Prime told me to look around. I assumed Prime wanted me to get familiar with the facility and staff."

"That makes sense."

Stanley cocked his head.

"Because the change happened so quickly. Your predecessor was here having coffee just hours before Prime announced you were the new Chief of Staff." She paused. "Your predecessor was here longer than most anyone. The abruptness of the change has people rattled."

Stanley said, "Prime told me I'd meet my predecessor." He wanted to ask if she knew what prompted this change but decided it was unsafe and it was unlikely she knew. "Back to my question. Where are the new people?"

Now, he understood people's apprehension. That information was unsettling to him as well. "My understanding is that they are being processed on the floors above us. As they go through orientation, they move down floor by floor. We should start seeing them in about six days."

Stanley glanced up, trying to imagine what orientation meant for those people. Would everyone reach this level? What would become of those who did not? Pam was still being evasive, and it wasn't helping. Yet, he understood and didn't enjoy continuing to probe, but he needed to know what was going on. "And how did you come to this knowledge?"

The fear in Pam's eyes told him instantly he'd gone too far. "I'm sorry. Let me rephrase that. Who could tell me about the intake process?"

Pam sipped her coffee, giving her a moment to think. "Todd, the guy standing in front of you in the coffee queue, works intake."

"Is that a full-time job?"

"No. It's an extra duty. Todd has been here for years. Prime trusts him."

Stanley sipped coffee, giving him a moment to think. "Did you go through the same orientation?"

"I did not. Different circumstances. The orientation is new."

"How's that?"

"I'm not sure." Pam paused. "I applied for my position. Vetting and orientation was part of the process. Given the number of people arriving, I don't think they volunteered to come."

Stanley nodded, and for the first time in a while, he understood. People were coming much like he did, although probably not led to a rooftop with hoods over their heads. No time for vetting line workers, scientists, technicians, engineers, etc., who did not work directly with Prime as he did. Prime had to ensure they could be trusted before they got this deep into the complex. "I understand. So, you applied to come here? I didn't know that was possible."

"That's not how it happened. I applied for a level one research position. It did not say where the position was. I'm not married. I have no children, so the location didn't matter. In the final interview, they asked if I would work at the central location. It shocked me," she paused, "and I'm not sure at that point there was a legitimate choice to be made. More like a test, I assume. However, I jumped at the opportunity."

Pam was a Primer. Primers were convinced Prime was a deity, one hundred percent certain in their convictions, unwilling to question their firmly held beliefs. They are unsure of nothing and would tell you quickly, should you try to interject any doubt into their world. Yet she seemed nervous, unsure of herself. His experience told him something was off. He drank the remainder of his coffee. He sensed Pam growing antsy, ready to leave, and probably needing to get to her next job.

He was running out of time and patience with Pam.

"What have you been told?"

Pam's eyes shifted. For a moment, he thought she might run.

He had touched a nerve, put her in a bad situation, so he changed tactics. "Something happened in Seattle. What have you been told about that? This isn't a trick. I'm just trying to help. Perhaps I can put some fears to rest." He doubted he could do that, but it was a Chief of Staff thing to say.

"You came from Seattle, right? Was everything there okay when you left?"

Stanley took a breath. Even if Prime was listening, he could make this conversation safe. Not so much for himself, although self-preservation was as instinctive for himself as it was for others. "Everything was fine when I left. I very much enjoyed working there."

"Yet you said—I don't recall exactly—something about being frightened when you left."

"I was. Looking back on it, I should not have been. Prime was simply protecting me. Safer if I didn't know where I was going." *Safer for Prime,* he thought. He shook his head. "It's hard to believe Seattle was destroyed if the rumor is true."

Pam sat quietly for a moment. He imagined a myriad of thoughts coursing through her mind, trying to determine if any were safe to speak, but ultimately, overwhelmed by her natural curiosity and problem-solving nature, she spoke. "Can I ask you a question?"

"Sure. I'll answer if I can." Stanley was pleased with his response. He was getting the hang of this Chief of Staff thing.

Pam glanced around again. "There's a rumor that one of Prime's experiments went wrong. Created a monster and that monster is trying to kill Prime."

Stanley hoped his face remained impassive. He had not thought of Derrick King as an experiment gone wrong, nor could he think of him as a monster, he was merely a teenager. However, a Primer would call Derrick King a monster and would always think of him that way.

Stanley knew all about Prime's attempts to kill Derrick and Miriam. Prime was the monster. So, his answer surprised him. "I have not heard of anything like that. I would put that rumor out of my head if I were you."

He wondered how Prime would judge his response.

Pam nodded. "Do you think Prime knew it was coming? The attack, that is. Perhaps that is the reason Prime removed you so abruptly. Think of it. Maybe Prime sacrificed himself to save you."

Stanley was glad he didn't have a mouthful of coffee, or he likely would have sprayed it all over her. He had hoped to probe her knowledge of this place and learn something helpful. That she might turn the tables on him had not crossed his mind. However, she had asked questions for which he wasn't prepared. Pam believed Prime had protected him. She was a Primer for sure. Convinced that Prime cared about people. Prime only cared about itself. "That is quite a thought. I don't know. Perhaps. Prime knows all. Right?"

He didn't believe that last part. Never did. Never would. But Prime would love hearing it if Prime were listening, and Stanley was sure that Prime was. But he had never considered the notion that Prime knew or sensed an attack was coming.

Still, he had underestimated Prime before.

14

AS STANLEY MIRES FINISHED HIS DOUBLE MACCHIATO at a simulated sidewalk café under a vast desert, Derrick, using the PFP, drifted down toward Prime's New York Complex, determined to save Anna and Rebekah Ford and his sister, Miriam. The PFP was virtually silent. Derrick had done nothing like this before and had only seen similar devices in old movies, which may have been props, but they were much different and used jet propulsion. Like the Prime aircraft, these did not have jets or rockets. He knew almost nothing about how things worked, given the Chosen doctrine forbidding technology. He'd never questioned that teaching. However, now he understood technology was everywhere, including Pacific Edge. However, even knowing next to nothing, he thought there was something strange about machines that could fly with no apparent means of doing so. No motors, no jets, no rockets, no wings. If he lived long enough, perhaps he'd ask how that was possible. Although it was more likely, he'd want to forget it all.

One thing he could not ignore was L. Linda Maxton. Her death was his responsibility. Nyx and Miriam could say it wasn't, but he knew it was. Her father, who wasn't her father, was also dead. Both gone. Although L. Linda's background differed from his, they shared similarities. Everyone in Potterville knew L. Linda, yet they did not. They knew the girl, L. Linda wanted them to know, not the real person. They did not even know the color of her eyes. He thought perhaps no one would even remember what color they were. But he would always remember their true color. That striking green was unlike anything he had ever seen. Unforgettable.

He had worn the helmet so he could communicate with the aircraft. Mostly, he needed the robot. "Hey, Five."

No answer.

"Sentry Five, I'm talking to you. Do you hear me?"

"Affirmative."

Derrick could see the robots as the PFP brought him down. The helmet allowed him to zoom in. He circled the stationary machines. They had not spotted him. He wished he'd grabbed something to toss at them. Perhaps if he hit one on the head, it would awaken the other controllers.

"Is there anything different about the drones and the controllers? Some way I can tell them apart?"

"The QR-2 and QR-3 androids are identical apart from the communication devices. The QR-2 is equipped with a receiver. The QR-3 has a receiver/transmitter combination. A small green light appears at the base of the head when connected. However, when a controller is transmitting, its light is red."

"So, there should be three with red lights. Right?"

"That is incorrect. Only one controller is transmitting. The other two are inactive. I have the active android target locked."

"You are certain there are three controllers?"

"There are three controllers in that group. The two androids escorting the third human are also controllers."

"You didn't mention that before."

"You did not ask."

"Feel free to tell me things I don't know to ask. Remember?"

"Affirmative."

"Can you destroy the two escorts? And her name is Rebekah."

"Who is Rebekah?"

"The third human."

"Noted. Is that important?"

"It is to me. About destroying those other two controllers. You can do that, right?"

"The tree cover is too thick. I cannot make a visual lock."

"But we'll need to destroy them before they get to Anna and Miriam, or we'll have five controllers instead of three."

"That is correct."

"Back to the inactive controllers. How do I make them transmit?"

"That will be difficult."

"You are full of good news."

"You requested I let you know stuff."

"True. So, how do I do it?"

"There are two prisoners, and the primary controller can monitor them. The secondary controller can assume that role should something happen to the primary."

"And the third can take over just as easily."

"Correct."

"I still don't have an answer," Derrick said, flying low enough to see the green lights as he passed over the robots.

"There is no technical answer to that question. What seems most logical is to be illogical."

"They have not noticed me yet, so let's keep it that way. Take me back up and then explain what you mean."

Derrick rose higher, but he kept his vision zoomed in.

Sentry Five said, "Androids function on direct orders. The controllers function based on direct orders or logic. The controllers were programmed to capture the intruders and to instruct you to surrender. Logic tells them to shut down two controllers for safety. Logic tells them to wait until you arrive."

"And then?"

"And then they will carry out the remainder of their programming."

"So, if they are programmed to kill us, when they see me, they will kill us before I can do anything?"

"You understand the situation correctly. They will carry out the programming unless they receive a change in that order."

"Great. So, they might not be programmed to kill us, but that might change."

"Affirmative."

"And to get the inactive controllers to transmit, I must do something illogical before they kill us."

"That is correct."

"Any suggestions?"

"I also follow orders and use logic."

"Anyone?"

Antonio said, "I don't know. Dance?"

Nyx said, "Sing."

"Sing?"

"I heard you were learning to play the guitar. You have a good voice."

Derrick thought for a moment. He could not remember singing for Nyx. They lived in the same building. Perhaps the sound carried. Maybe she had been in the hall outside his door. He felt a sudden bit of embarrassment but pushed it aside. No time for that now.

"Five, do you record stuff? Like Anna and Miriam being attacked?"

"Affirmative. Everything in our flight plan and observations are recorded."

"Review them. See if you can tell what the setting was on the robot's weapons."

Zooming in with the telescopic vision, Derrick inspected several weapons. What he saw wasn't good. Not good at all.

Five said, "The weapons were set to low. I believe that is meant to stun a human but not kill."

Derrick said, "I need a weapon."

Five said, "That is not advised. The androids would interpret it as an immediate threat and signal of noncompliance. Logic would dictate they kill you."

"They have no intention of capturing us. They mean to kill us. All the weapons are set to kill now. Bring me back up so I can get a weapon. We need a new plan."

"A drone can deliver a weapon."

"Great. Take me up farther. We can't risk the robots seeing me."

The robots were mere specks without magnification.

"Don't do this," Nyx said.

"I don't have a choice."

"It's too dangerous. Come back to the ship, and we'll figure something out. We can all man weapons and do it that way."

Derrick heard something unfamiliar in Nyx's voice. Panic. He felt an odd sensation—a bit of elation that she was worried about him, a bit of sorrow for causing her to worry. "I'm sorry. That won't work. It will only take one robot to kill Anna and Miriam. Even if we could hit them all before one got off a shot, shrapnel from our rounds could kill them. I can't take that chance."

His radio fell silent. Nyx had cut his transmission. Perhaps she was trying to bring him back to the aircraft. He studied the controls and found how to switch to manual if necessary. If Five didn't deliver a weapon, perhaps he could land some distance from the fray and pick one up from a fallen robot. However, that was not a good option. He needed everyone's help—especially the computer. Five was critical for them to have any chance at making this work. It was not lost on him how much his attitude had changed from when he first saw Charlie and grew angry at Miriam for treating the machine like a person.

A faint hiss indicated a radio channel had opened. Five said, "The weapon is on its way. It is set on high. You could change it if I misjudged the situation."

"Your conclusion is correct. Can you tell me which robot is a controller?"

"The active machine is one step ahead of the androids directly in front of Anna and Miriam."

A small drone floated down, carrying a familiar electronic weapon, which he took. The drone zoomed upward and disappeared.

Derrick knew where the logical inactive controllers stood. Two robots stood in a similar position to the active controller on the left and right. Triangulation—a standard operational tactic. It was a standard tactic for a reason. It worked.

The controller stood a yard in front of the others. The inactive controllers were likely mirror images.

Logical.

"Five. Do you see the robots on both sides standing in the same position as the active controller? Likely the other controllers. Do you agree?"

"Affirmative. Most likely."

"Also, logical."

"Correct."

"Which means at least one of them is not a controller."

"Exactly."

Antonio said, "You've lost me."

"The purpose of two inactive controllers is to increase the unit's survival if attacked. By keeping the controllers hidden until needed, they increase the success of the mission. So, placing the third controller in a position mirroring the other two is the most logical, which makes it illogical because it's too obvious. So, at least one controller isn't in the obvious position," Derrick said.

"Unless it is," Nyx said.

"Huh?"

"Robots are not the most imaginative bunch. Sorry, Five."

Antonio said, "Good point."

Five said, "Correct. There are six robots on each side for a total of eighteen. However, we know which robot is the controller in one group. In the other two groups, it could be any of them."

"Targeting two gets us almost to 20%. Not great. How long will it take for the third controller to signal the drones?" Derrick asked.

"Hundredths of a second," Five said.

Derrick said, "Here's the plan. Five, land me in front of Anna and Miriam."

Antonio said, "That makes no sense."

"Exactly. It's illogical," Derrick said. "Then, on the east side, I'm going to shoot the robot to the left of the one out front."

"Why that one?" Nyx asked.

Derrick hated this part. It made little sense. He wasn't good at it. Yet, it felt right to him. "Because I feel that's the controller."

"You feel it?" Antonio asked, the skepticism evident in his voice.

"Best I got. Five, I'll count down from three. We both fire on one. You take the active controller and the logical position on the west side. Fire again if you get a chance. One last thing. If we don't make it, save Rebekah and destroy that building. Got it?"

"Acknowledged."

"Derrick! No!"

He heard the anguish in Nyx's voice. He didn't want her to watch him die. Not how he wanted to be remembered. Nothing he could do about it. He cut her radio.

Coming down was like being in a free fall, although he'd never jumped from an aircraft, so he wasn't sure if it was that fast, but it might be even faster.

He aimed at the robot he felt was the controller.

You're sure this feels right?

15

IN ACCORDANCE WITH HIS TRAINING, DERRICK slowed things down. How slow was possible, he did not know. Probably not hundredths of a second that Sentry Five had predicted as the robots' reaction time. He had a robot in his sights as he floated to the ground. The one he had predicted was the third controller. Predicted on nothing more than a wild guess. A feeling. Not something that could be tested. Not something to be trusted. If he guessed wrong, Miriam and Anna would be dead before he touched down.

So, he did what he could not do in track or football but could certainly do in this situation.

He cheated.

It would have taken too long to explain his plan to Sentry Five and even implementing it was more difficult than explaining it. So, Sentry Five would fire on the count of one.

Then something happened. Something so unexpected it startled him. "Stop. Five, stop me right here."

The deceleration was fierce. Speed was part of the attack plan. He could not fall fast enough to be quicker than the robots. There wasn't much about his plan that was illogical. So, he changed the plan midflight. "Five, can the robots hear me if I talk?"

Five said, "Affirmative. Your suit has that capability." There was a pause. "Why do you ask?"

"I have an idea. I'm in a suit and a blacked-out helmet. I'm flying. Perhaps they won't recognize me as a human. Is there a way to alter my voice so I sound—mechanical?"

"Give me a moment."

Derrick kept his weapon trained on the robot he thought was a controller.

Five said, "I can modulate your voice. In addition, I believe it can be audible and transmitted directly to the robots' communication receptors."

"That would be unexpected. Illogical. Right?"

"Correct. However, robots are not confused like humans."

"What happens when they are confronted with unforeseen events?" Derrick asked.

Five did not answer for a moment. "The analysis of incompatible information is difficult to explain."

"Sounds confusing."

"Noted. What is the new plan?"

"I'm going down to talk to them."

Five remained silent for a moment. "I'm confused."

"Just follow my lead. When I fire, you fire. Questions?"

"Hundreds."

A new icon appeared in Derrick's helmet. "I see an icon that says broadcast. Is that what enables my outside voice?"

"Affirmative."

"Take me down. Slowly. The inactive controllers might activate before I touchdown. If that happens, take them out." Derrick scanned the area, hoping he'd see something to pick out the inactive controllers. Anna looked angry. Her head moved back and forth as if looking for an opportunity to grab a gun. Any such attempt would end in death. Miriam was expressionless, pale, blood once again oozed through her clothing. Whether she was shot a second time or had torn open the old wound, he did not know.

Sentry Five remained silent. Derrick started moving down again. He could make out minute details about the robots. Then he realized he had zoomed in on them, so he set his vision to normal. A minor detail that might have cost Anna and Miriam's lives. There was no margin for error. Which made the entire idea sound like one huge mistake. He considered asking Five what the odds of success were but decided he didn't want to know.

He didn't know what the robots' field of vision was but assumed it was greater than that of a human, so about fifty yards up, he activated the broadcast feature of his suit. His voice startled him. Thin and slightly metallic. He'd run this through his head a few times and never came to a satisfactory monologue. He didn't know how a robot might talk to another robot.

"Greetings earth-bound Prime androids. I come in peace."

The known controller's head rotated upward. Derrick noted that all the robots standing behind the controller rotated their heads in unison. The robots on the left and right had not moved.

"Are you Derrick King?" the controller asked.

"I am not. I come before Derrick King to ascertain your intentions."

"Derrick King must surrender."

"Mr. King requires more information and requests Prime meet him outside." The robots on the right turned their heads toward him. Two banks of robots were now staring at him. Their weapons raised in unison.

"Derrick King must surrender."

"Your request has been received and is pending a response. What does Prime intend to do with Mr. King?"

"Prime requires Mr. King's presence."

"For what purpose?"

"To initiate protocols."

Derrick wondered what that meant. Perhaps the protocol was deconstruction. The remaining bank of robots turned their heads toward Derrick, which he thought meant the third controller was now active. He had not discussed a signal to open fire with Five.

Sentry Five fired, and at almost the same moment, Derrick killed three robots.

None of the robots were moving now. Whether his first guess was correct or not, he'd never know. It didn't matter. The controllers were dead, and the remaining robots were frozen. Derrick took control of the PFP and spun toward Anna and Miriam. "Get behind the barrier. Shoot as many robots as you can."

"Derrick?" Miriam asked. "Why aren't they moving?"

"They need controllers. We shot them first, but two more are escorting Rebekah here. I'm going to stop them. If they get close enough to communicate with these," he motioned to the stationary robots, "they'll start shooting again."

And with that, Derrick flew away. He heard weapons firing behind him. Miriam and Anna, he hoped.

Once clear of the robots, he flew lower into the opening in the trees. Not a main road, but a service lane—narrow and dirt. The trees formed a canopy, creating a gloomy tunnel. Warm, moist air hung heavy in the darkness under the green ceiling that blotted out the sun.

Ahead, he saw an impenetrable wall of trees and brush. The damp air smelled of an odd combination of melting plastic from Anna and Miriam, destroying robots and something entirely different. Perhaps rotting wood, for he saw fallen trees half decomposed. How long did it take for a tree to decay? He had no idea. Such was the life of a boy raised in a laboratory as a test for an unknown purpose.

He drew closer to what looked like a dead end but was actually a 90-degree turn. Derrick hovered a few feet above the dirt path. Trees and brush could have provided cover, but safety was an illusion because the robots probably didn't see things the same as people. He was sure of that. The robots likely saw heat signatures. They would spot him instantly against the cooler forest. He was better off in the open, floating in the air, pretending to be a robot.

Rebekah appeared first. Hands raised. She wouldn't know what to make of him. He gave a little wave before the robots turned the corner, but she didn't seem to notice. He looked like another enemy, he supposed. The robots turned the corner, and Rebekah was back in front of them. What would be a robot's first reaction? Locate and kill the threat, or shoot the hostage? More importantly, could he shoot both before one of them could fire?

All unknowns.

Derrick didn't like unknowns.

He had no time to contemplate the issue. Each robot had a weapon pointed at Rebekah. Putting his weapon's sights on the first robot, he started to squeeze the trigger.

Then stopped.

Something told him he could not fire fast enough. He had killed three robots before they could fire but this felt different. He didn't know why.

Just a hunch.

Derrick hated a hunch.

Especially if it were his.

He lowered his weapon. "Don't shoot. I come in peace bearing a message from Mr. Derrick King."

The robots stopped in such unison that Derrick thought perhaps Five was wrong. Maybe only one was a controller. But he didn't think Five was wrong. He didn't know how robots thought, saw, or worked. He wasn't much more knowledgeable regarding people, but robots had no emotions—well, except Charlie, who now had Akira's emotions along with whatever it was he had developed over the decades of lonely existence.

Controllers function on direct orders and logic, as Sentry Five said.

The direct orders were unknown to Derrick, but since the robots didn't fire, he assumed the order was to not kill Derrick King. At least, don't kill Derrick King's messenger flying robot. Not yet, anyway. So, what was the logic? Since he hated operating on feelings, suspicions, and intuitions, logic should be his wheelhouse, which was a term he did not fully understand. Yet he did. Infer by context? That didn't seem much better than intuition. Assuming logic was his strong suit, suddenly seemed like a mistake.

He had nothing.

"Are you Derrick King?" one robot asked.

Lying had not served Derrick well in Potterville, but this was New York. Lying here felt right. "I am not. Derrick will come at my command. First, I must ascertain your intentions with Mr. King."

The robot didn't respond. The robot wasn't thinking it over. It was waiting for an order. It was communicating with Prime. Which gave Derrick a moment to think. Miriam said she had disrupted the outlier Primes from the central Prime. She said it was like a mirror—99% of communication was one way, downhill: Central Prime outward. The outliers usually just acknowledged receipt of the communications. Unless the Central Prime asked for a specific response, that was the end of the communication. Miriam's computer virus stopped the outliers from receiving the Central Prime's messages, but the computer acknowledge receipt. If the Central Prime demanded a response, the outlier reply would say it was researching.

It was possible the Central Prime would catch on, but Miriam had said that based on communications she had monitored, it was likely they could destroy the remaining outliers without the Central Prime knowing. All Prime locations knew about Seattle's destruction, but if Miriam's computer virus worked, Central Prime did not know what was happening here.

However, the New York Prime knew what was happening here. And, if the New York Prime could not contact the Central Prime, this Prime would think it was the last. So, what was this last Prime thinking? Prime's goals regarding him had changed more than once. First, it was bringing Derrick King back to Pacific Edge, albeit for deconstruction, but still, bringing him back alive. Then it was killing Derrick King. First with a missile that blew up Doc's house and then with a missile strike that killed four innocent kids outside the desert town. Prime had assumed each of those strikes would kill him and the others.

Derrick didn't know what Prime was thinking but hoped he'd created a bit of confusion. This Prime wasn't accustomed to making independent decisions. Did this Prime even understand what the Central Prime's motives were regarding the kids from Pacific Edge?

Maybe not.

That would be interesting to learn more about.

Based on a bit of logic that hinged on a hunch, Derrick thought a moment of confusion served him well.

"I shall summon Derrick King immediately. As soon as you tell me your intentions. Inform Prime that Mr. King would like to meet outside the building. No robots. No guards. Just the two of them."

And with that, he lowered his weapon and blasted both robots.

"What in the hell was that about?" Rebekah screamed. "You could have gotten us both killed."

"But I didn't."

Rebekah said, "Thank God. Now what? And can you turn off that stupid robot voice?"

Derrick didn't know how to turn off the robot voice, but Five must have heard because his normal voice, albeit loud, outside of his helmet said, "Help Anna and Miriam, and we then finish the job."

"Wait. Weren't you supposed to stay in the aircraft? Where is it?"

Derrick pointed up. "Still up there."

"Why are you here and not there?"

"Long story. Perhaps over coffee and a pastry at Donna's."

"Right. If we survive, and if Donna's is still there."

"You had better survive otherwise you'll never know this mystery regarding my presence here to save your life."

"Ha, ha. Your sister is rubbing off on you. I had this handled just fine until you showed up." Rebekah took up a weapon from one downed robot and shot both again for good measure.

Derrick turned and flew back to the clearing. Rebekah followed. The shooting had stopped. Some robots stood. Some were on the ground. Most had missing parts scattered here and there. A pile of batteries smoldered in the opening. It seemed they had the upper hand at last, which presented them with an opportunity.

Understanding what this isolated Prime in New York was thinking seemed almost as important as destroying it.

However, convincing Miriam would prove difficult. Derrick was sure of that.

16

AKIRA WAS BORED, WHICH RESULTED IN her noticing how sterile the room looked and how isolated she felt. Over the past couple of hours, Charlie had popped in occasionally to check on this and that, but she felt confident he was checking on her. Charlie was gone now. Red had left earlier. "Minor repairs were needed at the reactor. I'll be back soon," he had said.

But he wasn't back.

Akira was worried.

But that wasn't right. Worry was an emotion she lacked. Her emotions were drifting around inside Charlie.

What if Charlie malfunctioned, Red didn't return, and neither did Miriam and the others? Then what? Where did that leave her?

Alone.

That's where it left her.

She did not know what happened to her family. Yet she sensed they were no longer in Potterville. Either they left or Potterville no longer existed. The latter seemed entirely possible, given recent events.

Akira had been waiting to hear from New York for 30 minutes. Miriam and Derrick had cut radio transmissions when they arrived. Akira understood. Safer that way. But she didn't like it. Not one bit. She wanted to help.

She was helping no one. Red said he didn't need help. Easy job. She needed to stay here in case Miriam made radio contact. If the job was easy, why did Red leave so early? Why has he been gone so long?

It didn't make sense.

Except it did. Red didn't want her there. She had screwed things up the last time. That's why she got such a high dose of radiation. Red took responsibility. Kept saying it was his fault, but she realized during the night that Red was trying to cover up her mistakes. Since her head was so messed up, she didn't even know what she'd done wrong—no memory of it. But Red knew. The others did as well.

That's why they left her behind.

She couldn't do anything from here. It was all happening out there.

They didn't trust her. She didn't blame them.

Charlie walked in. "You should eat. Since everyone is gone, there's not much. Soup and sandwiches."

"Is Red back?"

"He is not."

Charlie probably sent food to Red. There were break areas in that section of the complex. Perhaps Red didn't want to be around her.

She didn't blame him.

"I'm not hungry."

"Are you okay?" Charlie asked, the concern evident in his voice. She didn't think Charlie could feel empathy. It was her emotions he was feeling, which meant she was feeling sorry for herself.

No surprise there.

"I'm alright." She paused. "Is Red okay? He's been gone a long time. He said it was an easy fix. I should check on him."

"I am monitoring his progress. Red is satisfactory, considering."

"Considering what?"

Charlie said nothing for a moment, as if thinking over how to respond, which made little sense because Charlie could process vast amounts of data in microseconds.

Perhaps having her emotions was disrupting his programming.

Messing him up.

No surprise there.

"Charlie, delete my emotions. They are slowing you down. Plus, you can't give them back to me anyway."

"This is a valid observation. But it's not your emotions slowing me down. I am processing much more data now. Unfamiliar information that is more gray than black and white."

Akira turned in her chair. "When I asked about Red, what did you mean, considering? And why did that cause you to pause?"

"Did I pause?"

"A very long pause, Charlie. Out with it."

"Red told you it was a simple fix. That was an inaccurate statement. It is a challenging job, even for trained technicians. Reactor one is in a critical state. I paused because there are many variables to consider."

"What variables?"

"How much should I tell you? Red didn't want you to know. I have analyzed many explanations, but determining the most accurate reason is difficult. There's a possibility that Red has multiple motives.

"I know why he didn't tell me."

"You do?"

"Yes. He doesn't trust me, not after what happened."

"This sort of thing does not compute. I find no data indicating Red lacks trust in you."

"Then why, Charlie? Tell the truth."

"Sometimes, the truth can hurt people. I find they often don't tell the truth, or at least they hide things."

"Like what?"

"Like L. Linda Maxton's death."

"What? Do you think Derrick hurt her?"

"Nothing like that. It's hard to describe."

"I'm confused."

"As am I. There are things he is keeping to himself. He's hiding something."

"Okay. Back to Red. Out with it."

"Based on my observations, Red trusts you. In fact, he admires you."

"Why on earth…"

"You saved his life. You saved everyone's life. You did nothing wrong. I've run the scenario multiple times, and you did everything exactly right. The odds of a trained staff member accomplishing what you did are very low."

"Then why did Red lie?"

"Again, my assessment. He knows you would try to help, and you cannot take more radiation. He's protecting you."

"Can he take that much radiation and fix what's broken?"

"Possibly not. But he is taking every precaution. He donned a high-rad protective suit before he started. I have QR-3s helping. Still, it's a substantial task. A successful outcome will take time."

Akira held back tears. "Is he going to be okay? I should go."

"As I said, you cannot. It is too dangerous for you."

"My decision. I've got to help Red."

"I must make another complex decision using data that is not black and white. However, this time, I can reach a decision without delay."

"What in the world are you talking about?"

"You're not going. I won't let you."

17

DERRICK HEARD NO SOUNDS COMING from what remained of the hangar. To be sure there was no further threat, he flew there. Adjusting his helmet display for the darkness, he understood what had happened. As Miriam had predicted, the majority of the structure was underground, much like the base. The aircraft were brought up using a huge elevator. The missile had hit the elevator shaft. The explosion had caused the shaft to collapse, creating a sealed tomb. He turned and flew back to the fallen robots.

Miriam's voice sounded in his headset. "I'm sorry. I was wrong. They were ready for us."

"It makes sense they were ready after Seattle. Or maybe your computer virus didn't work."

"I don't think that's what happened, but you have a valid point. It might not have worked," Miriam said.

Anna said, "Thanks, Derrick. I thought we were done for."

It was true. For all her doubts about Derrick, he had pulled through. Derrick had always been self-centered in Pacific Edge, so his concern for others confused her. Anna had not witnessed Derrick's time in Potterville. It had changed him. But maybe it was something else. Maybe there was more too it. Her purpose in the test program was to see how much it took to break a person's spirit. They teased and tormented her. That was her role. Although the mind wipe was supposed to erase all her memory of being a test subject, it did not change the girl they had created. She was shy and backward until Miriam gave her the code to the monitor's remote, and then she learned how to access her memories. She became the opposite of the girl they tried to break —bold and assertive. Perhaps at times she took it too far. Maybe Derrick flipped as well from being self-centered to caring. Maybe he just needed to find the right balance.

Rebekah joined them. Anna hugged her.

Derrick settled to the ground, removed his helmet, and stepped out of the PFP. Looking at Rebekah, he said, "What about the big gun thing back there? Is there still a robot we need to take care of?" Derrick asked.

Rebekah's eyes fell, just for a second, then she looked at Derrick, then at Miriam. "No. There were two robots and one man."

"So, we have one guy that's still a threat." Derrick thought for a moment. Knowing that he was likely the only one who wouldn't just kill the guy, he said, "I'll take care of it and be back in a minute."

"No need," Rebekah said. "They killed him."

Derrick said, "Who killed him? The robots?"

Rebekah nodded.

Miriam said, "There's more. After we surrendered, we heard screams and shooting inside. It's been quiet for a while now."

Derrick stared at her. "What happened?"

"I don't know. We were preoccupied, but I can guess."

"Go on," Derrick said.

"I think they killed the staff."

"The robots? Why would they do that?" Derrick asked.

"Prime ordered it."

"That makes little sense. Why would Prime kill the people who would protect him?"

"Fear and distrust. Here's my theory: When Prime realized it could not connect to the other headquarters, it concluded the others had also been destroyed. I suspect that although these outliers are Prime, they have no individual experience. They only follow directions. When this Prime thought it was the last one, self-preservation kicked into high gear. We could not know where this headquarters was located without inside help," Miriam said.

After a beat, Derrick said, "We had inside information from Stanley Mires. The Resistance guy who was supposed to be in Seattle."

"Right. He was supplying Professor and Wizard with inside information."

Derrick thought for a moment. "So, it's our fault."

Miriam said, "Excuse me?"

"Prime killed them because we showed up," Derrick said, feeling the color drain from his face.

"Not our fault. Prime killed them." Miriam paused. "We might have been forced to kill them to destroy Prime."

Derrick didn't like thinking about that. Thinking that because robots killed those people somehow made the situation better nauseated him. Those people were all dead. Directly or indirectly, he was responsible.

Miriam said, "Let's get this over with. Rebekah, go back to the aircraft and get it into the air. Pick us up when we are done. Derrick, go back to your aircraft. When we finish, we'll decide our next move."

Derrick had to go in. He had to question Prime. It was vital that they learn more about what happened here. What this Prime knew and what it did not.

"I'm going in with you."

Miriam started to protest. Derrick held up his hand. "Simple assault tactic. A three-pronged attack is much better than two."

Miriam nodded. "Okay. But Anna is lead."

"Sure thing," Derrick said, and then added, "Let me see what Five can tell us."

Derrick put on the helmet and ensured he had a private line to Five. "Five, this is private and must be kept confidential."

"Go ahead."

"Can you tell me where Prime is located in the building?"

"The one called Prime appears to be in the rear section on the top floor."

That surprised Derrick. He assumed Prime would be on a floor below the complex. "Five, I am going to open a channel with the others. You must sound as if I just made contact. Understood?"

"Yes, and not exactly."

Derrick opened the channel. "Five? Come in Five."

"Sentry Five."

"Is everything okay up there?"

There was a pause. Derrick thought perhaps the radio had disconnected, but then Five said, "Everything is functioning properly. There are no aircraft on the radar."

Derrick thought for a moment. "How far does the radar reach?"

"At this altitude, approximately 1800 miles. We could ascend to a higher position if you require additional range."

"Are you certain? That seems odd. There are no aircraft within 1800 miles?"

Five said, "There are commercial aircraft. I anticipated you were asking about military or enemy aircraft. I can start reading you a list. Do you want the closest aircraft first or the largest aircraft? Perhaps the fastest aircraft?"

Derrick said, "You had it right the first time. Can you tell me how many people are in the large building?"

"I see two heat signatures in the back. They are not moving, but both are alive."

"How many robots?" Anna asked.

"Twelve."

Derrick said, "Most of them were out here."

Anna said, "That makes sense. Prime wanted to stop us before we got into the building."

Derrick said, "How do we get in? The doors must be locked. They won't be easy to get through."

Miriam said, "It might be easier than it would appear." She walked over to a robot Derrick knew was a controller. She opened a small door on its side and removed something. Holding it up, she said, "Key."

It didn't look like a regular key. It was just a card, but Derrick figured Miriam knew what she was talking about. "Five, are there robots in the front of the building, behind the doors we are approaching?"

"There are no robots there. They are deeper inside. Six on the top floor and six on the bottom floor."

"How many floors are there?" Derrick asked.

Five said, "Two."

Derrick said, "I thought it would be bigger. I wonder what they do here?"

Miriam said, "Good question. My guess is that it is primarily for aircraft, like the ones we've flown."

Derrick walked to the double doors that led into the facility. Thick metal, painted rust-red. "I would have thought there were more robots."

Miriam said, "I think there are a lot more. They are sealed underground in the other building, trapped in there after you hit it with a missile." She paused, holding the key card near a port at the side of the door. "Are we ready?"

Derrick and Anna shouldered their weapons. Each responded with one word. "Ready."

Miriam said, "We'll work through the building together. Shoot first at anything alive or moving. No hesitation. Hesitation will get one of us killed. Any problems with that?"

Anna said, "No problems here."

"Derrick?" Miriam asked.

"No problem".

Miriam held the card near a small box by the door. A light turned green, and the door opened. It swung inward. Derrick saw nothing. Anna motioned him forward. He peeked around the edge of the door quickly and then back. He saw nothing, but a foul smell drifted from the open doorway. He motioned to Anna, who stood on the opposite side. She mirrored his quick glance inside. Pulling back, she nodded.

Derrick eased back around the doorway, leading with his weapon at eye level. Still nothing. He scanned the room, then the hallway, then back to the room. The room was small, stark, utilitarian. Nothing fancy except the walls were dark wood, perhaps walnut, maybe something else. To his left, against the wall, was a brown leather couch. It looked new, as if no one had ever sat there. Probably not many visitors. Maybe none. Perhaps they were the first.

On his right stood a counter made from the same wood. Polished. Expensive. The wall behind the counter was splattered with blood and bone, gray matter, and flesh. Two spots. Both large. Both fresh. The remains of two people. One bloody splatter had a long strand of hair the same color as L. Linda Maxton's. He didn't want to see what was left, and he feared seeing green eyes, but ensuring there were no threats behind the counter was necessary.

He took a quick look. Felt his stomach twist. Felt the blood drain from his face. Seeing the color of their eyes was not an issue. Two women, both unarmed, neither had a face left. Close range, probably a shotgun or similar weapon. Derrick said nothing. He just looked at Anna. Miriam had joined her. He shook his head. No threat. There never was from these two. Prime didn't see it that way. He had to learn what Prime was thinking. To do that, he had to get there first.

Derrick moved to the hallway. Miriam and Anna had taken a position on the other side. He motioned that he was looking down the hall at their side and that they were to look at his. Better angle. Standard procedure. The hallway was clear. Anna indicated she would go first. Derrick shook his head, motioned her to stay put.

Anna frowned. Miriam motioned they should hurry. Derrick shook his head. No reason to rush. The people were dead. The robots were not. The robots knew they were inside. Probably knew their location. Robots would not be impatient. Time was on their side. Haste equaled mistakes. Derrick hoped Prime did not share the robots' patience. Prime was scared. Odd as that seemed, Derrick knew it was true. Otherwise, Prime would not have killed its staff. Fear led to bad decisions. They were outnumbered by killing machines. Efficient. Patient. They needed the robots to make mistakes. But robots didn't make mistakes. They needed Prime to do that.

And Prime did.

Derrick saw a weapon appear at the intersection of the hall. He motioned to Anna. She nodded. Their weapons didn't shoot bullets. They fired a burst of energy, much like the one he carried. He didn't understand it exactly, but he understood the concept. Understood the weapon's capability. This hall was not hardened concrete. It was a half inch of chalky material pressed hard and covered with paper and paint. He didn't know the composition, but he believed the weapon's energy would pass through it. However, he did not know how much energy might be lost or if it would stop the robot. Depending on where the charge struck. Depending on a lot of things.

He aimed at the wall, so the electrical energy would pass through and hit the robot. That was the theory. Miriam and Anna responded correctly, both taking up positions at the edge of the hall entry, one high, the other low. One aiming at the left, and one aiming at the right. Killing the robot by shooting through the walls was a gamble. A head shot should do it. The designers, being humans, put a lot of important circuitries there, but hitting the head based on a guess of where the machine stood was iffy. Most likely, the robot would come out firing. Maybe somewhat disabled. Perhaps fully functioning. Accurate and fast. Others would emerge with weapons firing. Not the best scenario, but it was the scenario they faced.

Derrick calculated the size of the weapon, envisioned the robot standing, and aimed at the center of the robot's chest. Its human designers put important stuff there too. They couldn't help themselves. The human body permeated their thinking. That was his hunch.

The weapon was designed to kill people. That was its purpose. But it could also be dialed back. That was why he selected it. Killing people was something he wanted to avoid. It had also proven effective at stopping robots. Sometimes things work out.

Often, they do not.

He selected the highest setting. Best bet given the wall and the robot. It would have been safer to have been prone, exposing as little as possible at the corner where the wall and floor met. The robot would likely fire at where a person stood. Right at him. But the angle might reduce the bolt of electricity reaching the robot. Inflicting maximum damage seemed best. He glanced at Miriam and Anna and nodded.

They both acknowledged. Ready.

He fired. The barrel of the weapon moved fast into the hall. Derrick fired again into the robot's head as it cleared the corner. Miriam and Anna were firing as well. Two robots emerged from the opposite side. The robot Derrick shot fell sideways, knocking the first robot into the wall, causing its shots to go wild but also causing one of the girls to miss. The third robot's head exploded, and then the second did as well.

Derrick stayed on target for a couple of minutes, but no other robots emerged. Smoke curled from the machines and hung in the air, burning his lungs and stinging his eyes.

"Cover me," Derrick said, and before either Miriam or Anna could respond, he stepped into the hall and moved to the intersection where the robots had fallen.

He slid along the wall on the left, peering as far as he could into the right hallway. He could see a metal door with a placard that said *stairs*. He moved to the other side and repeated the process. Finally, he got on the floor and glanced at the full hallway.

Empty.

He motioned for Anna and Miriam.

Pointing, he said, "Stairway is there. Three robots left on this floor. Six below. Prime is probably downstairs. Safer there." He was lying and hoped it didn't show. Then he added, hoping his assumption would work. "I'll go downstairs. You guys finish up here."

Anna snapped. "I'm the leader, or did you forget? Miriam and I will go downstairs. That evens our odds. We each have three robots to destroy and then Prime."

Miriam said, "We should stick together."

This didn't surprise Derrick. It made sense. It was the best plan. Miriam was smart. Derrick was no match for her, but he had to have a moment with Prime. "That's a good idea, which means it is predictable. Five told me robots function on direct orders and logic. Our best bet is to be illogical."

Miriam nodded. "Okay. But Anna is right. We'll go downstairs. Be careful."

"You too." Derrick motioned to the stairwell. "The doorway will be the most dangerous. I'll go that far with you. I'll open the door. You be ready to fire."

Miriam and Anna took up positions on either side of the doorway. Derrick pulled it open, throwing himself against the wall. Anna fired immediately, before he'd even hit the wall. Miriam fired a split second later. A robot fell to the floor at his feet.

"That was close. Thanks," Derrick said.

Miriam patted his chest. "Don't get yourself killed, brother. I need you."

Derrick felt a bit disgusted lying to her, but it was for the best. He was certain of that. "See you in a few minutes."

The door closed slowly against the pneumatic control as Derrick eased down the hallway. He was completely exposed and didn't like it. Perhaps this wasn't such a good idea. The three-prong method is safest and most effective, and he was experiencing the reason in real time. Creeping down the hall, he kept the weapon at the ready, sweeping it back and forth across the opening. He wondered how many times the weapon could fire. He had a standard military pistol but hoped he didn't have to use it. It would not be as effective against the robots.

Considering the consequences of going against robots or Prime with a pistol caused him to dial the weapon back. He did not know if that setting would disable a robot. There were three robots remaining as well as Prime and one person. Although given Five's description, Derrick thought the last person was Prime's assistant, might be injured. Perhaps dead already. The other heat signature was Prime, and because Prime had ordered the robots to kill all the staff, Prime's assistant had likely not fared any better.

Derrick slowed at an open door. Peeking inside the room, he saw a vending machine like those at the base. A large chrome container for coffee. And a foot. The person was prone and still. He gave his usual quick glance.

No robots.

A room full of bodies.

Pools of blood.

Splatters on the walls.

Ten to twelve people. All dead.

Prime must have summoned them to the breakroom, where robots mowed them down.

Weapons erupted below him, muffled. Bolts of electricity shot through the next hallway intersection. The robots had fired in response to the gunfire. An automated response. A last-ditch effort.

A muffled three-shot burst sounded below his feet. Before the sound faded, bolts of electricity followed. The robots had switched weapons. The bullet-riddled bodies indicated guns were used in the massacre. Why did they switch? Perhaps they had used all their ammunition.

The air smelled of ozone and burned metal and blood. He knew virtually nothing about electricity or its properties. Knowledge may have helped in this situation. He had grown up with electricity all around him. Everything in Pacific Edge ran on it. Yet, the Chosen literally denied its existence, so engrained was their anti-science philosophy.

Miriam understood the foolishness in the Chosen ways. Rebelled against it. He had been oblivious. Fell in line with fervor.

What an idiot he had been.

What else was he not seeing? Something important, he feared.

He crawled to the corner, then positioned himself so he could inch just enough to see down the hallway. Derrick moved slowly until the first robot came into view, stopping before he could see the machine's head. He aimed for the shoulder, right at the joint, and squeezed the trigger.

As soon as he fired, he pulled back against the wall. Lightning bolts blazed down the hall, causing Derrick's hair to stand straight up. Perhaps the power was low, but the bolts were still deadly. Of that, he was certain.

Another wave of lightning surged through the hall. How many was that? Three? Four? He was running out of time.

A muffled scream. "Help me. I'm injured. For god's sake, help me!"

Derrick's chest constricted until he realized the voice was neither Anna nor Miriam. It came from the direction of the robots. Prime's assistant, perhaps.

He eased to the opening. The robot stood in the same location, except its right arm, the one holding the weapon was pointing straight down. The floor at its feet was blackened. His shot had disabled its arm.

Robots function using logic or direct orders.

These were drones following orders. Fire at anything threatening, which included the weapons on the other floor of the building.

At least, he hoped that was the case. If they were using logic, they would anticipate his next shot. Just waiting for his weapon to become visible.

He eased to the edge of the hallway on his stomach and peered around the corner.

The man screamed again. Lightning coursed just above his head.

This time he'd aimed at where he estimated the second robot stood. Whether he had hit it, was unknown.

He'd find out soon enough.

Switching back to full power, he fired where he estimated the third robot stood. No return fire. He stood and eased around the corner. The first robot fired another bolt of lightning at its feet. Derrick put a bolt of electricity into its head.

Six robots down.

One person and Prime remained.

Derrick eased past the ruined robots. Thought about taking one of their weapons but decided against it. He wasn't sure why.

He heard more gunfire downstairs. It lasted several seconds, probably the last of the robots. He took a deep breath, hoping Miriam and Anna were alright, wishing they would have stayed together, wondering if he'd made the right decision. Would he learn something important from Prime?

He eased the door open. A man lay on the floor, his face pale and wet. His body twisted in an unnatural way. He saw Derrick, his eyes pleading.

Then the voice Derrick heard earlier. "Is someone there? You must help me." It was coming from the other side of the room. He could not see the source.

Derrick went to the crumpled man. The man looked as if most of the bones in his body were broken. Derrick kneeled next to him.

The man whispered. "He was killing them. I'm sorry, but I had to do something."

"What happened?" Derrick asked, although he already guessed the gist of it.

"I shot Prime. I'm sorry. I was supposed to protect him, but …" a few words were lost … "was killing them."

"Prime? That's who is asking for help?" Derrick asked.

From across the room, the voice said, "I can hear you. I'm the one you should be helping. I am Prime. You must save me. It is written."

Derrick lowered his voice. "Does Prime have a weapon?"

"Prime *is* a weapon, but I destroyed the mainframe first. Prime cannot control any weapons except the robots."

"All destroyed." Derrick hoped that was true. He had not heard gunfire for a few minutes.

"Is it true? Were all the other Primes destroyed?"

One question answered. Miriam's block had worked. This Prime thought it was the last. That would likely be the case when they attacked the other sites.

Derrick shook his head. No reason to not be truthful with the man. He wasn't long for this world and wouldn't be repeating any information to anyone.

Derrick said, "We'll get help. Just hang on."

The man shook his head. Just a little. "There's no helping me." He took a ragged breath. "Are you him? Are you Derrick King?"

Derrick nodded.

"You must stop Prime. He has gotten worse. He's crazy. He plans to destroy the world."

The man was in shock, but Derrick had no doubt he believed what he was saying, and for good reason, because when Prime ordered the robots to kill all the staff, it must have seemed like the end of the world. It was the end of the world for the people here.

"I'll be back." Derrick started to stand.

"But you're Derrick King. You cannot …" The man drew his last breath. His eyes remained open but stopped moving. He was gone.

Prime said, "Derrick King! I command you to save me."

Derrick stood. A shot rang out from below. He walked toward Prime's voice. The weapon in his right hand pointed at the floor. *I can kill Prime after I learn what I need to know.* Why he was trying to convince himself of this, he did not know.

Stepping around a large, ornate desk, Derrick saw Prime lying in a pool of blood. This one was much different from the Prime in Seattle. Arms and limbs were huge and looked as if they belonged to an animal, but the face looked normal. The body was clothed, and it bled like a human.

Smoke drifted from a rack of computers against the far wall.

Prime looked at him. "Derrick King. You must save me."

Another muffled shot.

Prime said, "Who's still fighting? Your sister, I assume. The robots will take care of her."

Another shot.

"You're wrong. The robots are gone. Miriam is destroying your replacements." The stack of computers sent sparks flying into the room. "I assume your assistant ended your ability to replicate, or whatever it is you do."

"He was a traitor. Go finish him."

Derrick felt a strange sensation but didn't move. Instead, he said, "He's dead."

"Good," Prime said. "Now, send for help. I must survive."

Derrick said, "What did this location do?"

"Isn't it obvious? Aircraft. That was our purpose. By now, we have launched hundreds of aircraft to put down this rebellion."

"They didn't launch."

Prime coughed, blood sprayed from his mouth. Time was running out.

"Where's the Central Prime?" Derrick asked.

"You don't know? Then I was not the last. This is wonderful news. But I couldn't contact Central. All my communications were answered by routine responses. My assistant said it was like a prerecorded loop. He could not determine the ..."

Prime stopped for a moment and then said, "It was your sister!"

Derrick remembered that they had planted a phrase in his brain using hypnosis that would force him to obey. He had to kill Prime before the code words could be uttered.

But his arm wasn't responding.

The crack of a weapon startled him.

Derrick turned to see Anna holding a rifle. A whiff of smoke drifted from the barrel. He spun back and saw that the top half of Prime's head was gone.

"Why did you do that?! Prime was no longer a threat. I was trying to find out where the Central Prime is located."

"And did you learn where it was?"

"You shot before Prime could answer."

"You should have killed it."

"I was trying to get information. The assistant destroyed the computers." Derrick pointed. "Prime could do nothing. There was no danger."

"Was it still talking?"

"Yes. Of course."

"Then it was still dangerous."

18

MIRIAM APPEARED A FEW SECONDS LATER, three-shades paler than normal, holding her side, where blood stained the fabric. She looked at Prime, staring for a moment. They said nothing. Anna led them out. Derrick scanned the halls, hoping to see a closer exit, but there were none. No fire escapes. No escapes of any sort. One way in, one way out. He refused to look into the breakroom again. But the dead could not be unseen, and the stench remained unavoidable. He walked through the lobby. Past the rich walnut counter, past the hardwood paneling, past the wall splattered with blood, brains, and bone, finally bursting into the sunlight where thirty some dead robots smoldered.

Making a right-hand turn after exiting the building, Derrick made it fifteen yards and then threw up. A few minutes later, he rejoined the group. Rebekah had landed the aircraft. Miriam and Anna sat side by side on a concrete barrier pitted and pocked by bullets. The color had drained from both. Rebekah stood a few feet away. She had a little color in her face, but not much.

"Are you okay?" Rebekah asked as Derrick walked up.

"No."

"What happened in there?" Rebekah asked.

Derrick looked at Miriam. "You're bleeding."

Miriam said, "I'm okay. Pulled some stitches, I think." She looked at Rebekah. "The robots killed the staff."

"Slaughtered them." Derrick said. "They gathered them in the breakroom and killed them. At least a dozen, plus two women at the counter in the foyer."

Anna said, "We found five dead downstairs. That's where the replicants were. One had started birthing, or whatever the hell it is they do to become active."

"Is that what we are calling them now? Replicants?" Rebekah asked.

Anna said, "That's what Prime calls them. Written on the tubes that contain them."

"That's curious," Derrick said, joining them.

"That Prime calls them replicants?" Miriam asked.

"No. That one was activating. Prime's assistant destroyed the mainframe computer. Prime could not do anything."

"Prime was still alive when you got there?" Rebekah asked.

"Barely. The assistant had shot him. Prime was on the other side of the room. I couldn't see Prime. The assistant was still alive. Prime had broken every bone in the man's body. He could not move. He got a few words out before he died." Derrick paused. "Prime was unlike the one in Seattle. Huge arms and legs. It looked like some kind of animal. Except the face, that looked human. It was hideous."

Miriam stared at him. "You talked to Prime?"

"Yes. It was begging for help."

Anna said, "Sounded more like orders to me."

"You didn't hear all the conversation. Prime thought it was the last. It figured out it could not communicate with Central Prime." Derrick paused. "We are the reason those people were killed."

Anna said, "Prime killed them. Not us."

"We should go back to the base and rethink this. I don't want to be responsible for innocent people getting killed," Derrick said.

Anna stood. Fist clenched. "Innocent! They aren't innocent. They work for Prime, and Prime is a monster."

Derrick stood too, feeling more anger than he wanted. "True, but we don't know how much freedom they have. The assistant killed Prime."

"I killed Prime."

"The wounds were fatal. Prime was dying."

Miriam said, "Calm down. Both of you." She thought for a moment. "Derrick is right, we caused Prime to freak out."

"Could we have done something different?" Rebekah asked.

"No. But it didn't go as planned. Prime was ready for an assault. I didn't see that coming."

"So, we go to the base?" Derrick asked.

All eyes turned to Miriam. She remained silent for a moment, and then said, "No. We finish what we started. Chicago is next. We'll do better at assessing the situation. This headquarters had a lot of aircraft."

"It was their mission here," Derrick said. Their faces indicated doubt. "Prime told me."

"You should have killed it straight away," Anna said.

Miriam said, "Enough. That might explain the situation here."

"You lost me," Rebekah said, adding, "not unusual."

"This Prime focused on security. At least from the air, meaning it was more geared toward combat," Miriam said.

"Do you know what Prime does in Chicago?" Derrick asked.

"I do not, but we're about to find out. Chicago is close. We go there, take out that Prime. Then we'll find an isolated place between Chicago and Dallas. We'll make further plans. Derrick, I assume you can use the flying backpack thing to get back to your ship. You fly ahead, same as before. Scout the situation and send images. Nyx has the coordinates. Don't start anything until we get there."

Derrick said, "I'll do my best not to. One question. How are we going to find the Central Prime? If we can't do that, all these people have died for nothing." Derrick was mostly thinking about one life lost unnecessarily and far too soon, but he didn't say that.

Miriam said, "After Chicago, I'm going to contact the Central Prime."

"Is that safe?" Derrick asked.

"We'll soon find out. Go scout Chicago."

19

IT STRUCK DERRICK AS ODD THAT HE NOTICED birds singing as he walked back toward the PFP. The silent trees stood so tight that little light fell on the forest floor, which was covered with fallen moss-covered tree trunks. Ferns grew taller than his head. It was beautiful here. Except for the smoking robot remnants and the visions of dead bodies that he could not vanquish.

Other than that, it was great.

Miriam fell in at his side, sending Anna ahead to the aircraft.

"Can I ask you something, brother?"

"Sure."

"Why didn't you destroy Prime first?"

"I couldn't see Prime, but I knew it was wounded. The man, his assistant, was still alive, although his body was twisted and broken."

"You went to him because he was alive? Or because you wanted to do something for him? I don't understand. You could have destroyed Prime and then tended to the assistant. You didn't know Prime was mortally wounded. Right?"

Derrick didn't like where this was going. He felt certain Miriam was going to ask questions he had already asked himself and found no answers.

"I wanted to help him." Derrick paused. "I didn't want him to die alone."

Miriam laced her arm through his as they walked. "I want to come back to New York someday when this is all over. It's beautiful."

Derrick didn't respond. He knew more was coming.

They stopped in front of the PFP, hovering a few feet above the ground. Derrick wondered if Miriam understood how the backpack worked. If she did not, he wondered how much not knowing bothered her.

"Derrick, I'm worried."

"Me too. That's why I think we should go back to the base and rethink this."

"I don't mean that. Don't get me wrong, I'm worried about Chicago. I'm distressed about the people killed here. But I'm talking about you. I'm worried about you."

"I'm okay."

"I'm worried you have forgotten about the secret phrases implanted in our heads that turn us in to killing machines at Prime's direction. Do you remember that?"

Derrick looked down. "I have not forgotten."

"It seems you have. We are in danger when we are in Prime's presence. That's why we must destroy every Prime immediately. We can't risk Prime using whatever secret phrase or other device he has planted in our heads."

"I figured we had control over it now that we are aware of it," Derrick said.

"Maybe we do. Maybe we don't. There's only one way to know for sure and we can't take that risk."

"Is that why you didn't want me to come with you here?"

Miriam studied him for a moment. "I didn't know it would be like this."

"What about Chicago?"

"We'll see when we get there. Go. Let me know what you learn. We'll be right behind you."

Derrick backed into the PFP. It closed around him. He put on his helmet and said, "Five? Can you hear me?"

"I hear you."

"Can you get me back to the aircraft?"

"That is affirmative."

And with that, Derrick shot straight up.

The backpack released Derrick once the aircraft door closed. He removed his helmet. Something wasn't right. It took a few moments for his brain to unravel what he saw. The door opening was not silent, and his arrival was not easily ignored unless a person was totally consumed in their activities. Neither Antonio nor Nyx tried to hide what was happening.

Fortunately, he could not see everything because of a console.

He could see Antonio's bare shoulders. He could only see Nyx's legs and part of her back. She was on her knees in front of Antonio.

He said nothing for a moment. In part from disbelief. In part from being unable to breathe. Then anger boiled from deep within.

Finally, he said, "What's happening here?" The anger in his voice was clear as he stepped farther into the aircraft. Still, Nyx did not move. Now he could see Antonio's flight suit pooled at his ankles. Nyx's hand was between Antonio's thighs.

Antonio noticed Derrick. As if he had just appeared. Derrick saw Antonio was pale. Almost like a ghost. "Hey, bro. I'm glad you're okay. Is something wrong?"

Finally, Nyx turned toward Derrick. "He's been shot. A round pierced the hull. Shrapnel hit him in the leg. I almost lost him." Tears streamed down her cheeks.

Derrick stepped closer. He could now see that Nyx was holding a medical device against Antonio's leg, and an intravenous line snaked to his arm.

Five said, "Shrapnel hit Antonio, cutting his femoral artery. He almost bled to death before Nyx got things under control."

Derrick felt faint. A bullet had hit Antonio. It could have killed him instantly. It could have killed any of them, including Nyx. And his thinking went straight to something entirely different. It was his responsibility to keep them both safe.

"I'm sorry. I didn't … uh, understand what…"

Both stared at him. Before he said something worse, he asked. "Will he be okay? We should get him to a hospital."

Nyx frowned. "What were you thinking? Don't answer that."

She paused. "Five says he will be okay. I have to hold this medical unit here for a few more minutes while it finishes repairing the artery and then stitching the wound."

Five said, "I had small robotic devices clean up the blood and others repaired the hull. Antonio will need a new flight suit. In addition, repairs have been completed to the ship. We can be underway soon if we don't make any sudden moves because Nyx and Antonio cannot be properly secured until the procedure is complete."

Derrick set his helmet down and sat. "We can wait." He would later realize this would be one of the most important lessons he would ever learn. The lives of others were far more important than his personal comfort. His desires. It was a lesson that would serve him well one day.

Nyx said, "I'm glad you're back. Was it terrible? Five told us there was gunfire and then quiet. What happened in there?"

"Prime ordered the robots to kill all the staff. They gathered most of them in a breakroom and slaughtered them. I can't get the image out of my head."

It was true. The images of the dead people and of the wall covered with blood and bones kept popping into his head despite attempts to block them. Worse, he kept seeing L. Linda Maxton's green eyes and promising her he'd destroy Prime. A promise he might not be capable of keeping.

"Where are we going next?" Antonio asked.

Derrick said, "Chicago. Nyx, you have the coordinates?"

"I do. Are we waiting for the others?"

"We are flying ahead, just like coming here."

After a few minutes, Five said, "The medical unit has completed the process."

Antonio stood, pulled his blood-soaked suit off, and tossed it in a receptacle.

Nyx busied herself stowing the medical device while Derrick helped Antonio put on a fresh flight suit.

"I'm sorry I ruined your suit, Five. I'll try not to do that again," Antonio said, adding, "Thanks, Nyx. You saved me."

Nyx took her seat, buckled in. "Everyone strapped in?"

When both Derrick and Antonio acknowledged they were ready, Nyx activated the flight plan. "Flight plan entered, Captain."

Derrick counted down from three and engaged the flight plan, which was just pushing a virtual button. The aircraft spun around and accelerated, pinning Derrick in his seat. "How long?"

"It's only 700 miles, so we can't reach the altitude or speed we achieved coming here. ETA is fifteen minutes. Rebekah will get there about fifteen minutes later."

Derrick said, "I don't understand where these places are or comprehend the distances involved, but it seems fast. Antonio, do you think this thing is faster than jets and such? Like the plane you and Red flew in?"

"Dude, so much faster. It's unbelievable."

Derrick said, "I'll bet Red would love this thing."

"You're not wrong."

"I hope he's okay," Derrick said.

"He's probably having a late second lunch or early first dinner," Antonio said.

"Maybe," Derrick said.

"You sound worried," Nyx said.

"He said there was a problem in the reactor he had to fix."

Antonio said, "Yeah, but he said it wasn't a big deal."

Derrick said, "That's what worries me."

"You lost me," Antonio said.

"If it wasn't a big deal, it could have waited. What he said and reality might be unrelated. That's what worries me."

"Well, crap," Antonio said.

Their chatting subsided, and they traveled the next few minutes in silence.

"Arriving at Chicago," Nyx said.

"Unbelievable," Antonio said.

Derrick said, "Five, can we see the building yet?"

"Coming on screen now."

The image of the roof of a tall building materialized on the monitor inside Derrick's helmet. Amazingly clear and detailed. It was as if he was just a few feet away. And what he saw wasn't good.

The building had 19 floors. Nineteen floors that might contain people, innocent or otherwise.

A black angular aircraft with a large capital P on the side was sitting on the roof next to a small structure with a door.

"Five, can you tell me about the building?" Derrick asked.

"The building has 19 floors and is a steel-beam skeletal structure utilizing pre-stressed concrete floors and stone siding. Built in ..."

Derrick cut in. "Not that. How many people are in the building and how many robots. Most important, where is Prime?"

"An unidentified bio-mechanical life form is on the top floor. There are 12 additional bio-mechanical life forms with extremely low metabolic rates on the next floor down. One human is located on the top floor in a separate part of the building. Because the floors are concrete, I cannot scan the entire building."

"Is this like Seattle?" Nyx asked.

"It appears to be," Derrick said.

"Then we'll go in through the basement and up to the top?" Antonio asked.

Derrick said, "I guess."

Five said, "Is this an occasion where I should insert information?"

"Probably," Derrick said.

"Entry to the top two floors from below is impossible."

"Can you be more specific?" Derrick asked.

"The elevator is blocked from the 18th and 19th floors."

"That's not a problem. We would take the stairs."

"Also blocked."

"How is it blocked? You mean the stairs don't go all the way up?" Derrick asked.

"They have to," Antonio said.

No one said anything.

"They have to. Fire code," Antonio added.

"You know about fire codes?" Derrick asked.

"Student body president," Antonio replied.

"He wanted to wall up the school's second floor fire escape and add more snack machines," Nyx explained.

"Hey. It was my campaign promise."

"And they didn't allow that?" Derrick asked.

"They did not. And Mr. Snapp made me read the state fire code because of how much trouble it caused."

"So, not a total loss," Nyx said, adding, "anything that forces Antonio to read is a good thing."

"Hey. I represent that remark."

Nyx snickered and said, "You sure do."

Derrick stared at them for a moment and then said, "Five, are you sure we can't reach the 18th floor using the stairs?"

"I am certain. The staircase is there, but they have filled the stairwell with two rows of concrete blocks and welded a two-inch steel plate in place to protect the blocks."

"How does the assistant get up there?" Antonio asked.

Derrick said, "Maybe the blockage is new. After Seattle. Maybe he lives up there and doesn't leave." He paused, then said, "We have devices that can cut the hinges and locks."

Five said, "Did you miss the part about filling the stairwell with concrete blocks."

Derrick said, "Right. They did it after Seattle. Letting all the Prime's see what happened in Seattle was a mistake."

Nyx said, "Agreed. On the bright side, at least we know Miriam isn't perfect."

"That does not inspire confidence," Antonio said.

"Acknowledged," Nyx said.

"Five, how many robots?" Derrick asked.

"Two."

"Are you sure? That doesn't sound right. How about people below the 18th floor?" Derrick asked.

"I estimate twenty-seven, but that data is incomplete. Concrete."

Derrick didn't respond. That aircraft seemed problematic. It was there to ensure an escape route for Prime. It would probably be okay to let him leave. They could shoot the aircraft down. Probably. Unless that aircraft had technology beyond what they had seen in similar machines, including the one Rebekah, Anna, and Miriam were in. If any aircraft had additional abilities, it would be one that Prime used. If Prime escaped, they might never find it.

They had to disable the aircraft. They couldn't do it like Seattle. Landing on the roof also gave Prime advanced warning. Prime could seal the door, making getting in difficult and dangerous, if not impossible.

They could destroy the entire building. He was sure of that, given the damage their missiles caused to the aircraft bunker in New York.

Then a thought occurred to him. "Five, is there a way to disable that aircraft and create disruption on the 19th floor without blowing up the building?"

"Or starting a fire?" Antonio asked, and then added, "fires and smoke are dangerous in high-rise buildings."

"Or that?" Derrick asked, adding, "without killing everyone?"

Five said, "A disturbance might be possible. Shall I calculate how best to achieve that?"

"Yes. And, Nyx, send the images to Miriam."

Derrick opened a channel, pausing, hoping no one could monitor their communications. "Miriam? We are sending images."

Seconds later, Miriam said, "Got them."

Derrick said, "I think we should disable that aircraft. I can meet you on the roof."

Miriam said, "Stay put. If we disable the aircraft, Prime will know we are here."

"Prime expects us and probably already has defenses in place. The stairs and elevators won't work. We must enter from the roof," Derrick said.

"We could destroy the building," Miriam said.

"There are twenty-eight people in the building. One is Prime's assistant. The others are not involved."

Miriam didn't respond for a few moments. Thinking it over. Perhaps strategizing with Anna.

Derrick wanted to avoid Anna's plan. She seemed less concerned about innocent people than he was. He added, "Five is working on a solution."

Derrick cut the channel. "I hope you don't make a liar of me, Five."

"I do not see how that would be my fault. However, I have a solution."

"Tell me."

"I can alter the warhead, causing the missile to go through the aircraft, hitting its flight computer, disabling it."

"That sounds good."

Derrick reopened the channel. "Miriam, we have a plan."

20

DERRICK FLEW CIRCLES FOR WHAT felt like hours but was only a few minutes. Still, there was no reason for Miriam not to at least ask about his plan.

A hiss indicated Miriam had activated their radio. "Anna and I are going ahead with our first plan. Rebekah will hover right above the roof. We'll jump out and enter."

Derrick slapped the arm of his chair. She didn't even ask about his plan. "I will come using the flight pack."

"You stay put. We'll call you if we need you."

Derrick chewed his lip. He didn't like it, but it didn't surprise him. It was Anna. There was no *back-off* in that girl. He brought the aircraft around to get a better look at the door. In the upper right-hand corner of his display, Miriam's aircraft eased down toward the roof.

Something didn't feel right.

He zoomed in on the door, analyzing the jam. The deadbolt wasn't locked. Perhaps he was wrong, but he didn't think so. He zoomed in closer, inching around the doorjamb.

Derrick opened a channel to Miriam's aircraft and yelled, "Stop!"

And then to Five, he said, "Fire that missile."

Zooming back out, he hoped Rebekah wasn't too close, but he had told Five to disable the warhead, so there should not be a problem.

The Prime aircraft leaped a couple of feet off the roof, rebounding from the missile that pierced its hardened metal exterior. How the missile could do that without exploding baffled Derrick.

A split second later, every window on the top floor burst outward, sending shards of glass raining down like snow.

"What was that?" Derrick yelled to no one in particular.

Five said, "That was the warhead exploding."

Black smoke snaked from an open window.

Suddenly, the door to the small room on the roof exploded.

Miriam's voice pierced Derrick's ears. "What just happened?"

"We fired a missile," Derrick said, and then added, "I meant to disable the aircraft."

He cut the radio. "Five?!"

"Yes, sir."

"What just happened?"

"That door had explosives wired to it."

"I suspected that." More smoke poured from the window. "Why did the top floor explode?"

"You told me to disable the aircraft, but I understood the mission was to destroy Prime. So, I set the delay to put the missile in the center of the 19th floor when it exploded. I reduce the payload to 25%. So as to not destroy the building or start a fire that the fire suppression system could not manage."

"What about the assistant?"

"Still alive but not moving. Unlikely he sustained serious injury, other than not hearing well for a few days."

"But the fire. We have to get people out of the building."

Five said, "The fire suppression system will put out the fire."

Derrick noticed the smoke slow and then disappear.

"There. The fire is out."

The other aircraft landed. Miriam and Anna disappeared through a gaping opening that had once been a roof access door. They emerged a few minutes later. A man had his arm wrapped around their shoulders, his legs working, but just barely. All of them were soaking wet. Anna's hair was wet and stringy. Miriam's face was smudged with black.

As Rebel 1 lifted into the air, Miriam opened a channel to Rebel 2. "How did you know?"

Derrick hesitated. "Know what?"

"About the bomb on the door? We would have been killed."

"I inspected the door. The deadbolt wasn't locked. I saw contact points and wires."

Miriam said, "We found the assistant and decided to take him. We'll drop him somewhere after he answers a few questions."

"Drop him someplace?" Derrick asked. He imagined Miriam staring at the assistant, who was likely restrained by now.

Miriam said, "Depending on his answers, I might drop him off near a town or I might drop him from 20,000 feet."

Derrick didn't think Miriam would drop him from 20,000 feet. Ten thousand, maybe.

"Where to?" Derrick asked, feeling almost giddy given how easily Chicago had fallen. Maybe the worst of it was behind them. Later, Derrick would reflect on how wishful thinking like this wasn't a good thing.

Miriam said, "Follow us. We'll find a place to set down. We should eat before we hit Dallas."

Derrick wasn't hungry, and the images from New York still haunted him anytime his mind grew the least bit idle. Terrible as those images were, they prevented him from thinking about something worse: L. Linda Maxton's eyes and the promise he had made.

But Miriam was right. They needed to eat. It wasn't about being hungry. It was about being ready for the next fight. Despite his wishful thinking, Dallas might prove more difficult than Chicago.

During the flight toward Dallas, Derrick concentrated on weapons, both those of the aircraft and those he could carry, thought about attack strategies, and tried to block negative thoughts. If self-doubt ever became valuable, he'd be rich.

He tried to block memories of secret code words and other things Prime could trigger in his head, turning him into a killer over which he had no control. And he tried to block the realization that he had not yet been able to point a weapon at Prime. He rationalized this using differing methods, wrapped in the notion that he had been trying to extract information.

Rationalization was not better than wishful thinking.

Both could get people killed.

It already had.

Someone tapped his shoulder. Derrick lifted the front of his flight helmet. Antonio was out of his seat, standing in front of him.

Antonio tapped the side of his helmet. "Is your com not working?"

Derrick said, "I think it's working. Why?"

"Nyx has been trying to get your attention for a couple of minutes."

Derrick scanned his controls. His channel was open, but he'd turned the volume to zero. "Sorry, Nyx. I had the volume turned down."

"Just letting you know we are descending. Looks like Miriam has picked a spot."

"Where are we?" Derrick asked.

Nyx said, "Somewhere in Arkansas, I think. Could be Missouri. Or Oklahoma."

"What is an Arkansas?" Derrick asked.

"They are all states."

"It doesn't sound like we know exactly where we are," Derrick said. "Are the instruments that inaccurate?"

"The instruments are accurate, but it is in longitude and latitude, which I don't understand."

"What makes you think we are in one of those states?"

"Just how far we've gone, how fast we've flown, and my vague memory of a map we were supposed to learn in school, but since I never thought I'd get over 50 miles from Potterville, I didn't pay much attention."

Antonio said, "Well, we got out of Potterville. We have that going for us."

Nyx giggled.

Derrick didn't think it was that funny, but Nyx and Antonio had a lot of history. Probably some private joke between them. The thought caused a sinking feeling in his chest. So much for Chicago being easy. The elation had not lasted for long.

He wanted to ask if they'd seen a body fall from Miriam's aircraft but decided against it. Once on the ground, the man they'd pulled from the building would either step out or he wouldn't. Nothing Derrick could do to change that.

Nyx said, "We passed over a small town. Maybe a mile or two."

"More like five," Antonio said.

If anyone knew the distance, it would be Miriam. Probably down to the number of yards. He switched to a view of the outside, panning the camera, or whatever technology the aircraft used, to see 360 degrees. They were in a wooded area, but it didn't look like New York. These trees were rough, scrubby, and dry. Not mountainous, but not easy walking either. If it all looked like this, five miles could turn into ten. Maintaining a constant direction would be difficult. If the man was still alive and Miriam dropped him here, he might die before finding help. Perhaps that was her plan.

Witnesses were not good. Derrick couldn't argue with that. Especially one inclined to warn Prime. If that was possible. He didn't know if Prime had a phone one could call. A Prime assistant might know how to get a message through.

He saw a cloud of dust rise as Rebel 1 settled to the surface. He heard the radio hiss.

Miriam said, "Rebel 2. Stay inside. We are dropping off our guest. Then we'll move to another location."

Derrick should have felt relieved, but he did not. Anna might shoot the assistant as he walked away. Just to be safe. There was a good argument. The logic was sound. But he didn't like it. He thought about shutting off the outside view but didn't. The man walked away from Miriam's aircraft, and it lifted into the air.

He felt their aircraft moving again. Although he was the pilot, Nyx was handling the flight plan. In this case, the plan was to follow Rebel 1. The aircrafts were linked as if on a tether. He estimated they flew for two minutes and had traveled about twenty miles. The terrain looked the same as where Miriam had dropped Prime's assistant. Derrick was glad the man was okay. He hoped the man wouldn't do something that put them at greater risk.

The door slid open. Dust filled the air as the other aircraft eased to the ground. There were no rockets or jets, and Derrick didn't know why the aircraft still stirred up dust, but they did. It confirmed again how little he knew about technology, engineering, and mechanical devices. Add that to his lack of understanding people, and it added up to overall ignorance. He wasn't as smart as Miriam. He could accept that, but he wasn't stupid. At least he didn't think he was stupid. But he was ignorant. That's what living in the Chosen bubble did to him. Whether he could ever catch up with normal people, he didn't know.

How would any of the Chosen catch up? They were not special in the way they had been told. They were only special in that they were ignorant about the rest of the country. Perhaps the average person in New America was just as ill-informed regarding the rest of the world.

He stood still beside his chair, holding his helmet. *Even if we destroy Prime, what will become of the Chosen? What will become of us all?* He had to talk to Miriam about this. Maybe she had a plan. There had to be a plan. Otherwise, the country would fall into chaos. The solution might prove worse than the problem.

"Earth to Derrick."

Derrick turned around upon hearing his name. Nyx stood looking at him with a puzzled expression. "I did it again. Didn't I?"

Nyx said, "I'll say. What's happening with you? You have me worried."

Nyx touched his arm. He didn't have an answer. He didn't know what was happening to him. She was right to be worried. He was worried too.

"Just a lot on my mind."

She smiled—not a happy sort of smile, or I'm glad you are okay sort of smile, but an, I'm still worried about you sort of smile.

Antonio said, "Are you two going to stand there gawking at each other all day? I'm hungry."

Nyx laced her arm through Derrick's and led him off the ship. Miriam carried a dull green metal box and set it on the ground.

Opening the lid, she pulled out packages, handing one to each of them.

"What are these?" Antonio asked.

"MREs."

"MR what's?"

"Meals ready to eat." Miriam pointed at the front of a packet. "That's what it says. There's water too."

Antonio pulled a flat brown bar from the packet. "This is food? Why didn't Charlie send sandwiches?"

Anna studied the package. "These are military meals. They expired decades ago."

"This just keeps getting better. Doesn't it, Derrick? Better with each passing moment. I want a sandwich. There was a town back there. Why don't we go there and find a hamburger? And a milk shake? And fries?" Antonio asked.

Nyx giggled again.

Derrick felt that sinking feeling. History. Lots of history. And he wasn't emotionally mature enough to handle it. Another casualty of being Chosen. Another casualty of being Derrick King.

Miriam took a bite of a brown bar, just like the one Antonio was holding. "It's not great, but it's edible. It's fuel."

"I'll wait until we get someplace with real food," Antonio said.

Anna said, "Eat. It's not about enjoying it. It's about keeping our strength up."

"Do I have to?" Antonio whined.

Nyx said, "You have to. Now, do as Anna said and stop your grumbling." She gave Derrick a wink.

Derrick gave her a weak smile.

Miriam said, "I'm proud of you, Derrick. You saved our butts. Again."

Derrick said, "I got lucky."

"Luck had nothing to do with it. You studied the situation and made the right decision," Miriam said.

Anna said, "Yeah. Thanks, Derrick." She strained at the words as if they were hard to say.

Miriam said, "Detonating the missile inside the building was brilliant. Made our job easy. But run it by me next time or stick to the plan."

Derrick wanted to say there was no time for a discussion but didn't. He was too tired to argue.

Nyx took a bite of her bar, made a face, and then, with a full mouth, said, "You were not in there very long. What happened?"

Miriam said, "Prime was dead."

"In little pieces," Anna added.

"Some robots too. We went to the floor below. Met two robots racing up the stairs, made quick work of them, destroyed the replicants, and headed back up. We found the assistant. He had been in his quarters, which, as luck would have it, were shielded by a concrete wall, so he survived the blast, but he was in shock and needed help to walk," Miriam said.

"You let him go. Do you think that was a good idea?" Antonio asked.

"No," Anna said.

Miriam said, "It was my decision."

Derrick felt a bit of relief. "Did you learn anything from him?"

"No," Miriam said.

"We might have if you would have let me open the door," Anna said.

Miriam said, "He was plenty scared without doing that. He didn't know anything about Central Prime's location. He didn't even know where the other satellite facilities were."

"Did he know about Seattle?" Derrick asked.

"They all do. That was part of the plan," Miriam fired back.

Derrick said, "The last one was easy, but New York wasn't. Perhaps letting them know about Seattle was a mistake."

Miriam glared at him for a moment and then said, "You might be right, but I think it was necessary. Remember, we had to distract Prime from invading Mexico. And it was important for the next phase of the plan."

"Which is?" Rebekah asked. "I've been wondering if there was a plan or if we were just winging it."

"Of course, I have a plan."

"Could have fooled me," Anna said.

Derrick felt heat rising in his chest and feared his face would flush red. He knew Anna had a problem with his decisions and being the leader earlier, but now something had her at odds with Miriam as well.

Rebekah said, "Seattle *was* chaotic. New York was worse. I'm surprised we got out of there without someone getting killed."

Derrick felt his face go from red to white. "Someone was killed. In Seattle."

Rebekah stared at him for a moment. "I can't believe I said that. I'm sorry. I didn't mean anything by it."

Antonio said, "L. Linda was weird but not in a bad way."

"She was nice to everyone," Nyx said, adding, "I wish I'd been nicer to her."

Antonio said, "We all should have been."

Derrick blurted out. "Were people mean to her?"

Nyx stared at him for a moment. "Not that I know of, but we never let her in our circle of friends."

"We let her be secretary to the student counsel," Antonio said.

"Did we?" Nyx asked. "As I recall, she showed up at a meeting and appointed herself. Everyone sort of shrugged, and she came to every meeting after that."

This didn't surprise Derrick. Not now. Not knowing what he knew. L. Linda manipulated them so she would know what was going on. She wasn't there to get added to the council. Voting wasn't important. She was there to observe. To know.

Nyx turned to Derrick. "You worked with her. Did you get to know her?"

He did not get to know her at work, but he knew more about her than anyone in Potterville ever did or ever would. "Not really. I washed dishes in the back. She was out front with Donna."

"She had a thing for you," Nyx said.

"I don't think so."

"I saw it. Girls can tell. She liked you."

Derrick felt his face turning red again. Not because L. Linda liked him. That wasn't it. She just hoped he could help her destroy Prime. If L. Linda had known him better, she would not have wanted his help. She thought he was someone *special.* Like she was.

"Did you like her?" Nyx asked and then added, "It's okay if you did. She was kind of pretty."

You should have seen her eyes, Derrick thought, then tried to force the thought from his mind. Instead, he said, "I suppose, in a way. I mean, she was nice to me, but I hardly knew her." Which was true because the only honest conversation they'd had was a few brief minutes before she died.

He couldn't tell them about her eyes.

He couldn't tell them she was an orphan.

He couldn't tell them she was a trained assassin.

He couldn't tell them he had made a promise he feared he could not keep.

But did he like her? He didn't know her.

Rebekah said, "I had just met her, yet I'm sad that she's gone. She might have been different, but she was brave. We might have all died in Seattle if it were not for her."

"I'll miss her too," Antonio said.

Nyx nodded.

Derrick wanted to change the subject. He would rather talk about the dead people in New York than this. But he didn't want to talk about that either. Finally, he said, "I'm glad you let the assistant go."

Miriam said, "You're not the only one who doesn't want to kill people. Remember, this isn't just about saving ourselves."

Derrick looked at his feet. "I know. I never said it was."

"None of us do," Anna said. "Prime is the enemy. It's not our fault if people try to help him or if they get caught in the crossfire."

"So, how are we going to find the last Prime?" Derrick asked. "If Prime's assistants don't know the location, then how are we going to find it?"

"If he wasn't lying," Anna said.

Miriam said, "I believed him."

"You have more confidence than I do," Anna said. "You should have let me question him."

Rebekah said, "Anna, what's with you? You're acting strange. It's not like you."

Anna glared at Rebekah for a moment, but then her expression softened. "Sorry. You're right." Looking back at Miriam, Anna said, "Sorry. I'm scared. Plus, Derrick is right. Nothing is going to change if we can't find the last location."

Miriam said, "I know that."

Derrick asked, "So, what's the plan? How are we going to find it?"

Miriam chewed the last of her brown bar. "I'm going to start a dialogue with Prime."

Derrick said, "The Central Prime?"

"Yes."

"Is that safe?" Rebekah asked.

"Not entirely."

"Not entirely?" Anna asked.

"No guarantees. But if the VPN works, Prime won't be able to track us."

"How are you going to contact him?" Derrick asked.

"I still have an email address. Remember? From when he tracked us to Doc's house."

"It seems like days ago, but yeah, I remember that well. Prime almost killed us that time as well," Derrick said.

"You guys are crazy," Antonio said.

Miriam had a sly smile. "True."

"I'll admit to that," Rebekah said. "It helps if you're going to hang out with this one." She pointed at Miriam.

"I'm just an ordinary girl in an ordinary town with an ordinary sister," Anna said, citing her first attempt at writing forbidden fiction after Miriam's prompt regarding the remote control of the monitor that opened her world and her memories.

"You lost me," Nyx said.

"Private joke. From before times," Anna said, stepping over to Miriam and giving her a hug. "I'm with you, Miriam. Always was and always will be."

Miriam said, "First, I need to make a call. I hope AJ has his phone on."

"AJ?" Nyx questioned.

"Sorry. Allen. I want to know if he's heard from Professor or Wizard."

"You lost me again," Nyx said.

"Resistance people we met."

"The people Red and Antonio saved?" Nyx asked.

"Correct."

"Speaking of Red, I hope he and Akira are okay," Nyx said.

"I'll contact them too," Miriam said, and then added, "I set up an email at the base. It will go directly to Charlie.

"Tell Charlie to send real food next time," Antonio said.

Everyone glanced at him.

Rebekah said, "You have a one-track mind."

Antonio said, "Yeah. I can't help it."

Miriam said, "There won't be a next time. We finish Prime this time or not at all. And if not at all, then Prime will finish us, and it won't end there."

"Always with the cheery thoughts," Rebekah said.

Miriam said, "You know it, girlfriend."

Antonio shook his head. "Girls." He looked at Derrick. "Am I right?"

Not entirely sure he understood how one should reply, Derrick said, "I need to take a walk over behind those bushes."

Antonio said, "Me too. You girls can go next."

"Why do boys always get to go first?" Rebekah asked. "Don't take all day."

When they were out of sight, Antonio said, "Can I ask a couple of questions?"

"Sure."

"When this is over, would you be mad if I asked Rebekah out?"

The question surprised Derrick. Nyx had been on his mind almost every passing second since he first saw her from his condo window, sitting at a sidewalk table in front of Donna's. However, other thoughts, like how to stay alive from one moment to the next, had occupied his thinking of late.

"Why would I be mad?"

"Well, since I learned she was on your list of girls for the wife picking thing, you know, I thought maybe you still had dibs if things didn't work out with Nyx."

Derrick's thoughts swirled in a hundred directions, some pleasant, some not so much. "Dibs?"

"You know, first pick."

Derrick zipped up. "No. I have no control over Rebekah."

"So, you'd be okay with it?"

Derrick thought for a moment. "Sure."

"Now, here's the big question. Do you think she'd go out with me?"

"Like a date?"

"Yes. Exactly. A date."

Antonio, the kid who always seemed in control and comfortable in every situation, suddenly looked awkward, nervous. He looked like Derrick had felt many times. Interesting. "I can't say. Rebekah does her own thinking."

Antonio's expression changed. Discouraged maybe.

Derrick said, "If I were to guess, I'd say yes. She'll go out with you."

Antonio checked his zipper. "Fantastic. We'd better get back before we are in trouble."

In trouble meant Rebekah wanted the bushes next.

Derrick realized, maybe for the first time, that everyone has their doubts. Antonio felt out of place here. He was a farmworker's kid from a small farming town. Not a warrior, not a soldier, not an assassin, not Chosen. He should have been terrified, and maybe he was, but the thing on his mind was whether a girl he'd met a few days ago would go on a date with him. To top it off, Rebekah was clearly interested in Antonio. Even he could see that, and reading people was not Derrick's strength.

Interesting.

As they approached, Rebekah started towards them. The other girls followed right behind her. "Took you long enough," she said, as she did a playful bump to Antonio's shoulder.

Derrick and Antonio lingered next to the aircraft. Derrick couldn't think of anything to say. His thoughts were private. Unavailable for sharing. None of them were pleasant. None were wanted. All were warranted.

When the girls came back, Nyx looked at Derrick and said, "See you soon," and then she headed to the aircraft. Antonio followed her.

Miriam grabbed Derrick's arm and said, "We need to talk." She glared at Rebekah and then added, "alone."

Rebekah and Anna went to the other aircraft. Rebekah's reaction was unreadable. Anna's expression barely masked her disapproval.

Derrick said, "Did you get a hold of Allen?"

"No. I left a message. I think his phone was off. It went straight to voice mail."

"So, you didn't learn anything about the Professor?"

"I did not, but I sent an email."

"And Prime?"

"Last email I sent. Then I turned the computer off. The VPN seems to be working so far. No missiles are raining down on us." She glanced at the sky. "I'm not taking unnecessary chances. I'll be online for the least amount of time possible."

"I'm surprised there's an internet connection out here."

Miriam said, "There isn't. I used my phone as a hotspot."

Derrick didn't know what that meant and didn't ask. "I still don't see how you're going to find Prime."

"It's a work in progress. Listen, I've noticed something."

Derrick was afraid this would happen. "I'll be okay."

Miriam looked puzzled. "Okay." She dragged the word out, not quite a question. "I know what happened in New York and losing L. Linda was tough for you. Hang in there. I need you."

He wasn't sure about that.

Then Miriam said, "Anna hasn't been herself. She's edgy."

With a bit of relief, it wasn't about him, not yet, he said, "I've noticed that too."

"Hard not to. Truth is, I feel out of sorts as well. Are you feeling anything? I don't know, odd?"

He was feeling a lot of odd stuff, but he said, "I don't think so? Like what?"

"Hard to describe, but I think it's part stress and part Prime."

"What do you mean, part Prime?"

"Getting close to Prime. The whole hallway and doors and imbedded secret code stuff. I mean, what if Prime replies to my email and uses a code on me?"

"I've been thinking about that too. It was wrong for me to delay, uh, you know, with Prime." *Kill or destroy. Why is that so hard to say?*

Miriam studied him for a moment. "Right. We need to look out for each other."

"Absolutely."

Miriam paused again. Troubled. "You have to promise me something."

Derrick had already made promises he might not be able to keep. "What kind of promise?"

Miriam said, "It's possible you'll have to kill Anna or me. If Prime were to take control of either of us, you can't hesitate. It must be sudden, brutal, and final. You have to kill us. Do you understand?"

"Miriam! I could never."

"Stop! I'm serious. Promise me."

And for the second time today, he made a promise he feared he could not keep.

21

Saturday, April 10, 4:25 p.m.

IT WAS CLOSER TO DINNER THAN LUNCH, but Akira had not heard from Red. He must be hungry. She would take him food but knew Charlie wouldn't permit it. She had heard from Miriam. Just a few minutes ago. A brief and cryptic email. "Three down, four to go." That was it. There was no: 'Hey how are you?' Or: 'I can't wait to see you.'

Akira had not seen Charlie for almost two hours. He was probably tired of her asking about Red every few minutes. However, Charlie had not forgotten about her because he had stationed two QR-3 robots at the door to keep her from sneaking off. She wanted a cup of tea and was sure Charlie would provide one, but it didn't seem right. She should not be sipping tea when the others were risking their lives.

The double doors swung open, and Charlie walked in. "I have news."

"Do I want to hear it?"

"Given the circumstances, you do not have a choice."

"How bad is it?"

"Like on a scale from one to ten, one being the worst, ten being the best?"

"Yes. Like that."

Charlie paused for a moment, which was half a beat for a person, but a long time for Charlie. "I cannot make that assessment. I can say it is neither a one nor a ten."

"Not helpful. Why do I not have a choice? That's an odd thing to say."

"Red requested I deliver the message."

"You've heard from Red? Why didn't you say that in the first place?"

"Because you redirected the conversation."

"That's fair. Where is he?"

"He is in the medical unit. He would like to speak to you."

Akira jumped to her feet. "How long has he been in there?"

"A couple of hours."

Akira threw a notebook at Charlie, the pages fluttering like a wounded bird before striking him in the chest and falling to the floor. Charlie didn't move or show any physical reaction. "What did I do?" he asked.

"Why didn't you tell me sooner? I've been worried about him."

"Only him?"

"Of course not. You're evading the question."

"I did not tell you because Red asked that I did not. Not until the medical unit upgraded his chances of recovery to 70% or higher."

"Seventy percent? You mean there's a 30% chance he'll die?"

"No. This is the recovery estimate. The unit reassesses the patient every 30 minutes, measuring how successful tissues are healing. The best depiction is the percentage of full recovery or back to normal."

Akira said nothing, looking as if she were wavering between sitting and standing. "You mean he might only be 70% of his former self? What does that mean? That he will limp? Or have a deformity? Or that his brain won't function?"

"It could be any of those things, or certain organs could be affected."

Akira sat. "Thirty percent."

"The last estimate was 85% recovery. He is improving with each assessment. The unit estimates he will be released within 12 hours."

"You should have started there."

"I'll assimilate that information and try to improve my communication skills. Red would like to see you now."

"Why didn't he want to see me earlier? Is he still mad at me?"

"Mad as in angry?"

"Yes, damn it!"

"I do not believe so. Did you have a fight of which I am not aware? That might change my assessment."

"No fight. Angry about what happened earlier. When I screwed up … When I ended up in the medical unit and … well, didn't come out right."

"I am confident in saying he is not angry with you. My estimation is that he thinks quite highly of you. I explained this earlier."

"Right. But I figured you were just trying to make me feel better."

"Your assessment is not wrong. However, it was also my best assessment of Red's feelings in the matter. My assessment that Red does not blame you remains unchanged."

"He shouldn't trust me."

"I do not understand."

"It's complicated."

"I can process thousands of computations simultaneously."

"Not complicated like that. Can we go now?"

"We can go soon. First, I have information I believe is beneficial."

"About Red?"

"Yes. And about you. Red and you both blame yourselves for the situation that put you in the medical unit. I analyzed the event again to be sure. At first, I thought the data was incorrect because the projections indicated a 0% chance of completing the repair."

"Your data must be wrong because we did it. Despite almost killing me and frying my brain."

"Correct. By making an adjustment in the calculation, I was able to increase the estimate to a 5% chance of success."

"That's got to be wrong."

"It is not. I studied the computation from several angles."

"Okay." Akira dragged the word out as if she didn't believe him or could not understand what Charlie was implying.

"In that first repair, Red could have measured the valve before starting the installation. That would change the entire scenario and the outcome assessment. However, employees were never trained to do that. The part number was correct. A trained employee would not have checked the dimensions before starting. To expect Red to do that would be unrealistic."

"Okay." The word strung out a little less this time.

"What I'm trying to tell you is that fully trained and experienced staff would have had a 0% chance of success. That means you both did a—I think the word is fantastic. Far exceeding expectations. You should be proud of what you did."

"So, how did you get to 5%? What did you change in the assessment?" Charlie said, "I factored in that you willingly sacrificed yourself to save the others."

22

AKIRA FOLLOWED CHARLIE TO THE medical unit. She knew the way, but Charlie insisted they go together. Intellectually, she knew excitement and dread were feelings she should be experiencing. Excited to see Red and know he was okay. Dread because she almost died in the medical unit and lost a big part of herself. She should have felt these things but didn't. Knowing about emotions was not the same as experiencing them.

Instead, she felt hollow. As if she were an animation or a caricature rather than a real person. Charlie was no longer talking about coping with her emotions. He wasn't built to have them, and it was causing him problems, but he was no longer showing indications of stress. He must have found a way to block them, so they no longer affected him. Perhaps he had deleted them. He might as well. She was never going to be the same again. Even if Charlie figured out a way to transfer her emotions back, syncing them with events and thoughts would be impossible and she no longer wanted them back. Getting them back now, would only make her worse.

Outside the medical unit, she stopped, preparing herself. Memories flooded her mind. Most of them were nightmares. Things she must have experienced while undergoing treatment, neither awake nor asleep. Her thoughts were difficult, if not impossible, to describe, but all were dark and twisted.

Charlie had not yet opened the door. He seemed to sense her anxiety. After a few moments, he asked, "Ready?"

She nodded, and he pushed the oversized door open. Red lay on a table inside a treatment unit. The machine's arms were withdrawn, which helped because the arms were often present in Akira's memories and nightmares, probing and sticking her with needles, forcing what seemed like tiny machines into her veins. Sometimes she dreamed she was inside a microscopic machine that moved through her blood like a submarine, sapping this and gathering that.

Tubes attached to each of Red's arms snaked into the wall. Small circular disks stuck on his chest, neck, and head were attached to the machine with wires. Monitors displayed vital signs, heart rate, blood pressure, and oxygen were self-explanatory. Diagnostic information was mostly meaningless to her, except for one line that indicated Red's prognosis had improved to 88% full recovery and the time remaining a mere four hours.

Akira smiled.

Red raised his head a couple of inches and gave her a small wave.

"You may go in if you'd like," Charlie said.

Akira rushed into the room. "How are you feeling?"

"Tired. Mostly tired."

"Like you could sleep a hundred years?"

"Yeah. Like that. I guess you'd know."

Akira said, "I should have been there to help you."

Red said, "Too big a risk. Charlie said you wouldn't survive exposure to radiation again, and it was elevated everywhere."

"Charlie says a lot of things."

Red gave her a weak smile. "Accurate and true things."

"I guess. Still, you should have waited until the others were here to help."

"Have you heard from them?"

"Just a short email. They have destroyed three locations."

"I wanted to go with them, but I couldn't leave. Another valve failed, and the reactor was near critical. Good news, it's fixed."

"You lied to me. You said it was no big deal."

"It wasn't a big deal if I fixed it. But yeah, I lied a little. I'm sorry about that."

Akira took his hand. "No, you're not."

"True. I didn't have a choice. If I told you the truth, you would have ended up there despite being told you couldn't go."

"I suppose you are right. But it might have beat the alternative."

Red lifted himself up on one elbow, staring into Akira's eyes. "What does that mean?"

Akira broke his gaze. "Living like this. I'm not sure how long I can go on. It's … I'm not sure it's worth the effort."

Red lifted her chin. "Don't talk like that."

A tear coursed down Akira's cheek. "You don't understand."

"Perhaps not. You're talking about losing your emotions. Right?"

"Yes. You don't understand how important they are until they are gone."

Red looked into her eyes. "I suppose you are right about that. It's hard to imagine, let alone understand. But let me ask you a question. Why were you smiling when you came in here?"

She paused. "First, I want to apologize."

"For what?"

"For how I treated you in school."

"You never did anything to me in school."

"Exactly. I ignored you. I thought you were just a big dumb kid who played football."

"I hung out with Jimmy Priest. It was a mistake. I see that now. I don't blame you. You were smart to ignore me and Jimmy."

"Still, you're so much more. You're smart and kind and brave."

Red didn't respond. He just held her gaze for a moment. "Thanks for saying that. It means a lot to me. I always admired you. Kinda had a thing for you." He paused and smiled. "You didn't answer my question. Why were you smiling when you came in?"

"I was so happy that you were okay."

"I see. One more question. Why are you blushing?"

Akira smiled. "Am I? I don't know. Just what you said, I guess."

"But no emotions?"

A smile lit Akira's face. "Oh my God!"

23

IT WAS HOT BUT UNLIKE THE DESERT it wasn't dry. Sweat poured off Derrick's face, and his clothes stuck to his skin. Even the air somehow smelled of heat. The aircraft would be cooler. He was ready to leave, even if he wasn't ready to enter the next prime facility.

Derrick said, "I'm baking. Let's get out of here."

"It's the humidity," Miriam said.

"Humidity?" Derrick asked.

"Moisture in the air. It's high here and low in the desert."

"Why don't I know this sort of thing?" Derrick asked.

"It's meteorology. Science of weather. The Chosen don't teach science."

Derrick took a deep breath, blew it out. "I'll never catch up. Why do you know this stuff?"

"I read a lot when I was in Patel's office. You'll be okay. Just focus on the next few hours."

"Why did you contact Professor and Wizard?" Derrick asked.

"Have you thought about what's going to happen when Prime is gone?"

"I have. I wanted to talk to you about it."

"So, what do you think will happen?"

Derrick paused for a moment. "To us? To Potterville? To New America?"

"Yes. All of it."

"Mostly, I've thought about New America. Pacific Edge. Places like that. The Chosen will be angry and terrified. They think the outside world is dangerous. Maybe it is. I don't know much about the rest of the country, except that Potterville is apparently different. Better since Coach and Bill Collins started the councils. Jimmy Priest was like the Chosen. Believed the New Doctrine. People like that—well, I don't know how they will react. Disbelief? Fear? Anger?"

Miriam said, "All true. There will be a vacuum. No one in control. Prime is awful, but Prime maintains order. Without order, things will get bad fast. So, we need a plan. The Resistance can help. The people in the desert town were smart and resourceful. Plus, they have the commander of the military. I want them to take over. Maybe Collins and Browning can help too. Set up a council like Potterville."

Derrick felt relieved, at least for a moment. "I'm glad you're thinking about this."

"There's something else," Miriam said. "When this is over, we can't tell anyone about it. Nothing. We must act as surprised as everyone else that Prime is gone. No one can know about the base, and they can't know we were in Mexico. Nothing. We had nothing to do with it."

Derrick thought for a moment and said, "I agree."

"Tell the others on the way to Dallas. Do you think we can trust them to keep it quiet?"

"I think so. We should talk as a group before we return to Potterville. You know, make sure our stories are the same."

"That's a good idea. See you in Dallas. Same as before. Get info on the headquarters and relay it to us. Nyx has the coordinates."

Derrick was glad Miriam wanted to keep this entire thing a secret. Still, it was a lot to ask. Save the world, but don't let anyone know. He had more secrets than the others to keep. Saying nothing made it all a little easier. He hoped.

They were closer to Dallas than they were to Chicago. Nyx again took them high and flew them fast. Within a few minutes, Derrick started getting the first images of the Dallas headquarters.

"Which building is it?" Derrick asked.

Nyx said, "I don't know. One of those three. That's the coordinates."

Miriam would know. Derrick sent the images and opened a channel directly to her, shutting the other channels off for a moment. "Are you seeing this?"

"Yes."

"Good. Which building?" Derrick asked.

"One of those three," Miriam said.

Derrick stared at three large buildings. The parking lots were some distance, and a small lake sealed entry from the back of the building farthest west. Surrounding the three buildings were miles of rubble, as if it were once a city but had been destroyed. Perhaps there was a war here. Maybe it was just Prime laying waste to everything nearby.

A small stream separated the middle building from the two on the east side. Shuttle buses ran from the parking lot to the buildings. As they circled the complex, Derrick saw that the two buildings on the eastern side were joined with a narrow passageway. Technically, it was one building, not two. A tall fence topped with razor wire encircled the entire complex. The tallest building had three stories. Probably more underground. There was no way to approach any of the buildings without detection. The compound was too large and spread out to use missiles.

"Five, can you tell me which building Prime is in?"

"The buildings are not easily scanned."

"Why not?" Derrick asked.

"Reinforced concrete structure and in places, lead or steel plating."

Derrick opened a channel so everyone on both ships could hear. "Five is scanning the building but running into difficulty because of the construction."

Miriam said, "Keep sending us data. We are ten minutes out."

As Nyx circled the buildings, obtaining video of all sides, Derrick grabbed stills of each building and then magnified, found what he was looking for, and magnified more.

"The building to the east has something etched into the stone over the main doors. It says, 'Federal Bureau of Investigation.'" Derrick said.

"What's that?" Anna asked.

Antonio said, "That building is very old. Old United States old. They called it the FBI. It was like a national police force. They mention it in Old American history, but like all history, they don't tell us much."

Derrick continued to study. Magnify, search, and magnify more. "The one on the east says, 'US Drug Administration.' Antonio, do you know what that means? Is it a pharmaceutical agency?"

"Maybe. But probably focused on illegal drugs."

Derrick had heard of illegal drugs. Stories regarding drugs and drug-gang violence filled his New America Media feed. Since he had learned what New America Media portrayed was mostly lies, he wondered if illegal drugs were a problem. He didn't know if they still were, but apparently, they were in the old United States.

"Antonio, are illegal drugs still a problem in New America?" Derrick asked.

"Sure. Some places are worse than others. Is it a problem in Chosen Communities?"

Derrick thought for a moment. Drugs were a problem, but not in the same way. There was a pill or potion for everything. He had often taken mood enhancers before school. His eye color was fake, as was his hair color. His skin was artificially perfected by microscopic robots. "Yeah, but different."

This was not going to work. The place was too big. Too complex. There was no way in.

24

LORI MARTINEZ WAS WRITING THE PROBABLE cause affidavit in her head all the way to the sheriff's office, revisiting where she would find the correct forms, rehearsing how she would explain it to Judge Smith. Or perhaps she would just let him read the affidavit. It was self-explanatory and as shocking as any prologue she could create. She arrived at the courthouse without remembering driving there. Perhaps she was concentrating on writing the statement correctly. Maybe it was because Bill figured out how to make killing Prime legal. It occurred to her that daydreaming was dangerous. They were not out of the woods. Not by a long shot.

Lori parked on the street in front of the courthouse. The sheriff's office was in back, but she didn't want to circle around. The thought of obtaining a warrant proved more exciting than she had anticipated. After all, she had never written a document charging someone with murder. She dashed up the courthouse steps, slightly more aware of her surroundings than she had been on the drive there.

Suddenly, something felt wrong.

She slowed. Placed her hand on her pistol. Silly. Like an old movie.

When she reached the top of the steps, the pistol came out without giving it much thought. Automatic response to a threat.

But there was no threat. It was a bright, sunshiny day. Although the streets were quiet, and she could not remember seeing anyone on the drive here. Why she had drawn her gun seemed a mystery.

Until an awareness of something out of place entered her conscious thoughts.

The front door of the courthouse was shattered. Broken glass covered the cement.

She stopped. Took an involuntary step back. And then another, pointing her pistol into the darkness of the empty building.

Lori had forgotten about something.

She had forgotten about assassins.

25

STANLEY MIRES HAD CONSUMED WELL beyond his normal intake of coffee, and Pam appeared uneasy having spent so much time with him, so he found his quarters, which were comfortable but spartan compared to his suite in Seattle. He did not have a view of the bay. He didn't have a view of anything because he was buried under a desert. The desert was in California, according to Prime. California has a lot of deserts. Which desert was unknown because, despite his best efforts, Stanley had never learned Prime's central location. He didn't know where he was—and neither did anyone else.

Stanley Mires had failed his primary mission: learning the location of the very place where he was now imprisoned. He had never dreamed of getting here. One might say he'd exceeded expectations, but since there was no way for him to get any information to the Resistance, he was now useless.

Stanley had done many things. Bad things. But all for the cause. To help the Resistance and he hoped, to destroy Prime. The Resistance needed information. However, with nothing left to gain or to lose, the next time Prime ordered him to launch a missile, or sink a ship, or shut off a power station in the dead of winter, he would refuse. Prime would kill him, perhaps quickly, perhaps slowly.

He turned on his monitor, wondering what he might have access to. Probably not much. He felt certain people here did not know what was going on in the outside world. Only what Prime wanted them to know. It surprised him that a video feed from New America Media came up first. It was the only thing available. It showed the building in which he had worked for over two decades as nothing more than a smoldering pile of rubble.

The tape along the bottom read: "Unknown terrorists bombed the New America Bank building in downtown Seattle, killing over 200 employees."

The statement that it was a New America Bank was inaccurate. Perhaps it was a bank in the past. It was inaccessible to the public. There were not 200 employees. The building had more androids than people.

The media didn't mention it was a Prime Headquarters. Prime Headquarters were unknown to the public. The Resistance knew the locations. Thanks to Stanley. However, it occurred to him that the news feed here would likely undergo another level of editing. Perhaps outside of here people were hearing something different about Seattle.

Unfortunately, Stanley had not learned specifics about any of the locations other than Seattle. He knew the addresses, but that was all, which made penetrating them difficult. Although he was a key to the Resistance information-gathering mechanisms, he didn't know much about them or their plans.

He knew they were an information gathering organization, not a military organization. To destroy Prime, they needed information. Although, to be honest, he did not know if the Resistance planned to destroy Prime. That was just his assumption. If they did plan to destroy Prime, they would need key players in the government and military. Any strikes would be military operations.

The destruction of Seattle could only be attributed to a couple of people.

Derrick and Miriam King. Stanley knew that already. The Resistance must have provided information. How that occurred, he did not know. Perhaps the Resistance rather than Ravengers occupied that desert town.

Stanley was fortunate that Prime didn't kill him out of sheer rage when Seattle was destroyed. That Prime told him to take the weekend was perhaps the strangest thing Stanley had ever experienced while working for Prime. Prime didn't believe in assistants having time off. Especially, in a crisis such as this.

Prime gave assistants fine whiskey and gourmet food. Although he doubted there would be much gourmet food here, so that was more of a cruel sort of joke. "You're my slave, here have a glass of Scotch."

Perhaps Prime was watching him even now. Seeing what he would do with spare time, perhaps to monitor his reaction to Seattle.

At that moment, the speakers embedded in the ceiling crackled to life. "Mr. Mires, would you be so kind as to come to my office? I apologize for interrupting your time off. However, there are developments I think you'll be interested in."

"Yes, sir. On my way, sir."

Stanley didn't like the sound of this. Prime was too cordial and sounded far too calm, given the circumstances. It felt like a trap of some sort.

His stomach twisted into a knot, and he wished he hadn't had that last cup of coffee because it felt as if the entire contents of his stomach had turned to acid.

At least the office, as Prime called it, which was more like the lab of a mad scientist, was easy to find. It was on the bottom floor of the complex. The elevator would not go there unless one had clearance. Inside, Stanley pushed the elevator button. An automated voice instructed him to look into the retinal scanner. He did so. The elevator lurched and descended. The door opened.

"Mr. Mires, my good and faithful servant. Please, pour yourself a drink and have a seat. I have exciting news."

Stanley didn't want a drink, but because Prime had become more unhinged than ever, it seemed best to play along for now. He would pour his drink as usual for appearance's sake. "I must say, I did not anticipate good news, given what I just saw on New America Media."

"I admit. At first, I was upset. When they destroyed New York, I was furious. Really, quite beside myself."

Stanley stood in the middle of the room, glass in hand, unable to move. "New York? As in Prime New York."

"Yes. Can you believe it? Destroyed most of our AT aircraft."

"I don't know what to say," Stanley said, honestly.

"Sit, my good man. You have not tasted your drink."

Stanley sat. Took a small sip. "It's excellent, as always. Thank you, sir."

Prime paced for a few minutes. Stanley remained silent.

"Mr. Mires, you've worked for me a long time. You're about to hear things you've never heard before."

"Okay."

"I've made a mistake. I underestimated just how successful and brilliant my original plan had been."

Stanley wasn't sure how to respond to that, so he said, "I'm eager to hear more."

"The Derrick King experiment. They told me it failed. Derrick King was very important to me. Do you know why?"

"I do not, sir. I was not privy to the purpose of that test, nor should I have been."

"That's true. Not as an assistant in Seattle. But you're here now. Things have changed. You see, Derrick King was to be my first human embodiment."

"Embodiment?" The word slipped from Stanley's lips before he could stop himself.

"Yes. A sound mind and body that I could inhabit. Originally, they felt the control mechanisms used to ensure Derrick King would not fight me once my mind was downloaded into his had proved successful. However, when he hit Marcus Carver, they concluded the test had failed. They convinced me of the same."

Stanley felt himself hyperventilating. "Now, you believe the test succeeded?"

"Yes. Beyond expectations. Derrick King has proved more resourceful than one could have predicted. Do not worry. Once I get them here, I will ensure Derrick King is 100% ready before I make the transformation."

"Get them here?"

"Yes. The best part is that Miriam King is a genius and will serve as the perfect test subject for advanced memory cleansing. When she is reduced to a complete idiot who cannot stack simple children's blocks regardless of the stimulus, then we'll be certain."

"Stimulus?"

"Yes. I'll use her friends. 'Stack the blocks in numerical order, lowest to highest and do it correctly, or I will cut off Rebekah Ford's hand, or chop off a foot.' Things like that."

Stanley took a sip but said nothing.

"The best part is Derrick King will get to watch his sister become a brainless idiot."

Stanley felt a sinking in his chest unlike any he'd felt before, and he had witnessed many horrendous things in Prime's presence.

"There's more. I had an epiphany when they destroyed Chicago. It didn't upset me at all. It was the most marvelous feeling I've had for decades. I don't know why I did not see it earlier. I have Derrick and Miriam to thank for that. And I'll get to share this decision with them."

"Chicago? I'm sorry, sir, I'm not following."

"Stanley, people have always underestimated me. It was always a mistake to do so. They didn't think I could launch a nuclear bomb on my own country. They didn't think I could become King forever. My enemies and even some of my closest employees have thought they could outsmart me. Haven't they, Mr. Mires?"

A menace oozed from Prime's words unlike anything he'd ever heard. "One would have to be crazy to think they could outsmart you, sir."

"You would think so. Stanley, even my best scientists have failed. They have failed where I will succeed. Here's the key. Derrick King must first be ruined. His mind must be completely broken. He will watch as I destroy Miriam. Reduce her to an idiot. He'll watch his friends die. One at a time. None of them fast. None of them painless. It's brilliant. Don't you agree?"

Stanley drank the remainder of his whiskey and poured more.

"Derrick must finish what he has started. I shall not help him in that endeavor. Although he could fail, which would end my plans for him, allowing them to continue is important. First, it's time to close all of the satellite locations. I'll explain that to you later. And second, it is vital that Derrick King believe he has been successful. By Mr. King believing he has reached the ultimate goal, crushing him completely becomes possible.

"Once I have them here, he will watch his friends die and know that he killed them. That should be enough to crush him, don't, you agree, Stanely?"

Stanley downed his second whiskey. "Bring them here? Have you found them, sir?"

"I shall find them. They underestimate me, and that will be their biggest mistake. You see they think they can trick me. Deceive me. But is I who shall orchestrate the deception. Once here and broken, I have one final blow for Mr. King. How do you think Derrick King will handle watching civilization be destroyed?"

"And know that he caused it."

The End

Deconstruction is the final book in the Derrick King series. Who will survive?

Author's Note:
Thank you for reading my books. If they gave you a bit of an escape, I'm pleased. Please consider **writing a review.** To sign up for my newsletter, visit my website daniellcopeland.com.

Acknowledgements:
Thanks to the love and support of the love of my life and partner, Liz. She is also a writer and illustrator. Check out her books on Amazon Libby K. I couldn't do any of this without her. She is also my best editor and critic.

Special thanks to Rod Leonard for providing feedback and guidance.

More books from Daniel L. Copeland:
Available at Amazon.com in paperback, eBooks for Kindle, and audiobooks. Also available at Barnes and Noble and independent bookstores.

The Derrick King Series

About the Author:

Daniel is a lifelong Idahoan and grew up on a small farm in Southern Idaho. He worked in the criminal justice system for 35 years and is now retired. Daniel has published nine novels. In addition to writing, he and his wife, Liz love to travel on their BMW motorcycle. They have ridden in most of the US, including Alaska, the Great Lakes, and Florida. They have also ridden in Canada, New Zealand, and Australia. Daniel is an award-winning home brewer and a certified beer judge.